community, a part of our country that we rarely see so clearly.
His characters navigate a universe that rests on indifference and
resignation. Despite the relentless push toward degradation the
human spirit pushes back with strength, humor, dignity, and
imagination. Drunk or sober, Carpenter's characters speak their
version of truth, sometimes mean, sometimes tender, sometimes
violent, sometimes filled with humor and irony, always honest,
and always without rounding the rough edges. James Carpenter
is a gifted writer. This book is an important addition to our
understanding of contemporary America." ~ **Vern Miller**,
Publisher, *Fifth Wednesday Journal*

"*No Place to Pray* is located at the creative nexus where Faulkner,
Cormac McCarthy, and Richard Pryor converge. Rarely do
writers explore, much less depict with insight, irony, and comedy,
the endless lower depths of American culture. James Carpenter
accomplishes this feat with page-turning skill. A great read, a
historical story!" ~ **Larry Bensky**, Executive Producer, "Radio
Proust;" Osher Lifetime Learning Institute, UC Berkeley

"The musicality of the language is a pleasure, putting you under
its spell. Reading this novel is like wandering through rooms
suffused with a rich, smoky scent: simply furnished rooms filled
with complex characters stumbling through hard lives, finding
moments of grace. The crude and the lyrical blend strikingly,
sumptuously; lovers of tough lyricism in the Cormac McCarthy
vein will linger appreciatively over many of these lines." ~ **Sharon
Guskin**, author of *The Forgetting Time*

"In *No Place to Pray*, James Carpenter fires up the Southern gothic
intensity of ten mortal lifetimes. The conscience burns, the prose
sings, and his characters' dreams will haunt your own." ~ Kafka
Prize-winning author Edie Meidav, author of *Kingdom of the Young*.

To Dawn,
Best Wishes!

No Place
To Pray

James Carpenter

9/25/16

ISBN # 978-1-940189-14-7
Libriary of Congress Control Number: 2016930525

Cover art by J Carpenter

Klondike Gold Field quote is from *Alaska and
the Klondike Gold Fields* by A. C. Harris, G. W. Bertron,
publisher, 1897.

Printed in the United States

Twisted Road Publications LLC

Dedicated to Greenie and Jack

*Awake, ye drunkards, and weep; and howl, all
ye drinkers of wine, because of the new wine;
for it is cut off from your mouth.*

Joel 1:5

*For the countries of the spirit, to which he was
now admitted, were accessible only via many
dim and tangled trails.*

Louise Erdrich

Tabernacle Parish, August, 1963

The line of cars pulled in from the road and spread out across the yard and the men got out, their shadows dragging long behind them. They loosened their ties and took off their suit coats and threw the coats through the cars' open windows and came up on the porch and sat in the evening shade, some in chairs and others on the steps. One of them carried a jug of bootleg whiskey in each hand, his index fingers looped through the handles, and set them heavily by the door and stood and flexed his cramped fists.

They were unsure of how to start. One of them slid his straw fedora back on his head and said it was a damn shame and somebody else said it sure was. Then they were quiet for a long time. The man who lived there went inside and came out with glasses and tin cups and somebody said that's what they been waiting on and they poured out the whiskey and drank it down, most of them pretending it had no more effect on them than water. But one of them said fuck that has got a kick to it.

To Whiskey Davis! somebody said, lifting his cup, and the others lifted theirs and echoed the salute, their voices trailing off raggedly like a choir at practice preparing for Sunday a hymn they had not before this day ever sung.

The twilight thickened and they drank some more and waited until finally somebody said Whiskey was a son-of-a-bitch in a fight and he didn't ever back down and didn't care about what the odds was, he'd just haul right in like the time he came out of the crapper over Smoky Joe's and found them two skinny niggers talking up that white woman of his. Whiskey told them those seats was taken and they told him back that they didn't see no reserved signs on them seats and Whiskey gave them one last chance. Laid his hand on one of them's shoulder and told them real quiet he was pretty sure their table was over on the far side of the room and the other one quick flicked out a knife and sliced Whiskey's arm right open.

Somebody said that was a damn dumb thing to try on Whiskey and somebody else said no shit and they went back to the story, how Whiskey grabs the knife off the boy and throws it back of the bar and lights into both of them. How there was blood all over the place and most of it was Whiskey's but a lot of it was coming out of them boys and you had to give them credit, they was holding their own for a while until Whiskey got them both up against the wall and he's got one hand on each of their throats so tight they's turning blue and you want to see two scared-ass motherfuckers you should of seen them two. Whiskey asks if they had enough and they nod fast as they could that they did. Rolling their eyes like they was in a fucking minstrel show. Whiskey tells them to stay right where they was and he lets them go real slow and then yells over to Joe to toss him the knife and he tells the one who cut him to take out his shirttail. You think that boy was scared when Whiskey had him up against the wall, he damn near shit himself when Whiskey opens his own knife right in his face. But all he did was cut off the boy's shirttail and wrap it around his arm to get the bleeding stopped. Then he made that poor kid tie it up. Made him do it twice. Said the first time wasn't neat enough.

Somebody said if it'd been him, he'd a killed the little prick and somebody else said it was easy to say that if you wasn't the one in the fight and when things happen fast like that, you can't never tell what you would do.

They went on and told how Whiskey didn't hold it against them boys and even had Joe bring them over some beers and before the night was over, they was all drinking and laughing like they been best friends for years. Some of the men wondered if that part of the story was true, but the tribute went on, whether it was true or not.

Only thing Whiskey liked better than fighting and drinking was fucking.

Can't blame him for that.

Never did run around on that white woman though. That must have been some real sweet pussy. Somebody said it had to be more than that on account of how he took that boy of hers just about everywhere he went like he was his own and somebody else said he always thought the boy *was* Whiskey's.

It got all the way dark and they got quiet again, the ends of their cigarettes glowing in the night, cicadas buzzing from the trees. Somebody said damn, them fucking bugs is loud this year.

Somebody said it wasn't right Whiskey's woman got a white preacher for the funeral and she should have got a black preacher just out of simple respect and there was a general consensus that you can't know what goes on in a fucking white woman's head and they all of them had their head up their ass anyway, and then they amended that to mean any woman's head, not just the white ones.

Some more men came and the owner went in and switched on the yellow porch light. The newcomers had another jug and they passed it around. Damn that is smooth somebody said. Makes that other taste like shit and the one who brought the other jugs said he didn't hear them complain about it too much when they was hogging it down. There ensued a long conversation on the relative merits of bootleg whiskey, depending on who made it and if where you brewed it made a difference and what time of year was best and should you use branch or spring water and how long the

mash should set and how best to keep the copper from burning.
Those who didn't know how to make it nodded like they did and
said it depends on a lot of things. Somebody said something that
reminded them that they had started out remembering Whiskey.

They remembered how he didn't win every time and how when
he lost, he lost just as bad as he won. They recalled him coming
home busted up bad after taking on one of them Sharpsville
swamp niggers. Took ten stitches to close up his head and half his
ribs was broke and they had to bring him home in the back of a
truck. Whiskey said the worst part of it was he broke his hand on
the man's face and had to wipe his ass with his left hand for the
better part of a month.

They remembered how good Whiskey was with cars and
somebody told how his cousin had a old Plymouth and the brakes
wasn't working right. Took it half a dozen places and one of them
said it was the master cylinder and somebody else told him it was
the wheel cylinders and another one said it was the shoes and
after he paid for all that, they still wasn't working right. He said his
cousin takes it to Whiskey and Whiskey drives it up the road and
back and gets out and tells him he's got a brake line rusted out on
the inside and tells him to get in and step on the brake when he says
to. Whiskey goes around to the wheels one at a time and gets down
on the ground and tells his cousin hit it after every wheel and taps
on the lines with a wrench and then gets out from under the car
and goes in his shed and comes out with a piece of brake line. He
splices it in and puts in a little fluid and bleeds 'em and they worked
perfect and he only charged his cousin five dollars.

Your cousin count his change?

If he didn't, he should of. Old Whiskey could count seventeen
dollars into your hand all day long and make you think it was twenty
every single time. Find a way to make you thank him for cheating
you. Be in and out a house so quick, the man living there'd think all

he heard was his old lady having a bad dream. He had rules about stealing though, when it was smart and when it wasn't and when there wasn't nothing wrong with it.

The talk rambled off into a long meandering meditation on the ethics of theft. Who it was okay to steal from and who not. Was it all right to steal from a poor widow if it was okay to steal from a rich one with a dried-up pussy? Or a man with kids? Or a white man with kids? And they went on so until those of them with the habit of larceny felt assuaged of guilt and justified of their sins and they went back to Whiskey and how good he was at stealing and somebody said he sure was, right up until that last time. They all got quiet again and tried to think of a better story to end up with, so they could all go home laughing instead of contemplating how it could have happened to them and they landed on the time Whiskey laid out the ape over at the Canfield fair.

They had a tent across from the striptease show set up with a boxing ring and a trained ape and anybody could go three rounds with it, you would win a hundred dollars. Cost fifty cents to get in and another two dollars to try and they was lining up to take a shot like kids been told they was giving away free ice cream. But hardly nobody even made it through a single round. Soon as that ape came at them, they'd jump right out of the ring. If they did stick to it, the thing'd throw three punches for every one they'd throw and kick their knees and jump on them if it got them down. Even bit one guy and he yelled to the carnie, your goddamn ape fucking bit me and the carnie told him so bite him back.

Whiskey went and watched every day while the fair was running, just studying up on the ape, and on the last day paid his two dollars and climbed up to the ring. He had on a pair of steel-toed, lace-up work boots and the carnie told him maybe he wanted to take them off, they was gonna slow him down. Whiskey said he'd take his chances.

For a while he just did whatever the ape did. Ape drag his hands on the canvas, Whiskey drag his. Ape bang his chest, Whiskey bang his. Ape scratch his ass, Whiskey scratch his. Ape show his teeth, Whiskey show his. Ape go oo-oo-oo, Whiskey go oo-oo-oo. Looked like a goddamn Tarzan movie and when Whiskey's got the ape all worked up, it comes flying across the ring about as pissed off as anything you ever seen. Whiskey just stands there and when it gets close, hauls off and kicks it in the balls and down goes the ape and doesn't fucking move even one little bit. The carnie starts yelling you killed my ape and Whiskey says it was just a little love tap. Might be awhile before he gets himself in the mood for making any baby apes, but he's going to live. He goes over in the corner and holds out his hand and you could tell that crook was trying to figure out a reason not to pay him but must have thought it through what Whiskey could do to him if he could knock out his ape with just one kick and he counted out the hundred.

The men agreed that would have been a thing worth seeing and thought to themselves how they would have fared against the ape. They poured out another round and somebody asked what time it was and somebody said who gives a fuck, it's late.

You know what we need?

What?

We need to go find us some whores.

They stood up from the steps, some of them swaying, and got in the cars and went off in a line toward town, their glowing taillights like a string of beckoning lanterns guiding all prodigal wayfarers home.

Tabernacle Parish, 1953

Agnes cried when she saw that her baby was black. The midwife turned away and wiped the blood from her scissors and forceps and put them in her bag. She folded the bloody towels and laid them in a basket, then wrapped the afterbirth in newspaper. She took it downstairs, out into the damp, twilit alley and discarded her oozing parcel in a garbage can. She held her hand above her eyes to shield them from the rain and sought vainly for the setting sun from which she might divine some augury of this fallen mother's future. When she came back, Agnes had stopped crying and the baby was moving his head from side to side. The midwife told her the boy wanted her breast and showed her how to hold him. Agnes sighed when she let down, her own lips parting. The midwife wiped Agnes's forehead with a damp cloth and hummed What a Friend We Have in Jesus. When the infant child was done, she showed Agnes how to diaper him and heated her some broth and told her to sleep if she could and in the morning she would come back and tell her more about how to take care of him. Agnes asked her how long it would be before she could start working again and the midwife told her to just keep it to blowjobs for the first six weeks and then they'd see. Agnes said what about in the ass and the midwife told her I put two stitches in you and you rip them out, you going to be worse off than out of work. The midwife sat awhile longer and watched Agnes as the baby rooted again for her breast and she gave it to him and the midwife said she was doing good and just let him whenever he wanted to, the baby knew better than them what was good for him. She asked Agnes did she want to know anything else and Agnes asked should she take him with her when she went to the bathroom. He aint going to break if you aint right there every minute. You start treating him like a china doll, that's what he'll be. Lord knows, he's going to need all the strength he can get. They looked at each other, Agnes's eyes saying please save me and my little boy and the midwife's saying I would if I could but it aint up to me. The midwife asked Agnes did she have a name for the boy and Agnes told her not yet. The midwife said she needed it for the parish and don't wait too long and took up her bag and left.

Agnes couldn't stop watching her baby. He nursed for a long time and went to sleep with his mouth still on her breast. She stroked his face and his head and held his tiny hand in hers and murmured I got you. She lifted him away from her and smiled when his mouth made a soft plopping sound like a pebble dropping into still water when it came off her breast. She laid him down on the bed and pulled the comforter over him and set a pillow up against him on both sides and stroked his face again and got up and went out to the front room. She went to the closet and had to stand on tiptoe to get what she was reaching for and it hurt and she had to stop and rest and do it again. She brought down a brown paper package and laid it on the table and went to the counter and got a pair of shears and cut the brown twine tying up the package. She pulled away the paper and unfolded a small white quilt. She traced with her fingers the blue-grey diamonds stitched across its breadth and ran her hands lightly over the checkered squares around the edge. She held it against herself to warm it and took it back to the bedroom and undid the baby from the pillows and the comforter and unwrapped him from the bunting the midwife had wound him in. She put the quilt tight around him and got into the bed with him and told him about the quilt.

She told him her grandmother made it for her on the stand in the sitting room with rollers on both ends with cranks, one to roll out the cloths for the bottom and the top. The batting went in between the two lengths of cloth and her grandmother turned the crank at the other end to roll the quilt up after they stitched on the patterns. Her grandmother taught her how to work the spindles and how to cut the pieces for the pattern and fold their edges back and sew them on. How her grandmother kept burlap bags full of rags and old clothes and how those old things nobody wanted came back in the quilts and sometimes in rag rugs. Agnes said when I got old enough she told me she made this one for me when I was a baby and someday I had to give it to my own baby. So here it is.

Agnes kept on telling him about her grandmother until she ran out of things to say and then she just went back to looking at him and after a while he woke up, working his mouth like he was trying to say something. He started to whimper and she gave him her breast again. When he took her into his mouth she felt his warmth meld into her and run along the nerves of her neck and her arms and into her legs. She said to him I had a little sister for a while and my grandma taught me songs to sing to her and asked him if he wanted to hear one and she felt him say yes through her breast and she started singing, *Hush little baby, don't you cry,* but he wasn't crying and then she thought ahead to Papa's going to buy you a diamond ring, and saw that nothing about that song was right because that song was for a little girl and he didn't even have a daddy. So she started singing *Rock-a-bye baby*, but thought ahead about that too and couldn't even think about her baby crashing down from a tree.

For a little while she just hummed the way the midwife had, but with no tune in particular until the humming turned into This

Little Light of Mine, and she sang the words softly and laid her fingers on the baby's chest so he would know she was singing to him. She went on and sang Jesus Loves Me and then Joy, Joy, Joy but slowed it down and made the words long and hushed and didn't clap because she couldn't clap and hold on to him at the same time and it would have scared him even if she could. She told him those were Sunday school songs. My grandpa was the superintendent and he got up front before the classes started and he would say a prayer before the kids all went downstairs and that's when we sang our songs. Some of them had motions to them so you could act out the parts. Grandpa had gray hair all the way down on his shoulders and I thought it was so he would look like Jesus but I found out when I was older it was because he was a major in the army. He always wore the jacket Grandma sewed for him. She didn't sew the whole jacket, just embroidered the signs on the pocket. After he got sick and couldn't be the superintendent anymore, he wore it every day. What Grandma sewed on the jacket was a picture of a crown and a sword and a lion. She told me the picture came from Grandpa's mother's name and she gave Grandpa her last name for his first name. She came from France and was a Catholic and so was Grandpa when he was a baby but he gave up being a Catholic and got baptized the right way. He couldn't have been the superintendent if he didn't and I wouldn't have learned the Sunday school songs.

Agnes went back to singing and while she was singing, she remembered that she was supposed to think of a name and thought for a while and saw her grandfather again standing up in front of the whole Sunday school and said to her baby would he would like it if she named him for her grandpa and he kicked hard through the quilt and Agnes took that as a sign that he did and named him LeRoy James after her grandfather. Then she told him she didn't mean it when she cried because he was black.

Brigard County, March 1993

Harmon snaked his way through the maze of flames flapping like wings, the walls glazed in liquid amber, the smoke vaulted and blinding. He made his way by the sound of windows imploding as the fire breathed in what air it had not already consumed and sucked the glass inward with it, the last rattling breaths of his home, the shattering panes points of reference by which he triangulated his place within the conflagration and mapped his way to the door, a pint bottle clenched in his hand, a grease-stained barn coat under his arm. He took his hat from its peg by the door and stumbled out and across the ground and donned the coat and leaned against a tree, entranced, watching his cabin burn in the chill night. Sparks flumed up toward the stars as his cabin's clapboard skin splintered and crackled and sloughed away. He raised the bottle and drank to the fire's success and resealed it and said fuck it anyway and collapsed as his home's bones gave way altogether and slept where he fell until morning.

The cold roused him early to light pale and watery. He blinked and remembered. Before him lay ashes. He worked his way to his knees and set one foot on the ground and arose unsteady. Among the remnants of his home, ribbons of blue smoke weakly rose from the last of the flames flickering leaf-like among the ashes. The refrigerator and woodstove stood askew in a pond of ash. The TV lay molten on a pair of blackened floor joists, curled in on itself like the lips of a toothless derelict.

He went around to the side. All that remained of the back porch were the cypress pilings. He realized he had never thought to wonder who had driven them and from what far reaches they had come. He looked again down to the river, from which a keening breeze rose, smelling of ice, sharp and bitter, and up to the roiling sky, turbulent and iron gray. Rain was imminent. He turned to go and as he did, the bottle in his coat pocket slapped against him and he took it out and opened it and pulled hard from it, the sting of it wasp-like in his stomach.

He put back the bottle and left, walking along the macadam road, pocked here and there with potholes from the long winter. In another month they would come out and patch them so the summer people would arrive to smooth roads. There would be motorboats on the river and fishermen wading out with new waders and fly rods and the store keepers would be happy about that but nobody else would. Sycamores, yet unwilling to arouse and bud, arched over the road, their branches black and spindly, their trunks blotched and scaled. Harmon followed them until they turned to pitch pines and followed those a little farther, past old man Montgomery's abandoned cabin. He stood on the road and looked at it and thought if it was shelter enough and would it stand up through the storm and decided it wasn't worth taking a chance on. If it had been worth anything, somebody would have taken it already. He turned and continued on and came to a place where the road bent in toward the river and a narrow path cut crooked through brown brush down to the bank and he took it until it came to another path running along close to the water and on to a small clearing where a rough plank table stood leaning toward the river with weathered benches and a circle of stones on the ground where a fire might be built but no one had built a fire in it since last summer and he had had enough of fire for this day.

Harmon lowered himself down to the bench on the side away from the river and grunted and held his hand on his side. The river glittered in spite of the darkling sky, the light spinning in silver spokes off the water. He took out the pint and looked at it and twisted off the cap and thought better and reset the cap and slipped the bottle back in his coat. A barge whistle blew from somewhere he couldn't see and he thought about how when they were kids they would swim out to a barge with a rope and tie it on and the barge would drag them upstream, and the crew on the barge yelling at them were they trying to get themselves killed and get the fuck off and they would yell back what could they do about it. And then they would take off the rope and float back down toward home, indolent and at peace under the sun, the river like a pair of cupped hands holding them afloat.

The breeze came up harder, scattering the wheels of light, wrinkling the water with its breath so that the river took on the cast of a great and ancient reptile, its scaled skin bulging and threatening to split open as it rose to the surface, its back humped, and slipped down again into atavistic darkness. Shards of rain came with the wind, stinging him about the eyes. He got up grunting and moved on. He came up to where the old man had his houseboat. He had fashioned a slip of sorts, a gangway of discarded planks lashed to pine logs salvaged from other storms long past, and tied his houseboat up to it, his lodging but a skiff with a PVC frame holding up a cracked brown tarp to keep out the rain and a pallet with musty smelling blankets laid across its thwarts.

The old man had a fire going under a second tarp and a pot on the fire with root vegetables and onions boiling. He picked up a wooden spoon and stirred. A bloody, gutted catfish lay on the jetty, its eyes cloudy and bewildered. The old man squinted out from under his hat and through his cataractic eyes saw it was Harmon and said hey Harmon and Harmon said hey back. The old man said for him to have a seat and nodded to a wooden box. The old man took up a filet knife and deftly went to it on the catfish, cutting it into chunks. He spread them across the top of the water boiling in the pot and took a church key from his pocket and opened a can of milk and poured that in too, gently, with an up and down gesture and told Harmon it wasn't going to be but a couple minutes more and he had an extra pan. Harmon was welcome to it if he wanted some. Harmon told him he already ate and he had a place to be and couldn't stay, but thanks anyway. The old man asked him was he sure and Harmon lied again, saying yes he was.

The old man lifted the pot off the coals but kept stirring. He told Harmon he saw the fire last night and it was a shame, and asked what happened. Harmon said he didn't altogether remember what happened and the old man said he knew how that was. They sat for a while and the old man asked Harmon if maybe he didn't have a little taste on him and Harmon said he was fresh out but he had a cigarette if he wanted it and the old man said he did. Harmon took the pack out of his shirt pocket and flipped it so one stuck up and held it out to the old man and took one himself. The old man held a twig in the flames until it took fire and they lit their cigarettes off it and sat back on their boxes under the tarp and relaxed. The old man coughed and told Harmon he would give him a bed if he had one, but there wasn't hardly space enough for just him to stay dry and Harmon said I know you would and there's places you can go to when you know where to look. That's so, the old man said.

Tabernacle Parish, 1953-1955

When she had healed, Agnes only left LeRoy alone for the little bit of time it took to go out and bring back a customer. At first she kept his bassinette on the far side of the bed but near enough so she could still hear him if he cried. She stopped doing that after a white customer saw the child right after he got inside her and screamed Jesus Christ and pulled out and jumped up and grabbed his undershorts off the floor and went to rubbing himself with them like someone poured lye on him and threw the undershorts on the floor and lurched around the room cursing and reeling like he had got a cerebral hemorrhage and was going to die in the next minute and never got around to getting himself right with God. He pulled on his shirt and went to hit her, and she saw in his eyes that he was afraid to touch her at all, even to lay his rage on her. He put on the rest of his clothes, pushing his undershorts away with the toe of his boot like they were a dead rat, and reached for the money Agnes had foolishly left on the dresser, but he wouldn't even touch that and pulled back his hand and stumbled down the stairs muttering Jesus Christ and fuck, his erection still bulging through his jeans.

After that she put the bassinette in the back room when she went out to work up business, but as soon as the customer left, she would go back and pick her baby up and tell him she was sorry and it might look like she was ashamed of him, but she wasn't and it wouldn't be like this forever. But it was still like that when he learned to walk and she had to put him in a playpen and if it was early, give him something to play with so he would be quiet.

One night he figured out how to escape the playpen and came out when a black customer was getting dressed. When he saw LeRoy he smiled and said what's this and Agnes went over and picked up the child and said he wasn't supposed to come out and the man said it was okay, bring him over. He tickled him under his chin and called him little man and said he had a baby boy himself somewhere and a child is a precious thing and when he left, he laid two extra dollars on the dresser.

Agnes got to know which men would despise her for the boy and which wouldn't care one way or the other and which would take to him. When he was old enough to talk, she worked out signs with him for when he was supposed to stay hidden and when he was supposed to come out. She showed him how to look shy with his thumb in his mouth and half hide between the curtains separating the front room from the kitchen and look cute. He was good at it and she was a little bit ashamed for teaching him to be that way. She said to herself it was only for a little while and he wouldn't remember it when he was older that he had watched his mother fuck strangers for money.

Brigard County, March 1993

First light seeped under the boathouse door feeble and gray and under the walls reaching out over the river. Harmon had taken the black canvas cover off the boat and folded it into a bed on the floating deck, and now he gathered the cover up and straightened it out and put it back on the boat, snapping down the grommets so no one would know what he'd done. He moved stiffly, sick to his stomach from the night of wind-fueled eddies lapping against the boat and rocking the deck. If he had held off with the Paramount, it would have been enough to settle his stomach, but he hadn't been able to and now he was sick. He got up off the deck and went to a window and looked out into the rain. There was a light on in the house. He took the empty pint and held it under the cold water and let it fill until it sank down into the bit of river like a tongue in the mouth of the boathouse. There was a workbench with a stool and an old fly vise on the bench clutching a half-made black fly. He sat on the stool and stared at the fly and took out a cigarette and smoked it halfway down and snuffed it out and put the butt in the pack and by then the hiss of the rain had gone quiet and the light under the door had gone sharp white and it was time to leave before whoever was up at the house came down.

He shuffled up the ramp to the door and stepped out and looked over the leaf-littered grass toward a row of swamp maples drooping bare limbed over the river. A cawing crow came from behind him and alighted awkwardly on a low-hanging branch.

Harmon coughed and the crow twisted its neck and looked at him and cawed some more and swept out its ungainly wings and set out again, flying low over the river, and turned upstream and out of sight. Harmon turned too, to go up across the brown grass to the road. A woman in a bathrobe sat on the back porch drinking coffee from a mug. She came down across the yard in a hurry, the mug in her hand, and came right up to him and told him he was trespassing and he said he knew he was. She asked what was he doing in her boathouse and he told her sleeping and she asked him had he taken anything and he said he hadn't, he thought the house was empty, it looking like a summer house, and he was just getting out of the rain. He told her he would be going and wouldn't bother her and was sorry if he scared her.

She looked at him for a while and then asked him if he wanted something to eat and he said thank you, he would. She told him to come up to the house with her and wait on the porch. She walked in front of him up across the yard, holding the front of her robe closed with one hand and the mug in the other. She led him up the porch steps and motioned him to a chair and went inside. Harmon looked over the railing and out over the river, its water a darker gray than the sky. A skiff with an outboard struggled up the current. The rain had stiffened the force of the river and it would run strong for another day or so. He could see the summer houses across the river. He thought about that. How someone could be well enough off to have two houses, and one of them for just being near the water and here he had been near water all his life, and how much did it cost to have one house you lived in and another for being near the water? Not as much of a price as he had paid for his own life by water.

The woman came out with a tray holding a plate of eggs and potatoes and a mug of coffee. She looked out over the river while he ate, his gorge pulsing against the food going down. When he was done she took up the tray and told him she'd be right back and went inside. She brought back another mug of coffee for him and one for herself and sat down. She told him if he had any respect for himself he'd pay for staying in the boathouse and would he want to work it off raking up the yard. Harmon nodded. She pointed to the garage off from the side of the house and told him he'd find tools in there and work gloves and it wasn't anymore locked than the boathouse and went back inside. Harmon stood at the top of the porch steps looking out over the narrow acre of damp litter lying heavy on the ground. The eggs tried to come up and the gorge burned the back of his throat and he swallowed it back down.

A set of red-stained stairs ran up the side of the two-story garage to a landing and a door. A dormer jutted out from the center of the roof, its rain-streaked, latticed windows showing dust from the inside. He went in through a side door. The garage was dim like the boathouse, with the smell of gasoline and the metallic smell of cold concrete. An old white Lincoln convertible, mammoth and gleaming. A wooden workbench like the one in the boathouse, but empty except for a bench vise, its red paint unscuffed, and a pair of leather-palmed work gloves. Professional red tool chests bookending the workbench. Harmon took down a rake from its hook on the side wall and went back out into the yard, leaving the gloves on the bench. On the far side of the property, the yard abutted a vacant lot gone to bramble and thorn and on this side faded gradually into brush and scrub. His work lay in between. He started at the side in a line from the porch and worked his way across to the brush and started back. The tangled brown grass under the wet leaves lay long and stringy and clung to the rake's tines, making the job harder. After three crossings the pile was too thick and heavy to manage. He went down near the bank and raked from there toward the river and into the water and went back up a little way from where he had begun the second time and raked a new line. He went back up to the first pile and started again from just below that and made another line and then from below that another and kept on that way until the yard was striped with windrows of piled leaves. Sometimes as he reached out with the rake, his side would torment him and he grimaced. But as he worked, the ache became familiar and tolerable. He found a rhythm to his task, reaching and clutching and pulling, the upturned leaves darkly glistening, smelling of rot, the path living things take on their way to becoming soil. The clouds gave way altogether and the sun came through and warmed him and the stiffness in him loosened. He took off his hat and wiped his brow with his sleeve and put his hat back on and returned to his work.

The woman came out the door carrying a box of trash bags and walked down to him and said he would need them and he told her he was just raking the leaves into the water. She asked if that was allowed. He pointed down to show her where the river ran speckled with leaves the storm had blown into it and told her the river didn't care. She looked where he pointed and nodded and went back into the house. She'd put on a black dress cut low in the back and showing her shoulders, her muscles creased like a man's, her spine like a sapling bending and straightening in the breeze as she walked.

Harmon worked all through the morning, rolling the fetid lines all the way down to the water. He began near the bank with the first line and followed with the next one higher up and by noon had traversed the yard a half dozen times with that many more still to go, covering the same ground over and over. The leaves roiled over groaning, weary, the color of rust and the color of shit and the color of dried blood. Webs of grass clutched at them, clinging and holding on, the rake a conduit between the denial of a body alive and the truth of the cavernous earth ravenous for more bones. Nausea thrummed up from the earth and through the rake like angry voices arguing along a telephone wire. He staggered and stumbled in a rush down to the river and got down on all fours behind a tree so she wouldn't see him vomit into the water and know that he was only being polite when he accepted her offer of breakfast.

Brigard County, March 1993

From time to time, Edna rose from her paperwork and went to a window and watched Harmon wrestle with the leaves. Drunken and homeless, she thought, but no stranger to work. And went back to her own work. So many documents. So many Latin words. Attorney's fees. Insurance forms. Her husband's estate's tax returns awaiting her signature, the ghost of him reincarnated as legal entity. From flesh to paper. This Harmon fellow emerging ghostlike himself from the boathouse.

She picked up yet another spurious claim from yet another faraway stranger, one of those who suspected her an easy target, an indolent widow bred from an indolent wife, as if stupidity follows naturally from marrying a wealthy man. She placed it along with some other papers in a large manila envelope addressed to the attorneys. She imagined the claimant opening the gilded envelope they would in turn send him, his starry-eyed avariciousness evaporating as his gaze traveled down the stiff beige letterhead demanding that he cease and desist and the threat of litigation if he did not.

Paper by paper she continued on until midafternoon and went again to the window just as Harmon came up from the river's bank, rake in hand, the yard cleared. Part way up, he bent down and picked up a dead tree branch that had blown in over the winter and as he passed the garage, tossed it into the weeds beyond. She went out onto the porch with her purse and waited for him to come back from putting up the rake and called him over. She told him she had underestimated the amount of work she'd asked of him and took fifty dollars from the purse and handed it to him. He took the money and thanked her and apologized again for his trespass and turned and walked toward the road.

She told him to come back. There was more work here if he wanted it and could he come back tomorrow. He said he could and left. As she went into the house, she realized what she had done, given a drunkard money, and wondered if she would ever see him again and thought about following after him, shouting for him to cease and desist, but simply returned to her paper-laden table and sat and took up another government form and signed it.

Tabernacle Parish, 1957

Agnes went up her stairs, the big man behind her. They went in and he pulled the money from his pocket and put it on the dresser. She saw LeRoy peeping from the slit of the curtain with his little bright bird eye and fluttered her hand with the sign that when it was over, LeRoy should come out and say he was thirsty. She reached behind herself to unzip her dress and the man said wait and went to her and took her face in his rough-skinned hands the color of strong black coffee and just looked at her for a while. Then he kissed her forehead with no more pressure than if he was brushing her face with a wildflower.

He took off his denim work shirt and laid it over the lamp by the bed, the air in the room turning to the soft blue of the shirt. He asked her did she have a radio and she turned it on and he asked her if she wouldn't mind changing the station to something not so loud and maybe slower. He took her into his arms and set his hands firm on her, one in the small of her back and the other between her shoulders and held her cheek against his broad chest and she nestled there, feeling him breathe and after a while heard his heart strong and steady. He smelled like the ground after rain. He swayed, slow, like the massive, barely discernible rhythm of the night melding into the morning and she let him lead her in a gossamery dance. He slid his hands up her back and took her dress's zipper in his fingers and drew it down one click at a time, and when her dress was undone and he slipped it from her shoulders, her breath came out of her with a little quavering sound in the exact same way she knew not to.

He undressed her one garment at a time, kissing her in between each one, and guided her to the bed and let her down and undressed himself the rest of the way and lay down beside her and pulled her to him and laid his hand on the back of her head, holding her against him like she was his child. He stiffened against her thigh and she opened her legs and let him swell between them, the blue air embracing them and the music from the radio rising.

He turned her over on her belly and kissed her neck and shoulders and between her shoulder blades and down across her waist, no tongue, just lips, and breathed on every inch of her, all the way to her feet. And then he lowered over her and came into her from behind, resting his weight on his elbows so that she would not have to bear the enormous might of him. She willed herself open and caressed him from within and closed tight around him and sighed again. He nestled into her neck and rubbed her cheek with his and began to rock, filling her with the heat of himself, and he warmed the entire room. He filled her completely, the strokes of him suffusing through her like a glass of wine that awakens the skin and then warms you all the way down to your bones. She climaxed twice before he did and when he came he made a sound not like the feral gnarr that other men make when they are released, but like a kitten suckling from its mother.

Still within her, he rolled the two of them on their sides and wrapped his arm under her neck and took up her white hand in his dark one and wove his fingers into hers and touched her shoulder with his other hand as he softened within her, barely touching her, his light caress the most sensual she had ever felt. They lay together, his chest to her back for a long while and then he asked her how much it was for all night. Agnes signaled for LeRoy to go to bed and the little bird eye disappeared from the slit in the curtain.

When Agnes awoke, Whiskey was looking at her. He asked her did she have any coffee and she went to get up. He told her to just stay there and tell him where it was, he would make it. She pointed to a cabinet. He got up and found the can and opened the pot sitting on the stove and threw out the old grounds and the old coffee and rinsed the pot and filled it and scooped in new grounds and set it to boiling. He asked did she have any eggs and she pointed to the refrigerator and he asked where there was a fry pan and she laughed and said are you sure you don't want me to do that? He asked how she liked her eggs and he got them started and by then the pot was perking and he turned down the flame. He looked in the cupboards and found plates and forks and set them out on the table and when the eggs were done, served them out on the plates and poured each of them coffee and told her she could get up now.

Agnes slipped on a nightdress and went to the table and they ate. They didn't talk for a while. Then she asked him how he got that name Whiskey.

Names is a complicated thing he said.

Brigard County, Summer, 1973

The chief drove up to the bridge and stopped and turned off the engine and the headlights. He tilted back his hat and scratched at his chest through the buttons of his khaki shirt and drummed his fingers on the outside of the door. Drivers coming over the bridge saw him and slowed down and sometimes they nodded if they knew him and sometimes they didn't nod because they knew him. Across the river, a set of headlights wound down the gravel road to the boat ramp and then along the service road to under the bridge and the lights went off. A semi lumbered down the hill, compression breaking. A motorcycle with straight pipes went spitting up the road on the other side. And then quiet. The rank, sweet scent of the river wafted up from under the bridge and spread out over the street and in through the car windows. He turned on the radio and listened to a cowboy song and then turned it off. A motorboat came up the river and turned in at the public dock and three men got out and tied it up and walked across the lot. They carried a cooler and tackle and he saw a match flare from all the way up here as one of them lit a cigarette. They got in a car and drove off. All of these things went on like a stray dog going along the back of your yard and you watch it vaguely from the porch. Watch it stop and sniff to see if what lies in the grass is worth eating and lifting its leg and stopping and going on again, the dog a trespasser but doesn't know it or even know what a trespasser is and you let it go because of its ignorance. Or maybe you go in and get a .22 and come back out and kill it because of its ignorance.

A skiff with a shadowy figure sitting in it came downriver, slow, the figure facing forward toward the bow and working the oars awkwardly. From time to time he stood and poled with an oar to get the skiff farther from the bank or to straighten its course. The chief watched him without looking until the skiff got to the light by the bridge and he saw that the figure was black. He sat up and paid attention then as the oarsman let the boat drift down and, poling again, steered into the dock where the fishermen had tied up and slipped in beside their boat and stepped out onto the dock and took up a line from the skiff's bow and stood looking at the motorboat with the line in his hand. He tied up the line and went over to the boat and stooped down on the dock and stared into it. The chief started up the car and drove down and when he got close put the spotlight on the interloper and saw that he was a young man. The chief got out of the car and spat in the water with a little chirping sound like an insect and asked him what did he think he was doing and he said admiring the boat and wishing he had one and then he wouldn't have to keep on working so hard to go down the river. The chief asked him how could he know he wasn't fixed on stealing something out of the boat and maybe even on stealing the whole boat. The young man said because if he was going to steal it, would he be so all out stupid to just walk up to it. He would have gone on past to see who was watching and tie up someplace else and work his way back on land and figure out how to do it without getting caught. And then he told the chief that there was a better way for him to know he wasn't thinking about stealing the boat and the chief asked him what that was and he told him because the boat was still here. The chief hit him with his stick.

Get out the car the chief told his prisoner and took him by the arm and led him inside. Under bright lights a deputy had his feet up on a chair, watching the news and drinking coffee from a paper cup. The chief took his prisoner over to the deputy and told him to process him and the deputy asked him for what and the chief told him for now make it loitering and they'd figure the rest out tomorrow. Just get him settled.

The deputy put his feet down and told the prisoner to sit in the chair. He turned to his desk and took a form out of the side drawer and a pen from a glass jar. The deputy asked him what his name was and he said LeRoy James. The deputy snickered and looked at the chief and they shook their heads. The deputy said did his mama give him that name so everybody would be absolute sure they was dealing with a dumb-ass nigger in case there was any doubt. LeRoy looked doe-eyed at the deputy and said he supposed so. The deputy asked some more questions and said to the chief where did he want him and the chief said to put him in with Harmon, no sense dirtying up two cells and he left.

The deputy slid back the cell door and took LeRoy's cuffs off. LeRoy looked around baffled. The deputy told him to go on in. LeRoy asked the deputy what was he supposed to do. The deputy told him what he could do was get in there and stay quiet. LeRoy stepped into the cell and saw a young man lying on a cot with his arm over his eyes. LeRoy said hi and Harmon looked up and nodded and put his arm back on his eyes. The pipes clanged. LeRoy watched Harmon for a while and then sat on the other cot. They were close enough together that LeRoy could have reached out and touched Harmon. LeRoy asked were they going to get blankets, it was cold in here. Harmon told him this was just a holding cell, he'd get a blanket if they decided to send him over to county.

LeRoy got up and walked the length of the small cell and back and did it again and asked Harmon wasn't there supposed to be a window. Harmon didn't say anything and LeRoy sat back down and tapped his fingers on the edge of the cot. He started humming, his fingers keeping time to the song. After a while Harmon peeked out from under his arm and went back in under it and squirmed back and forth trying to find a soft spot on the cot. LeRoy hummed louder and Harmon looked out again a couple more times and finally told him why didn't he just lay down and go to sleep. LeRoy said how could you sleep with the lights on and Harmon mumbled you get used to it.

Harmon swung his legs over the side of the cot and sat up and asked LeRoy was this his first time and LeRoy said it was. LeRoy asked Harmon what he was in for and Harmon told him for being drunk. LeRoy asked how was that a crime and Harmon said it wasn't, they just brought him in here to keep things from getting out of hand and they would let him out in the morning. LeRoy said they got me for loitering and how bad was that. Harmon told him it just meant the chief was checking him out and if there wasn't any warrants would let him out in the morning too.

The deputy came in early and told them the chief had called and said to let them both out. He unlocked the cell door and pointed to the office and they went out and the deputy followed them. He got their wallets out of a desk drawer and gave them to them and said for them to stay out of trouble. LeRoy asked wasn't there a paper for them to sign and the deputy said no there wasn't, they wasn't arrested, they was just here for their own good. Harmon asked if the deputy had any idea where his truck was and the deputy told him he imagined it was where he left it. Harmon said he didn't remember where he left it and the deputy said most likely it was at the Lone Pine. Harmon said shit, and asked if they had his keys and the deputy told him no. Harmon said you left my truck up there with the keys in it? The deputy said his truck was safe. Nobody there sober enough to figure out how to steal it or drive it if they did figure out how. Harmon asked him what was the chances the deputy would give him a ride. The deputy just looked at him. Harmon walked off, LeRoy trailing.

LeRoy wanted to know where was they going. Harmon said he didn't know about LeRoy but he was going home. LeRoy asked him where that was. Harmon pointed across the river and downstream. LeRoy looked confused. He looked over across the river and then in the direction they were going. Aint that the long way round? Harmon kept walking. LeRoy said I got a boat and Harmon stopped and looked at him and said where was it and LeRoy told him he wasn't altogether sure because of him being dizzy after the chief hit him but it was tied up next to a motorboat and there was a bridge. He remembered the bridge. Harmon said that was the way they were going.

The skiff lay heavy in the river, green water sloshing in the bottom, bare wood showing weathered gray through its dirty yellow paint. Harmon said where you'd get it and LeRoy said he borrowed it. Harmon walked to the end of the dock and went into a trash can and came back with a styrofoam tray. He scraped a French fry out with his finger and flicked it into the water. He bailed what he could out of the skiff and tossed the tray aside and got in the boat. LeRoy slipped the rope off the post and stepped in and stood in the stern and took up an oar and pushed them from the dock.

Harmon told him to sit down before he drowned the both of them and hand over the oar and he'd show him how to work the skiff. He took the oar and got the other one from where it lay in the bottom and slipped them into the oarlocks. Harmon spun the skiff around and began to row, the bow pointed a little upriver and pulled strong and full through with each stroke, pushing with his feet. LeRoy said he thought they were going the other way. Harmon said be patient. When they got out in the river's surging channel, he brought in the oars and let the river take the skiff. The river turned them down and into its current. Harmon leaned back on his elbows and closed his eyes and let the rising sun shine full on his face.

The Story of My Life

By

LeRoy James

Chapter 1

I got the idea to write this book after I watched some girls getting
baptized in the river. There was some old men watching with
me. They wanted to see the girls get their baptizing dresses wet
so they could see through them. They had a bottle of whiskey
and they gave me some. The preacher looked at us drinking the
whiskey but he didn't say nothing about it. When the preacher was
done saving everybody, he came over and said we was welcome
to come to service any time. Then he went in the church. One
of the old men said maybe we should take him up on his offer
next time because them girls would be getting changed out of
their baptizing clothes and putting on their real clothes and that
would be worth seeing. But they have rooms for that so they
can do it in private without people looking at them, so he didn't
know what he was talking about. I do know because I been in
a church right after people been baptized and saw the changing
rooms with my own eyes. Then he told some dirty jokes and one
of the other guys said he should write a book. Probably make a
million dollars. I been thinking about it for a while and decided to
get this composition book and write a book of my own. Part of
what I was thinking about was what I would put in the book and
decided to tell the story of my life, because it would be easy, all
I would have to do is write down what I saw and what I did, but
it ain't is not easy. The hardest part so far is figuring out what to
start with how to get it started. You can only go back so far. Like

you cannot remember getting born. ~~About the furthest I can go back is about when I was 4.~~ I sort of remember some things from before I was 4, ~~but not like I really remember them~~ but in pieces and not real clear. Like I remember looking up at Mama when she was standing next to the sink but not able to see what she was doing. I remember looking out the window at a man getting out of a car but I do not remember where he went or remember if it was somebody I knew. I can guess why he was there but you should not say that kind of thing about somebody if you are not 100 percent sure of it. There is one thing from when I was 3 that I remember all of. It was a dream. ~~People~~ You will probably think it is strange that the first thing anybody could remember is a dream but it is true. ~~The dream started at the top of the stairs~~ The first thing I remember in the dream was looking down the stairs that went from our apartment down to the outside door. I remember I wanted to go outside. Then ~~the next thing~~ I was flying down the stairs except not really flying. More like I was floating in the air like a balloon. I was scared. ~~I was afraid~~ I would fall on the stairs. I tried to lift up so I would fly straight ahead instead of being pointed down but I kept on going down. I never hit the stairs but I came close a couple times. When I got to the bottom I came up in a little circle and floated down real easy and landed light as a feather on my feet by the door. It is ~~weird~~ odd how I remember little things in the dream. I remember the color of the light brown paint on the walls. And the stairs was dark brown. I even remember how the boards was worn through the paint all the way to the wood and that the front door was black and had a window at the top. It was the kind of window divided into windowpanes and I even remember that there was 9 of them. 3 across and 3 down. I could not see the street out the window being that I was only 3 and too short but I did see a tree and a bird on one of its limbs. ~~So that is it for chapter 1.~~ I have just read this over again and I am wondering how I could see out the window and watch the man get out of the car but I could not see out the window in the door. The window I saw the man out of was a regular window in the wall and not a door window so it would have been lower down, but even so, it would be too high up for somebody who is only 3 to see out of it. I must of stood up on something. Maybe a chair? But Mama would have yelled at me if I stood on a chair like that, she would be afraid I would fall. Maybe that memory is made up and not a real memory? So now that really is it for ~~chapter 1~~ Chapter 1.

Brigard County, March, 1993

Harmon stood at the foot of the steps and looked up at the solder-gray sky framing Ruby's slate roof. The darkening street stretched before him and he turned to follow it and stopped and said fuck it under his breath and turned again to the steps and went up and across the porch to the door. A ragged tear still gaped in the screen and would go on unrepaired for yet another year, and in the summer flies would scavenge inside as had their ancestors through simmering summers past. He reached for the handle and heard a voice call from below. Hold up, Harm. Harmon looked down toward the street at Old Johnson grinning up. I heard you got burned up he said. Harmon told him just his cabin and Old Johnson said aint that a blessing and came up the steps and they went in together.

Silent men with beers in front of them sat in spindly chairs at round wood tables. Ruby leaned on the yellow Formica counter reading a newspaper and when they walked in she looked up and said Harmon, I been waiting on you and asked him was he all right and he said no worse than before, just poorer was all. She asked Harmon did he have a place to stay and he told her he was working on it. She lowered her voice and said if he needed it, she was down a girl and could hold a room for him no charge for a couple of nights and he said he'd had a day's work and could pay for it and he could pay for it now up front if she wanted and started for his pocket. She laid her hand on his and told him if there was anybody deserved a reprieve from his worries it was him and what he did with his own money wasn't her business. But it didn't matter how much his pay was, it wasn't enough for the night and a room both and the last thing he wanted was to be begging her for the money back so he could keep on going. He nodded and said he'd have a sandwich and a beer and asked Old Johnson if he wanted a sandwich and Old Johnson said he already ate but he'd take a beer. Harmon told Ruby make it two. She patted his hand and got the beers and made the sandwich and he gave her a ten and she made change.

Harmon asked her who was back there and she told him you know and he said he probably shouldn't go back empty handed and told her to give him a pint of Paramount. He put the pint in his coat pocket and took the beers and the sandwich to a table and sat. Old Johnson sat down at the table with his beer and watched Harmon eat. He drummed his fingers on the sticky tabletop and looked out the window and said the days was getting longer and Harmon said he guessed they was. Old Johnson said Jesus, Harm, you going to make me beg for it? Harmon told him it was for in back and he was welcome to come along but he just wanted to sit here and finish the sandwich first and Old Johnson worked his mouth like a dying fish but didn't say anything. Two young men in denim jackets came in and got a 30. Ruby told them to have a good time and they said they were counting on it. Ruby told them they could have a good time right here if they knew what she meant and she canted her head up in a knowing little jerk and pointed her slant eyes toward the ceiling. They said they didn't figure they were that desperate yet and went out. They looked sideways at Harmon and Old Johnson on their way past and one of them smirked and said now *there's* desperate and Harmon said to Old Johnson let's go back.

They went down the hall to the back room. LeRoy was there and Biker Wayne and Darryl. LeRoy said have a seat and moved over on the couch and when Harmon worked himself down, he grimaced and pressed his elbow into his side where the ache lay. Darryl was taking a drink from a bottle. He pulled the bottle away from his mouth and said shit, but that was nasty and LeRoy said didn't he know it and wiped at his rheumy eyes and the sweat on his forehead with a white handkerchief. Darryl asked what is this shit and LeRoy told him to look at the label and see what it says and Darryl said he didn't have his glasses but he didn't need no glasses to see it was bad whiskey and Biker Wayne said there aint no such thing and he wasn't too high class to have another turn, waving with his tattooed arm for Darryl to give him the bottle. Muddy sediment snaked up from the bottom and Old Johnson said Christ, at least they could have strained it. Darryl said that's on purpose to give it character. Harmon reached over and took the bottle before Biker Wayne got it and took a long pull and started choking and coughed and said Jesus fuck, that is about the worst I ever tasted and LeRoy said you always was a top shelf man and he wouldn't be surprised if he had a bottle of his own on him and Harmon pulled the Paramount out of his coat. LeRoy said he knew Harmon was holding out on them. Biker Wayne said why didn't they mix them together and Old Johnson said what and risk it exploding and burning Ruby's to the ground? He looked at Harmon and said he was sorry, he didn't think first and Harmon said he didn't have nothing to be sorry for and for all he knew maybe that's what happened. LeRoy said he was going to miss it wasn't he and Harmon said no doubt he would. LeRoy said they used to have some good times there and Harmon said that was a fact. LeRoy asked him did he remember those girls that robbed them that time. Harmon said you aint going to bring that up again are you, everybody already heard it and LeRoy said yeah I am. It's a funny story you got to admit and Harmon said he guessed it was. Old Johnson said *he* never heard it.

LeRoy said him and Harmon and Eli picked up some girls at the Hogshead and the girls said they wanted to go someplace private. Harmon said what about his place and they said it sounded good to them. The girls had a car and LeRoy and Eli went with two of the girls in the car and Harmon took the other one in his truck. One of them was fat as a corncrib and that one was LeRoy's on account of him being black and lucky to get any white girl at all. Eli was in the front with the skinny girl and the fat girl got herself straddled over LeRoy in the back, dry humping him and damn near crushed him to death before they even got to Harmon's. The girls said they wanted to be outside but someplace out of sight and they all six of them went out on the back porch and the girls said they figured since it was still just in the afternoon and they had a long night ahead of them, maybe they ought to blow them first so they could take their time later on and they all said sure, if that's what you want. Who wouldn't?

Biker Wayne said he knew LeRoy had a silver tongue but he always liked the way Eli told it better, even if it wasn't real elegant, and he picked it up from there and told them the story the way Eli always had. He said the girls made them lay down on their backs on the porch with their feet pointed toward the river and the girls unbuckled their belts. LeRoy put his hands under his head and laid back like he was a big shot and said it would work better and save time if they took their pants off altogether and didn't just unzip them and pull their dicks out and the fat girl said that's just what they had in mind, the deeper the better, and she gave LeRoy a dirty wink that said she knew what it was he really wanted. The girls took off the guys' shoes so they could get their pants off over their feet and then they got down on the porch floor and started blowing them. Eli said he looked over and the fat girl was bobbing up and down over top of LeRoy like a beer truck with busted springs on a washboard road. And LeRoy's dick was coming in and out of her mouth like a blacksnake rooting around after a ground squirrel. Now that he saw how good she was at it, he wondered if maybe he didn't make a bad pick and from his sideways angle she didn't look all that bad. LeRoy started howling like a cat in heat and Eli looked over at Harmon and Harmon's just had the end of his between her lips like she was trying to get down an oyster for the first time and doing her best not to gag on it. Harmon looked back and they was both of them laughing and Eli thought they were like the three musketeers with their swords drawn and all for one and one for all. LeRoy started yelling and cursing, Jesus Christ I'm going to blow the fuck up and Eli was just about there too when the one on Harmon spit him out and yelled time to go. They all three of the girls jumped up and kicked them in the nuts and you think LeRoy was screaming when he was getting ready to come, you should have heard him then. Rolled over into a tight little ball and had his face down on the floor and there was his little bitty ass sticking up like a couple of cupcakes with chocolate icing and he was yelling motherfucker!, she fucking kicked me in the nuts and then he couldn't say nothing because he couldn't hardly breathe and Eli wanted to say no shit, on account of how funny it was, but when he tried to say it, all he could get out was a prissy little hiss like piss was coming out his mouth instead of words. That's how far up his throat his girl rammed his nuts. The girls grabbed their pants and ran in the cabin. Harmon's didn't get him as bad and he was able to get up and start after them, but just because she didn't get him as bad, didn't mean she didn't get him and he was staggering back and forth and banging into everything and knocking over chairs and falling down and he was yelling son-of-a-bitch and motherfuck every time he ran into something. By the time he made it out front, the fat girl was taking the keys out of his truck and the other girls were in their car and yelling at her to hurry up and laughing like crazy and when they saw Harmon on the porch, just started laughing all the more and throwing him kisses. The one driving leaned out the window and held up his wallet and yelled out did he have any more friends would like to get blowed. The fat girl threw Harmon's keys way out in the weeds and got in the back seat and off they went and Harmon started up the road after them before he remembered he was naked from the waist down, just kind of dangling in the wind and he started jumping up and down because the hot blacktop was burning his bare feet and his dick was flopping around so much it looked like he was trying to beat himself to death with it. Everybody laughed and Darryl said he would just about have paid money to see that.

LeRoy said it was surely a lesson learned. They had enough cash in their wallets they could have gone over to Harrisville and got blowed and laid both for a lot less money and it would have been for all night too and they wouldn't have had to go and get new driver's licenses on top of it. And besides that it took the better part of an hour to find Harmon's goddamn truck keys.

Biker Wayne asked if them Harrisville whores took care of black boys back then and LeRoy said shit, sure they did. Even back then, whores didn't care what color you was, just whether you got any money. And as a matter of fact, he lived there for a while doing chores and they gave him free rent on top of his pay and nobody there ever treated him different than any other whorehouse swamper. Darryl asked him did he ever take his pay out in trade and LeRoy said just the one that was his girlfriend and that was free anyway, so he supposed not.

Old Johnson said there wasn't no such thing as a free girlfriend and give me that bottle again and he looked at the label and read out loud Angel Wings Bonded Whiskey and said he never heard of it before and they should have called it Buzzard Wings. LeRoy said don't all good whiskey taste like varnish and Darryl said more like varnish remover and stop hogging it for yourself and pass it over here.

Biker Wayne said he always liked the way Eli told that story and it was a shame what happened. Harmon and LeRoy looked at each other. Biker Wayne saw them and said he was sorry and he shouldn't have said that.

People went out and some came back and others didn't come back after they left and new people came in. They had names like Road Kill and Wood Pile, and there was for a little while Smokestack John, who sat on the arm of the couch and passed on the Angel Wings. He had some Jack Daniels and when he pulled it out Darryl said did he rob a bank. The Jack Daniels was gone before it got all the way around and Biker Wayne said LeRoy's whiskey was really going to be shit now and he left.

Wood Pile asked did they hear about Tony Young and some of them said they had and some of them hadn't.

Got himself killed over half a pack a cigarettes. Him and his brother was down to their last dollars and they was both out of smokes and Tony told Bobby give him his dollar and he'd get a pack and they could split it. Except he got the cigarettes and didn't give his brother none of them. Just got in his car and went home. Bobby figured it out and went over there and slit his fucking throat.

Over a pack of cigarettes somebody marveled.

Bet he wished he got cut up over stealing a car instead.

There came then a moment of quiet wherein they contemplated the wisdom of what had been said and then they went back to the quarrelsome sound of companions drinking.

Two of Ruby's whores came and stood in the doorway and smoked cigarettes. Wood Pile asked them was they coming in and they told him no, they were just on their break and business was slow. The whores looked around and saw who was there and one said there's nothing here and the other one shrugged and they went out. Somebody said they would have stayed if they saved some of the Jack Daniels and somebody else said he didn't think so, Jack Daniels aint money.

Harmon opened up the Paramount and took a drink and looked around and saw how many they were and drank again and handed it off. The room tilted. Somebody was asking if Ruby was half Chinese or half Japanese and LeRoy said it didn't matter, all that mattered was her black half. Harmon went to say something but stopped. LeRoy said if Ruby had been born in Louisiana she would be a voodoo queen instead of running a whorehouse because people there would think the way she looked gave her magic powers. Darryl said he didn't think it would make a difference, she would be running a whorehouse down there too. People do what they are good at no matter where they are. Somebody said what if she was in New York City?, and Darryl said the only difference was the girls wouldn't be as ugly and passed the Paramount back to Harmon and asked how come nobody ever thought Ruby was half Korean.

Harmon and LeRoy unfolded ponderous and apelike from Ruby's door. They descended bandy legged down the steps to the street where patches of darkness lay scattered like leaves upon garish light shed from street lamps. They held each of them a pint in one hand and clung to the railing with the other, reeling as if orbiting umbral dance partners. Harmon looked up past the lights to what fraction of the stars pierced the street lamps' lavender veils. The stars spun in a short arc and jerked back again to where they had started and spun again and again went back as if shackled to some ordained place and prisoner to it. He looked down to the sidewalk to abate the nausea such spinning drew up from deep within him, where the shit whiskey nestled like a half-satiated ambush predator. The sidewalk slipped sideways, but not as much as the sky. He lit a cigarette and refocused, looking down the hill along the streets carved like stairs into the town all the way down to the river which spun not at all.

LeRoy drew up abreast of him and again said that Angels Wings really was some rough whiskey. LeRoy wheezed and then he rested, his hands on his knees, and looked down to the river too and asked if Harmon was drunk enough yet. Harmon said he was getting close. LeRoy said where you want to go?, and Harmon told him someplace else and they started up the street toward Merchant and turned there and went on past the shops with their corroded metal gates shuttered against thieves and went up a narrow alley and leaned against the bricks, one on either side like debris a flood had washed up on the flats under a bridge. LeRoy said you hurting much? Harmon said he was, but wasn't everybody and he didn't want to talk about it. LeRoy drew on his pint. He held it to his lips, sucking hard. He took it down and held it toward the street at eye level and saw that it was empty and said all good things and dropped the bottle and kicked it clattering down the alley. Harmon drank from his and passed it to LeRoy across the space between them and LeRoy drank and passed it back. Harmon felt in his coat pocket for the cap and screwed it on and put the bottle in his pocket. He said it worked out for the best that LeRoy didn't ever take him up on his invitation to move in with him. Who knows? LeRoy said. Maybe it wouldn't have burned up if LeRoy had of.

Who knows is right.

You know what they say about best friends and fish.

Harmon said he did and then he asked LeRoy was he hungry. LeRoy said he wasn't but he wouldn't mind finding a place to sit down for a while. They went out the alley to the street and went on again in the way they had come, all the way down to the River View Diner.

Shotgun Lenny sat slumped in a booth drinking coffee and they sat on the bench across from him. Harmon called over to Marvin they would have coffee too and Marvin said come over and get it. They asked did Shotgun Lenny want a refill and he said he did. LeRoy started over to get it, lurching, and Marvin said sit back down, I'll bring it. Marvin brought the cups and set them on the table. Harmon got his pint and poured a half shot into Shotgun Lenny's cup and then his and LeRoy's. Marvin said they couldn't do that in here and Shotgun Lenny said fuck if we can't and Marvin went sullenly back behind the counter. There was dispute over the circumstances but none over the results of the altercation that lent Shotgun Lenny his name. When it was done, the flesh of his enemy's shoulder lay splayed and shredded like confetti and a pink froth of blood fogged the air seemingly forever before slowly settling. The man lost his arm and Shotgun Lenny his freedom and when he came home, people like Marvin who knew the story avoided all argument with him.

Shotgun Lenny said he heard and Harmon said everybody heard. Shotgun Lenny wanted to know if they had plans for the rest of the evening and Harmon said his was to get a little bit drunker. Shotgun Lenny said him too. LeRoy dozed, a thread of drool webbing down from his chin. Shotgun Lenny said where should they go. Harmon said maybe Eugene's and Shotgun Lenny said he wasn't so sure they'd let him in. Harmon said you don't know if you don't try. Shotgun Lenny said Harmon did know it would be full price didn't he and Harmon said what difference did what it cost make. Cheap or expensive the money was all going to be gone by morning either way. He poked LeRoy and LeRoy started and looked around vacant-eyed, curious as to how he had arrived. Harmon said him and Shotgun Lenny were going to

Eugene's and did he want to come and LeRoy thought about it for a while. He said he didn't think so and he probably should head for the warmth of his hearth. He asked did Harmon want to get another couple pints and just come there instead and he could stay the night if he wanted to. Harmon told him there wasn't enough room but you know I appreciate it. LeRoy said there was plenty of room under the bridge, he'd just kick the billy goats gruff out, and if you change your mind. Harmon said you know what they say about best friends and fish. LeRoy nodded and shambled out and waved through the broad window as he went back the way he and Harmon had come.

Shotgun Lenny asked Harmon did he have any left. Harmon took out the pint and held it up and stared at its amber dregs circling the bottle's bottom and said maybe a swallow each and took one and handed it to Shotgun Lenny and he finished it off. Marvin watched them. I told you, you can't do that here. Shotgun Lenny said that's the end of it and if he wanted to throw them out go ahead. Marvin went back to wiping coffee cups. Shotgun Lenny asked if Harmon had any money and Harmon said a little bit and what about him. Shotgun Lenny checked and said almost enough.

Harmon said let's go then. They heaved themselves up from the booth and went out into the night. They cut down an alley and went past a row of garages and came up to the back yard of a house. A mongrel dog raced at them snarling and enraged and snapped at the end of its chain and fell and got up and roared at the interlopers. Shotgun Lenny reared back and said fuck, scared the fucking shit out of me. He held up his arms like he had a shotgun aimed at the dog and said bang motherfucker. They went on a ways and the dog stopped barking. Shotgun Lenny said that fucking dog don't know how lucky he is. Harmon braced his hand against a stone wall and said I need a minute and they rested. Harmon looked up to see if the stars still spun. Harmon said you know how bad an idea this is and Shotgun Lenny said he did, but did he have any different idea. They went on and came to Eugene's and no one said they couldn't go in, so they did.

The tavern was soft lit and smoky and the music low enough not to bother anybody. Beer signs glowed green and orange in the windows. Hey Harm somebody called and Harmon looked to see who it was. Ab sat at a table with a woman Harmon didn't know. He said come on over. Shotgun Lenny and Harmon went over and sat down. The woman was embroidering. Shotgun Lenny asked her what she was sewing and she undid the hoop and smoothed the white linen on the table. It said JESUS WEPT inside a border of thorn-adorned flowers. Shotgun Lenny said that was a first and Ab said she got it out of the Bible and Shotgun Lenny said how come she picked that one instead of something prettier. Ab said that's just the way she was. I told her she should have spelled out a beatitude, but she aint got no sense of humor at all.

Why you think Jesus did that?

Did what? Make women too dumb to laugh at a good joke?

Weep.

Cause he just that second figured out how bad he fucked everything up?

Everybody laughed except the woman. She snapped the linen into the hoop and went back to her needle and Harmon considered whether she was mad because of what they said about women or Jesus. Harmon told Shotgun Lenny to give him his money and he added that to his and went to the bar and came back with two pints and three beers and two glasses. Shotgun Lenny asked was that it, and Harmon said was he expecting change. Ab and the woman left. Harmon watched them navigate among the tables and bodies crowding near the door and wondered if the well from which Ab's misery bubbled had at last gone dry and hoped for the woman's sake it had, or Jesus would be weeping for her soon.

Harmon twisted off the cap from his pint and poured his glass half full and slid the other pint and glass over to Shotgun Lenny and opened one of the beers. He crossed his arms on the table and leaned over on them and watched the legs of people walking past and the crossed legs of young women salacious and their tattooed thighs tender and yielding under the tables, their slippered feet brushing the booted feet of young men. He drank. Shotgun Lenny finished his beer and asked did Harmon want to fight him for the last one and Harmon said they could split it and they drained the whiskey from their glasses and portioned out the beer in equal measure, precisely, with the slit carnivorous eyes of usurers.

They finished their half glasses of beer and raised their pints in pantomime of a toast and saluted one another and drank from the bottles. The sounds in the bar, laughter and quarrels and maudlin music and the clinking of ice in glasses, merged into a homogenous visceral murmur and separated again and proceeded so, like a broken band of soldiers marching in and out of step. When the voices came back, they came back rendered not in the cadences of speech but in the coarse screech of rutting cats and the frantic gurgling deep in the throats of the drowning. The room dimmed and before Harmon's eyes patches of blackness like inkblots drifted, so that bodies became detached from their faces and there opened in the gray smoke voids wherein all light was lost and the barroom became a patchwork of dismembered figures. Harmon looked again beneath the tables and saw a hand creep under a woman's skirt and her legs parting in welcome and then closing to embrace the hand. There was in his pint a double shot or so left and he lifted the bottle and like an infant greedily sucking the life from its mother breathed the whiskey in, too fast, so that he choked on the last of it and it stung up behind his nose and clotted rank as sewage in his throat and he staggered up from the table like a dancing bear and lumbered toward the bathrooms gagging.

The men's door was locked and a girl stood before the women's. The women's door opened and Harmon grabbed at the door and tried to shoulder the waiting girl aside and ran into the woman coming out. The girl yelled what the fuck you doing? I'm next and that's the ladies'. And it came up gushing with the taste and smell of rancid cheese and Harmon spun about desperately trying to locate a vessel to receive it and splashed both girls and heaved again as he tried to turn away and he baptized them once more with the distilled yellow bile of Ruby's sandwich and slipped into the wall and fell on hands and knees to the floor. A man came out of the men's room and saw and said you motherfucker and pulled the girl who had been waiting aside and told her to go in the bathroom and he would be in in a minute as soon as he was done with this motherfucker. He turned and placed his foot on Harmon's back and pushed his face to the floor greasy with vomit and kicked him twice, in the face and in his belly where the soot-black fetus of his death lay curled and grinning, and the pain welled up dark and thunderous, and then they came for him. They didn't even throw him out the front but dragged him through the kitchen, his legs trailing, and out to the back lot where they dispensed him like trash and went in and washed themselves clean of him, saying Jesus who let him in? Harmon tried to rise and stumbled and fell again and made his way half crawling to a cavern of wooden boxes and empty beer kegs and sat with one leg folded under him and the other reaching toward the alley, the blood seeping from above his eye the only evidence that he was not dead and as he sighed and went under, the warmth of piss diffused through his groin as gently and lovingly as a motherly kiss.

Harmon awoke to church bells and squinted against the sun. He unbent his leg from under him and waited for feeling to return to it and tested his legs and arms and rose with great effort and shuffled to the alley and made his way to the street and walked with one hand balanced on the storefronts the half-block to an intersection and read the street signs to see where he was and looked down through the cross street to see where the river was and thus knew which direction to take. He stopped twice to rest and another time to heave again, though there was nothing left to come up, and he bucked on all fours, his knees scraping on the sidewalk, moaning and shuddering with the strain of it, and came to Ruby's steps and rested again and climbed the stairs and went in. Ruby looked up at the sound of her door opening and said O Jesus, Harmon.

Brigard County, March 1993

Witch, he thought. Gypsy maybe. Slant eyes set snake bright in her calla face. Hoop earrings and iridescent skirt. Brass and silver-plated talismans braceleting her wrists, dangling prayers on chains to sundry gods. Turquoise and onyx. Witch or gypsy, it don't matter, I aint fucking with either one, and he shrank back into his dwelling's thick foul air, wherein he wrapped himself in the refuge of hearth and spat into a can. From within his gray-black shack, its thinning tarpaper siding dried to alligator scales, the old man squinted out his jaundiced window until she was beyond sight along the crumbling brick alleyway and he let himself take a normal breath.

Ruby went upward through grimy streets where the hopeless prowled, slinking around corners like smoke, mucus soaked and ulcerated. A rattle-backed old crone, trembling on her cane, looked up and met her gaze and looked away, whispering a charm of protection. The old woman crossed herself and drew her coat up tighter around her throat. A young mother with a wisp of a child lurking in the folds of her skirt disappeared in a doorway. Ruby went on through the clammy, refuse-cluttered morning.

She went into Jones's rag store and the bell clinked. Jones looked up. He laid his brittle hand on the pile of faded old clothes he had been sorting, the fingers bent and fragile as dogwood twigs. He said to her what happened, all the uptown stores go belly up?

She told him she thought this was an uptown store and maybe she should go someplace more modest, she didn't want anybody thinking she was putting on airs and he said don't worry, no chance of that and what was she here for. She told him clothes for Harmon.

He asked her was she taking on charity cases now and she told him Harmon lost everything. He said why didn't she just get it new, she could afford it, and she told him Harmon wouldn't take it if it was new. Might not take it at all.

Jones asked her what did she need and she told him pants and shirts and he went to a wooden bin marked CLEARANCE and ruffled through the heaps of castoffs thrown there randomly, gangly limbed like limp arms and legs braided together in a mass grave. He asked her did she know what size and she said large and he said there appeared to be some and pick out what she wanted. She chose two pairs of work trousers worn a little in the knees but unpatched and two work shirts. She checked that the buttons were all there and told him she would take these and he asked did she want anything else. She asked did he have underwear and socks and he said did she want new or second hand. She asked him did he wash the second hand and he laughed. She asked him where was the new and he pointed a gnarled finger to a shelf where lay underwear and sweat socks wrapped in plastic bags with masking tape price tags.

A little on the high side she said.

You want the best you got to pay for it.

She said she would pay him twice what he paid for it which was still nothing and he laughed again and said he would give them to her half price. She picked out some and took them to the counter. She asked him did he have something Harmon could use for a suitcase and he went through the doorway to the back, drawing aside a frayed wool blanket draped over a dowel. He came back carrying a scuffed briefcase with a shoulder strap friction-taped to the buckles, its side pockets yawning through broken zippers. He told her because she was such a good customer he would throw it in for free and maybe she would remember that and return the favor if he came over on Saturday. She said she couldn't cut the girls out and he could have it for cost, same as he gave her on the briefcase. That's fair he said and put the clothes in the briefcase and added up the price and she paid him and went back out into the pathways of the discarded.

She stopped at a drugstore, its smoked-smudged windows papered in sun-bleached flyers for charity fundraisers held years in the past and handwritten signs that said No Checks and No Unattended Children and bought shave cream and bar soap and a toothbrush and what other such items men needed and went out again into the street and threw the receipt into the gutter. A derelict who sat leaning against a door, his legs stretched out straight before him, reached out his hand and seeing it was her, let it fall back into his lap and sighed and belched raggedly. A truck hulked idling, its wheels up on the sidewalk, so Ruby had to walk out into the street through acrid diesel exhaust to get past. The boy unloading from the truck crates of already rotting cabbage leered at her as she passed. The storeowner saw him and told the boy he better watch himself, she'd cut his nuts off and feed them to her pet snake. The boy said he had a snake he'd like to feed to her and the shopkeeper shook his head at the idiocy of youth. Ruby went on home.

The gonorrhea-addled girl sat on the bottom step. She looked up, her idiotic eyes darting and rolling and said to Ruby she had to let her come in and Ruby said there wasn't nothing more for her here and what did she do with the bus ticket.

Turned it back in.

That was for you to go home.

Ruby said to her she knew she was going to die if she didn't get cleaned up, didn't she, and the girl said she didn't care, she was just hungry was all and just let her have a couple customers and she wouldn't bother her anymore. Ruby told her she already filled her spot and if the girl didn't care about dying, Ruby's customers did, and she wasn't going to risk losing all that business.

I aint got nowhere.

Go up to the doctor and get a shot and tell him to send me the bill. After that, you do what you want, but you can't do it here.

I tell him that, he's gonna know everybody knows. If you just give me the money, it'll be like I showed up on my own.

Ruby considered the request and went into her bag and came out with a twenty and rethought and put it back and gave the girl a fifty. If there were in the world any mercy at all, the fifty would kill the girl when she needled it into her arm.

Inside, Harmon sat at a table, nothing before him. Ruby asked him did he want some eggs and he said he wasn't quite ready for that yet but maybe a biscuit if she had it. She set the briefcase on a chair and went behind the counter and took a plate of biscuits from last night and opened two and laid them on the grill. You want a drink? He told her he sorely did but he should see how the biscuits sat first. She turned the toasted biscuits onto a plate and buttered them and took them and a glass of water to him. She sat across from him and waited for him to take a bite and get it down and take a sip of water.

I got you a present.

She took the briefcase from the chair and set it on the table. He pulled it open and looked inside and went to say he couldn't take it, but she said it was just a loan before he could get it out and he nodded. He took another bite of biscuit and sipped again from the water glass. Ruby lifted a finger, half pointing to the counter and he told her no, but pretty soon.

I got to get my coat.

It's in the closet. I had Maxy do the best she could with it, but you surely tested it.

It's one of my bad habits.

Harmon told Ruby she knew he appreciated what she did, didn't she. She said she knew. He took up the briefcase and went back and up the stairs, stepping the faded rubber runner upon which thousands of footfalls had left their impressions on their way to countless loveless copulations. In the hall he passed an early rising whore coming out for the bathroom. She smelled of sour sweat and wore a flannel robe tied at the waist but open enough up top to show her sagging breasts. She nodded to Harmon and he wondered if it was her sweat he smelled or a customer's and maybe more than one. An all-nighter came out of one of the rooms. Harmon looked in and saw the girl naked on the bed, dollar bills scattered on the rumpled sheets. Her arm lay across her eyes and she held her legs crisscrossed at the shins in the figure of an X, her C-section scar idiotically grinning like the mouth of a demented old man.

Harmon went into his borrowed room and opened the closet where his coat hung on a wire hanger and took it down. He saw where Maxy had stitched it back up under the arm and how she'd tried to wash away the stains, but there are things indelible and their shadows played across the corduroy in irregular rings like the burnt remains of grass after a wildfire. The coat smelled of his bender, but it was all he had and he put it on.

He went back down and asked Ruby was that offer for a drink still open and she poured him a double shot from which he sipped and set back on the counter and then took up again and swallowed half of it and savored it sifting through his veins. He closed his eyes and took in the rest like a sacrament and the trembling within him subsided. His side still hurt, but because of the whiskey, he didn't care.

Ruby went into the till and took a twenty and laid it by his hand and said don't refuse it. Through the window he saw Old

Johnson accost an old woman who clutched her handbag closer as she scuttled past him. He remembered the two young men who'd called him and Old Johnson desperate and put the twenty in his pocket and nodded to Ruby without looking at her. He took up his bag and went out. He went again down the stairs to the street and walked off hurriedly away from Old Johnson and turned down toward the river to avoid the old man. Late morning mists rose up from the water. He ran the list of what he needed, food, shelter, drink. And where they might be had and what means he had by which to get there.

He went by alleyways up toward Merchant, past back lots scabbed with winter detritus among which sprouted dandelions sucking up filth. Against a rusting chain link fence, a row of daffodils, heads bent, humble supplicants sans begging bowls and soon to die. A woman came out onto a back porch with a throw rug and shook it out over the railing. She lit a cigarette and breathed the smoke up through her nose and shook the rug a final time and went in.

On Merchant he went into a diner and asked for change for the bus and they told him he had to buy something. He started to say they could go fuck themselves, but saw his bruised face in the mirror behind the counter and just went back out. He went into a drugstore and got cigarettes and matches and asked if they would make change in the right coins for the bus and they did and he took the change and on the bus watched the city as it painted itself on to the bus's dirty windows.

He got off at the end of the line and carried himself and his bag up a gravel lane at the edge of the city to a salvage yard and went in through the clutter of rusting dead cars and appliances and stacked piles of things alike. Furniture and garden tools and rolled bales of wire and the leavings of demolition lumber left from buildings long ago gone to rot. Communes of inhabitants huddling with their own kind.

A dog barked from within a listing Airstream whose skin was corroded to dusty white and whose wheels were but memories. Rister came out blinking, holding a beer, and saw it was Harmon and grinned with his gums and asked was he here to buy or sell and Harmon asked since when did Rister have anything worth buying. Rister said aint that the truth? He said he had an extra beer and Harmon said it sounded like a good idea. Rister went in and got the beer and came out and motioned for Harmon to sit and they sat on failing wicker chairs and set their beers on a grimy wicker table.

Harmon asked if Rister heard about his cabin burning. Rister said he hadn't, it takes some time for news to get all the way out here and was Harmon okay and Harmon said he was. They drank some more and after a while Harmon said I need a place for a couple days.

I would, you know I would, but I can't. After that last time, she said she going to kill you and me both I ever brought you around again. Harmon asked him what if he just slept in one of the cars for a few days and Rister said he couldn't chance it. Rister said what about with LeRoy? Harmon said LeRoy already offered but he didn't even have enough room in that shack for himself. Rister said there be other bridges and Harmon allowed that there were and that was maybe the thing for now and finished his beer and threw the bottle into the weeds and told Rister thanks for the beer and I'll see you around. Rister said we cool? Harmon said always and went back out and down the gravel lane and waited for the bus along with a Jehovah's Witness who gave him a pamphlet and asked him was he a true Christian and he said he sure as shit fucking was so she wouldn't go on bothering him.

Brigard County, March 1993

Edna opened her door at Harmon's knock and looked at him. She told him he was supposed to come back last week and he turned and started toward the road. She called him back and said the mail carrier had asked her if the fire last week frightened her and how she hadn't even been aware there'd been a fire.

Was it your house?

It was.

You should have told me, I wouldn't have been unkind.

Didn't give me a reason to sneak in like I did.

She asked him if he still wanted the work. He nodded and she led him through the front room to the kitchen. She told him to sit and poured coffee from a black and chrome coffee maker into mugs and set them in the microwave and set the timer.

Let me take your coat.

He took it off and handed it to her. She started to hang it over a sweater on a hook by the door but stopped and took down the sweater and hung the coat in its place and draped the sweater over the back of a kitchen chair. The microwave chimed. She set the mugs of coffee on the table and sat down across from him, trying not to look at the green and yellow bruise on his face dragging itself down from the ragged scab above his eye.

It looks worse than it is he said.

Did you fall?

Harmon looked down and toyed with his mug's handle and looked up again and said he made the wrong man mad. Edna asked him what was the right kind of man to make mad and he told her the kind that don't kick you in the face when you do.

Edna said it was going to rain again tonight and did he have somewhere to stay.

No.

Were you able to save anything from the fire?

What I had on.

She told him there was an apartment above the garage her husband used for an office during vacations and he was welcome to spend the night there if he wanted. There was a bedroom and a kitchen and a bathroom with a shower.

Won't he mind? Harmon asked.

No, she said.

Brigard County, Summer, 1973

Harmon brought the skiff in hard, the bow sliding up on the muddy bank. The two young men got out and heaved the boat by its gunwales to ground and tied it to a weathered post loosely pinioned in the slippery clay. LeRoy followed Harmon on a path winding uphill to a cabin. LeRoy said are we supposed to be here? As they went inside, Harmon told him don't worry, it was his. He opened the refrigerator and took out a beer and handed it to LeRoy and took another for himself. They went back out on the porch and leaned on the railing and drank. LeRoy wanted to know what was next and Harmon looked at him and said he didn't know what was next for LeRoy but he was going to go get his truck. He dropped the empty bottle in a rusted steel drum standing crooked against the railing and told LeRoy to come with him and he'd buy him dinner. They went out to the road and turned and walked downriver.

A car came up behind them and on past and stopped. The driver backed up and yelled out the window to Harmon and asked him where he was going. Harmon said hey Barker and told him the Lone Pine, he left his truck there. Barker asked did they want a ride. Harmon said he would appreciate it and he and LeRoy got in the car. They drove down the road and turned into a gravel lane and went up the wavering route it took over the hill. LeRoy looked out the back window and watched the twin plumes of pale beige dust rolling inward toward one another and rising upward and sifting back to settle on the broad leaves of white oaks and sumac leaning out over the road.

Barker remembered how one time he woke up and his car wasn't there and all he remembered was starting out the night with K. L., and thought maybe K. L. gave him a ride home. He called K. L. and K. L. said he did. Barker had to ask him from where and K. L. told him the Hogshead and did he want a ride back to get his car. So K. L. picked him up and when they pulled into the Hogshead, there was *both* Barker's cars. How the fuck is it possible to go someplace with two cars and forget both of them? I aint ever figured out how I could of done that.

They came up to the Lone Pine, a faded sign in front with a tall pine tree and a whitetail deer and in red letters across the bottom, *Lone Pine Inn – Sandwiches, Steaks, Spirits.* Barker laughed when they turned into the lot and pulled up next to Harmon's truck and saw Eli asleep on the driver's side. A girl lay curled up under his arm, both of them naked from the waist down, the girl's fingers wrapped around his flaccid penis. Harmon beat on the window and Eli awoke and blinked and looked at Harmon and smiled. He rolled down the window and asked where he'd been. Harmon told him he knew damn well he got locked up and he didn't fuck her did he.

Who?

Harmon pointed to Vicki. Eli looked at her and jumped and said shit, maybe I did.

The girl woke up and saw Harmon and asked him what was he looking at and did he want a turn, half price, she was holding a special. Eli looked around in the cab and said to Harmon to look in the back and see if his jeans were there and they were, Eli's and Vicki's both, laid out on top of each other in the truck bed, the girl's on the bottom, the legs wrapped up over the backside of his and crossed over where her ankles would have been if she were wearing them. Harmon handed Eli his jeans and got a stick and used it to pick up Vicki's and passed them to her. Vicki told him how would he like it if she turned them inside out and rubbed them in his face. She said the half-price special was only good for right now and Harmon said he would pass. Barker said he had to get going and went.

Eli twisted himself back and forth behind the steering wheel getting his pants on and opened the door and got out and buckled his belt. Vicki just got out and put hers on where she could stand up. A red crease from the truck's upholstery ran across her backside. A car turned in from the road and the driver honked and Vicki flipped up her middle finger without even looking at him. Eli told her she better be careful about pissing off some strangers and he'd have to get into it with them just because she happened to be with him right then. She asked him would it make a difference if he knew who they were and he said he guessed not. Eli reached in his shirt pocket and took out an empty cigarette pack. He crumpled it up and threw it on the ground. Harmon took one of his and handed it over and took one for himself, the last one, and threw the empty pack in the cab. Eli asked him for a light and Harmon asked him back how was he fixed for spit. Eli said he had enough spit, but thanks anyway and asked if Harmon saw his shoes back there. Harmon looked around and found them under the truck, set upright with the work socks tucked in and Vicki's pink patent leather high heels nestled up beside them. He handed them their shoes. They sat on the tailgate and put them on. Eli asked Harmon was he hungry, it must be close to dinner time. Harmon said it is and I am. The two of them started across the gravel lot, LeRoy and

Vicki behind them. Vicki asked LeRoy if he wanted the special and Harmon told her no he doesn't and then he told Eli how he met up with LeRoy in the jail and how he helped out with the skiff. Eli slapped LeRoy's shoulder and told him welcome to the family.

A rough pine rail ran around the tavern's veranda, the bark shaved off on the sides and bottom, but left on top, shellacked so it looked new and fake next to the veranda's faded planks and the tavern's weathered clapboards. A dusty pine-cone wreath with a Santa Claus in the center hung on the green door. It lifted away from the door when they went in and slapped back with a scratching sound. They asked Jimmey was the grill up yet and Jimmey said it was damn near noon wasn't it and what did they want. They told him hamburgers all the way round and a pitcher. Jimmey asked them if they had any money left after last night and they checked and said they did and he said show me and they gave him thirty dollars and said let us know when that's gone. Then they said might as well make it two pitchers. Jimmey poured out the two pitchers and set them on the beer-stained bar. They carried them over to a booth. Vicki asked did anybody have any change and Harmon gave her a couple dollars. She walked over to the bar, shimmying in her tight pants. LeRoy watched her the whole way and Harmon said if he valued his health he'd stay away from that and Eli should have known better and if he was lucky maybe all that went on was she gave him a handjob in the truck. Eli said whatever went on, there wasn't nothing he could do about it now. He just hoped if he did catch something, he could get it fixed with a shot of penicillin. Vicki got change and put some country songs on the jukebox and came back to the booth and sat down and tapped her fingers on the table in time to the music. She asked could she have a cigarette, but nobody had any. Eli gave her some more money and she went to the bar and bought a pack and they shared them. In a little while the blue-gray smoke hovered in layers across the room. Jimmey hollered that their hamburgers were ready and LeRoy and Vicki went over to get them. Harmon told them to get a bottle of ketchup and a salt shaker while they were at it. They ate their hamburgers and smoked some more and talked about last night. Vicki didn't know either if Eli fucked her and said if he did, it was for free because she didn't have any money. She asked LeRoy was he from around here, she didn't ever remember seeing him and he told her he wasn't. Vicki told him she guessed she should have known, she would have remembered him because he didn't talk like a nigger and LeRoy said that's okay, he would have remembered her too because she didn't talk like a whore.

They drank pitchers through the afternoon and by then the tavern was filling up and there were waitresses to take orders. Jimmey turned off the jukebox and turned on the sound system and put dance music on. Harmon and Eli went over to some girls and asked if they wanted to dance. Harmon's wore strawberry perfume, sickly sweet and stale. The perfume mixed with her sour cigarette breath, but he danced with her anyway. He leaned on her too hard, stepping on her foot and they stumbled. He grabbed her hip to keep from falling and she slapped him and they went on dancing. Harmon looked over her shoulder at the neon beer signs and shelves of dusty curios. Mounted small game animals, their glass eyes opaque and morose. An Esso sign. A rusted Union Motor Oil can. A cast-metal toy fire truck.

A fat woman with ruby-red lipstick came in and Harmon looked at her too. She cackled and pulled her skirt up to show her thick dimpled thighs and said was this what he wanted. There was a break in the music while Jimmey was changing it to something better for night time. Harmon and the girl went back to the booth and Eli had a different girl with him than the one he'd been dancing with and was looking around for one for LeRoy. Harmon asked where Vicki went. Eli said she got a customer. They moved to a table to make room for the girls. They were talking about last night and Eli said he would have done the same thing if he was Harmon, who'd that fucker think he was anyway. But maybe they should take it easy tonight because the chief wouldn't be happy about coming out two nights in a row and Harmon said he'd try, but sometimes you can't help yourself. Harmon asked what day it was and Eli told him Saturday and Harmon said that's good, we don't got work. Then he remembered and asked did they miss last night and Eli said shit, he forgot all about it.

Harmon got up and headed for the bathroom weaving. Someone he didn't know sat on one of the two commodes, his jeans all the way down on the gritty cement floor. The man groaned, clutching at his stomach. The light hurt. Harmon pissed in the galvanized trough where rust spread in rings around the roofing nails tacking the sheet metal to its wooden frame. The trough was buckled on the bottom from endless seasons of warmth and cold, so that little puddles of piss lay in small stagnant pools along the bottom from which the stench of ammonia drifted. A cricket crouched in the corner of the trough. Harmon's piss ringing against the stippled zinc sent the insect into a furious thrashing of legs and antennae as it vainly sought purchase by which to escape and slipped down to lie helpless on its back among uretic seas. Harmon finished pissing and with finger and thumb took up the creature by its legs and gently set it on the floor. A bit of vomit slipped up his throat and he spat it out in the trough. He rinsed his fingers under the single cold-water tap and wiped his hands on his jeans and went back out.

LeRoy had a girl leaning all over him. Eli was pouring out shots from a bottle of Jim Beam. Each of them had a shot, lifting them up and waving to each other. Harmon drifted when the whiskey slid down his throat warm and promising. Something mean and rasping came on over the music system and the girl with LeRoy asked did he want to dance and he told her yes. The girl giggled when she stumbled against her chair and said they better dance close, she didn't think she could handle fast dancing just now. She wrapped her arms around LeRoy's neck and pushed herself into him and he put one hand in the small of her back and helped her push. They swayed back and forth for a while and another even meaner song came on and the girl turned around and put her backside into his groin and writhed like she was working her way into a tight dress a size too small. She took his hands and pulled them down over her hips, her eyes closed and her head rolling on her neck in a rapture, her face and neck sheened with sweat. The girl with Eli said there was a big fucking difference between not being prejudiced and letting a damn nigger go too far and enough was enough and said we need to get the fuck out of here and she went out on the floor and grabbed the other girl by the elbow and they left. Eli said more for us and did another shot, the last of it dribbling off his chin. Harmon watched the girls go and got up from the table and lurched across the floor and went outside himself. They were gone. He steadied himself against a post and closed his eyes and listened to the music coming out muffled. It sounded better from out here than from inside. With his eyes closed, the world spun and he had to open them up or retch. He didn't want to go back inside and he didn't want to stay on the veranda. He went down the steps and looked around vacantly and walked around the side, brushing his fingers lightly against the rail for balance. Vicki was with her customer, the man leaning against the wall, his face dimly lit from what light bled around the side of the tavern, his eyes closed, Vicki kneeling in front of him, her head bobbing, the man grimacing. She lifted her hand from the man's scrotum and waved to Harmon and went back to stroking it. Harmon walked on around to the back and sat on the steps and looked off toward the woods. Two rats the size of house cats fought over garbage spilling from an overturned trash can. He went over to them and one ran off but the other reared up and hissed at him. Harmon kicked at it and it ran off after its brother, its claws scratching against the gravel, a scrap of fetid meat in its jaws. Harmon went on, through the high brown grass behind the tavern and on to the woods and went in a little ways and sat with his back against a spruce, its needles like spun glass haloed blue in the starlight. He sat quiet and listened. Dark things slithered among the trees. He rose and followed them. An owl flew before his face, screeching, a tiny terrified night creature wriggling in its talons. Harmon stopped and looked up. A meteor streaked across the sky, its tail stretching from horizon to horizon. He heard Eli call him and he turned and worked his way back to the tavern.

Eli and LeRoy were sitting on the truck's tailgate. They told him he missed last call but they got another bottle of Jim Beam. They passed it among them for a while until it slipped from Eli's hands and they watched it spill out on the ground. Eli said it must mean they were supposed to go home but no way he could drive and Harmon didn't look that good either. LeRoy told them he could drive and they said did he remember how to get there and he said just go down the hill and turn right and they said close enough. Eli got in the cab with LeRoy. Harmon crawled in the bed and lay down. LeRoy drove with one eye closed, his face tight up over the steering wheel, driving slow to keep from going off the road, but wallowing back and forth just the same, enough so that Harmon had to get off his back to keep from puking and held his head out over the bed, taking the sultry night air into his face and taking in the road dust with the air, so that its grit grated between his teeth when he tried to swallow down what was trying to come up.

Tabernacle Parish, 1958

LeRoy awoke to the murmur of Whiskey and his mother talking and came out in his pajamas. Whiskey said hey LeRoy. The boy ran over and stood expectantly and Whiskey asked him was there something he wanted. LeRoy shrugged his shoulders and Whiskey said he thought he knew what it was and went through his pockets one by one. Nothing here he said and checked another one and said nothing here neither and after he checked them all, LeRoy pointed to Whiskey's watch pocket and Whiskey said oh yeah, I remember and poked his fingers into the watch packet and came out with a quarter and held it out and the boy took it. Agnes told him what do you say?, and LeRoy said thank you. Whiskey said he was welcome and to go put it in his bank and Agnes said for him to get dressed while he was back there. LeRoy flitted across the room and behind the curtain and a minute later came back, his shirttail partly tucked. Agnes told him to come over and she fixed it.

Whiskey said LeRoy was buzzing around here like a skeeter and come to think of it he wasn't too much bigger than a skeeter and he better be careful if he saw somebody coming with a flyswatter. Agnes told LeRoy to sit at the table and got a bowl and put it at his place and another one for Whiskey. LeRoy poured out cereal and milk and then Whiskey did too. LeRoy watched Whiskey eat and took a bite every time Whiskey did. Whiskey asked him what he was going to do with all the quarters he was saving and LeRoy looked at Agnes and told Whiskey it was a secret. Whiskey said it would still be a secret if he whispered it to him and leaned over and put his ear down so LeRoy could whisper into it and LeRoy told him he was waiting until he had enough quarters and he was going to buy Agnes a new dress. Whiskey put his finger to his lips and nodded knowingly. Agnes asked Whiskey did he want any more coffee and Whiskey said he had enough. The man and the boy went on eating, the syncopated rhythm of their clinking spoons slowly measuring out the morning to make it last.

When they finished their cereal, Whiskey leaned over conspiratorially and asked LeRoy did he think they would be able to talk his mama into going on a picnic with them and LeRoy brightened and looked at Agnes and asked her if they could and she said she didn't have anything to fix. Whiskey said all they needed was a blanket, they could stop at the store and get sandwiches and pop and Agnes said okay.

Whiskey said, Skeeter, you got a ball we can take with us and throw around? LeRoy said he didn't and Whiskey said they could stop at the five and ten and get one.

The Story of My Life
By
LeRoy James

Chapter 2

The most important thing that ever happened to me was when
Mama took me with her to see the witch. I was 5. I remember it
was real hot so it must of been in the summer. Mama had on her
purple dress, the one I only ever saw her wear to church except
for that day we went to the witch, and she was wearing a red
bandana around her head. The reason Mama was going to the
witch was to get something to give Daddy so he would be safe.
We lived in a pretty rough place and there were a lot of bad guys
lived around there and they were all the time starting up trouble.
Then Daddy would step in and make sure nothing happened to
any of us. I had 7 brothers and sisters, so counting me and Mama
that made 9 people he had to take care of. He did a good job.
Nothing too bad ever happened to us, but sometimes he would
get hurt trying to protect us and Mama didn't think that was right.
She was going to the witch to help him out.

The road to the witch started out like a regular road, dirt
and gravel, but the further we got the weirder the road got. First
was the ditch started to go, so that there wasn't no difference in
level between the road and what was beside it and then the road
turned to green grass, which there should not of been because
it was so hot back there in the summer and the grass should of
been all dried up. Pretty soon I started seeing eyes shining out
of the woods. Some of them eyes had mouths to go with them

and some was grinning and some was growling, but I was the
only one that could see or hear them. Mama just kept walking. I
started picking up stones from alongside the road and throwing
them at them eyes. Every time I threw a stone at some eyes, they
would blink a couple times and then look mad. When I got too
close for them like when one of the stones hit smack on the tree
the eyes was hiding behind, the eyes glared at me and then ran
off and that was the first I saw there was beasts behind them
eyes. And then I hit one right in the middle of his forehead and
it yelped like a beagle that just got kicked in the belly, and he ran
off scared ~~shitless~~ and howling like a beagle too. I was proud
of myself for that because I was taking care of my mama, who
didn't have ~~no idea~~ any clue how much danger she was in. ~~There
was other things different about those woods. There was~~ I saw
a little creek running out of a spring, and where it started at, the
water was crystal clear ~~like spring water supposed to be~~. Little
silver fish was swimming in it and where the sun got in through
the trees, it shined like jewels. But the further the water got from
the spring, instead of running like a normal creek with ripples
on top and rocks on the bottom covered up with moss and you
could see them rocks because the water was so clear, the water got
darker and darker and thicker and thicker until it look like clotted
up blood only it was black. So thick the water was that it did not
flow anymore, but just oozed along like a sewer and every once in
a while it would spit like there was little volcanoes inside it. ~~And
there weren't no little fish living in it after that but I knew there
was monsters down under there because of the spitting, even
though no one not even me could see them.~~

When we finally got to the witch's house, I expected it to be
like a castle, with a moat and a tower like in a book, but it was just
a cabin like ours. ~~Mama stopped walking when we got there and~~

~~I could tell she was thinking over in her mind whether this was a thing she was really sure she wanted to do.~~ There was one thing that was weird about the cabin though and that was the chimney. ~~It was a stovepipe chimney, just like ours, except bigger across and went up higher.~~ What was strange about it was the smoke. When us kids would play out back of our cabin, we could tell what Mama was doing by the color the smoke was coming up out of the chimney. Black meant she had just started up the fire and was getting ready to cook. Then it would lighten up and how much it lightened up would tell you something about what she was fixing. If it only lightened up a little bit and stayed dark gray, that meant she was frying something on top of the stove. If we was lucky, it would be eggs, and if we was not so lucky that day, it would just be fried bread. But if the smoke turned white and then went to no color at all, just ripples in the air, that meant she had built up a hot fire and turned down the damper and was going to put something in the oven. And that was going to be a good day.

The witch's chimney had smoke coming out of it too, but it was not black or gray or white or no color. It was red when we first saw it and then it was blue for a while and then a big puff of yellow blew out the top, but it did not drift off in the air like smoke supposed to. It fell back down and hugged itself around the chimney stack and then rolled down onto the roof and fell off and covered the ground, walking around like it was a bunch of barn cats. And then it faded away like the ground had soaked it up. And that is when I knew the witch was really inside this place and she was doing magic.

That smoke would of scared a lot of people, but it ~~didn't~~ did not scare Mama. She just went across the porch and raised up her hand to rap on the door like nothing happened, but the door opened up before she could and there was the witch. And the way she looked was a surprise. Sometimes you do not know that you are expecting something to be a certain way until you see it. She was pretty young and stood up straight and when I saw that, I realized that I was expecting some bent up old evil-looking woman with a black dress and a cone hat, but she had on a red dress and no hat at all.

The witch said, "What you want?" I always imagined that when a witch said something, it would come out like a hiss, like she had a snake down in her throat where a regular woman would have a voice box. But her voice came out like it was smoke, that smooth and husky, and fluttery like she was holding a moth in her mouth gentle so's not to kill it and the moth was flapping its wings and ~~that's~~ that is what made her voice flutter. She sounded a little bit mean too, but not a lot.

"I need a spell of protection," Mama said.

"Who for?"

"This boy's daddy."

The witch said, "What did you bring?"

Mama pulled two dollars out of her pocket and held them up. The witch looked at the money and nodded her head back at the room behind her, and we went in. You could barely see in there at first. The witch had her windows all covered up with black cloth. She had candles set up all over and they gave off enough light so that after a little bit, the sun from outside worked its way out of my eyes and I could see better. It was all one big room with shelves hung up all around and a big table running down the middle all covered with mason jars and bottles, all different colors, with little lights bouncing off them from all them candles.

The witch held out her hand and Mama handed over the two dollars and that was the first time I really looked at the witch. She was real dark skinned, even more than Mama. She looked like she was made out of coal, even the palm of her hand when she put it

out to take the money. Her eyes were black like coal too, and not
shiny black like her skin, but empty black, like they were holes in
her head and what was inside was so dark nobody in the world
would of been able to see what was in there. She had dreadlocks
with little red stones that must have been rubies tied on the ends.
I heard something off to the side, and when I looked to see what
it was, I got the witch out of the corner of my eye, and looking
at her that way, I saw that she was not dark skinned at all, she was
like she was a mulatto, but her eyes went up at the sides like she
was half Chinese instead of half white. And those eyes were not
black at all, they was bright blue, with X's of light in them that
made them shine. She still had her dreadlocks, though, but with
blue stones at the end, blue star sapphires I think, to match her
eyes, instead of rubies. And then she gave me a LOOK. That was
because she could see that I could see her the way she really was
and she did not like it. Not one little bit.

Her and Mama went over to the table and the witch was
asking Mama things about Daddy, how big he was and was he
usually asleep at midnight and had he ever seen the sun flash
green in the morning. They was too busy to bother about me,
so I went off and looked around the cabin but I did not touch
nothing. Anything in that cabin could have had a magic spell on
it and you touching it just might be the thing that would set it off
and turn it into something that wanted to devour you or send you
off to hell.

I was looking at a little oak keg sitting on a shelf that had
a red skull and crossbones painted on it when I saw something
looking back at me from behind the shelf, like it was standing in
front of the wall and stuck back behind the wall both at the same
time. I could not see what it was, so I looked away so's I could see
it out of the corner of my eye and see if that made a difference
and I could see it better like with the witch, but it did not make

a difference. I figured I better move on to something else before whatever that was had a chance to turn into something I did not want to be no part of, but it slipped out of the wall and went with me.

That thing followed me everywhere I went around that house, and then I went outside and it followed me there too. I said to him, "You a ghost?" It laughed and said, "I kind of am, but I am really more like a genie bodyguard."

I said, "What are you doing following me around."

He said, "You are next on my list to protect." I asked him what his name was and he said that was up to me. He let whoever he was guarding decide that. He told me he had one time or another had just about any name you could think of. He been called Captain and Old Crow and Abraham and even funny nicknames like Booger.

I had to think about that for a while. A name is a thing you should be careful about. A name ought to fit a person because people are going to call them that for a long time and it changes what people think about you. I can see how somebody would call him Crow, being how black he was. But him being black wasn't what made him what he was, like a crow is not just something black, but a thing you could touch if you could catch it. This thing was just <u>there</u>, but not so's you could touch him. He was like a hole in the air and he was cold even in that day's heat, and the space he took up was like it was just black without there being something in there that <u>was</u> black, an empty spot where nothing was alive. But there was. The more I thought about it, the more I thought about how much he really was like a ghost and then I thought about how ghosts sometimes walk around with their bones showing ~~through~~.

"I think I got one," I said. "How about I call you Mr. Bones?"

"Hmmm," he said. "I like that. Makes me sound kind of like a elder or a deacon. Mr. Bones it is!"

Then I asked him why he picked me. He laughed and the laugh was all cold and joyful at the same time, like there was someone who was happy laughing from way down inside a pitch dark cave. "I am going to take care of you, boy, because you are going to need a lot of taking care of from here on out."

"How do you know that?"

Mr. Bones laughed again. "I see the future, boy. Don't you know that? And yours, boy, is going to be one ~~hell~~ heck of a future, and there ain't no way I am going to miss it. No ~~fucking~~ way I am going to miss that show!"

Pretty soon Mama come out and she was putting a little blue bottle in her pocket and we started back off for home, back through those weird woods with the mud stream in it and the eyes that was beasts and Mama could not see none of them things going that direction either. But Mr. Bones could. He went right alongside me all the way, but it was not like he was walking, more like he was floating along an inch off the grass road. Mama could not see him and she did not hear him when he told me what to be careful of in them woods and what I should just plain be afraid off. I could see he knew what he was talking about and he was dead serious about taking care of me. After that, I was not often without him. He even stayed in the bedroom with me at night, stuck up under the ceiling, and staying awake all night long. I know that because whenever I woke up in the middle of the night, I would see him looking down, but my brothers and sisters could not see him.

Whatever it was the witch gave Mama did not work. Daddy still got hurt sometimes when he was protecting us and sometimes it was harder on us seeing him like that than it would of been if we got clobbered ourselves. Me and Mama should not of been surprised that the potion did not work. You cannot ever trust a witch to ever say one single thing that is true. You just about should of expected her to lie about what she gave Mama and to steal her money too. I always thought Mama should of gone back to that witch and got her 2 dollars back, but she never did. The trip was not a total loss though. I had Mr. Bones for the whole rest my life ~~so I guess it all worked out okay~~. And that is it for Chapter 2.

Brigard County, Summer, 1973

LeRoy walked down from the cabin and stood by the skiff and looked out over the water. He undid the skiff's rope from the post and coiled it fist to elbow and laid it in the bow. He pushed the boat off the bank and stepped in, trying for grace but nearly capsizing. He crouched down fast, gripping the gunwales and made his way crablike to the rowing thwart and sat there facing the stern the way Harmon had yesterday morning. He took up the oars and practiced working the water, jerking the boat in awkward maneuvers, the oars at first slipping from the locks. He continued on working them in random ways and saw that the oars wanted him to let them do the work and when he tried not as hard, they stopped popping from the locks. He went on practicing, practicing rowing straight and in turns, left and right, and by the time he could spin the skiff all the way around and get himself going in a more or less straight course as he willed, the river had taken him and the boat a quarter mile downstream and a hundred yards from the bank and he could see enough of both sides of the river to know that where he wanted to go was on the other side and upstream, back to town where there would be better chances.

He got the skiff pointed upriver and across but he couldn't hold course and the river kept taking him downstream. He remembered how Harmon had pulled into the current aiming upstream first toward the bridge and then letting the river carry them down to his cabin. LeRoy elected to get across first and if he could get there, he could from the far shore get upstream to town where he wanted to go, even if he had to pole his way hugging the bank. He bent to his task, but the river more so, in a wide sweeping bend to his right and the great current kept sweeping his tiny craft to the near bank and he made no headway. He lifted the oars from the water and rested. The skiff drifted and came to a ridge of gray cliffs hovering above him like a row of robed nuns, the current strong against them and in places had worn shelves into the stone where small surges of water rippled like probing fingers searching for soft flesh beneath the cliffs' skirts. Past the cliffs the river began an opposite bend, long and slow, and took the skiff with it out into the slight lift of the bore, the river's breath. The sun blazed down. A large fish came up and took a skimmer from the surface and looked at LeRoy and slid back down into the water. LeRoy took up the oars again and rowed toward the far bank and the river aided him this time, its serpentine path seeming to draw the land toward him rather than the boat making its way shoreward. The river came up to a narrow landing laid out flat and sandy, where young trees stretched out over the water. The current undercut the bank and there was no gradual scrape of the bow up on the land as there had been when Harmon beached them below his cabin. LeRoy grabbed at a bush with an oar and pulled himself and the boat in tight and stood and hopped out onto the land and the boat went the other way. He rushed to grab hold of it, but it was by then a half-dozen feet out in the water and the current had caught it. LeRoy lost his balance and fell.

An old man sitting on a hummock a ways off laughed and said she's gone unless you want to swim for her. LeRoy went up to him and started to say something, but a sputtering of engines came across from near the cliffs and the two of them looked over to see what it was. A brace of barges came around the bend, a tug pushing them and trailing ochre oil slicks behind it. They watched the barges come lazy down the channel, the tug's exhaust rising in a blue fog over the river, catching the sun in twitching glints. A small falcon swooped down from the cliffs and dipped and vanished into the cloud and came out again, a songbird in its grasp, frantic and thrashing and bloody feathers shedding from the songbird's wings down into the river like ash.

The old man held a rod over the water, a plastic bobber floating from the line and a can of worms writhing in woodchips beside him. The old man leaned to his side and spat a tobacco-stained hawker onto the sand and asked him where was he going and LeRoy said to town. The old man said that was a pretty far ways and it was getting hotter'n hell for such a walk. LeRoy said he knew how far it was and was there a road he could take. The old man pointed up the rise behind them and said there was some railroad tracks just a little way up and they was in the same direction as the road but you didn't have to go all the way over the hill. He told LeRoy the tracks and the road came together a mile or so upriver. The bobber dipped and the old man felt through the rod, down the line and below the water but whatever had been there was gone. He said I seen you come across. You and that boat was having a mighty battle. LeRoy said he was new at it was all. The old man told him that as good as he was at it, it was just as well that the skiff run off on him. LeRoy said he thought maybe he could have sold it to somebody and the old man said it wasn't likely. Everybody needed a boat already had one and that one he let get away would have cost whoever bought it more to fix than to buy one new.

LeRoy admired that it was surely hot and the old man said it was. LeRoy asked was it always this hot and the old man said yes it was except when it wasn't. LeRoy asked was it cold here in the winter and the old man said colder than now but the river don't freeze all the way acrost, if that's what he was asking.

LeRoy asked where there was work around here and the old man told him a couple places. There was the Bessemer. It's over where you already came from. It's a hell hole the old man said but it pays. LeRoy asked him could anybody work there and the old man said did he mean did they take on niggers and LeRoy said he guessed that's what he meant. The old man spat a globule of phlegm into the grass and said shit, they take on anybody. LeRoy asked him what else there was. The old man said you can work on the river and you can work in a store. But they don't pay as much. There's farms too he said. They pay even less than in the stores. Just decide what you want, hell and money, or quiet and broke.

LeRoy said he was going to get going and the old man said he'd walk a little of the way with him and reeled in the line and pushed the hook into the rod's cork handle and took up the can of worms and threw it in the water. The can floated for a moment and then tipped over and filled with water and sank. Have them worms if you want them, they're free now. It's what you been waiting on, aint it, he told the fish and cackled again, self satisfied, as if no one had ever told that joke before.

He led LeRoy up from the bank toward a path through the weeds. From the bank, the weeds had appeared pale green, lush and yielding. But closer up there was brown among them and brambles. Rodents scurried out of their way. A dead lizard lay curled on the path. They came up to railroad tracks laid down in crushed, soot-stained limestone, the ties gray, what creosote they'd once held long since leached out by rain and sun. The old man pointed upriver and said that's the way up to the road and see you around sometime. LeRoy told him thanks and the old man nodded and went on up the path into the woods and LeRoy walked along the railroad tracks towards town, the limestone crunching under his shoes and heat shimmering up from the ties.

The sound of singing came down the tracks, growing louder as LeRoy walked. The tracks bent around in front of him and where they turned, he came to a dirt road, the crossing of the tracks and the road an elongated X, the tracks receding from the river and the road winding down toward it. From where they crossed he could see a church from which the singing drifted, its white clapboards bright in the sun. There was a graveyard and benches for respecting the dead where a small huddle of men sat, passing a bottle among them. Their voices rattled like wet gravel in their throats. One of them called over to LeRoy was he here for the show and LeRoy told him he didn't know about a show. A tambourine shook from within the church and a new song started up and the man said it's getting ready to start, have a seat. He offered the bottle up to LeRoy. LeRoy took it and started to lift it to his lips and looked at the man quizzically and the man told him to go on ahead, none of them was against going after a nigger and LeRoy took a drink. He grimaced and the man said he knew it was some rough shit but it got the job done. LeRoy sat.

A man on the far side of the bench said here it comes. The church doors opened and a large man in a purple robe appeared at the top of the steps, his arms uplifted, a Bible with gilt-edged pages in his right hand. A stout woman in a red robe followed behind him, shaking and slapping a tambourine and chanting, and behind her a line of singers, they too in red and flinging back what she sang, *Lord help the sinner man,* and they came down to the ground and stepped in time to the tambourine and lifted their arms and ducked their shoulders. *Lord help the gambling man.* As the last of the singers emerged from the church, there came behind them a clutch of barefoot followers, women and girls in white shifts and boys and men in white shirts with bow ties, some of them looking around confused and blinking and others steel-eyed and some rapturous. They followed the singers in single file on down toward the river and after them the rest of the congregation, the women fanning themselves, the men stepping with solemn determination.

The malingerers on the benches rose and followed, LeRoy with them, on down to the grass above the river but stopped short of the water and lay on the grass, propped on their elbows, and went back to passing the bottle. It gonna get good now one of them said. And another said this is the only way, drizzling don't count and another said it was all bullshit anyway. Another with missing teeth said he got it both ways, drizzled and immersed and neither one of them took.

The big man in the robe handed his Bible off and pulled the robe over his head and handed it to an attendant and stood in the sun in white pants and a white shirt and took off his shoes and waded into the shallows at the river's edge up to his waist. That's the preacher the immersed one said. He the real lucky one. Have his hands all over them. The singers started up another song, slow this time and no tambourine, a petition to the water. They swayed like reeds, their faces uplifted and shining with sweat.

The preacher raised his arms and in a voice vibrant and swamp dark, started in. The gap-toothed man said he wouldn't be taking too long, he already gospelized them for better than an hour and they wasn't ever gonna be more ready than they already was. The preacher shouted I indeed baptize you with water, but one mightier than I cometh, the latchet of whose shoes I am not worthy to unloose. He came down hard on *mightier* and *I* and *worthy* and *unloose*. His voice rolled over the water. He reached toward the bank and said come unto me and two men gently took the arms of a young woman and guided her to the river's edge. The toothless man sucked in his breath and said them deacons is pretty lucky too. This the best part said another as the girl stepped into the water, her shift floating up over her calves. She went up to the preacher and he put one hand on her face and the other between her shoulder blades and said something to her and she took both her hands and clasped onto his forearm. The preacher shouted out in the sweet name of Jesus and in an action swift and practiced threw her beneath the water and brought her back up, the water coming after her in an arc radiant with color. He let go her face and held his hand on her back and steadied her and said go and sin no more and the assembly on the grass shouted praise God and hallelujah and the singers sang. The girl came up out of the river, the wet shift clinging tight on her hips and her taut nipples pressing through and the hair beneath her belly risen against the shift like lace. The man with the bottle shouted praise God and the gap-toothed man leaned over to LeRoy and said if there's anywhere got a for-free show better than that, I aint never seen it.

Tabernacle Parish, 1958

Agnes stood with LeRoy across the road from the African Methodist Episcopal Church. Through its open windows, she could hear the preacher winding down and then he said let us pray and he started in on a prayer and she thought it wasn't going to be much longer, but he just kept on praying and praying, and when he finished up with that, he started in singing, just him without the organ, his voice low and soulful and Agnes heard him say come on now like he was reminding a child of his manners, and other voices came in, a woman's strong voice leading them and then the organ started and more voices with it and there was clapping and a tambourine and then the singing stopped and the preacher's voice came again, rolling thick and deep like far off thunder. *The Lord bless thee, and keep thee: The Lord make his face to shine upon thee, and be gracious unto thee: The Lord lift up his countenance upon thee, and give thee peace.* And Agnes was hopeful this might be a church for LeRoy, because she had heard that same prayer when she was a child herself in her grandfather's church.

The doors opened and the preacher stood at the top of the steps while the people came out and every one of them had something to say to him. Agnes kept on waiting through it all, even when the last one to come out, an elderly man in an old-fashioned suit, started in on a long conversation with the preacher about how they couldn't put off fixing the roof too much longer.

She waited until the preacher and the man shook hands and then she moistened her thumb with her tongue and rubbed LeRoy's forehead and smoothed the shoulders of his new white shirt and took him by the hand across the street. The preacher was on his way back in and she called up to him excuse me Pastor and he looked down at her kindly and asked what he could do for her.

She asked if there was room in his Sunday school for LeRoy. The preacher came down the steps and said of course there was room. He asked her why she thought there might not be and she told him she already tried at the Baptist Church and they said they were full up but they could put LeRoy on the waiting list if she wanted. The preacher told her when Jesus said suffer the little children, he didn't add provided there's a spot. And to himself thought, and provided he aint half black, but he didn't say it because the woman already knew that and her trials must be hard enough without him bringing them any more attention. He said if he knew she was waiting out here he would have cut the last prayer short and she smiled and said it did go on awhile, but she liked the sound of it even if she couldn't make out all the words. He said the Bible says pray without ceasing and I maybe take that a little too serious sometimes and she asked was he praying now and he said he guessed maybe he was. He said they had an adult class too and she was welcome to come herself and she told him she didn't think that would work out too good. He asked her why and she told him I done some pretty bad things and he said all have sinned and come short of the glory of God and there's some people find shelter within this sanctuary who have led quite troubled lives and there's not a one of them who doesn't belong here, Mrs. James. She told him it was Miss James and looked away from the preacher's face and to her son's. She waited for the preacher to quote some Bible verse about how if you confess your sins and promise Jesus not to do them again, he will love you for it and you could go to church. If promising to confess and saying she was sorry was the price to pay for getting LeRoy in, she would pay it and nod and say she was grateful to Jesus and maybe she would start coming. But instead he took her hand softly and said, Miss James, the Bible says Not by works of righteousness which we have done, but according to his mercy he saved us. He told her Jesus loved her just as much as she loved this boy and he didn't know what her story was, but Jesus must have given her this child for a reason and there was no possibility of shame in Jesus's reasons. He said Sunday school started with everybody together for singing at quarter to ten every Sunday and he looked forward to having LeRoy join them and her too. Any time she wanted.

Brigard County, March, 1993

After Harmon's first night above the garage, Edna told him they should work out what the rules were, what she would pay him and how many days a week he would work. Harmon said whatever she thought was fair and they settled on two hundred fifty dollars a week and Monday to Friday. She said she would take care of his meals for a few days until he got himself settled in but after that he should use the kitchen in the apartment. He said he appreciated that but he been taking care of himself for a long time now and didn't need anybody waiting on him.

During breakfast, she said she wanted him to paint the house before he did anything else, that the old paint had started to blister and peel and she was worried the weather would get to the wood. He said he could see it needed doing but it wasn't an emergency yet and there were a couple of other things she might want to think about taking care of first.

She asked him what things and he took her outside and pointed up to the roof gutters where green maple seedlings sprouted and said that trees growing in your gutters is a pretty good sign it's time to clean them out. If she didn't do it pretty soon, she'd end up having to put up all new gutters.

He said that when he'd showered the night before, the best he could get was tepid water. He asked her if she kept the water heater set low. She told him she didn't know, that the water was warm in the morning but less so as the day went by. She said she'd never been here this early in the year and thought that had something to do with it, that it would get better when summer came. He said it was more likely to be something with the water heater and he'd take a look at it. Edna began clearing the dishes and he asked how to get to the basement. She showed him the stairway and he disappeared. In a short while he came up and said there was definitely something not right with the water heater. He'd have to turn off the water for a little while and he needed to get some tools from the garage. He said it could wait if she needed to wash clothes or anything.

Just let me finish with the dishes.

You might want to use the toilet, too. Won't be able to flush it while the water's off.

By the time Edna had washed the dishes, Harmon was back from the garage with a toolbox.

Did you find everything you need?

He said he did and that she had a lot of tools out there. She said her husband used them to work on the car. It was his favorite, the only one he ever brought here. He took all their other cars to mechanics. Harmon returned to the basement. He was gone a long time and came back up holding some misshapen, ash-colored branchlike thing. He said one of the elements burned out and held it up to show her. He said he'd have to put in a new one. There's two of them. Might as well replace both while I got it apart. She asked if he could do it today, she wouldn't want to be without hot water at all.

There's a place in town. I can be up and back in an hour and a half.

Walking?

Yes.

I could drive you.

If we do that, you'll have hot water by dinner time.

So long?

He looked puzzled for a moment and then smiled and said by lunch time.

Just over the bridge, Harmon told Edna to turn right and they went down a winding road lined with a motley assortment of drab businesses. A garage. A scrap yard. A discount furniture store. A beauty parlor. A laundromat. The air smelled oily and of things burnt and bleached. He told her to turn in at the lot of a place whose sign read Martin's Plumbing and Electrical Supply. He asked if she wanted to come in with him. She said no and asked how much money he would need.

No more than twenty for the elements. I should get new insulation for the pipes while we're here.

She took fifty dollars from her purse and handed it to him.

It won't be anywhere near that much.

Just in case.

He took the money and went in. Edna could see him through the plate glass windows where he leaned on a wooden counter across from a man he obviously knew and showed him the burnt element. The man disappeared among rows of shelves running farther than she could see towards the back of the store. A truck with a huge load of large white pipe strapped down in the back drove in a little farther along on the lot and on through the gate of a high chain link fence and up to a large utilitarian-looking building. A man came out and motioned for the driver to back his truck inside. Edna marveled at the elegance of the maneuver, the driver deftly gliding his elephantine machine in a sweeping forward curve and then backwards, looking only in the truck's mirrors, until the building had swallowed all but the cab. The driver stepped down, holding a clipboard, and went inside.

Another customer drove up and went in. He too knew Harmon. They talked and at one point Harmon nodded toward Edna in the car and the man looked at her and then back at Harmon and laughed and clapped him on the shoulder. The counterman came back with a box and three long black tubes that flopped as he carried them. The counterman worried the cash register and said something and Harmon handed him money and got back change.

Harmon came out and asked her to open the trunk. She told him that her husband said never to use the trunk. He was afraid of something bumping against all that mysterious machinery and setting some necessary thing out of adjustment. She told him just to put everything in the back seat. He hesitated and she told him it was all right. He took off his jacket and laid it on the seat and set the box on that and laid the tubes of insulation on the floor. He got in the car and handed her the change. Only came to twenty-one, sixty-four altogether he said.

On the way home, he asked her how long the house had been empty. She told him nearly three years. He told her what probably happened was the pump hung up for some reason and the water level in the heater fell. The element just melted when there wasn't any water for it to heat. Heat's got to go somewhere. Take that away and it'll just burn itself up. He said he'd show her how to turn the heater off before she left for the winter so it wouldn't happen again.

As they turned off the bridge toward home, he asked when was the last time she had the septic tank pumped out

I don't recall its ever being done.

This close to the river, you ought to pump it out at least every other year. You're taking a chance it'll back up into the house if you don't. Then you got a real mess on your hands.

Brigard County, Summer, 1973

 T he chorus swelled with new voices coming up from the water praising God and glistening with the irrepressible joy of redemption. The tambourine fell silent, the slower hymns of assured salvation not needing it. *I will cling to that old rugged cross* they sang and *Softly and tenderly Jesus is calling* and *He walks with me and he talks with me.* The last woman carried an infant with her to the water's edge. A stout matron went to her and touched her shoulder and reached for the child. The woman said you got to walk by yourself this time, I'll keep him for you. The mother clutched the baby tighter to herself and looked at the preacher hip-deep in the river. He offered out his hand palm up in an avuncular gesture meant to tell her the child would be safe with his flock and she with him and she gave up the child and went in the water and was baptized and came out again and took back her baby, both of them crying.

The preacher came out of the water and raised up his hands and said let us pray, the river raining from his arms. LeRoy lowered his head and listened. He had in his short life heard countless prayers like this one, the preacher's sonorous words of praise wafting heavenward with the precise passion of countless rehearsals. We thank thee Lord for thy *saving grace* and ask thee that you might burden the hearts of them which are *still lost* and awaken within them the same *hunger for salvation* as these who have this day come unto thee and *met thee in the river* as did your holy son in the River Jordan and may your spirit *descend upon them* as a pure white dove.

LeRoy wondered how come God never got bored with that same prayer every Sunday and then thought maybe he *was* bored with it and that would explain a lot of things. The preacher finished and the congregants started up again with the tambourine and sang all the way back up to the church and they were still singing as they filed in.

The gap-toothed man said the show was over and he'd be on his way. LeRoy watched him totter toward the road and disappear. The preacher came to the church door and the people inside came out, the newly baptized back in their church clothes. The preacher shook hands with some of them and others he embraced and one or two he clasped their shoulders and said he shared their joy. Most climbed into battered cars and pickup trucks, their motors coaxed into one more coughing life, and went off, their eructating exhausts a flock of blue-gray angels winging heavenward. Some walked and when offered rides, said it was a nice day and they'd rather walk. Some went up the road toward town, but most went the other way. When there was no one left to come out, the preacher came down and said good morning and one of the men said good morning back. The preacher smiled again and told them they were all welcome to come inside next Sunday and there was a prayer meeting every Wednesday night and they were welcome there too. One of them said maybe they would. When the preacher walked away, he said yeah and maybe I'll stick a shovel handle up my ass, which was the exact same place that preacher could stick his fucking tithes.

LeRoy asked if the people going downriver were going to another town and they told him it depended on what you called a town. LeRoy said he didn't know there was different kinds and the man rolled his eyes and said some folks thought a real town had to have stores and doctors and places to go for what you needed and not just places to live and other folks thought you just needed the people. LeRoy said he guessed this one just had people and they told him that was right. LeRoy wanted to know where they bought stuff if there wasn't any stores. They told him there was a store and a gas station straight over on the other side of the river. LeRoy said how is that better than just going to town? One of them spat and said you are truly a dumb fuck, aint you? There's a ferry and some got boats of their own to get acrost on.

LeRoy looked tightlipped at the loungers braced on elbows in the grass and considered the age and the degree of drunkenness aligned against him. He looked out over the river and then back at the man who had insulted him and said if it is not too much trouble, can you tell me one more thing? The man said sure, if it aint too complicated a question and the rest of them snickered. What do you want to know?

Does being such a big asshole come naturally for you or do you have to practice a lot?

The man came off his elbows and pushed down on his hand and rose up enraged and LeRoy came up with him looking straight into his face and they stood there silent. A mockingbird ventriloquized a crow from high in an elm across the road. One of the men on the ground giggled and slapped the man beside him on the thigh and cackled that LeRoy had Jackson just about pegged, that ever there was a natural born asshole, it had to be old Jackson. Jackson looked away muttering.

LeRoy walked up past the church and wound through the graves to the road and turned downriver, the mockingbird hooting owl song at his back in a raucous, peregrine accent redolent of the crow still crouching in its throat. One of the men said you got to give that nigger son-of-a-bitch credit. He sure enough got a set on him.

The asphalt lay buckled and ran thick with sinuous welts and runnels. The road curved, bending inward away from the river and rose into the hills and the woods, and for a while the river glittered through the trees and then disappeared. The grade flattened and the asphalt fell into a web of cracks and then bled into a slag road coming toward it, pocked deeply. An old black sedan came toward him, billowing feculent clouds of dust behind it, and slowed as it came up to him. LeRoy nodded his thanks to the driver and the driver lifted a finger from the wheel. The woman beside him turned her face to LeRoy and then looked away.

LeRoy came upon a wooden bridge, its timbers and planks weathered like driftwood, road dust tattooed deep into the grain. Arms of angled rafters ran along the sides for parapets and reinforcing planks had been laid along the tire tracks, warped and twisted. Half way over, LeRoy looked down to a trickle of a stream in whose center a shirtless boy waded, the water coming only to his ankles. LeRoy thought it was a lot of bridge for so little water. He went on.

The woods opened out and fallow fenced fields lay among patches of scrub oak and birch, ragged with unkempt grass and gnarled brush. Dust clung to fences, split rail and rusted barbed wire stippled here and there with bits of hair. The road bent downward and LeRoy came upon a house set back from the road. An old man and woman sat in rockers on the narrow porch. The man raised his hand as LeRoy approached and LeRoy waved back and the road bent riverward and came to another house and another and then more frequently, some with stovepipe chimneys and outhouses and others where sagging wires ran in from utility poles and where plank coverings lay over cesspools. Animals grazed in side and back yards and dogs lolled on porch steps and under shade trees. A cow looked up, vacuously curious, and then, surprised to see this stranger, twisted her head back and forth like a dog shaking off water and turned back to the grass in this integrated land whose census held all, men and women and children and animals, as citizen peers.

Through the viscous air there flowed streams of insect mating calls and the whirling of their wings. LeRoy wiped his forehead with his sleeve. The road bent again and through the buzzing air LeRoy smelled water and looked down through the trees and again there was the river. The road widened and came up to where it melded in a shallow lip to macadam and in a short while to houses one upon another and gravel walks and a pitted street sign reading *Richardson Street* through peeling paint.

Three men sat in wicker chairs on the porch of a dirty whitewashed building. A sign next to the street said Ruthy's Diner and another sign on the door said CLOSED. LeRoy went up to them and heard one of them working on a story. The man said old Butler aint never been the same since. That foot never all the way healed up and when it came time, he would still be limping when he went through the pearly gates.

You giving him a lot of credit. Maybe someplace a little bit warmer than the pearly gates.

Maybe so. He said he figured it was worth it though and he'd do it again if it came down to it.

Pussy will do that to you.

Nothing fuck you up quicker'n pussy.

One of the men picked up a pop bottle from the porch floor and drank from it and saw LeRoy and looked at him and asked him if there was something he could help him with. LeRoy said he been told there was a town this way, but whoever told him said it didn't have stores, so he must have missed a turn.

You didn't miss nothing. There aint no other town except here.

LeRoy asked them what its name was and they told him this town he was standing in was what they called unincorporated and that meant it wasn't anyplace at all but everybody called it the Crossings. LeRoy wanted to know why.

You are one curious nigger, aint you? Curiosity what got you that eye?

No.

How'd you get it?

Ran into something.

That something have a police on the other end of it?

LeRoy asked how did he know and he told him there wasn't that many choices. It was one of a woman, a fight, or a cop and he just got lucky guessing which one and for LeRoy to come on up and sit down. One of them reached into a bucket of ice and handed LeRoy a root beer and a bottle opener. They looked out toward the river.

LeRoy asked them where was the Bessemer.

You looking for work?

I am.

Over on the other side and past the ridge.

They said there was a ferry.

They pointed down the street and said it was not even a quarter mile, just go down until you hit the highway and you'll see it. LeRoy asked them how much did it cost and they told him a nickel if you was walking and a quarter for a car and LeRoy said he didn't have a car and could he walk to the Bessemer from the ferry and they told him he couldn't but the company had a free bus picked you up at the other end.

You take the six o'clock ferry in the morning and when you get off, there'll be the bus. Just tell the driver you putting in a application and he'll take you right where you need to go.

They sat and drank their pop and spat over the railing. One of them pointed down to the river and said them boys got themselves a treasure. Three boys knee-deep in the water, barefoot and bare chested, their jeans soaked, pulled at the rope of a skiff. They dragged it to the bank and heaved to bring it up but hadn't the strength. LeRoy went down and said what you doing there? The oldest of the three looked at LeRoy and told him what did he think they were doing, hunting frogs. LeRoy asked did they need any help and the boy said they would manage. LeRoy told them to get in the water and push from the back and he'd pull up from the front and together they brought the skiff ashore.

LeRoy asked them did their boat have a name and they said they didn't get that far yet, they just found it and LeRoy asked them where. The oldest pointed out to a sandbar and said it was hung up there and LeRoy asked them did they think maybe somebody left it there for safekeeping and the boy said fuck'm if they did. LeRoy said he found a boat like that one time and he got his use out of it and that they should take care of it if they wanted to get their use out of this one. He wished them good luck with it and went back up to the diner. When the boys thought he was out of earshot, they started talking about what name they should give their boat.

LeRoy asked the men was there a place he could stay until morning. Mrs. Briggs lets out rooms they told him, if you got cash for it. He said did they know how much and they said there was a range, but cheapest was four dollars a night. LeRoy said he had enough for the ferry and for something to eat if it didn't cost too much but not for that and the room too and did they think she would carry him until he got paid and they said he was counting on a lot wasn't he. She maybe would if he already had the job lined up, but she didn't get to owning that house free and clear taking in down-and-out niggers. They told him not to be in such a hurry and sit back down and finish his pop.

They sat and sipped at their pops and spat some more and took out cigarettes and gave LeRoy one. One of them pointed downriver and said here comes the ferry. He said it don't run too often on Sunday, there must have been a truck come through. It was midway across, looking like a dull red and brown monument to a long ago war nobody cared about anymore. From where they sat, you could just make out the stars and stripes flying from above its bridge.

A big man with a sack over his shoulder came up the street. That's what you need they told LeRoy. They yelled out to the man hey Catfish and he looked up. He only had one eye and it rolled in its socket and found them and he came over and set his sack heavily on the porch. He had the look of a man who is often looked at. What you got in there they asked and he told them none of their fucking business and what were you fools doing here when the place wasn't even open and they said because that way they couldn't get throwed out. Fuckin idiots he said and they said they didn't dispute that.

Catfish rolled his eye on LeRoy and asked what's this and they told him a world-weary traveler and did he have any room. He said not in the caboose but there was a whole car empty and how much did LeRoy have to pay for it. They told him he didn't own them cars and all they were trying to do was help the young man out and did he want to help or not. Catfish said maybe he didn't own them cars but it was him laid down rat poison and swept up and sprayed them down to keep out the ticks and had blankets and if you want it that's okay and could LeRoy do fifty cents and if you don't that's okay too, just find someplace else. LeRoy said he would take a look and did Catfish want help with the sack. Catfish said no thanks and picked up the sack and nodded for LeRoy to follow him. As they went down the steps, the men asked LeRoy what was his name and LeRoy told them and they told him theirs. They said Ruthy opened up at five and had a good breakfast special for a dollar if he wanted to eat before the ferry left. And then they went back to their story about the man who ended up goat-footed on account of pussy.

Brigard County, Summer, 1973

LeRoy followed Catfish up the street and through a dirt alley and on past clapboard houses where the alley narrowed to a needle-strewn path threading into a copse of dwarf spruce. Catfish's sack rattled from within and he adjusted it on his back, switching hands. LeRoy asked him was he sure he couldn't use some help. Catfish set the sack on the needles and said he guessed he could if LeRoy was going to keep asking. LeRoy took up the sack and they went out from the trees into a barren space through which ran a rail spur where the end of a freight stood, a caboose and several gondolas and boxcars. Catfish climbed the caboose's forward steps and took a key from his pocket and undid a padlock on the car's door and opened it and motioned to LeRoy to come up and they went in. Catfish pointed to a cot made up taut as a military bunk and told LeRoy to put the sack there.

Everywhere wooden shelves ran floor to ceiling, braced by brazed angle iron brackets. They held a motley collection of objects neatly arranged. A menagerie of small stuffed animals and tin toys and street signs and clusters of bones and antique hand tools. A row of alarm clocks all set to different times. Above a dresser a shield-shaped mirror from which dangled bits of colored ribbon and bunting. Like bookends, two framed pieces of corkboard on either side of the mirror held pinned to them campaign buttons from elections long past, some still shining and others rusted.

Catfish saw LeRoy looking and asked him did he like his museum and LeRoy said he supposed he did. When I get it big enough, I'm going to charge people to get in and see it. He asked LeRoy did he think a quarter was too much and LeRoy said that sounded about right.

Catfish emptied out the sack item by item, inspecting each one, turning them this way and that and holding them up against the light from the windows. He laid them on the bed and ran his hands over them spiderlike, his long fingers fretting like an old woman's. He took special interest in an old pipe wrench, its rusting knurl seized up tight. He looked about and went to place it among the arrangement of hand tools, but reconsidered and took it back and set it at the other end of the car between a brakeman's blue lantern and an oilcan. I aint crazy he told LeRoy, where it goes is more important than what it is. Everything can go more than one place. You got to figure out the one's best. That's what people will pay to see and they won't even know why that is, but they will.

With languorous deliberation, he found a place on the shelves for each thing he'd brought in and then folded the sack and smoothed it with the palm of his hand like a priest caressing his vestments and delicately laid it in the top drawer of a dresser. Next to the dresser stood a bookcase with glass doors and filled with books. LeRoy asked Catfish had he read them all and Catfish told him he read some but not all and those he had read, he only got half of what they said because of him having only one eye. He slapped the dresser and laughed snottily through his nose.

He asked LeRoy was he hungry and LeRoy said if he was offering, he figured he could eat. Catfish went to the end of the car where stood a table and a pair of chairs and where an icebox cowered and a ledge attached to the wall held a Coleman stove. Catfish said all he had was leftovers and LeRoy thanked him and said it sounded like Sunday dinner and what could he do to help. Catfish told him just have a seat and opened the icebox and took out a jar of stew and opened a cabinet and took out a pot. He pumped up the Coleman and lit it and poured the stew in the pot and placed it on the burner. He got bowls and spoons and set the table and then went to stirring the stew until it was hot and turned off the burner and with a rag, took up the pot and poured stew into the bowls. He sat and laid his hand in his lap and asked LeRoy did he want to say the prayer. LeRoy looked at him and Catfish again laughed his snotty laugh and said I fucking got you, didn't I?

When they were part way done eating, Catfish said it was hard not to look at it wasn't it. LeRoy was going to say what did he mean, but said instead that it was. Catfish said he used to have a glass eye, but it never looked the same direction as the real one and that was even stranger than just having one eye and did make him look crazy to a lot of people and he had to clean it every day and it was a pain in the ass getting in and out and sometimes made his face sore. So he stopped using it and went to a patch, but it kept slipping off and there would be just the socket looking out and that made folks even more uneasy than the glass eye so he went to a vet and had him sew it shut. He had to cut both lids so they would grow together after he stitched them up and it for the most part worked because the eye wouldn't never open again. But it didn't altogether work because it was supposed to look like he just had it closed was all, but it sunk in and made that half of his face look like it was dead.

LeRoy asked him how come if he didn't like the way it looked, he just didn't go back to the patch. Catfish said he had calculated on it and decided that when he got the museum opened up folks would tell other folks about it because of the way he looked, like he was part of the exhibit. They'd say, they got a nigger up there is dead on the one side and you got to see it and it only costs a quarter and free advertising is free advertising. Aint nothing cheaper than free. LeRoy wanted to tell him that more often than not free was pretty fucking expensive, but he didn't.

They finished eating and Catfish gathered up the dishes and pot and told LeRoy he could help him wash them if he wanted. They went outside and around the side of the car to where a pair of laundry tubs clung to its side and a pitcher pump was lagged onto a weathered wooden table, the pump's spout, like a sniffing dog, just clearing the edge of the first tub. Catfish pointed under the tubs to an enameled steel cabinet and said there's soap and rags and scrub pads in there and when he was done bring the dishes back in. He went back into the car.

LeRoy worked the pump and watched the water run into the tub and saw a rubber stopper on the table and put it in the drain and pumped some more and took out the things Catfish had told him about from the cabinet and washed and rinsed the dishes and took them inside. He asked Catfish where the well was and Catfish said he dug it himself and ran the lines and pointed out the window to a wooden cover a dozen yards from the car. LeRoy said that must have been a hell of a job and Catfish said not really, everywhere around here first water aint far down. The hard part was running the drain far enough away so it wouldn't sicken the well.

Catfish waved toward the bed where lay a blanket and a sheet and part of a loaf of sliced bread and a can of Spam. He told LeRoy you can take that over to the far boxcar and make up the bed and it wasn't much of a supper but it would get him to morning. LeRoy said he'd done with a lot less and what did he owe him. Catfish said he just said that over at Ruthy's because he had a reputation to keep up and he was glad for the company and if things worked out, LeRoy could maybe take him up to town for a beer someday and LeRoy said he could count on it. Catfish said that was just if it was a couple of nights. If it got permanent, he would have to charge him and LeRoy said he knew that.

There's a lantern out there if you need it, but there'll be enough of a moon tonight, you can see good enough to get up and piss. The lantern'll just draw in the bugs. But don't worry about the bed having bugs in it. I sprayed it. If you got to shit, there's an outhouse. You can see it from the car. I don't care where you piss, but don't shit anywhere except in there. And don't worry about waking up in time to get the ferry. The birds'll start up with time to spare.

LeRoy thanked him and started out and stopped to look at the books and asked Catfish did he mind if he borrowed one for the night. Catfish said aint you the educated nigger and help yourself. LeRoy ran his finger across the glass. Most of the books were old and some the spines were torn or missing altogether. There was a pile of paperbacks sitting on top of the case. He thumbed through a couple and saw they were fuck books and put them back. He went to the other case and looked and next to a line of books with all the same covers but different names he saw one with a different color cover, a dingy bronze that said in sunk-in, crooked letters *The Klondike Gold Fields.* It had a picture of a river with trees behind it and a tent right on the bank of the river and above that clouds and birds. A man stood right next to the water.

LeRoy took it out and opened it. There was a map folded up inside, glued to the cover. He opened the map and it had all of Alaska in pink with broken red lines showing all the ways to get to the gold fields and there was printed on the map in big red letters where the gold fields were and there were a lot of them, across almost the whole of Alaska. Over top of Alaska and just beyond a stretch of water, a white map said Eastern Siberia. He told Catfish he'd take this one if he didn't mind and Catfish said it was okay with him and LeRoy said thanks again for everything and gathered up the bedding and supper and put the book under his arm and went out and over to the boxcar.

There was a rickety wood table and two chairs in the middle of the car. A straw tick mattress was rolled up against the far end and there was a frame bed with squares of woven rope to hold the mattress. A blue lantern like the one Catfish put the wrench next to sat on the table and a box of matches. LeRoy rolled the mattress out and laid out the sheet and the blanket and looked around for a pillow. There was no pillow, but a tick mattress makes its own pillow when you sink down into it and it would more than do.

LeRoy went back to the door and looked out and saw where the outhouse was, along the woods on the far side of another track and he wondered if a train would come through in the night and would it blow its whistle. He sat down with his legs dangling and leaned against the door and took up the book and turned to the first chapter, which was a Preface.

Klondike is the magic word that is thrilling the whole country. It stands for millions of gold and great fortunes for hundreds of miners, who have risen from poverty to affluence in the brief period of a few months. Thousands are reading of fortunes made in the Klondike Gold Fields, and thousands of others are turning their longing eyes toward the new El Dorado.

The old Spanish dreams of a wonderful realm somewhere in the Western Continent, made of gold and precious stones, seem almost on the point of being realized. Not since 1849, when the marvelous discoveries of gold were made in California, has there been such excitement among all classes of people.

There were pictures in the book of beaches with seals and mountains and the book said how to get there and what to take and what the dangers were and where there were places miners had already found gold and how to make a claim when you found yours. LeRoy saw himself walking down the street in an Alaska gold town, dressed in an expensive old-time suit and wearing patent leather cowboy boots and smoking a cigar and a white girl on one arm and a black girl on the other and they are wearing those old-time southern gowns and talk in a soft drawl so beautiful you would know for sure they were not whores but ladies and who cares if both kinds of women like you better if you are rich? Thinking about the ladies in Alaska made him remember the girls last night and that made him think of Harmon and how in three nights he would have slept in three places not too many people ever sleep in one of, let alone all three, a jail cell and a cabin on a river and a boxcar. And maybe that was enough of an adventure for this place along the river and he should go and steal back his skiff from those boys and keep going, just light out for whatever there was downriver. But he decided him landing here and sleeping in these strange places must be a sign and went on reading until it was too dark and then lit the lantern even if it did draw bugs and sat at the table and read some more until he came up to the end of a chapter and put down the book and snuffed out the lantern and went to the bed and lay down. He looked out the boxcar's door toward the woods, where stars hung brightly above the trees. He picked one out and wished on it and lay back and closed his eyes. The last thought LeRoy had as he slipped into a sleep wherein he would dream of camping on a bank above the Yukon with the midnight sun brushing the mountains and the fire's smoke scented with pine branches, was would the day ever come when he would fuck a rich woman?

LeRoy dreamed of birds flying across the river, their songs louder and louder until they awakened him and he realized that they were real birds and remembered he'd slept in a boxcar and not in a camp on the Yukon. He pulled back the blanket and stood in the dark and looked out through the open door toward the moon just over the trees. He went to the door and let himself down and walked over across the main line and pissed. He started toward the path where he and Catfish had come through the woods and remembered the book and went back to the car and got it. He considered keeping it but decided that stealing from Catfish after what he did for him wouldn't be right. He took the book back along the row of abandoned cars to Catfish's caboose, an amber light glowing through the little tower on the roof. He reached up and set the book on the deck where Catfish would at least see half of it.

By the time he got to Ruthy's, the sky was filling up with a vague and silver light. He went in and sat at the L-shaped counter. On the other side of the L sat the man who was telling the story yesterday. He called LeRoy by name and asked did he make out okay and did Catfish try to gouge him and LeRoy said he made out pretty good and the price was fair enough. A tall thin woman came over and with strong hands wiped the counter in front of him and asked did he want the special and he said he did and she asked did he want grits or potatoes and how did he want his eggs. He told her potatoes and sunny side up. He asked would she get him some coffee and she said it comes with it and poured him a cup and went behind a curtain. LeRoy asked the man did he know what time it was. The man took out a pocket watch and said not quite five yet. You got plenty of time.

The man asked LeRoy what he thought of Catfish's museum. LeRoy said he guessed it was all right and the man said it was a fucking junk shop was what it was. Catfish thinks just because if he had a extra quarter he would spend it to look at junk, every-fucking-body else would too. The woman came back out with a plate and gave the man a look and he said sorry Ruthy and she said sorry my fucking ass and they both laughed. The man looked at LeRoy and said Ruthy don't want bad language in here on account of it keeps out the church people, not because it bothers her.

He told Ruthy LeRoy's name and how he was going over to put in an application at the Bessemer and she said she knew they were hiring, so it was good timing and she hoped he wasn't afraid of work because if he was, he might as well take the morning off and go up to town and put in for relief. LeRoy waited for her to ask him where he was from but she didn't, just filled up his coffee and told him when he was ready it was a dollar and went back in the kitchen. Even thin as she was, she had strong hips to go with her strong hands and LeRoy for a second imagined her naked and him wrapped up safe within her with those hands on his back holding him down hard to one place. He shook the thought away and drank down the coffee and mopped up the last of the plate with a biscuit and put four quarters and a dime on the counter and started out. The man got up too and said he'd walk LeRoy part way to the ferry and they went out together.

LeRoy asked the man did he know what he could expect when he got to the Bessemer.

All they care about is are you going to show up and can you handle a shovel. They're going to make you show ID. You got that?

I got a driver's license.

Where from?

LeRoy told him Louisiana and the man said being out of state is going to make them think twice and he will ask you what you are doing here. You tell him there wasn't no work where you come from and you came here to stay with a uncle.

Will he ask who he is?

Shit no, he just take it for what it's worth. They already think we all related. But if he does, just tell him you staying with me.

They walked on a ways and the houses became scattered and the sidewalk ended. They came to a squat cabin with a sun-bleached wooden porch and a newly plowed field behind it. The man said it was his and he had to get to work himself. He told LeRoy the main road was just around that turn and when he got there he would see the big wharf where the ferry was tied up and where to get his ticket.

From up top of the ferry LeRoy could feel the diesels chugging and heaving through the river. He looked down into the brown water and watched the ripples angling off from the ferry's sides and looked to the stern where the water splashed up in white coils and rolled over and curled back down into the river. He wondered if fish ever got caught up in the roiling water and would they be bewildered by their world suddenly spinning and them not able to do anything about it and would they wonder was the boat a monster come to hunt them down.

He marveled at how the boat could hold a tractor-trailer and a dozen cars and all the people who had come on the deck with him and what kept it all up. There had to be a reason for why a thing so big could float. He had watched the truck roll onto the deck, the airbrakes sighing and the lurch of the tractor against its load and how the driver had taken the truck to the very end of the ferry and just stopped there and climbed down from the cab and stood in silhouette against the morning sun and lit a cigarette, leaving the engine slowly throbbing. LeRoy wondered how often it happened that a truck just kept on going and slipped over the front of the boat and went down into the water and disappeared, the driver frantic at the brakes and the wheel all the way down into the river where he drowned.

For all its churning, the ferry seemed mired in the water, the other shore never closer. LeRoy wanted it to speed across, to just get him to whatever the next thing was, but the ferry was crossing in its own time and there wasn't anything he could do to get to whatever was over there quicker than what the ferry wanted. Whatever was coming was going to come when it did. He walked back to where there were some benches where people sat and looked across the water to where they had come from. The wharf was smaller and fading so that he could just make out the workers resetting the gate and another truck coming down from the hills and pulling up in the lot to await the boat's return. Moving away from where he had been meant that he really was getting closer to what was next and he sat on one of the benches and let his impatience drain out of him. He wished he had kept the book. It would have helped pass the time.

The Story of My Life
By
LeRoy James

Chapter 3

The next thing I am going to tell you about is how me and Mr.
Bones saved my teacher Miss Wells from a ~~bunch~~ hoard of
demons when I was 10. She was a real good teacher and she was
strict too. She would not put up with no sassing and you had to
do your lessons or she would make you stand in the corner with
the dunce hat on ~~and nobody wanted that~~. If you made it through
eight years of Miss Wells, you would know your numbers and
how to read and write and your countries ~~and what their main
crops was~~ and just about everything there is to know about the
thirteen colonies and the Civil War and the other wars. A lot of
people only know their times tables up to 10, but Miss Wells
made us study them up to 12. And she ~~didn't~~ did not just make
you do one kind of lesson in the part of the day she had set up
for it. You could be right in the middle of geography and for no
reason that anybody could of seen, she would up and say, "LeRoy,
what is 12 times 6?" and you better ~~by Jesus~~ know. Sometimes she
would try to trip you up, ask you first what 12 times 6 is and then
say, "OK, LeRoy, now what is 6 times 12?" It was on account of
that lesson I learned that some things you have to figure out by
looking at them backwards. Like if you want to know the wind
direction, you just look to which way the wind is going and turn
it around. So say if the wind is blowing down the river toward the
Crossings, which is south, you turn that around and that makes it

a north wind, and if the wind is blowing across the river toward town, you turn that around and say it is an east wind.

But I am getting away from what happened with me and Mr. Bones and Miss Wells. I woke up in the dark with Mr. Bones floating about a inch from my eyes and what woke me up was he was blowing the dark against my face. (This is not a thing I can explain, him blowing the dark out of his mouth and if I did, you wouldn't believe me, but it's true.) Well, he just about scared the complete ~~shit~~ devil out me, me waking up and seeing him that close. I almost yelled, but he yelled first, "Shush up, boy, or you will wake everybody up and we will never make it out of here and we got important work to do." (Don't forget, he could yell all he wanted because I was the only one who could hear him.)

Then he said, "Get dressed, then go out to the shed and get yourself two feed sacks. Make sure they don't have ~~no~~ holes in them and get a couple pieces of wire to close them up. Get the hatchet and shovel while you are at it."

All this was a strange thing for him to be telling me to do in the middle of the night, but I did it just like he said, and even if he allowed me to, I wouldn't have asked him any questions. By the time I was 10, I had figured out that when somebody who's older than you and has done some things over and over that you have not even done once, you are a lot better off doing it their way. I think I most learned that particular lesson when Daddy took me squirrel hunting with him for the first time. There was a big, fat gray chattering down at us and Daddy gave me the shotgun and told me to hold it real tight against my shoulder, but that did not make sense to me because I had seen how a shotgun kicks and holding it tight would make that kick hurt like hell. So I held it off of my shoulder a couple inches and then shot at the squirrel. And that ~~fucking~~ gun whammed back into me like I had got kicked by a horse. I asked Daddy why he did not tell me what would happen if I did not hold the gun tight in and all he said was, "I told you not to do it. That should of been enough for me to say." What I learned from that was to just do what an old person says even if it does not make no sense and then contemplate on it later on when you are by yourself and then make up your mind what you will do the next time you are in the same situation. Maybe you will do it their way the next time and maybe you won't. As far as the first time goes, you are better off doing it their way. So I did what he said and got dressed.

The bedroom where I slept was off the kitchen so I had to go through there and was a little nervous because sometimes Mama would get up in the middle of the night and sit at the table and drink a cup of cold coffee left over from supper. I saw her sometimes when I had to get up in the night and go to the bathroom. She would be sitting there with her elbows on the table, holding the cup up under her mouth like she forgot it was there and then remembering and taking a sip. I watched her one time for a good long while when she didn't know I was there and she just sat there taking a sip every once in a while but mostly looking into the air like there was something she wished she could see, but wasn't there. When I saw that, I wanted to be big like Daddy and sit down next to her and put my arm around her shoulders so she could lean her head on me and I could tell her everything was going to be all right. I wanted to even though I knew it was her place in life to comfort me and not the other way round, but for some reason that don't seem right to me. There ought to be a way a child can comfort his own mother when she seems to need it, when she is sitting in the dark looking at something that ~~aint~~ is not there but should be.

But the coast was clear and I snuck through the kitchen and outside and went out to the shed like Mr. Bones told me. I

could see the shed okay, because it was the week before Easter
and there is always a full moon right before Easter and it was a
clear night so the moonlight didn't have to fight its way through
no clouds. I made it to the shed and there was enough moonlight
getting in through the open door for me to see where the hatchet
and shovel was, so I got them pretty easy, but it was harder with
the sacks. Mr. Bones had told me to make sure to get sacks that
didn't have no holes in them. But just because there was enough
light getting in the shed to see where the sacks was, there wasn't
enough to see how good a shape any one of them was in. I
tried feeling for holes with my hands. But it's a strange thing:
it's a lot easier to feel around for something that's there than for
something that ain't there and what I was really doing was feeling
for holes that ~~wasn't~~ was not there. You just try imagining that.
Think about what a thing with no holes in it feels like and how
would you know you had felt all the places there could of been
a hole. While I was trying to figure this out, Mr. Bones appeared
beside me in the shed and said, "Just bring a bunch outside where
you can see them better. Take a lot less time than the way you are
trying to do it." I felt a little stupid that I hadn't thought of it first
myself. I grabbed up a dozen or so of them sacks and took them
outside and put them on the ground and then I went through
them one at a time until I found two that didn't have even one
single hole in them. I threw them over my shoulder and carried
the other ones back in the shed and put them on the pile with the
other sacks. Mr. Bones didn't have to tell me to do that. Daddy
told me that when you are trying to get away with something that
some folks might think was a crime, the best way to go about it
is to leave wherever it is that you are doing the crime looking like
you never did it in the first place. If ~~your~~ you are lucky they never
will notice it, or at least won't for a long enough time that nobody
will think to put you and the crime together in their head. The

way Mr. Bones was sneaking around and shushing me had got me to feeling like this mission of his was going to have some kind of a crime be a part of it and I figured there's no better time to be thinking about getting away with something than when you are first getting started. It turned out that what me and Mr. Bones was going to be doing was all for good, but I didn't know it right then in the dark with nothing but the moon for light.

I still had not got the wire, so I started back into the shed to get it and the nippers too, to cut off the pieces. But before I could even get to the shed door, Mr. Bones was coming out of it with the wire in his hand already cut up. He handed them pieces over to me and told me to loop them over my belt so I could get at them quick when the time came. I asked him if he had trouble finding the nippers and he said, "Didn't need to, bit them off."

"We almost ready," he said. "Just a couple more things left to do." Then he reached around behind him. He looked like he was rooting around in a dresser drawer for something that was mixed in with a whole lot of other things and he knew it was there, but not exactly in what place. Finally he brings his hand back out where I can see it and he is holding a piece of bone tied onto a string. He said, "Come here, boy," and waved me over. Then he tied the string around my neck so the bone hung down on my chest. I said, "What is that for?"

"It is a charm to stave off bad magic."

I took a closer look at the bone. "Shit, Mr. Bones, it ain't nothing but a piece of chicken bone."

"It might look like a chicken bone to you, boy, but that bone come out of a Aztec bird-of-war. The bird that bone came out of been dead 500 years. Them Aztecs used war birds to warn them when enemies was coming. That bone you got on been on the winning side of more battles than you got hairs on your head. There is powerful magic in that bone, and you better believe me when I say you are going to need some magic on your side tonight."

I looked on the bone with more respect after he said that. "You said a couple more things. What else?"

"Got to get you purified, boy. Get rid of any black evil swimming around in your blood. Got to make you a 100 percent bona fide hero."

"How are we going to do that?"

" We ain't going to do nothing. I am going to take care of it. You just do what I tell you."

"Okay, then," I said. "I will try. Tell me what you want me to do."

"Get down on your knees and look straight up at the moon and then close your eyes. Keep them closed until I tell you it is OK to open them."

I did what he said and kneeled down and looked up at the moon and just at that exact second, something blood red that had wings that looked like they was made out of fire and smoke flew right past it, and when it did I saw the moon shiver and shake right up there in the sky and I do not mind admitting that it scared me real bad. I felt like the moon shivering was like a lightning bolt had come down in a channel cut in the dark right into the top of my head and ran all the way down my spine and into my knees stuck down in the dirt. Mr. Bones saw that and said, "You are going to see a lot worse than that before morning. Now close your eyes."

I closed my eyes and at first I couldn't hear nothing but the tree frogs. And then there started up a rushing sound like water falling over a big stone in a freshwater branch. And then it got louder and I felt the air swirling around me, except I knew it wasn't the air, it was Mr. Bones. There is a difference between the way air feels and the way Mr. Bones feels. I couldn't see because

of my closed eyes, but I could imagine in my mind what was
going on, with the sound of Mr. Bones whirling around me like a
Arabian dervish, spinning hard as a twister. And then the rushing
sound turned into a roar and the roar turned into a shriek. I read
a story one time about banshees and how they come out at night
when someone is dying and I got scared for a minute that maybe
what I was hearing wasn't Mr. Bones at all, but a banshee coming
and the one he was coming for was me and that meant I was
dying. Nothing will make you more scared than wondering if you
are about to die, and I got about ready to ~~say fuck it and~~ open up
my eyes so I could at least see what was about to kill me, but I
didn't. Pretty soon the shrieking calmed down and was the roar
again and that calmed down too and it was the rushing sound like
water and then it was just the tree frogs again. Mr. Bones said,
"All right, boy, you can take a look now." I opened up my eyes and
there was the moon still there, but not white anymore, but pure
silver, like a mirror up there in the sky.

I heard Mr. Bones say, "Almost there, boy." His voice came
a little from the side and I looked over at him and he was holding
a big tin bucket and the bucket was filled up with moonlight,
sloshing back and forth. Then he said, "Bow down your head,
boy," and I did. Then he must of stood over top of me and
poured the moonlight out of the bucket onto my head because I
felt it falling all over me, cool and fresh, and it streamed down my
face and all over my clothes and spread around in a circle around
me on the ground and I was kneeling in a circle of light. It felt a
little bit like water was pouring over me but it didn't make me wet.
It just glowed on my clothes and skin and on the ground too. I
stayed like that for a while and watched the light on the ground
fade away, but a part of it stayed on me for the whole night and
didn't go away altogether until the sun came up. Mr. Bones said,
"Look back up at the moon," and when I did I saw something

else fly across it, another creature with wings, but this time I think it was an angel and not something to be afraid of because its wings was pure white and they shined from inside, bright as a candle in a dark room.

Mr. Bones said, "You are as pure now as you are ever going to be, though I expect it ~~won't~~ will not last long. Time to go. You take the sacks and the hatchet. I got the shovel." He put the shovel on his shoulder and started down the road. I was glad it was the middle of the night and nobody would be around to see me walking down the road, because even though I have been lots of places with Mr. Bones, he never carried nothing before, and because nobody but me could see him, I'd sure ~~as shit~~ make people suspicious that I was a man witch if they saw me walking down the road holding a hatchet and there was a shovel floating in the air next to me. Could even get me lynched or nailed up on a cross and set on fire. There is a lot more to this adventure, but it is late now and I am running out of gas. I think it will be better if I take a break and tell the rest in a different chapter. So I will see you then.

TO BE CONTINUED

Tabernacle Parish, 1958

LeRoy liked some parts of Sunday school more than others. He didn't like the opening exercises as much as he liked the singing downstairs, but he did like the way the women looked in their big hats and white gloves. They'd chuck him under his chin and sometimes they would give him a mint and then Pastor Johnson would walk up the stairs to the pulpit and everybody had to get real quiet. LeRoy was proud of himself because he knew what words like *opening exercises* and *pulpit* meant. If it was sunny, the pastor would say what a glorious day to be in the sunshine of the Spirit and if it was raining he would say how wonderful it was they could come together and find refuge from the darkness and the storm in the house of God. Then he would say let us pray and he would pray that God would open everybody's heart to the teachings they were about to receive. The first time LeRoy went to Sunday school, the lady next to him showed him how to fold his hands and bow his head and after that he knew what do to, but he snuck looks anyway once the pastor started praying and the ladies had their own eyes closed and he saw that not everybody closed their eyes. Some of them were looking around too. After the pastor finished his prayer, they would sing a song and then they would all go to different places in the church. LeRoy went downstairs to the basement with the other little kids where there were chairs lined up in rows and the teachers would take turns leading them in more songs. Some of the songs were the same ones his mother sang to him and some were different. He liked the ones with motions best, making your feet go like you were a soldier when you sang *I may never march in the infantry* and pointing in and out for *One door and only one* and holding your hands way out when you got to the part in Do Lord about how Glory Land outshines the sun.

After the songs they split up again and went to their classes. LeRoy was in the five to eight class with Miss Wells. The first thing they did was go around and everybody said the Bible verse for that day and if you got it right without any mistakes, you got a star in your workbook. At first LeRoy had a hard time understanding what the other kids said until he saw that most of them talked like Whiskey and then they were easier to understand. He thought about that and how other people talked. How Pastor Johnson had a way of making words longer than other people, like he was part singing them and only partly saying them. And how Miss Wells talked more like his mother than she did the other ladies at church.

After the verses, the kids who were in regular school took turns reading parts of the stories in the lessons. The story about the coat of many colors and the ark with all the animals and the rainbow's promise and how the lions couldn't hurt Daniel and Jesus throwing out the money changers. He thought Jesus must have been a lot like Whiskey when he threw the bad people out of the temple and when he was bigger, maybe he could beat up the bad people like Jesus and Whiskey did. After they finished reading the story, Miss Wells told them about why the story for that day was important and how they should take the lesson home with them in their hearts and use it to be better in how they acted and how they treated other people. Like when they got to the story about Zacchaeus, she told them how he didn't have to climb up in the tree so Jesus could see him. Jesus could see you no matter how little you are and he especially saw the little children and when he told Zacchaeus to come down because he was going to his house today, it meant Jesus came to your house every day and that's why you should be good because it made Jesus happy when he came to your house and saw you were being good. Then she had them sing about the wee little man.

One day when they were having the lesson on Moses and the girl reading got to a word that was too hard for her, LeRoy told her it was *bulrushes*. Miss Wells looked at him like she was surprised. After the lesson, she asked him how he knew what the word was and he said he just knew. The next week she gave him a letter and told him to take it home and give it to his mother and not to be worried about what it said. The letter was just about how well he was doing and how proud she was of him.

LeRoy skipped and skittered all the way home that day, the letter tight in one hand and his workbook in the other, his shirttail hanging out and him singing out loud *Be careful little eyes what you see*, except when he met somebody on the sidewalk. Then he kept on singing the song, but not out loud, just in his head. And without the motions.

Tabernacle Parish, 1958

Helen Wells sat at her desk in her house on Youngquist Street, preparing Monday's lessons. She graded yesterday's arithmetic tests, affixing gold and silver stars when warranted and sometimes when not, sad that for some of the little ones whose time with her would be brief, the mystery of carrying the one would never unravel and what stars she gave them were among the few lights they would ever know. But there were those who had with some luck navigated the rocky waters of their lives and made it to the upper grades where they were adroitly solving for the unknown x, and she was hopeful that one or two of them might attend high school. She marked their essays, correcting *were's* to *where's* and for the eighth graders admonishing their run-ons and fragments and noting, in the metallic tone she often regretted needing to use, where neatness was sparse and how she would not tolerate laziness and how she knew they could do better. She recorded the grades and took up the eight spellers the Board had granted her and wrote out the week's words, ten for each grade, the eighty words she would write on the blackboard for her charges to copy down and which most of them would quickly master, spelling a rote subject for which their wish to please her was sufficient motivation to goad them to success. She traced spidery maps onto ditto paper to run off on Monday morning and made notes for the geography and history lessons and reviewed the selections for reading and gauged how long before she would again have to seek money for ink and composition paper from the Board for her penmanship lessons. When she was done, she placed all her work in a scuffed portfolio case, her desk clear for tomorrow's Sunday school lesson about the temptation of Jesus. This one they universally liked because it had the devil in it. She would let them draw pictures for this one with the scraps of crayons she kept in a shoebox and some of the pictures would have Satan with horns and a pitchfork and one or two with the devil knocked out on the ground and Jesus standing over him. At least one child would draw a brother or sister burning in the flames of hell and she would quietly turn that into a lesson on loving one another and on forgiveness. She thought about the best way to get across the meaning of the week's verse. *Thou shalt worship the Lord thy God, and him only shalt thou serve.* She decided to keep it simple. Tell them how Satan was always trying to tempt them to do bad things and if they gave in, they weren't serving Jesus like he told them and that would make him sad. She contemplated her own temptations and tried to honestly measure how closely her life aligned with the impossible theology of Luke Chapter 4, Verse 8, and on how far short of that exhortation one could lag before falling from grace. When she was finished with her lesson preparations and her introspection, she took up a yellow tablet and a pencil and began to draft the letter she had been thinking about all week.

Dear Miss James:

I am writing to tell you what a pleasure it has been having LeRoy in Sunday school these last few months. He is always attentive and ~~generally~~ well mannered. He gets on quite well with the other children. He is always prepared, never having failed to memorize the week's Bible verse.

~~But you know all of this already.~~ Recently I have noticed that even though he has not yet attended regular day school, he appears to be reading the lessons and understanding what he reads. ~~I am curious as to whether you have been teaching him to read.~~ I believe he is ready to begin school, even though you are not required to send him until next year. I am sure that if I interceded with the Board of Education, they would admit him even though we are in midyear.

Perhaps we could get together to discuss this? Could you meet me for coffee at Arlene's Café on Summit Street on Wednesday afternoon at 4:00?

Helen put down her pencil and imagined the two of them sitting together at Arlene's and wondered which sight would raise more eyebrows and worse trouble, two young women, one black and the other white, having coffee together, or a teacher and a prostitute. She took up her ivory nib holder, put in a fresh point, and on her letter stationary wrote out a one-sentence note asking if Agnes could meet her at the church this coming Wednesday afternoon to talk about the possibility of LeRoy's starting day school.

Tabernacle Parish, 1958

LeRoy came down the church steps amid a laughing gaggle of children and heard someone call from across the street hey Skeeter! He looked over to Whiskey leaning against the fender of his truck. He ran down the steps and into the road and Whiskey hollered for him to watch out, there was a car coming. The boy waited for the car and ran over and wrapped his arms around Whiskey's legs. Whiskey opened the truck door and lifted him up to the seat and climbed in beside him. He asked him did he behave himself in Sunday school and LeRoy said he guessed he did.

What was the lesson about?

Jonah and the whale.

You learn your verse?

LeRoy said he did and Whiskey said let me hear you say it.

When my soul fainted within me I remembered the Lord: and my prayer came in unto thee, into thine holy temple.

Whiskey told him he did good and asked what the teacher taught them about Jonah.

LeRoy said Miss Wells told them Jonah being in the whale and then getting spit out meant you sometimes have to go through a lot of darkness to get to the light and Whiskey told him Miss Wells sounded like a pretty smart lady.

Whiskey pointed to a paper LeRoy was holding and said what's that?

My whale picture.

LeRoy held it up. A grinning figure stood on a beach holding up one hand. The whale was swimming away, a tear dripping down from its eye. Whiskey said he didn't know Jonah was black and LeRoy said it wasn't Jonah, it was him.

Whiskey wanted to know how come the whale was crying and LeRoy said I didn't give him no chance to eat me. Soon as he tried, I smacked him good and he ran off crying like a baby before I could hurt him any more and that's me holding up my fist so he would know what he was fucking in for if he came back.

Whoa, Skeeter. That aint no way to talk. You kiss your mama with that mouth?

LeRoy said you talk that way and you kiss her.

Whiskey looked at LeRoy as if the boy had slapped him and said he was right. Let's you and me both watch how we talk around your mama. You didn't tell that to your teacher, did you?

I told her I was waving goodbye to the whale and I was laughing because I was happy for coming up out of the darkness and the whale was crying because he was sad that he wasn't going to be seeing me no more.

What'd she say about that?

She said it was good and she put a star on it. He showed Whiskey the star.

Whiskey tousled the boy's head and said he guessed getting a star meant it all worked out, but he better be careful about what he told the teacher. Skeeter didn't want her catching him in a lie. He started the truck and told LeRoy to look in the glove box and drove off down the street. LeRoy opened the box where lay a Three Musketeers. LeRoy asked could he have it now and Whiskey said go ahead but maybe just have a little bit. Save the rest for later. And maybe keep it a secret. They didn't want his mama scolding them about spoiling his dinner. Whiskey told him he could remember when he was about as old as LeRoy was now, Three Musketeers had two lines on them where you could break them up and share them with two friends. LeRoy asked him who he shared them with and Whiskey said whoever was with him at the time. Then he said that wasn't altogether true. What he usually did was eat one right away and put up the other two pieces for himself for later. He lit a cigarette and said he would drive slow so LeRoy could make the candy last.

Whiskey parked in front of Agnes's building and asked LeRoy was there anybody up there and the boy told him there was last night but he left before LeRoy got out of bed. Whiskey took a blue bandana from his pocket and held it taut over his finger and told LeRoy to spit on it. He said they didn't want to leave any evidence of the crime and wiped around LeRoy's mouth.

Show me your teeth.

LeRoy pulled back his lips. Whiskey rubbed his teeth with a dry part of the bandana. He took the candy bar and wrapped back up what was left and put it in the glove box.

You go up and ask your mama if you two want to go get something to eat.

LeRoy got excited and said why didn't Whiskey come up with him and ask her himself.

Ladies don't want somebody busting in on them before they got a chance to comb their hair. You just ask her and you wave out the window if she wants to go or not. LeRoy said okay and started out of the truck and Whiskey told him to remember not to say anything about the Three Musketeers. He got out too and sat on the running board and after LeRoy went in, he lit another cigarette and watched the upstairs window.

It was Agnes who pulled back the curtain. She smiled down and waved and shook her head yes and disappeared. Whiskey stood up and looked at himself in the side mirror and adjusted his collar. He tucked his shirt in a little tighter and centered his belt buckle and sat back on the running board and pretty soon they came down. LeRoy wanted to know where they were going to eat. Whiskey told him it was a surprise. He drove them back the way he and LeRoy had come, past the street where the church stood at the edge of town and into the Quarters. He asked Agnes did she see the star on Skeeter's picture and she said she did and she was proud of him. They came up to a small yellow house and pulled in the driveway. Lilacs nestled up against its sides and there was a front porch with a porch swing. A white wooden sign at the edge of the yard in crisp lettering said Ezra Davis, Automotive Repair and in all different colors: Brakes, Alignments, Oil Changes, Flats Fixed, Engine Work, Mufflers and Exhausts, Tune-ups. All Makes and Models. An old Ford coupe in the side yard faced the road with For Sale signs taped on the insides of the front windows. Whiskey drove to the end of the driveway and shut off the truck and looked at LeRoy and Agnes and said this is me. A Bluetick hound trotted out from behind the house. Whiskey said old Jigger wouldn't bite and wouldn't even bark at them. He got down from the truck and petted the dog and told LeRoy to come over and pet him and then told the dog to go back and lay down. The dog romped sideways. Whiskey said not today, Jigger. We'll play tomorrow. Now go. And the dog disappeared again behind the house.

Whiskey led them across the back yard and up onto a porch with two metal rocking chairs painted green and through a screen door into a kitchen full with the smell of roasting chicken. The table was set with three places and a mason jar with sprigs of chicory and buttercups nodding. Whiskey asked did they want some pop. He said he had grape and Coca-Cola and if Agnes wanted one, he had some beer. She said she would take a coke and Whiskey asked LeRoy what about him and he said he'd take a grape. Whiskey got their pop from the refrigerator and a coke for himself and pried off the tops and handed the bottles to his guests. He asked them did they want to look around and Agnes said that would be nice. He took them through the kitchen into the front room where a pair of curve back hickory rockers sat at angles to one another and a swing couch was pressed up against the wall. Whiskey pointed to a small television and said he didn't watch it much but the picture was pretty good. You could see the front yard and the road through a wide latticed window. The window had been recently cleaned, but not well, streaks angling along the panes through a light layer of dust so that the sunshine coming through bent in inexact colors.

Whiskey showed them the two bedrooms with the beds made and then took them out on the porch. He pointed across an expanse of cut grass and said the property goes all the way back through those woods and down to the creek. It's real pretty sitting here in the morning he said. The sun comes up over them hills. He pointed to low-lying mountains off in the distance where the last of the morning's mist was fading.

He led them across the driveway to a pole barn. He took his keys from his pocket and unlocked a padlock and slid the doors open and reached around the side to flip a switch. Two bays of fluorescent utility lights came on, casting their harsh light on an old car, its hood gaping open, tools neatly aligned on orange shop cloths draped over its fenders. Whiskey told them this was his garage and pointed to shelves stocked with all manner of fluids and lubricants. A long bench ran across the back wall with a drill press and a grinding wheel and different sized vises and wooden drawers with wrought iron handles. A thick round post squatted on the floor, bearing the weight of an anvil.

Whiskey said let me show you something Skeeter. He took LeRoy over to the car and pointed to the top of the engine and its exposed valve springs and rockers. He picked LeRoy up and told him what the different parts were for and said he was almost finished putting this job back together but one of these days he would show him one when it was all in pieces. He took them back out and showed them the beds he'd spaded up between the lilacs and told them how they'd make a good place for flowers if he could find somebody who could teach him how to plant them. He showed them the remnants of an old rail fence covered in green leaves flowing down like a waterfall. You should see that in the spring he said. It's all honeysuckle. A lot of folks say honeysuckle's just a weed and cut it out and tell me I should too and get rid of the fence before it all goes to rot, but I just let it grow. If it's a weed, it is for sure a pretty weed. LeRoy pointed to a small weathered outbuilding and asked what it was. Whiskey told him it was the springhouse and walked them over. I probably ought to paint it he said but he liked the way the old grey wood looked, like a wise old man. A ragged swamp maple's limbs swept down over the roof and across the back. Whiskey took hold of an old brass handle on the door and pulled it open. The door lurched a little and Whiskey said the bottom hinge was rusted through and he kept meaning to fix it but something else more important always seemed to be coming up.

Water murmured in a circle of smooth stones a foot or so high in the middle of the dark building. Whiskey told them it was an artesian well and where he got his water. He showed them the pipe he had driven down into the gravel from which the water arose and he told them you drive the pipe down like that so you only get clean water. Dirt gets in on top and you don't want to be drinking that. He said there used to be a runnel went off out the side of the springhouse and down to the creek but he had dug out a trench and run a drain line and covered it over to keep the yard even. I got a electric pump in the basement and the line going in to it is buried too.

He told them that the old lady who lived here before him had a lever pump up next to the house and a pitcher pump inside and they both ran off a line that took from the top of the water and how she kept milk and butter in the water to keep it cold. He said that was before there was electric in the house and it wasn't too sanitary but back in those days there was a lot that wasn't sanitary and people just lived with it. He said sometimes when it was real hot he brought a chair out here where it was cool and just listened to the water. He said it's a good place for keeping potatoes and onions but you have to put them in wire crates so the animals can't get at them. LeRoy pointed to some crates on shelves and asked was there potatoes in them and Whiskey said yes there was. He took one of the crates down and showed him. LeRoy asked how come there were green things coming out of the potatoes and Whiskey said they been here almost too long and they was sprouting and you could plant them in the ground like that and get more potatoes for next year.

Whiskey said they could sit on the porch while he got dinner on the table and Agnes asked could she help and he told her he pretty much got everything ready last night. All he had to do was heat up a couple things and it wouldn't be too long and she should just relax. Agnes and LeRoy sat in the rockers on the porch and drank their pop and listened through the screen door to the sound of rattling pans and cupboards banging shut. LeRoy asked her if men could cook dinner. Agnes smiled and said sometimes they can if their mothers taught them how. After a while Whiskey came to the door and told them it was ready.

This time the table held a platter of cut-up chicken and a bowl of mashed potatoes and a bowl of greens and gravy in a gravy boat and a plate of Wonder bread still in the wrapper. Whiskey waited for them to sit down and sat himself. He said don't be shy, there was plenty and he made two chickens in case Skeeter was real hungry and it would only take a minute to cut the other one up if he was. He said he knew there was some lumps in the potatoes and gravy, he was better at making breakfast than he was at dinner. Agnes said everything was delicious and reminded LeRoy to watch his manners. Whiskey told them about how when he was a kid, they didn't have electricity or gas, but had to use kerosene lanterns and cook on a coal stove. He told LeRoy him and his brothers and sisters would go outside early to play before breakfast. They could tell what their mother was fixing from what kind of smoke came out of the chimney, what color it was and whether it was thick or not. When they were finished, Whiskey put coffee on to perk and Agnes asked if she could wash the dishes. Whiskey said they were his company and he wasn't going to put company to work and he would take care of it later and they should all go out on the porch and take in the afternoon.

Before they sat down, he whispered in Agnes's ear and she smiled and nodded. Whiskey said Skeeter I got something for you. He led the boy around the side and over to the truck and got out what was left of the Three Musketeers. Whiskey said there was something he wanted to talk about with LeRoy's mama just between him and her and would LeRoy want to watch some television. LeRoy asked would it be okay if he went down to the creek instead. Whiskey said you have to ask your mama. They went back and asked her and she said yes but didn't look too sure about it. Whiskey said it would be bragging to call it a creek. Might be deep enough to drown a field mouse but nothing for her to worry about and she looked less afraid. Whiskey told her Skeeter could take Jigger with him and Jigger would let them know if the boy had got himself into any devilment and she said okay again, sounding happier about it this time. Whiskey whistled for the dog and told LeRoy to pet him and run off a little ways and the dog would go with him. LeRoy ran and he and the dog scurried down the rise and out of sight. Whiskey said the coffee should be ready and went in and came out with two cups and they sat down.

They sat there for a while and then Whiskey said there was something he wanted to talk to her about. He asked her what she thought of his place and she said it was real nice. He told her what all work he had done on it. How it was all brush in the back yard when he got it and how the paint was down to the bare clapboards. He'd paid for the electric line in from the road and wired the house and the barn himself and cleared the brush and put in an electric water heater and a septic tank so he could have an inside toilet. He pointed over to a little tuft of ground where the grass was a brighter green than the rest of the yard and said that was where the outhouse had been. He told her how he was planning to put in an oil burner but he would keep the wood stove when he did, just because he liked the way it warmed the room.

He pointed to the few trees in the back yard and told her what they were. A plum tree and a pair of old apple trees with their gnarled branches intertwined and a pear tree. He said somebody had planted them years and years ago and there were a lot of them he had to cut out because they were rotting in the trunk. But he kept a few that he thought would live. The fruit isn't much good he said. But he kept them because of the flowers in the spring. And there's a dogwood out front and a mock orange and something I don't know what it is and in the spring when they all come out and the lilacs with them, you can open the windows and let the smell of all those flowers fill up the house. He sat there quiet for a while and then he asked her again what she thought and she told him he'd done a lot of work.

He took a deep breath and looked toward the woods and without looking back at her asked her if she thought maybe she might want to move out of where she was and come stay here with him. Her and the boy. And then he looked at her and it was her turn to look down toward the woods. She was quiet for a long time.

Finally she said she wasn't expecting him to ask something like that and he said he'd been thinking about it for a while now and what did she say.

It would be taking a big chance.

He told her he wasn't going to lie to her and say there wouldn't be some tongues wagging and she would maybe get called some nasty names but most of them wouldn't tell her to her face and she said I don't know.

It's closer to the school he said and closer to the church too and Skeeter would have all this yard to play in and lots of kids lived around here to play in it with him.

Aint it against the law?

What you doing now is against the law and you don't seem to mind it too much.

Agnes looked at him hard and halfway lifted up her hand and Whiskey saw he had gone too far and sat still as a stone and thought if she was going to hit him, he was going to let her and it seemed like days before she finally touched him, but she didn't hit him. Her eyes softened and she nodded that she knew he was right and she reached her hand over and laid it on his arm, her white fingers thin as a debutante's spread out on his dark skin, those white fingers like thin rivers of snow melting into rich and fertile soil.

Can I put up some curtains?

You do anything you want.

LeRoy came up from the woods, swinging his arms and marching in an exaggerated goose step and Jigger prancing beside him, bounding in the same rhythm. LeRoy had a stick threaded through his belt.

Hey there Skeeter, what you been up to?

LeRoy pulled the stick from his belt and brandished it in the air. I just slayed me a dragon he said. And Jigger howled.

Brigard County, Autumn, 1973

The whistle blew on the precise instant of midnight and the foundry disgorged men from the maw of the guard shack, a horde of bent backs and scurrying feet like rats tumbling from a sewer. Out into the clear night they came, lighting cigarettes and talking loudly so that they could hear one another, the main floor's pandemonic clamor a dusty palimpsest clogging their ears, their speech sprinkled with the spice of *fuck* and *shit*. Some of them had showered and came out with freshly scalded faces, others with the filth of the foundry still ground into their skin, their eyes raccoon-ringed. They hawked and spat black-speckled clots of phlegm onto the parking lot's gray stones and dispersed in ones and twos into their cars and trucks, and some climbed into the company buses waiting with their engines idling to channel them home.

Eli leaned against Harmon's truck and waited for him and LeRoy. LeRoy said he was fucking glad that week was over and Eli said he should be happy he learned a new skill and he could put it on his resume. LeRoy said he would be sure to do that as soon as he got home, put on there that he was getting real fucking good at damn near blowing himself up running twelve pounds of gas and a hundred-forty pounds of air so he could cut up a fifteen-inch crankshaft just because some asshole craneman dropped it and put it out of true, and it would no doubt be just the little extra oomph he needed to get that executive position and then they would be begging him for a job and he would tell them to go fuck themselves. Just go back to the Bessemer and burn scrap, you motherfuckers.

Eli said Jesus Christ, who would want to work for you? Then he said it was Friday, so what should they do. Harmon said he felt like it was about time for Harrisville and Eli said did Harmon think they knew LeRoy long enough to trust him with that. The Lone Pine and Hogshead is one thing, but Harrisville is a whole different level.

Harmon figured they did and Eli said yeah but did Harmon think LeRoy was ready for Harrisville.

Nobody's ready for Harrisville.

LeRoy wanted to know what was so special about the place, he heard it was just another whorehouse. Eli told him you'll see.

Harmon said pile in then, and LeRoy said why didn't they take the ferry and drop Harmon's truck off at LeRoy's place and he'd drive them. Eli said it was surely a sign of how pathetic he was that LeRoy was that fucking proud of that pile of junk he called a car. They ought to throw it in the scrap pit so LeRoy could cut it up like he did the crankshaft and did LeRoy think them Harrisville whores would give him a special price on account of he drove a convertible with rusted through fenders and six taillights, half of them burned out. LeRoy said he was sure of it and he wouldn't be surprised if they told him they would pay *him* if he promised to take them for a ride in old Black Beauty when they were done.

Eli clapped LeRoy on the back and said his confidence was an inspiration and he did know it was an act of faith on him and Harmon's part that they believed his old Black Beauty would actually get them all the ways to Harrisville and back without breaking down, didn't he.

Harmon told LeRoy to pull in here and LeRoy said it didn't look like much. Eli said just wait. They pulled in and LeRoy turned off the key. The engine turned over a few more times before it finally coughed and quit. Eli said he wasn't going to say anything. They got out of the car and went in. LeRoy said it still didn't look like much and if this was supposed to impress him, it wasn't working.

Be patient.

Harmon thought it would be a good idea to have a couple beers to loosen them up and they sat at the U-shaped bar. Eli tapped his fingers on the bar in time to the song coming out of the jukebox about a long woman. LeRoy wondered what that meant. The young, black bartender came over to them, moving with determined grace as if there were rails on the floor behind the bar upon which he glided. They ordered drafts and the bartender set them up, serving LeRoy first. The three friends talked about work.

Eli said LeRoy picked up on how to burn steel faster than most and LeRoy said it was because his daddy was a mechanic and taught him how to weld when he was just a kid and it wasn't that much harder, just a whole lot more pressure was all. Eli asked him was it his intention to put his mechanical knowledge to work on Black Beauty and LeRoy said it was, just as soon as he could figure out how to get by without a car while he had her down. Eli said shit, he'd pick him up for work if he wanted and how long did he think it would be. LeRoy said probably not more than a month. The compression was good and he wouldn't have to tear her down, just a lot of little things and the body work. Eli said no problem. He said they had a long weekend coming up and was LeRoy planning on going to go see his dad and LeRoy told them his dad was dead. All three of them drank from their drafts and went back to talking about the foundry.

LeRoy asked how it worked here and Eli pointed to a door at the back of the bar where behind a little counter there sat on a high stool a large man in a suit and bowtie. He said you go over there and pay and then there's another building and you go in there and take your pick and the girl takes you out to a cabin. The cabins is pretty nice. They got them all decorated up like a Louisiana cathouse and they each one got a bathroom of their own and they change the sheets in between every time they use it. LeRoy said it must cost a lot. Eli said not as much as you think.

They got another draft and two black men, already drunk, came in and sat at the end of the bar along the U and the two sets of companions nodded to each other. One of the new men was telling the other one about how the northern lights worked. Eli asked Harmon was he loosened up enough yet and Harmon said he guessed he was and they took their beers and went over to the gatekeeper. He told them fifteen dollars apiece and they reached for their wallets and Eli told LeRoy it was his treat. LeRoy told him it was too much and Eli said consider it taxi fare. LeRoy said okay and Harmon paid for himself and Eli paid for him and LeRoy. Harmon said he'd get the next few rounds when they came back. Eli asked the man if Marilynn was working and he told she was and they did know she was extra, didn't they. Eli went again for his wallet and asked how much and the gatekeeper said you pay for her back there. He gave them each a ticket and gestured to the door and said straight back. They went out into the quiet and across to the cathouse.

Inside was warm with light and the music was softer. Girls sat on couches or stood leaning against another small bar. Some of them wore see-throughs and others just underwear. Two or three were black and the rest white. Eli said to LeRoy was he getting impressed yet and LeRoy said he was getting close. An older woman who had all her clothes on came over and said to Eli who's this?, and Eli told her his and Harmon's new friend LeRoy. He and Harmon handed her their tickets and told LeRoy to give her his. Eli told LeRoy that Katie made sure everybody got took care of. He said she was better than a nurse and she said to LeRoy welcome to heaven and just look around and see what he liked.

Eli said they thought since it being his first time here, they'd start LeRoy off with Marilynn and was she busy. Katie whispered into Eli's ear and he pulled out his wallet and the fifty dollars he took from it melted into her fingers. She told LeRoy to wait and took both Eli's and Harmon's arms and walked them to the girls and said take your time and went back for LeRoy and took his arm. She told him to leave his draft on the bar and walked him through a curtained doorway and up a carpeted, curving flight of stairs. LeRoy said Eli and Harmon told him there was cabins and Katie said not for Marilynn and that LeRoy's friends must hold a special affection for him. She took him down a broad hall and stopped at a white enameled door and rapped lightly and opened the door and led him in. A young woman in a long black dress, tight on her form and sequined, sat in an overstuffed chair with a book in her lap, her hair tied high on her head with beaded pins, her face so perfect it looked to have been carved from some rare African hardwood. She sat with her back straight, her face uplifted, her legs crossed so that all of their lissome curves showed against her dress. Katie said this is LeRoy and his friends brought him and went out and left them alone.

Marilynn smiled, her face alchemizing into liquid radiance, and when she set aside the book and unfolded herself to rise, the full length of her leg flashed from the slit of her dress, from thigh to ankle, as ghostlike as smoke and as elegant as if it had been cast in glass. She came to him, nearly as tall in her heels as he, and took his face in her thin hands soft as a child's and kissed him lightly on the lips, and when she breathed into his neck, he stopped looking around to see if there was anybody else in the room watching them.

When Marilynn brought LeRoy back down to the sitting room, Harmon and Eli were already there, holding glasses of whiskey and bantering with the girls. Eli was looking deep into a chubby whore's eyes and telling her he had a three-story house on fifty acres over by the county seat and a Cadillac and a Lincoln too and a big-ass yacht he kept on the river just for special occasions and if she wanted a life of luxury, all she had to do was marry him. She asked him did he get those callouses on his hands from driving that Cadillac and he said hell no, them's from counting all my money and how about it? Harmon said look who's here. Eli looked up from the whore's face and said Jesus Christ, LeRoy, you better sit the fuck down before you fall down.

Marilynn kissed LeRoy on the cheek and turned and left. LeRoy walked to a couch, weak-kneed, his eyes glazed and sat and looked around like a man lost among strangers and said Jesus Christ. Eli asked him did she do that thing with her pussy and LeRoy just looked at him. Eli laughed and looked at Harmon and said yeah she did and Harmon told LeRoy now *that's* what's special about Harrisville. He went to the bar and got a whiskey for LeRoy and fresh ones for him and Eli and told LeRoy it looked like he needed it.

LeRoy sat and said holy fuck.

That's about right.

Somebody came in and picked Eli's chubby whore and Eli told her she did know she was blowing her chances and she said oh well, sometimes you eat the bear. She took her customer's arm and as they walked toward the door to the cabins, asked him did his name happen to be Chances. She glanced back at Eli and winked.

Harmon said he didn't feel like going home yet and why didn't they go back to the bar. The gatekeeper nodded when they came in and asked was they satisfied customers. Harmon put his hand on LeRoy's shoulder and said this one sure as shit is. They sat at the same places they'd sat in before. The same two men were sitting at the end, considerably drunker that when they'd left them. The storyteller was explaining to the other how Arabs use their camels to navigate across the Sahara. He said they only go at night and they get where they're going because camels can draw a straight line from just where the moon is, but if you try it on your own, you end up going in circles and you die of thirst. And them Arabs walk behind the camels because the camels got a cleft foot and they can tell by squiggling their toes in the sand where quicksand is.

There was no order to what then happened but these things did.

Eli told the man there wasn't no quicksand in the Sahara and camels weren't no compasses neither.

The gatekeeper slipped his cashbox into a drawer and locked it.

The bartender sidled to the back end of the bar.

Eli told the teller of tales that what he was saying was at least the second dumbest thing he ever heard.

The storyteller hit Eli on the side of his forehead with a beer bottle and Eli fell to the floor, blood gushing from the slit the bottle opened in his head.

The storyteller tumbled from his stool.

The storyteller's friend reached behind him and under his shirt.

LeRoy tackled the friend's bar stool and the man fell one way and the .38 he was going for clattered another way.

LeRoy got hold of the gun and straddled its owner and pushed the barrel into his mouth.

Harmon kneeled down over Eli.

The entire room went silent except for Hank Williams's voice crooning Blue Eyes Cryin' In The Rain from the jukebox and the flow of time returned.

Eli said Jesus, who the fuck played that shit?, and everybody wanted to laugh but no one did. He asked Harmon how bad was it. Harmon said he'd seen Eli get worse than this, but it was pretty bad and it was a good thing he was drunk or he would be in a lot of hurt. Harmon told the bartender to throw him a rag and he pressed it on Eli's wound and it helped some, but blood still came. The storyteller got himself to his knees and stumbled to his feet and made a move toward LeRoy. LeRoy looked him straight in the eye and said you take one more motherfucking step and I will blow this cocksucker's head off and put the rest of the load in your chest before you can count the shots. Everything stopped again. Nobody knew what to do.

Harmon said to LeRoy to give him his car keys and LeRoy reached in his jeans with his free hand and got them and tossed them to Harmon. Harmon motioned with his head to the gatekeeper to come over and help him with Eli. He told Eli to hold the rag tight on his head and they got him up and dragged him to the door and out into the parking lot and over to LeRoy's car. They folded him into the back seat. Harmon slid behind the wheel and started the engine. He told the gatekeeper to go tell LeRoy to get his ass out here and the gatekeeper went back in and LeRoy came out running, still holding the gun, and jumped in the back with Eli. Harmon backed out and took them out onto the road, the car's spinning tires throwing a wake of gravel behind them.

Eli said Jesus Christ, it's starting to hurt. Harmon said no shit, this time the bone was showing and Eli was lucky his skull was too thick for that motherfucker to break it. We gotta go get you stitched up. Eli said shit.

LeRoy said what the fuck was you thinking calling that guy a dumb nigger? Eli said he didn't call him a nigger and LeRoy said it didn't matter what he said, it was what the man heard. Eli said now you are really making my head hurt.

LeRoy asked did they have to worry about them calling the police and Harmon said no, Katie wouldn't let them but the hospital might if they didn't have a good reason for Eli's head. Eli said just tell them I fell down.

Nobody falls that hard.

How about we ran the car into a pole?

LeRoy told Harmon to just drive the car, he'd make up something the hospital would believe.

Eli said Jesus Christ, Skeeter, where'd you learn how to fight like that?

Daddy.

What, he was a mechanic *and* a fighter?

He was a lot of things.

He give you lessons?

Some, but mostly he told me it comes down to two rules.

Them being?

First rule is hit him before he hits you and two is the one who fights fair is the one who gets their ass kicked.

Your daddy teach you how to shoot a pistol too?

LeRoy said fuck, I got no fucking clue how to shoot this thing, and he threw it in a long arc over his head and into the weeds flashing past them like a quarrel in the night.

The Story of My Life
By
LeRoy James

Chapter 4

In case you took a break from reading the story of my life and
forgot what was the last thing that happened, here's where
Chapter 3 left off: With me and Mr. Bones walking down the
road and him carrying the shovel and me being worried about
somebody seeing us. So now I will pick it up from there. Me and
Mr. Bones walked on a little ways and then he said, "We got to
be going a lot faster than this." He stopped and took the shovel
off his shoulder and leaned on it and looked down at the ground,
very serious. I seen that look on him before. It meant he was
thinking real hard about whether something he wondered if he
should do was going to be something he would be sorry for if he
went ahead and did it. Then he looks up at me and says, "LeRoy
I am going to give you a one-time gift tonight." I knew right then
that whatever he was talking about was real important and had
maybe some bad tanglements in it, because he only ever called me
LeRoy when he was being real serious. Usually he just called me
boy.

"LeRoy," he said, "I am going to give you the gift of flying.
It's got to be just for this one night and I don't want you asking
for it again. And you are going to want to ask for it, because
you ain't never the same after you have gone flying, and you will
be wanting to do it over and over. But I ~~can't~~ cannot give it to
you after tonight. I ain't even supposed to give it to you at all,

but tonight is a special situation and I can't see no way through without breaking the rules."

I could see he was asking me to promise him I wouldn't go begging him for the gift some other time, but he wanted me to promise without him having to ask me. Any other time I wouldn't have. I would of just stood there like I didn't know what he wanted from me and make him ask me for it. But that night was different being we was going to save Miss Wells. That made it urgent and I let go my stubborn streak and said, "I promise you that I will do anything to help Miss Wells and if that means keeping my mouth shut about any gift whatsoever you give me tonight, I promise. You won't never hear one word from me about wanting to fly ever again after this." I can tell you I kept that promise, but it was a ~~goddamn~~ very hard promise to keep. Once you been flying, it is something you want to do again for the whole rest of your life, and I expect even after you are dead, it is that powerful a thing.

Mr. Bones said, "All right then." He laid his hands on me, one on my back between my shoulder blades and the other over my face and he leaned me back so that I was looking right up at the stars. I remember seeing a shooting star right then. I have seen lots of shooting stars before then and since then, but never one like that. Most shooting stars is just little specks of white light that burn out so quick you cannot be 100 percent sure you even saw them, but this shooting star was big as Mr. Bones and glowed green and went all the way across the sky and over the horizon still on fire. If I had any doubt up to that second that this was going to be a night of omens and signs, I ~~didn't~~ did not have any after I saw that giant green shooting star. Mr. Bones tilted me back and then straight up again three times and every time he did he said, "Fly," with something after it. First he said, "Fly like a bird." And then, "Fly like a angel." And then the last time he said,

"Fly like a comet." And then he let me go. "It is going to seem a little strange at first, but you will get used to it real quick. All you got to do is think where you want to go, you don't have to think about <u>how</u> to fly, you just do it. Like you don't think about how to walk. You just decide you want to walk someplace and then you walk there." He took back the shovel and the sacks and the hatchet too and said, "We are going to practice for a minute." He pointed up to the top of a big oak tree and said, "That is where we are going to fly to first." And then, like I saw him do a million times, he just rose up off the ground and swooped up to the top of that tree. "Come on up here, boy," he yelled down and I just kind of pointed my shoulders his way and there I was, rising right up into the air, and the way it made me feel was the strangest I had ever before felt in my whole life. Mr. Bones was right. This was just like walking, except walking through air and nothing on me had to move to do it. I didn't have to kick my legs like I was swimming or flap my arms. All I had to do was think it and there I was, standing on the topmost branch of that oak, right alongside where Mr. Bones was standing. He pointed over to the neighbor's barn and said, "You go there next and I will follow you this time." I pointed my shoulders toward the barn and just that fast I was racing through the air and there I was, right up at the peak of the roof. I sat myself down and leaned up against a lightning rod and looked over where I had come from and there comes Mr. Bones, all loaded down with the tools and the sacks. I must have had a pretty wide ~~shit-eating~~ grin on my face because he laughed and said, "You look like a preacher about to pass the plate, you so ~~damn~~ smiley. It is fun, I do admit that. But we got to get to the schoolhouse, so let's get to it." He gave me back the hatchet and the sacks and flew off with the shovel and I flew right behind him. (It seemed to me at the time that we should of been heading to Miss Wells's house where she would be asleep if we was out to save her, but like I said before, it's better just to stick to them who has done this already and not ask a lot of questions.)

Things are a lot different up in the air than they are on the ground, especially at night. For one thing, there is a lot of night birds flying around up there that you do not see from down below. That is because they have plain black feathers so that when you look up, you can't see them because the black of those feathers mixes in with the black sky and it is like they disappeared up there. But when you are flying up above them, they get lit up with the moon and stars and you can see them. Then there is some things that if you thought about them, would make sense they were there, but most of the time you don't think about them. Like ghosts. In every graveyard, ghosts ooze up out of the ground every night. They kind of seep up out of the dirt and at first from up high they look like little patches of fog rolling over the ground. They stop creeping like that when they get to their tombstones and kind of stick themselves up against where their names is carved into the stone and then they slither right up the stone like a snake working its way up a tree and gathering up speed like they are getting ready to jump over a little creek and I guess that really is what they do, except they go right up into the sky and do not land on the other side of anything like they would if they was just trying to get over a creek. What they are crossing over is the wall between the realm of the dead and the realm of the living, so they just keep on going up.

Me and Mr. Bones seen a lot of ghosts that night. They was gray and you could see through them and their bodies (except they ~~wasn't~~ was not really bodies, because their bodies was dead and rotting away, but that is the only way I can think to say it (the only words you can use is the ones you got)) kind of got strung out like old raggedy spider webs hanging down in the weeds and waving back in forth in the wind. I seen blood clot up like that,

all stringy and sticking together. They all came up to the same
height in the air, just a little bit below where me and Mr. Bones
was flying and then they headed off. I asked Mr. Bones who they
was going to haunt and he laughed. "~~Fuck,~~ Boy," he said. "~~You
don't know a lot about a lot~~. Them ghosts are not going to haunt
nobody. Well maybe one or two of them might, the ones that
are holding onto a grudge against somebody that is still alive.
Haunting for a ghost means being cooped up inside a house all
night long and being cooped up is what they are trying to get
away from. Can you imagine what it is like to have to stay in a
casket in the dark all ~~goddamn~~ day and not be able to see anything
but the inside of that box and your ownself laying there and
rotting away? They are just getting out to see stuff, just the same
way you get out of the house first thing you can in the morning.
Would you want to spend the night inside after being in a casket
all day?" I did not say nothing, because he was right.

We went over houses and barns and fields almost ready to
be planted. There was one field we went over where there was
a white boy and a black girl without their clothes on laying on a
blanket. That girl was asking herself for a whole lot more trouble
than she was going to be able to handle if she did not watch it.
But girls can get real stupid if some boy tells her she is pretty.
My sister Abby moved in with a boy because he told her she was
pretty. They live in a shack over the hill from where we used to
live and so far she has had six babies with him and all's she got to
show for it is a lot of work and being able to brag that she used
to be pretty. I could go on about a lot more things I saw, but that
ain't the point of what I have to say about that night. I got to get
to where we was at the schoolhouse and the demons started in on
us.

When we got there, the way the Easter moon was lighting
it up, you could just about see everything all around it: The wood

slat cover over the well and the pump sitting on the cover, though
you would not know it was a pump from up high except the
moon made a shadow of a pump on the cover and the ground.
It was like the moon had drew a picture of a pump down there
and that is what I saw, the picture of the pump, and from that I
could tell where the real pump was. You could see the school bell
out front and you could even see where there was patches of the
school roof that was going to need fixing pretty soon. You could
see the outhouses too, the one for the boys and the one for the
girls and the tall walls that went around so nobody could see in
to where you was doing your business and how they was open
over the top, and I thought then how I would not mind being
able to fly all the time and come up here during recess and watch
the girls go in there and pull up their dresses and pull down their
underpants. I grew out of that kind of nonsense not too long
afterwards, but when you are 10, you are naturally curious about
that kind of thing.

Mr. Bones pulled up right then and reached his arm out
and put it on my chest and we held up. Then he whispered real
soft, so low I could just barely hear him, "LeRoy, we got to be as
quiet as we can be right now." Which was real strange, because
like I already told you more than once, nobody but me can hear
Mr. Bones, and he could have yelled whatever he had to say to me
as loud as he wanted and it wouldn't of made no difference. He
said, "I know what you thinking, LeRoy, but what we up against
ain't like the normal beings you used to being around. Demons
are bad ~~motherfuckers~~ motherfuckers, but they are a lot like me
too. Not too many people can see them and the people who do
pretty much always wished afterwards they did not, and that goes
for the ones that is still alive after they come across a demon and
the ones that ~~ain't~~ is dead. It is worse for the ones the demons kill,
because they will be in torment for the whole of eternity because

the last thing they saw on this earth was the face of the demon and that is pure evil and it will send you straight to hell. Demons can hear me and they can see me too, and it is going to be a touch and go thing tonight whether you and me kill the demons or they kill us. So just stay piped down while I tell you what we are going to be doing."

He took my arm and guided me up a little bit higher, I guess so it would be harder for the demons to see and hear us, but I did not ask to find out for sure. "First off," he said, "I am going to tell you why these demons are after Miss Wells. She is just about one of the only things in this parish that is pure good. She is here to help boys like you and girls like your sisters and she hardly don't get paid for it. She does it out of the kindness of her heart. And if there is one thing that demons cannot stand, it is natural pure goodness. I been feeling the presence of these demons for a couple of months now and I knew they was coming for somebody, but I couldn't figure out who it was. At first I thought it must of been the preacher, but good as he makes out to be, he ain't is not altogether pure because he sometimes gets people to trust him and then takes advantage of them. Then I thought maybe it was the sheriff because he is so clean and polite, but even though he ain't a mean man and don't does not go looking to make people suffer on purpose, in his deepest heart he is still pretty greedy and somebody that greedy cannot be pure at the same time. So a couple days ago, I went out while you was asleep and had me a look around and that is when I saw one of the demons for real. I followed him every place he went. After a while he came here and there was three of them up on the roof. Where they was sitting on their haunches is where those worn out places is, they put a rot on everything they touch. They was saying that just as soon as the rest of the gang got up here from hell they was going to fuck up that schoolteacher <u>real</u> bad. That's when I knew for sure. They were going to wait until Good Friday, when school is out and they know Miss Wells will take that day off to come and clean things up a little in the schoolhouse. That and they thought it would be a good joke to do it on the day Jesus died. They celebrate Good Friday just like us, except they do it because they are always hoping Jesus will stay dead this time. They figure to rip Miss Wells up like she was a dead thing on the road and you kids will find her with hers guts all hanging out when you come back to school after Easter and that will ~~fuck~~ mess you up a lot, especially the littlest ones, for a long, long time. Tonight is the night they are all here, so what we are going to do is trap them and put them where they can't hurt nobody at all."

OK. So I can see that I am taking a long time working up to the real adventure and besides I am getting tired again. So I am going to end this chapter and start up again when I have thought some more about what happened and what is the best way for me to remember it so I do not bore you. That happens sometimes. There was books I started out liking a lot but got tired of when I was part way through them because they was just going on and on and I never did read the whole story. So I am going to do you a favor and make sure my book will not be like that. But I will tell you that what happens next is not the kind of story you would ever want to read to a little kid for a bedtime story. They would have bad dreams if you did.

TO BE CONTINUED

Tabernacle Parish, 1960

Most times when Whiskey went out, he asked Agnes did she want to go with him. She liked that he was proud to be seen with her and she liked that there was always the hint of danger to it, that anytime they went out, trouble could flare up sudden as a struck match. And she liked that he never let anything happen to her and was a little bit ashamed that sometimes she wished there would be a fight just so she could feel what it was like to have him protect her. She liked it too when he won and they would go home and he would lie on her lightly, holding his weight back with his arms under her on the bed, and she could feel with her hands the strength in his back and the rasp of his face on hers. And the couple times he lost, she liked taking care of him.

Sometimes she told him no, just go, that he needed a night out and he would come home those nights a little drunker than when they went out together, but not so it would disgust her and he was on those nights as gentle with her as if she were a newly born child and he was like a new father afraid the slightest touch might break her infant bones. He didn't smell like other men when he was drunk, sour and rotting. He smelled like leaves and roots thick in the earth and like freshly split stove wood.

On occasion he would slip from their bed in the middle of the night and gather up his clothes in the dark and go dress in the kitchen. Sometimes she heard him and sometimes she didn't, but she never told him, not when he was getting up and not when he came home. Those nights, he never came back drunk and the next day or maybe the day after, there would be some little shining thing left for her on the bedside table or in the bathroom or by the kitchen sink. A ring or a brooch or a pair of earrings. Once she found a delicate chain bracelet arranged in the shape of a heart on the dresser.

She told him he shouldn't spend all that money on her and he always said whatever it was didn't cost anything. That somebody couldn't pay their whole bill and gave him the trinket to settle it. Or he won it in a card game. Or found it under the seat of a car somebody sold him. Then he would ask her to put it on and when she did, he always said that she was the best thing that ever happened to that sparkler. She made it look pretty.

Brigard County, June, 1993

Edna and Harmon fell into a kind of shadow domesticity. He rose early and set to work and a little later she got up and made them coffee and they had it together out on the back porch. Every morning she offered him breakfast and every morning he said no but he appreciated the offer. At midday, he climbed up to his apartment and if the day was heating up, closed the windows and turned on the wall air conditioner. On temperate days, he left the windows open and Edna could hear the television and the kitchen sounds of his preparing his lunch. Then it would be quiet for a while. Napping, she thought, though for all she knew he read from a Bible and prayed. In the afternoons, Harmon went back to his work, at the painting project or the grounds if some part of them needed to be tended to or some repair demanding his attention. In the evening he went back up and had his supper and she hers in the house.

After a while, he would come down and they would sit on the back porch and watch the sun setting over the river. Edna would get them a drink. Sometimes two or three. She found pleasure in the ceremony, in the hazy shift an evening drink lent the sunset, how it smoothed the jagged edges of awkward conversations. In the threads of wellbeing it wove into her arms and legs.

One night as they watched the boats on the river, she told him how her husband had meant to have a patio built on the bank, a place to gather by the water. A place for guests. She asked him if he knew where they could find someone to build it. He said he could do it cheaper, that it wasn't hard at all. She told him that her husband had thought about putting down a wooden deck. Harmon said that was a bad idea, the seasons would heave against the wood and warp it, so that she'd end up replacing much of it every spring and that leaves would gather beneath it and they would be hard to get out and their rotting would stink it up. She asked him what he would do. He said put down a barrier edge of wooden beams and fill in the space with crushed limestone. Easy to build he said. Easy to take care of too. She asked him when he could start and he told her he'd check in the garage in the morning to see what tools he needed and they could go in and get them and order the materials at the same time. That is, if she didn't mind holding off on the painting for a couple more days.

Brigard County, June, 1993

The six-by-sixes and the lumber for the furniture arrived on a flatbed. The driver and his helper laid stud scraps on the ground next to the driveway and pulled the lumber off the truck and set it across the scraps. Harmon asked them did they bring the rebar and the driver said it was a good thing he remembered and climbed up to the bed and slid the bundle of rust-tinged, fluted rods to the tailgate and climbed down. He and the helper struggled with the weight. Harmon said don't set it on the grass, put it on the drive. The driver said that is a shitload of rebar and was Harmon sure he needed that much.

Going to drive it in down by the bank he said. Has to go pretty deep.

As long as I aint paying for it the driver said. How come you didn't just have us unload it down there? Them six-by's is heavy.

Electric's up here and I don't want to tear up the grass.

You better be getting paid by the hour.

When they were all unloaded, Harmon said to give him the bill and he went inside the house and a few minutes later returned with a check and a twenty each for the driver and the helper. They looked questioningly at each other, then at Harmon. Harmon asked them if they didn't want it and they said fuck no, they was just surprised was all. The driver wrote *Paid* on the bill and the check number and handed it to Harmon. He asked when he wanted the stone and Harmon said day after tomorrow and they climbed in the truck and drove off.

Harmon swallowed down more Advil and rubbed his side and began. He carried string and wood stakes and a hammer down to the water and measured out where he wanted the beams to lie and staked out the lines with the string to mark the edges so the trenches would align true. He sprayed plant killer within all the space he'd circumscribed, soaking it twice, so that when he spread the stone, there would be no chance for any green resurrection among the jagged grey pebbles. With spade and mattock he trenched a narrow, shallow ditch along the strings in which to lay the timbers. He piled the soil he'd taken up in a long hummock beside the trench. She came down and said she made sandwiches and don't say no. They went up to the house and had lunch together. In the afternoon, he hacksawed a length of rebar and bent the end into a J-hook, clamping it in the bench vise and leveraging the bend with a length of galvanized pipe. He measured the width of the J to know how far to space the holes in the timbers so they would seat and then began on the timbers themselves, lifting them one by one onto sawhorses, the weight of them drawing the ache up from his side and into his neck and shoulders so that his progress was measured in lengths of pain, a tick mark for each timber. He drilled eight holes in each, four all the way through and four blind in which to latch the J-hooks. As the bits dulled, he threw them in the trash can and started again with new ones though there was a grinding wheel in the garage where he could have sharpened them, trivial waste no longer a thing worth worrying about. He worked into the evening and she came and said wasn't that enough for one day and he went up into his loft and showered and ate and came back and they sat on the porch and talked about what he had done and why. She had a bottle of Jack Daniels and they drank more of it than they should have, but less than he wanted. The evening was mild enough to open the windows and she put psychedelic music on inside that both of them remembered from when they were young and the memories the music invoked drifted out through the windows on the sound of it.

On the second day he cut the rebar into three-foot lengths and fashioned the hooks and wire-brushed the rust from the loops and spray-painted the ends and laid them across the horses to dry. He barrowed the timbers down to the river one at a time and set them in the trench and toed the ends together with twenty-penny galvanized nails, on the sides and the tops, and tamped in the dirt left over from the trenches tight against them. The grass he'd sprayed was already yellowing. It would all be dead by tomorrow. She came down late in the morning and said she was going in to buy groceries and did he want to come. She thought maybe they could stop and have lunch. He started to say no and she said Dutch treat and he said okay and they both saved face, even though whatever money he would lay down had all come from her anyway. They drove to the River View Diner and sat by the windows, Marvin watching them with a suspicious curiosity from behind the counter. She asked why they called it the River View when you could barely see the river and he told her you used to be able to before everything got built up. They ate and talked about the morning's progress. Harmon told her it was going quicker than he'd thought it would. They left and got groceries and went back to the house.

Harmon loaded the hooks into the wheelbarrow and rolled them down to the set timbers and drove them through the holes and into the ground with a hand sledge, each thud a blow both to the metal and the thing lurking in his side. From time to time he stood and pulled his lips tight and looked out over the water and let the thing thrash for a while until it had spent itself and he could return to his work, he and his pain arriving at an uneasy accommodation. Some of the rebar caught on hidden stones and he left them jutting up from the timbers until he had driven down the rest and finished off the stubborn ones with a ten-pound sledge, against which no river stone could stand for long. The stone would resist and the shock of the hammer slamming to a stop carried through his hands, stinging all the way to his shoulders, and he would hit the rebar again and again until the stone surrendered and he could feel it splitting apart down under the dirt like a woman giving way. When all the hooks were sunk flush into the timbers, he brushed fresh paint over where he had hammered through to the metal and stopped for the day. She had the music on again and a warm supper and another bottle of Jack Daniels. They took it out on the porch and talked about those young days again and she put her hand on his arm to get his attention and said look and pointed with her other hand toward the river where a hawk drafted upward, silhouetted against the sunset. She touched his arm a few times more to punctuate some embarrassment she was telling him from her past, the reckless escapades of her adolescence.

In the morning the stone came and again the driver said wouldn't it be easier to just dump it down where it was going to go and Harmon told him he did enough work on the grounds and didn't feel like reseeding any more of it and just dump it on the drive but leave enough room to get the car out and the driver said you're the customer. He dumped the stone and Harmon took the bill in and came out with a check and two twenties and gave them to the driver. The driver asked did she know it was just him and no helper this time. Harmon told him she knew.

Jesus, Harmon, you got yourself a pretty sweet deal here, don't you?

Maybe.

There just aint no justice the driver said.

Using a transfer shovel, Harmon filled the wheelbarrow and set a bow saw on the stone and wheeled the load down to the river.

He stood and leaned over to stretch out his side and put his hand there again and held it tight in and it helped some, but not enough. He cut off some of the swamp maple saplings with the bow saw, as low to the ground as he could get, and heaved them into the water where they floated out into the current in slow sweeping pinwheels, the fingers of their leaves vainly clutching for some line of rescue. He left a few for the way they would look when everything was done, trying to see through a woman's eyes some vernal arrangement which would be pleasant for her to look at. He dumped the stone in the middle of the work space and wheeled the barrow back up and loaded it again. He took a garden rake this time and spread the stone and left the rake by the water and fell into this day's routine of shovel and wheel and rake, a contemplative labor devoid of all thought. She had a lunch for them again and afterwards he took Advil and asked was there any beer left. The beer helped more than the Advil. In midafternoon she came down with more beer and said now that it was coming together, she saw what he meant. Stone was better than a wooden deck and she liked that he had cut back the trees and where did he put them. He gestured to the water. She asked him how late he was going to work. He said he wanted to get all the stone down today even if he didn't get it all spread out and maybe until about seven. He went back to work and on his way for another load saw her drive out and turn toward town.

By evening he had moved all the stone and was sweeping the drive when she came out and told him dinner was on and it was time to stop. He said he should shower first and she told him he was fine the way he was. He put up the broom and followed her in where she had spread a white cloth on the dining room table and lit candles and set places for the two of them facing across the narrow side of the table and asked him to pour the wine and if he would carve the roast. He started to tell her she didn't have to go to all this trouble but told her instead she was full of surprises wasn't she. She told him he couldn't even begin to guess. They finished their meal and she said why didn't they take the last of the wine out on the porch and enjoy the evening. She asked him what was next and he told her he was almost done with the stone and by this time tomorrow he should have a pretty good start on the table and chairs so maybe by the day after, it'd be all done. She said that meant they could start sitting down there instead of on the porch to watch the sunset and he allowed as how that would be a pleasant way of ending the day.

In the morning he laid out on the workbench the plans for the six-sided table and the four Adirondacks and studied them so they would be in his mind while he finished spreading the stone and how they might be changed for the better and then went down with his rake. He carried down a spade as well to smooth out the small knolls of soil he had not noticed were there until he laid the layers of stone. He worked back and forth as if he were brushing the stone onto a canvas until it was as level as it was going to be, though there remained here and there imperfections.

For the rest of that day and all of the next and with the same deliberation, he built the chairs and the table, assembling the chairs in the driveway and wheeling them down to where they went. He built the table twice, using galvanized lag screws so that he could take it apart and carry it down to the river in pieces he could manage and put them back together on the stone. He kept a sketch of where he had put each board and numbered them underneath in some hidden place and wrote those numbers on the sketch. He used a power drill with a socket bit to screw in the lags the first time, but down by the river he had to ratchet them. There was another supper with candles at the end of the day and wine again on the porch. She asked how the furniture would stand up to the weather and shouldn't he paint it. He told her it was all pressure treated and it was good for thirty years just like it was but you can paint it if you want, but you should wait a year.

On the last day, he worked into the twilight, determined to finish because that's what he told her. The last thing he did was cut a length of PVC and secure it through a hole in the table to hold an umbrella for when she would want shade. He put what few hand tools he'd taken down into a toolbox and set it beside one of the chairs and sat himself in the chair and felt how it would be to relax by the water. Fireflies flickered among the leaves of the remaining trees. He was pretty sure she would like it, but not a hundred percent. He'd have to see what she said. In the last of the light, her music slipped down across the grass and he thought of the drink she would have for him and took up the toolbox and went up to the house. Even though the lights were low, he could see her through the open window. She had on the same black dress she wore the day he awoke in her boathouse. She held her arms above her head, a cocktail glass in her hand, sinuously swaying, her hair brushing back and forth across her face, her eyes closed. He stood and watched and the song ended and a new song came on, the muted wail of the guitar giving way to a rock drummer's imitation of primeval rhythms and a blues harp. She rolled her shoulders and worked her thighs and lifted her head and opened her eyes and saw him. She looked at him straight on and worked herself harder and, still writhing, set her glass down and reached behind her and undid her dress and as the song's dark lyrics spat out the window, let the dress fall from her, under which she wore nothing at all. She lifted her chin. Harmon set the toolbox on the ground and went in.

Tabernacle Parish, October, 1962

You got enough money?

Whiskey shuffled his feet and put his hands in his pockets and looked down at the ground and said it depend on what it cost, sir.

Five dollars for a jug and two for a pint.

I heard it was one dollar for a pint, and that's just all what I brung.

The man said for him to show him. Whiskey reached into his bib pocket and brought out a crumpled dollar bill and held it out.

The man asked him what his name was and Whiskey said Daniel Watson, sir. The man took the money and nodded to a boy who was not quite a man sitting on a stump and cradling a shotgun. When Whiskey went to follow the man, the boy gestured with the gun and told him he could wait right there. Whiskey watched the way the man went and listened until he heard leaves rustle in the woods not so far up and studied where the sound came from, its direction and its distance. He turned to the boy and remarked how hot it was for October.

Whiskey took off his coveralls and hung them on a peg and went to the workbench and scooped lanolin from the can and cleaned the grease from his hands and wiped them with a rag and went in the house. Agnes laughed when she saw him and he asked her what was so funny. She told him he had grease on his nose. He went in the front room and looked in the mirror and came back and told her he put it there on purpose on account of he was thinking of running off to the circus and this was his clown costume and did she think he would have a better chance getting the job if he told them he was a happy clown or a sad one. She told him she thought he should wash his face.

He went in the bathroom and washed the lanolin smell from his hands with the bar of Lava. He washed his face and dried off with his work towel and put the Lava back down beside her bar of Camay. He went back to the kitchen and told Agnes he hoped she was satisfied now that she had ruined his chance for being famous. She said he was already plenty famous and how come he stopped so early. He told her that the next part of the job was going to take a full day and he didn't want to stop in the middle and break the rhythm of it. He'd finish it tomorrow. He told her he was thinking about going out for coon tonight and she told him it would do him good. He'd been working hard and deserved it. He got a beer from the refrigerator and stood leaning against the table. Agnes said what else?

You mean besides you ruining my chance with the circus without even hearing me out on what a great idea it is?

Yes.

I was thinking maybe I'd take Skeeter with me.

Agnes's face clouded over.

Whiskey said it was a hard thing going from a boy to a man and an even harder thing for a mother to watch. He waited.

He's got school tomorrow.

Whiskey said he knew it and he wasn't going to take the boy if he didn't get his lessons done and Agnes said what about his chores and Whiskey said them too.

Agnes said didn't Whiskey know she wouldn't be able to sleep until they got back, and she'd be afraid he would fall in the dark and that he'd catch a cold, and she was worried sick just when he took LeRoy out for rabbits and that was in the daylight.

Whiskey told her there was a full moon tonight and it was warm for fall and did she know anybody who would take better care of the boy than him. And that was the end of it.

Whiskey took his beer out to the porch and sat in his rocker and waited for LeRoy. When the boy came, Whiskey told him he was taking Jigger out tonight, so don't feed him anything and did LeRoy know why and LeRoy said fat dogs don't hunt and Whiskey said I guess I told you that one before. Whiskey asked him what about fat boys, do they hunt? LeRoy said probably not and Whiskey said you better go easy on your supper then. LeRoy thought for a second and then understood and looked toward the kitchen and Whiskey said I already asked her. Go change your clothes and get started on your lessons.

It was nearly dark when Whiskey backed the truck into a brush-lined lane, far enough in so nobody could see it from the road, and turned it off and opened the door and stepped down. LeRoy went to take the shotgun from the rack but Whiskey told him leave it there, just get the flashlight out of the glove box. He reached behind the seat for a length of rope and tied it to the ring in Jigger's collar. He told LeRoy there were two feed sacks in the bed and to get them and to wait here for a minute. Whiskey led Jigger a little farther back up the lane and tied him to a sapling and told him to lay down and then came back to the truck. Moonlight had begun sifting silk-like through the trees at the top of the hills across the valley. Whiskey lit a cigarette and leaned against the truck. The sounds of the day faded away and quiet descended and after a while the sounds of the night began to come up from the woods. Something rustled in the leaves and Jigger barked. LeRoy shifted around, restless and anxious to get started.

Whiskey dropped his cigarette beside the truck and ground it out with the toe of his boot and put his hand on the boy's shoulder and asked him did he think he could keep one more secret and not tell his mama about it and LeRoy said he could. Whiskey said everything they were going to do tonight had to be a secret and LeRoy asked again what it was. Whiskey told him he'd see soon enough and let's go and started down the road on foot. LeRoy went along beside him. Their shadows lay down across the leaves into the woods and the trees put down their own shadows across the road as if they had shorn themselves of their branches and laid them down in a carpet for Whiskey and LeRoy to walk on. An owl hooted somewhere above them. LeRoy switched on the flashlight and Whiskey told him to turn it off, they didn't need it yet.

They walked a few hundred yards down the road and Whiskey pointed to a path running off into the woods and they turned and followed it. A soft ruffling sound came from a little ways up the path and Whiskey stopped and stretched his arm out so LeRoy would know to stop too. Whiskey turned to the side and when he turned back around, he was holding something wrapped up in wax paper in his hand. Whiskey made no sound in retrieving it, as if he'd conjured it out of thin air. Whiskey said real low, not quite whispering, for LeRoy to just stay behind him and he took a few more steps and LeRoy heard the ruffling again and looked toward where Whiskey was going. In the soft light he saw a yellow dog, mostly hound, but bigger than a hound, the legacy of the feral mongrel lurking within it, angry and mean. The dog showed its teeth.

Whiskey unwrapped the wax paper and showed the dog the leftovers it held. He made little kissing sounds at the dog and moaned out soft and real slow. Yo boy. He made more kisses. The dog lifted its ears and gave out a little bit of a bark and Whiskey said shh and the dog went quiet but shifted its weight back and

forth on its forelegs like a fighter. Whiskey cooed like a dove and
LeRoy felt himself unsettled at the sound, soft and feminine, not
a sound he would ever expect from Whiskey. The dog took a little
sideways jump and whimpered and raised up its head set to howl.
Whiskey threw a piece of the leftovers between the dog's feet and
the dog lowered its head and sniffed at them and then looked at
Whiskey and then at LeRoy and bolted down the leftovers in one
bite. Whiskey murmured atta boy, but a little louder than when
he'd cooed. He took another step and tossed some more of the
leftovers to the dog and the dog ate them and then looked up at
Whiskey, the dog's face lined with a beggar's disregard for himself
or anything around him other than the alms giver. Whiskey walked
to the dog and squatted down and set another bit of leftovers on
the ground and when the dog was eating them, put his hand on the
dog's massive neck and scratched under his ears and murmured
hey, boy, you remember me from last night, don't you? We's best
buddies aint we? He motioned to LeRoy to come over to the dog
and told him to pet him too. Whiskey said for him to show the
dog the back of his hand. The dog licked it and Whiskey said okay.
Whiskey placed his palms on his knees and pushed himself up. He
gave the dog one last pat on its hindquarters and started back up
the path, motioning to LeRoy to come along. They came upon a
crumbling, wood-shingled cabin, its porch roof propped up with
dead tree branches, its windows all broken. Gangling saplings grew
up spider-like along its sides.

 Whiskey told LeRoy to stay close and they went up the path
and into a thicket of evergreens within which a circle had been
cleared and where stood a pole barn, newer and smaller than
Whiskey's. Whiskey guided LeRoy around the side of the barn and
motioned for him to hand over the feed sacks and the flashlight.
He pointed to a space where the barn's siding was a little off the
ground and told the boy he wanted him to crawl through it and tell
him what he saw inside.

LeRoy lay in the moss next to the barn and stuck his feet under the siding and slid back and forth like a snake until he was in up to his neck. He turned his face sideways and dug with his heels and pulled himself through. Whiskey held the flashlight in the opening and turned it on and LeRoy took it and sat up. The smell of the hard dirt floor rose up in the dark, not much different than the moss smell outside. Whiskey asked him what he saw in there.

LeRoy stood up and swept the flashlight across the walls. The barn was almost empty except for some tools leaning against one wall and a set of wide shelves stacked up in the middle of the floor. LeRoy told Whiskey what he saw and Whiskey asked him was there anything on the shelves. LeRoy said they were filled up with glass milk jugs.

They got anything in them?

LeRoy shone the light on the top shelf and felt the jugs. They were empty, and then he went down one shelf at a time until down near the bottom he found jugs filled with what looked like water. He told Whiskey and Whiskey told him to push one of them under the wall. It wouldn't fit and Whiskey told him to see if there was a shovel. LeRoy went over to the tools and found a shovel and came back to the wall and pushed it through. Whiskey dug the hole out a little deeper. He said to try again and LeRoy started the jug through and felt Whisky pull it the rest of the way. Whiskey said to just wait a minute and LeRoy heard a sloshing sound and Whiskey saying that's it.

Whiskey told him to bring over any more jugs had something in them. LeRoy brought them over one at a time, keeping count. When they got up to eight, Whiskey said that's about as much as we can handle in one night and for him to come over and get the shovel and to put it back and then come on out. When Whiskey helped pull him through, the boy's pant leg caught on a splinter and opened a tear in the cloth and scratched his calf. LeRoy grimaced but remained silent.

Whiskey took up one of the feed sacks and put two of the jugs in it and walked out a little ways from the barn and gathered up an armful of moss and came back and tucked it around the jugs and told LeRoy that was to keep the glass of one jug from breaking the glass of the other and asked LeRoy did he think he could manage carrying it. LeRoy said he thought he could. Whiskey put the other six jugs in his sack, padding them in the same way. He threw it over his shoulder as if it held only dried leaves. He helped LeRoy get his sack up on his back and told him to hold onto it with both hands. Just the two jugs was a heavy load for the boy, but he didn't say anything, only wondered if he would ever be as strong as Whiskey as he followed him past the yellow dog which lay quiet as they went by and back to the road and to the truck.

Jigger was howling and Whiskey said it sounded like he smelled something he wanted to chase. He put the jugs in the truck bed and told LeRoy to get the shotgun and some shells from behind the seat and he took LeRoy with him to where the dog was lunging against the rope. He untied him and said go get him and the dog bounded off. LeRoy started to run after him and Whiskey told him to just slow down and follow Jigger's calling. Whiskey splayed the flashlight's beam back and forth before them as they went. The eyes of small animals flashed briefly as they ran from the light and looked back terrified to see if they were about to die. Jigger appeared in the light, up on his back legs, scratching at the trunk of an ancient oak whose brown leaves hung down like an old man's wrinkled flesh.

Whiskey shone the flashlight up into the branches and said son-of-a-bitch, there's two of them. He stood LeRoy in front of him and squatted and set the flashlight at the level of LeRoy's eyes and asked him did he see it. LeRoy said he didn't and then the coon turned and the light caught its eyes and he did. Whiskey told him to load the shotgun and be careful like he showed him and remember to pull the stock tight into the side of his chest and not on his shoulder bone and squeeze off slow and LeRoy did all that and shot. The coon skidded over the branch it was standing on and tried to hold on with just its forepaws but they slipped from the branch as well, first the one and then the other, slow, like what was happening wasn't happening now but in some other time and the coon fell. Whiskey went over. The coon's spine was laid open and though crippled, was still alive, mewling and frantically trying to crawl off in crazed desperation and Whiskey put his foot on its head and with his pocket knife slit its throat and it died. Whiskey helped LeRoy locate the second coon and when he shot this time, the coon fell directly off the branch and was dead when it hit the ground. They field dressed what they'd killed and Whiskey sorted through the viscera and found the hearts and livers and gave them to Jigger and they went back to the truck and started toward home.

Whiskey was quiet for a little while and then he asked LeRoy did he remember that time Miss Wells gave him that book about the Arabian nights and LeRoy read him the story about the forty thieves. LeRoy said he did. Whiskey said tonight is like that and LeRoy asked him if he meant the part about stealing from thieves wasn't stealing. Whiskey said it was something like that. LeRoy asked if the man whose moonshine it was, was a thief and Whiskey said he was pretty close to it. They drove on.

Whiskey asked LeRoy what Miss Wells was having him read now and LeRoy said he was in between books, he just finished up *Huckleberry Finn*. Whiskey said he heard about that one, wasn't it about some boy went down the Mississippi on a raft? LeRoy said him and a runaway slave Jim. Whiskey wanted to know if Miss Wells asked him what the real story was and LeRoy said she did.

What'd you tell her?

I told her they should have called the book *Jim* because the real story was about him and the real story was that you are the only one can make yourself a nigger.

What'd she say?

She told me she was proud of me.

LeRoy looked ahead at the road and told Whiskey she kissed him on the forehead too and Whiskey asked him did anybody see her do that and did they make any trouble for him. LeRoy said not for long they didn't and Whiskey said he bet they didn't.

The moon was high when they pulled in the driveway. Whiskey told LeRoy to go in the house so his mama could go to sleep and tell her they got the two coons and Whiskey was going to skin them before he came in. He told him she would want to know about the scratch on his leg and to tell her he got caught up in some brambles in the dark. LeRoy asked him where he was going to put the moonshine and Whiskey told him he was going to bury it. The boy went in the house and Whiskey took the stolen moonshine and a shovel and dug out a shallow trench in the soft soil in which cucumbers had grown and buried the jugs, camouflaging their grave with the sere, withered remains of the summer's abundance. He took the coons into the barn and while he skinned them, thought of what LeRoy said about *Huckleberry Finn* and recalled when he himself left home.

They were sitting outside on the porch after Sunday dinner and Uncle George was going on again about how they got their name on account of their family was owned by kin of Jefferson Davis and that meant they carried with them the mark of Ham two times over. He told Whiskey again you got to mind your place and don't never forget you a brack man and Whiskey had heard it one more time than he could stand and he got up out of his chair and said how the fuck could he forget with Uncle George telling him all the fucking time and being a brack man is just another name for a nigger and that's all you are ever going to be, you dumb fuck, because you aint got the balls to be anything else. Uncle George came rearing up like he was going to slap Whiskey and Whiskey told him to go ahead and try and stood to his full height and Uncle George sat down looking like he was going to cry. Fuck you brack man Whiskey said and turned and walked off with just what he had on, walked off that porch and out of that yard and out of that town and out of Concordia Parish and never went back. He was sixteen.

The Story of My Life
By
LeRoy James

Chapter 5

This chapter is not about my life, because I am going to take a
break from telling you my adventures and tell you something I
just thought about last night about how I could be doing it better.
I do not think this will take long, but if it does, I will tell you up
front that I am sorry about that. But here is what I want to tell
you:

Miss Wells was a hard teacher. I already told you that you
could not get away with nothing with her. When most people
hear that about a teacher, they think that means that teacher was
real strict about how you behaved, like you were not allowed to
talk without raising your hand up first and not pulling girls' hair
and things like that. That was true about Miss Wells, but it was
not something anybody held against her like I have heard some
people say about teachers they had. Miss Wells was so nice about
it, you just wanted to behave right, because you did not want
her to be disappointed in you. That was the worst thing you
could hear from her. She told that to me once in a while, if I did
something that was out of line. I remember when she said, "I
am disappointed in you, LeRoy," how bad it made me feel. Just
writing that down right now made me feel real bad and it has been
a long time since I even saw her.

But your behavior, that was not what she was most strict
about. What she was most strict about was how you did your
lessons. You had to line up your arithmetic problems in perfect

lines and if you did not do that, she would lower your grade even if you had all the answers right. And you had to have the right heading on all your papers. Most of all she had real strict rules for your essays. She gave us a different essay every week. Sometimes they were about geography and you had to write about why you would want to go to whatever country we was learning about. Sometimes they was about history and you had to write about what you thought about a king and if you thought he was a good king. Almost nobody liked writing essays but I kind of did. My favorite ones were when she made us write about the stories we read. One time she made us write a essay about what person in a story we would like to be. I wrote that I would like to be Jim in <u>Huckleberry Finn</u>. She did not allow you to just tell who you wanted to be. You had to tell her why. I told her I would be Jim because of how he made friends easy and said that he was rich because he owned himself. I got a A on that essay.

It was not easy to get a A on one of Miss Wells's essays. That was because of all the rules she had. If you broke any of them rules, she would take points off. Like with spelling. In the first couple of grades, she would take 1 point off every time you spelled a word wrong and then by third grade, it was 5 points off for every one. And in 7th grade, you could not spell one single word wrong. She said that was what we had dictionaries for. She gave everybody a dictionary. I think she bought them herself with her own money. They was paperbacks and cheaper than a real dictionary, but that was still something pretty nice of her to do.

Also you were not allowed to use no contractions. She said that people who used contractions was being sloppy. (I am finally getting to what I wanted to tell you, so just be patient.) We had to write our essays in composition books and we had to write on every other line, so that she could make her corrections on the in-between lines. If you used a contraction, she would write it out in the correction line. Like if you said, "Jim couldn't go on shore by himself, because he might get caught and sold down the river," she would scratch out couldn't like this: ~~couldn't.~~ She did it with a red pen and then would write "could not" in the space over top of it. So here is the thing. When I been writing my adventures, even though it has been a long time since I been in school and out of practice, I have been trying to follow Miss Wells's rules, because I respected her very much. And that includes not writing no contractions. But when I went back just before I decided to tell you about this and read the adventures I already put down to see how they sounded, I did not like the way they sounded. They sounded like I was trying to be a big shot and that is not what I was trying to do. What I was trying to do was write adventures that people would want to read and tell other people about and then I could be a millionaire because I sold so many books. But the adventures do not sound like that. I am embarrassed to say that they make me sound stuck up. I think that is because when people talk, they do not follow rules and if you make them do that in an adventure, they sound stuck up too. Which is not what you want an adventure to be like. It is supposed to be about how some normal person has to step up and do something brave even if ~~they are~~ they're scared of it.

It is probably not just contractions either that make me sound stuck up. It is probably some other things too. I am telling you this because starting with the next adventure, I am going to try and not be so careful and I ~~did not~~ didn't want you to think that I had all of a sudden got real ignorant. I will be doing it on purpose. So ~~that is~~ that's that and you will know I am doing things wrong on purpose. The next adventure will be something you never in a million years could ever expect. So goodbye until then.

Brigard County, September, 1975

Eli cut off the outboard and tilted it up out of the water and drifted. He took up his rod and baited it and cast toward shore and leaned against the gunnel. He pulled his hat over his eyes and pretended to fish. A red tail called and plummeted from the cliffs and streaked out over the river, shoveling the air. The bird flared its wings wide as it came to the hardscrabble bank and braked, the white of its nether feathers majestic, and without touching the ground, took up in its talons a gopher and rose up again through the trees gossamer with the morning, the gopher flailing and squealing, the red tail sedate. Eli watched and went back to pretending to fish.

He drifted through the morning until a bend drew him up toward the bank and his craft's hull scraped against a log and awakened him. He reeled in the line. It had broken sometime in the morning. He tied on a new leader and hook and set the hook in the rod's cork handle and laid it in the bottom and went to start the outboard. Hey there, he heard and looked to the bank where a man stood. Hey he said back. The man said they was broke down on the road and where was there a gas station. Eli looked at the farther bank to see where he was and pointed upriver and said five miles that way. He said there was one closer downriver but they didn't have a mechanic and asked what was wrong. If it was just a part, they might have it.

The man said they was overheated and probably the thermostat. Eli told him they would have that. He said give him a half hour and he'd give him a ride. The man said they didn't want to put him to any trouble, he could walk it. Eli told him he was just getting ready to put in for the day and it was pretty much on his way. The man said he sure was grateful. Eli started the outboard and the man went back up to the road and in a little while Eli pulled up with his truck, trailering the boat. He worked hard not to laugh.

The man sat in an old sun-faded lawn chair in the shade of an awning billowing out from a homemade travel trailer, a bug-shaped contraption huddling on a rusting angle-iron utility trailer, its house-sized storm door opened and held to the side with an eyehook. Askance windows in two-by-four frames. Aluminum siding in motley colors and widths, cobbled together and spliced and patched with roof flashing and sheet metal screws. A stout woman and a girl and a boy, both nearly grown, sat on a blanket at the man's feet.

The man saw Eli looking and said me and the boy built it ourselves, every bit of her except the trailer. Show him, Ashley, he said. The boy looked up annoyed.

He already seen it.

Jesus Christ boy. Show him the inside. He aint seen that.

Ashley got up and stood sullenly by the door and pointed and said this is the inside and went back to the blanket and sat down.

The man said eighteen years old and still dumber than a pine cone. He's a fighter though. Emma there made me name him Ashley. Thought with a name like that he would turn out a gentleman. I held out for John or Bill, a real name, not no pansy-assed Ashley, but she wouldn't have none of it and she outlasted me. Wore me right down. I tried telling her. But no. Shit, with a name like that, you gonna grow up being good at one of two things. Fighting or getting buggered and Ashley here aint no faggot. He got in trouble so much, they finally threw him out of school altogether. Just as well they did. He aint one for books. Aint that right, Emma?

Emma looked up from where she sat with her legs folded beneath her, her face etched about the eyes in the deep veins of worry long endured. That's right Jesse she said. She looked out over the river and resumed worrying.

Emma thinks we shouldn't of pulled Sarah Anne out of school last spring. I said what good's it gonna do her? Pulled her right out the day she turned sixteen and it was legal. Besides that, how she gonna work out being in school when we got to be someplace?

Eli asked him where they was going and Jesse said they hadn't altogether figured that out yet. Maybe somewhere around here if the trapping and hunting's any good. Eli told him he guessed it was as good as any place else, but pretty hard to make a living at it.

Don't need to make a whole living with it. Just a little bit and a little bit someplace else. Maybe fish some too. Do some things on the side if you know what I mean. It don't take all that many and you got yourself enough to get by on. He pointed to the ancient pink Fleetwood station wagon to which the trailer was hitched, the wagon packed and stuffed full with plastic trash bags and bundles pressing up against the glass like the faces of madmen straining against their asylum's windows. Got us that he said, pride in his voice. Eli said you don't see too many of them anymore and why don't we take a look and they went to the front of the car where the hood yawned open.

Eli asked Jesse did he have a rag and Jesse told Sarah Anne to get a dishtowel out of the trailer. She smiled shyly at Eli when she handed it to him and he smiled back. He told her to stand off a little bit in case it blew. With the towel for buffer, he pressed gingerly down on the radiator cap and steam hissed forth and he let go and pressed again and twisted it part way and let the pressure bleed off. Damn he said. I'd say she's overheated. He said don't touch nothing and went to his truck and came back with a socket wrench and an extension and a screwdriver. He undid the thermostat housing and gingerly pried out the thermostat and held it up in the towel and said that was it, see how it's corroded all the way shut. Spring might as well be welded. Sarah Anne twisted her head forward to see and he told it was safe now and she could come look. He showed her the white fur on the spring and told her it was supposed to be clean. Little things can make a big difference he said. He handed it to Jesse and asked was he ready. Jesse said hold on a minute and went in the back of the Fleetwood and came out with a jacket draped over his arm.

Jesse, Emma said. Don't.

Jesse said don't what? Emma went back to watching the river.

Eli and Jesse got in the truck and started off. After the first bend, Jesse looked back through the rear window and settled himself in the seat and pulled a pint mason jar out from under his jacket and unscrewed the lid and lifted it under his nose and sniffed. Pure perfume he said and sipped from the jar and snapped his head back and forth. Damn that is strong he said and asked Eli did he want some. Eli took the jar, driving with one hand, and smelled and jerked his own head back. Holy shit he said. Singed my fucking nose hairs! He asked Jesse where did he get it.

With the same pride with which he had claimed the Cadillac Jesse said he didn't get in nowhere, he made it.

Take a slug.

Eli said was he sure it was safe and Jesse said shit, it sure is, I take some ever day for my health and took the jar and drank deeply. Sweat beaded from his brow.

Here.

Eli took a sip. Jesus!

Jesse slapped his thigh and cackled and said you have to take enough to numb up your mouth a little bit and then it goes down pretty good.

What is it?

Hard to tell. I take whatever's to hand and mash it all up. There's corn in there and apples and sweet potatoes. Never the same twice is my motto. And I don't water it down hardly none at all. Keeps the customers satisfied.

Jesse asked did Eli know anybody might want to buy some and Eli said it depends on what it costs. There's out of the way places around town where folks'll drink just about anything if it's cheap enough.

When we get back, maybe you can point me out where they are.

They came up to the gas station and Jesse asked was that a ferryboat there going across and Eli told him it was.

What's it cost?

A quarter a car.

Shit, I'll bring the kids down. They like riding on things. Anything to do over there?

Come back.

Eli slid the truck up over the oil-stained gravel by the gas pumps and got out. A man came through the station's door and said hey Eli and Eli said hey Walter and told him to fill it up and held up the failed thermostat and asked did he have one.

Back of the counter. Just root around.

Eli and Jesse went in, past two men in the midst of dispute, both regaled in the livery of sweat-stained blue denim and leaning back against the front wall of the station in old wood chairs, the stain on the lower spindles worn away to bare wood where years of work soles had lingered and rubbed. They wore baseball caps to shield their squint eyes from the sun's glare and they held each one a beer and one raised his to Eli and the other said hey and the two of them went back to their argument. It aint the same thing one said and the other replied it sure as fuck is.

Eli found the row of thermostats in cubed boxes and checked a couple and found the kind that matched and handed it to Jesse.

He told Jesse they ought to get a new radiator cap while they was at it and Jesse said it made sense to him. He asked did he think them guys out there would be interested in some of his whiskey and Eli said it depended on if they were drunk enough. They went out and while Jesse engaged the men in conversation, Eli asked Walter did he have some old jugs he could use for water and would he mind letting them have the water too. Walter said there was some old Prestone jugs in the dumpster. Make sure you rinse them out. Might be some butts in there.

One of the men by the station yelled motherfuck!

Jesse joined Eli by the dumpster and they fished around among its bent cans and tattered rags and oil-soaked cardboard and unearthed a half-dozen antifreeze jugs. Jesse asked was six enough. Eli said if it wasn't enough to fill it, it would get them to where there was enough.

While they were driving back, Jesse said it wasn't hard at all getting them boys to take his whiskey and he got two dollars from both of them and would have settled for just two dollars between them. He thought maybe around here would be a decent enough place for them to catch their breath and figure out their next move. He asked Eli did he care about him selling the whiskey being it wasn't altogether legal and Eli said he didn't care as long as he didn't have to drink it. Jesse asked what if he was to set up someplace around here.

Like I said, as long as I don't have to drink it.

When they got back to the Fleetwood, Emma stood over a card table with folding chairs arranged around it, cutting bologna from a half-used block and laying the slices out on white bread, the fat above her elbow wobbling with the strokes of the knife. She asked Eli would he like a sandwich and he thanked her and said he already had his dinner on the boat. He scraped off the old thermostat gasket and set in the new one and bolted the thermostat housing down tight. He and Jesse took the jugs from the truck and filled the Fleetwood's radiator, the jugs' sides sucking in and out in time to the chugging water. He pushed on the new radiator cap and set it and Jesse started the car and let it idle. He got out of the car and stood with Eli looking at the engine, their arms crossed. Every now and again they bent over and spat. After a bit, Eli said that ought to be enough and for Jesse to check the gauge. Jesse stuck his head in the driver's window and said she's holding right where she's supposed to. He asked Eli what he owed him and Eli said not a thing, he was glad to do it. Jesse asked if Eli knew where there was a spot they could put in for the night. Eli thought a little bit and said, I got plenty of room if you want. Jesse said he didn't want to be no trouble. Aint no trouble. I got space to throw away.

Brigard County, July, 1993

Edna asked if Harmon knew how to operate a motorboat and he told her it depended on what kind. She told him the one in the boathouse. Her husband said it should be exercised from time to time. Harmon said he'd take it out in the morning and would she want to go with him. She said maybe.

In the morning Harmon stayed in the boathouse a long time and came out and up to the porch and told her the battery was dead and he'd try putting it on the charger. He went into the garage and wheeled the charger down to the boathouse and came back and told her it would be awhile and returned to scraping paint. He checked the battery after lunch and told her it didn't look like the battery was going to take a charge, but give it a little bit longer.

In the evening he checked again and said the battery was past saving. He said he'd poked around a little and wasn't comfortable with what he'd found. He suspected there was more wrong with the boat than he could handle. Edna asked what he thought they should do. Harmon told her he had a friend who was a mechanic and asked if she wanted him to ask his friend if he would take a look at the boat and she asked did he trust this friend. Harmon said his friend was about the best mechanic there is, but that he lived across the river, a little farther than would be easy to walk, and was there a chance she would let him use the car. With some hesitation she said yes.

The garage door's motor hummed, its chains rattled, and its diminutive aluminum wheels squealed in their tracks. Like a theater curtain rising, the door opened to the midmorning sun towards which the car faced, a narcissistic stage star in the limelight. Harmon slid behind the wheel and laid his hand on the white leather seat and just sat. It had been a long time. He started the engine and pulled out into the driveway and stopped and looked around for the switch to open the top and pressed it and the car came alive, its trunk devouring its own roof and closing down again tight upon itself.

He pulled out onto the road, turning downriver. The sun glinted through damp green leaves and called forth laced threads of multicolored light from the silk of countless spider webs and the beads of pure water suspended from them among the lush and abundant growth along the road. He drove until he came upon the remnants of his cabin and stopped and got out. From rusty steel stakes driven in the ground, there fenced about the ashes a line of yellow tape, a demarcation between where you could be and where you couldn't, proclaiming in bold black letters, NO TRESPASSING and CONDEMNED. In places where the tape had broken from its anchors, it lay limp and soiled on the seared ground. A clear plastic envelope with a red tag fluttered from the mailbox where someone had taped it. Harmon pulled it free and opened it and found an official township notice with spaces where someone had typed his name and the address and the name of the township's fire marshal. The form referenced title numbers and the numbers of codes and told him the above-referenced property was unsafe for habitation and he was hereby ordered according to law to demolish the property and remove from the site all resulting debris within thirty days from the date handwritten in the space provided for that purpose, after which he was subject to criminal penalty, the thirty days of grace a point in time already in the past. He taped the notice back on the mailbox and opened the box and took out a stacked bale of envelopes and advertisements. Electric and phone bills and weeks' worth of faded circulars from the Save-A-Lot. A handmade flyer. Lost dog, it said. Male border collie, two years old. Reward. A phone number. A photograph of the dog, Xeroxed into blackened obscurity. Harmon carried it all across the yard and threw it among the ashes of his cabin and went back and again peeled the notice from the mailbox and threw it among the ashes too. He looked closer. The refrigerator and woodstove were gone and small ditches ran in ragged lines among the rubble where thieves scavenging for scrap metal to fund their vices or relieve their economic despair had dug for the copper wire and plumbing which the fire would not have consumed. They'll steal anything he thought. He remembered how much in his life he himself had stolen and the reasons for it and how he held within him insufficient repentance to redeem him from his crimes. Fuck it he thought and forgave the thieves.

He went around back and down the path to the river. Already weeds sprouted from cracks opening in the path's packed earth. On the bank, a makeshift fireplace of stones ringed yet more ashes and scorched beer cans and the afterthoughts of crumpled cigarette wrappers and tin foil. A speedboat snarled past trailing a skier who, attempting to jump the boat's wake, fell in a frenzied thrashing of arms and legs. Harmon went back to the car and drove to the ferry crossing and onto the ferry as the Day-Glo-vested attendants directed him.

From both sides of the river there stretched the hands of the new bridge, their fingers reaching one for the other. When they would at last come together and interlace, there would be no further need for the ferry. By Thanksgiving they said, end of the year at the latest. Too far off for Harmon. He wondered what the boats' fate would be. Maybe somebody would buy one and turn it into a saloon. Name it The River Fairy. Decorate it with pictures of winged naked women brandishing magic wands and trailing clouds of misty dust flecked with gold. He'd drink in a place like that.

On the way across, people came to him and admired the car and asked was he going to be in the parade. He told them no and they said they don't make them like that anymore. Somebody asked was it for sale and he told them it wasn't, but to himself he thought everything is for sale. The ferry heaved up against the wharf's wooden ties and workmen bound the vessel fast with ropes thick as his legs and opened the gate and let down the ramp and waved him through. He piloted the Lincoln up toward the hills and turned off at the Crossings and on through and stopped on the side of the road at LeRoy's bridge and threaded his way through a nest of nettles spread across the shallow slope and down to the trickle of water beside which huddled his friend's shack of plywood and tarpaper.

Yo Skeeter he yelled and waited and yelled again and LeRoy opened the door, its bottom edge scraping on the brown, pebbled scratch of dirt upon which his home was founded.

Jesus Christ, Harmon. What are you doing here? Aint you supposed to be working?

Jesus Christ yourself. You got anything cold in there?

Nothing cold, but something wet. LeRoy went back in and came out with a pint almost empty. Not much he said.

Enough for a toast?

You here to celebrate?

If you want some work for yourself I am.

They sat on a wooden bench back out of the light. LeRoy asked was he serious about some work and what kind it was. Harmon asked him did LeRoy ever know him not to be serious and did it really matter what kind.

LeRoy said he guessed it didn't, unless it was something not exactly legal and as flimsy a roof as his bridge was, it was better than being locked up.

It's legal.

LeRoy raised the pint and said here's to it then. He drank and passed it to Harmon and told him to finish it and Harmon said here's to it and drained the bottle. He asked LeRoy did they have recycling out here. LeRoy said they did, right over there, pointing toward the bank. Harmon threw the bottle into the nettles. A car came across the bridge, thumping the warped lane boards and rattling the trestles.

So what's the job?

She's got a boat won't start.

What'd you try?

Nothing. Battery won't take a charge. It's been sitting close to three years.

I'd have to see it.

I got a car.

Anything I'd feel safe riding in?

Come see.

Harmon led LeRoy out from under the shade of the bridge and pointed to the Lincoln.

Jesus!

They went up through the nettles and stood by the car. LeRoy asked whose it was.

Hers.

She know you got it?

Her idea.

What is it? '64?

'63.

She ought to be wearing antique plates.

LeRoy ran his hands across the fender, stroking the car. He said, Jesus, Harm, if cars was whores, she'd be a thousand a night.

Harmon gave LeRoy the keys and told him to take it easy until they got on blacktop. They got in and went up toward town. Harmon said he had to make a couple stops and told LeRoy to drive by the doctor's. LeRoy asked him how bad was it and Harmon said bad enough but the pills helped. LeRoy asked was he sure the doctor would be there. Harmon said he told him he would be home until 11:00. LeRoy threaded through back streets to avoid the holiday traffic and came to the doctor's and pulled to the curb. Harmon got out. LeRoy said if Harmon didn't mind, he was just going to sit in her while he was gone and feel her up and Harmon said do what you want but don't go jacking off on the leather. He went around to the back door and rapped and the doctor's wife opened the door and told him to come in, he wanted to see him. Harmon went into the kitchen and the wife called out that Harmon was here and the doctor came in smoking a cigarette. He had the prescription in his hand. He told Harmon to lift up his shirt. Harmon hesitated and the doctor said you want the pills don't you? Harmon undid his shirt and pulled it up. The doctor pressed with his fingers and asked did that hurt and Harmon said what the fuck do you think?

The doctor said when the time came, he could get Harmon in the hospital on a charity claim.

Harmon asked would it make a difference how things turned out.

Maybe draw it out a little.

Is that a thing you'd want for yourself?

No.

Make it hurt any less?

Some.

Harmon said hospitals wasn't for him either, and the doctor gave him the prescription and said if he changed his mind, call him. Harmon told him thanks and went back out and LeRoy took him to a drugstore. By the time they got the prescription the parade had started and they had to wait on the other side of Merchant for it to pass. Gray-haired old men in tight military uniforms and wheel chairs on the back of a flatbed. Acne-faced Boy Scouts, mimetic soldiers in shorts and long socks. High school girls with bare thighs twirling batons and high kicking, the mayor behind them in an open car with nowhere near the class of the Lincoln, His Honor leering at the young asses flickering before him and occasionally remembering to wave and smile to his constituents. The local reserves marching raggedly, the less deft among them skipping now and then. A sergeant calling cadence over the ruffle of snare drums, *Hup, Two, Three, Four. Left...Left...Left/Right/Left!* Harmon thought back: *I don't know but I been told, Eskimo pussy is mighty cold. Sound off!* A for-show rifle with a white stock clumsily dropped with a thud on the pavement. Flags and ribbons. Clowns. Bicycles with red and blue crepe paper woven through the wheels and pasteboard taped to the forks to rattle against the spokes.

LeRoy asked was they going to watch the fireworks when it got dark. Harmon said it would be pretty hard to miss them from her house. Then he asked didn't LeRoy have a big birthday coming up pretty soon himself.

Yeah, the big four-oh.

Time to grow up?

Way past time.

Harmon said you better pull over and let me drive the rest of the way. LeRoy turned into an abandoned service station's debris-cluttered lot and shut off the car. You didn't tell her about me did you?

Didn't think of it until now. But it wouldn't matter. I wouldn't want to take a chance with nobody no matter who they were. Took her a long time just to trust me with it. And I don't think she's like that.

But you aint sure.

I aint sure.

Pretty much everybody's like that.

Not everybody.

Damn near.

I know.

They got out to switch sides and LeRoy asked Harmon did he have another cigarette. They went to lean against the hood and LeRoy said they shouldn't take a chance scratching her and they walked to the station with its boarded windows and leaned against its graffiti-latticed wall of concrete block, smoking and looking at the road where cars with boat trailers rattling behind them sought out a public ramp. Remember when we used to come up here on beer runs?

You mean do I remember when we had money for it?

That too.

You remember when they got robbed that time and they shot that kid who worked here?

What was his name?

I don't know, but he was a fucking little shithead. I do remember that.

They stood quiet for a while, remembering. Harmon finished his cigarette and flicked the butt out onto the lot. Let's go he said.

What's her name?

Edna.

What we gonna do? Walk up to her and say hey Edna, this here is my personal nigger LeRoy. He a real polite little nigger and hardly don't never make no trouble and he a real hard worker long as you gots your eye on him. And if he do give you any lip, you just give him a slap across his nappy head and he'll toe the line sure enough. Just be sure if it come down to that or if you maybe touch him by accident, you go and wash your hands right away. You don't never know where he been and you don't want to take no chances on catching something off him.

Harmon snorted out a laugh and winced with the pain. LeRoy asked was he okay and Harmon said he would be soon as the pills took hold. They got in the car and Harmon drove them to the house. He backed in the driveway and put up the top and backed the rest of the way into the garage. LeRoy looked at the tools hanging and went through the drawers of the tool chests. Christ, Harm, there's enough in here to start a whole fucking shop.

Harmon led LeRoy to the house. Now you got me so all I can think of is explaining how I got my own private nigger.

Don't think about it.

You try not thinking about it.

All the goddamn time.

Harmon knocked on the door once and opened it and they went in. Edna came into the front room from the kitchen and saw LeRoy and stopped and started again as if she had not seen this strange thing and crossed the room and said you're back. Harmon said they would have been back sooner, but they got caught on the other side of the parade. He told Edna and LeRoy who the other was and Edna offered her hand and LeRoy took it gently and said it was a pleasure, Miz Connor. She asked could she get him something and he told her that was kind of her but he probably ought to take a look at the boat first. She said just let her know if they needed anything and Harmon led him back out the front and around to the side and down to the boathouse.

She aint been around a lot of brack people has she?

How would I know?

You should've told her. Fucking near gave her a heart attack.

Not her.

Harmon switched on the boathouse lights and LeRoy whistled and said Jesus Christ. And then he looked around and said holy fuck, Harm. What'd you fall into?

He stepped on board the boat and checked around and tested the controls. He asked Harmon did he know where the registration was. Harmon said he didn't. LeRoy fished around in the storage compartments by the wheel and found the registration. '81 he said.

He snapped open the engine compartment latches and lifted the lid, the struts soughing and lightly squealing before setting and holding. He searched among the tangle of hoses and wires, pushing them aside and testing them with his fingers. He took off the coolant cap and smelled. He said it was good she wouldn't start. Half the hoses is dry-rotted and there's mud in the cooling system. Better look underneath.

Harmon helped him with the lift. They roped down its broad canvas straps hand over hand and threaded them under the hull and drew them taut. LeRoy asked where the switch was and Harmon pointed to the panel by the door. LeRoy said he couldn't fucking believe they had a lift for a river boat and pressed on the button's mushroom head. The lift thrummed and heaved and the boat sucked up from the water and he let off on the button. He walked around the decking and examined the hull and came all the way around and stood before the prop and swept it with his eyes and said uh-oh. Harmon said what?

Looks like a crack. You got a plank or something we can lay across here?

Harmon told him she had a couple ladders they could use and some five-eighths plywood and LeRoy said that would do. They hauled down the ladder Harmon was using to scrape the house's old paint and another from the garage and the plywood and assembled their scaffolding. LeRoy stepped out under the boat and ran his fingers lightly along the prop casing and said yeah, it was cracked. He pointed to where a jagged, thin line ran, dark gray where the aluminum showed through the black paint.

Must have hit a log or something.

How bad is it?

Can't tell for sure until I get her apart and see if the shaft's bent. Seals might be bad too.

How hard is it?

Not hard. Just gotta take a lot of shit off first. I'll need a shop manual. Think Gardner's done being pissed off?

Maybe. Let's go give her the news.

They went up and into the house and LeRoy told Edna what he'd found and she asked him how long he thought it would take. He told her as he had Harmon that he'd have to open up everything before he could tell her for sure. He said it partly depended on how long it would take to order parts and how a lot of them he could get at Pep Boys and that would speed things up some. She said wasn't Pep Boys for cars. He explained that some parts was just plain engine parts like spark plugs and wires and the dealer's parts were the exact same ones, just different labels, and three times as expensive.

LeRoy asked her if he could use the phone and did she have a phonebook. She nodded to the phone on the wall and took a phonebook from a drawer. He looked up the number he wanted and dialed. Edna saw that he had opened the Yellow Pages to MARINAS. She and Harmon listened to LeRoy's part in the conversation.

Is Marty there?

LeRoy.

Ask him anyway.

Hey.

I know.

A shop manual.

I know that too.

Side job.

'81 Ambassador.

Twenty-four.

Eight.

I know you don't.

Okay.

Today?

I will.

You too.

He got off the phone and said Marty would lend him the shop manual and then he explained to Edna what that meant. Edna

asked him was that the marina up above the bridge. LeRoy told her
it was. She said that was where her husband always took the boat
and why didn't they just have them do the work.

LeRoy told her they could do that but they would tell her
they was real busy, it being July and all and people coming up for
the 4th, and they would be tied up taking boats out of storage and
doing maintenance and they wouldn't be able to come and get it
for maybe three weeks and they wouldn't come then and she'd have
to call and ask when they were coming. They'd tell her they was
just getting ready to call and how about tomorrow morning. Now
you're way into August and they'll wait another week and call and
tell you there are about three times as many things wrong with the
boat than there really are and they're going to have to order some
parts and they'll say they'll call you when they come in, but they
won't. Then it'll be September and when you call them, they'll say
they are busy putting up boats, but you're next in line. Then it'll be
October and they will say the best thing to do is put it up for the
winter and worry about it next year and they have to charge extra
for the storage because they have to take special care to keep from
making things worse. Then in the spring they'll call and say it's done
because they put a rush on it like they're doing you a big favor, but
it cost a little bit more than they thought, and a little bit more on
top of what they told you it was going to be is about ten times what
it really should cost.

Edna asked him how he knew that.

I used to be their head mechanic.

Harmon and LeRoy left, but Harmon came right back. He
said that he didn't want to embarrass LeRoy by telling her this in
front of him, but LeRoy was between jobs and living in a shack
under a bridge and would it be all right with Edna if he stayed in
the garage apartment while he worked on the boat.

The Amazing Adventures of LeRoy James

Me and Mr. Bones Kill the Demons

The last I left off, me and Mr. Bones was up over the schoolhouse and the adventure was getting ready to start for real. So here goes:

Mr. Bones looked across the top of the trees and toward the ridge way off where you could see it winding back and forth in the moonlight like a big fat snake. Finally he said, "LeRoy, you know I said that I purified you to make you be like a hero?"

I got a cold chill then because when somebody starts off telling you about something they said, it either means they was lying or not telling you everything about it they should have. Then he said, "Just like demons hate folks like Miss Wells with a hatred black as midnight, they hate anybody that has been purified and they will come for you. LeRoy, you are going to be the bait tonight. I should of told you from the start and let you make up your own mind about it. I did not didn't have no right to do it without telling you. If you want to, I can dis-purify you."

I thought about that for a minute, how that glow I had on from the bucket of moonlight was like the scent trappers put around their bobcat traps and then I thought how after they are trapped, them bobcats would of wished they had not let themselves get taken in by that scent, and I thought to myself that whatever danger I was going to be in wasn't nothing compared to the danger Miss Wells was facing. After everything she had done for me, being bait for a demon trap was the least I could do. I told Mr. Bones I was proud he had faith in me.

Mr. Bones said, "OK, boy, here's what we are going to do. Your job is to bait lure them out of the schoolhouse. Then what we do is we cut off their heads with the hatchet. That will not all the way kill them, because they are demons, but it will suck almost all the power out of them. Then we stick their heads in one sack and their bodies in the other. We got to be careful how we do it though. If a demon that's lost his head can figure out where it is and nestle the end of his neck up against it, the two pieces of him will grow back together and we will have one real pissed off demon on our hands. So make sure you wire them sacks up tight."

Then he said, "OK, boy. We going to fly down real slow so we do not make no wind noise. You go all the way down and set yourself up by the bell. I'll stay up in the air a little bit. We each take one of the sacks and I'll hold on to the hatchet. When I give you the signal, you give that bell just the littlest bit of a ring that you can. Then you wait a little while and do it again. It'll probably take three or four rings to get them demons curious and they will send out one of the youngest ones to see what's going on. Then when he comes out and sees that you are perfectly purified he is going to come straight at you. You just hold your ground and I'll whack off his head before he gets to you. You go for the body and leave the head to me. You stuff the body into your sack and tie it up and I'll do the same thing with the head. You set?"

I nodded that I was, and then we started down, real, real slow. Mr. Bones stopped about twenty feet above the peak of the schoolhouse roof and I floated down all by myself, kind of rolling my shoulders so they pointed down and then up and that way it was like putting on the brakes. While I was doing it I remembered that dream I had way back when I was 3, and I thought for a second maybe that dream wasn't a dream at all but it was a prophesy. Mr. Bones made a motion with his arm like he was pulling on a rope. I pulled on the bell, and the bell went <u>ding</u>, so light there wasn't no slow winding down of the bell sound like there usually is when you make a bell ring. I waited about a half minute and gave it another ding like he told me and then dinged it again. Sure enough, I heard the door to the schoolhouse creak on its hinges and the next thing I saw was a actual demon standing on the porch. ~~That motherfucker~~ That ~~demon~~ motherfucker looked like he was on fire, he had yellow and red and orange blotches moving all over him. He had scales and big claws and a long sharp beak like an eagle and big leather bat wings. He come straight at me on a beeline, and at the exact same time he was getting to me, Mr. Bones did too. Mr. Bones swung that hatchet like he was Paul Bunyan and off went that demon's head. It kept flying a little bit further along the line he was flying in before Mr. Bones got there, but his body just turned black like all the color had just bled out of it all at once and he collapsed on the ground like he was a balloon somebody just shot with a BB gun. Mr. Bones said, "Get that body in the sack before it shakes itself off and starts running around without its head." Then he grabbed up the head, which was trying to warn the other demons but couldn't because without no body it didn't have lungs to yell out of, and Mr. Bones shoved it in his sack. By the time I got the body in my sack, it was already starting to squirm around and I was sure glad we got it trapped. I for real didn't want to see no demon running around without no head.

"Goddamn, Mr. Bones," I whispered back. "If that is one of the little ones, I ain't real sure I'm looking forward to meeting up with the big ones."

He just laughed and said, "One down and six to go." Then he went back up in the air to wait for the next demon to come out. This time it only took two dings. Me and Mr. Bones dispatched him just like we did the first one and I started thinking that this wasn't going to be so hard a thing to get done as Mr. Bones had been going on about. But, man oh man, was I ever wrong.

The next time, three of them came flying out all at the same time. Mr. Bones got one just when it was coming out the door, but I could tell right away that fast as Mr. Bones was, there wasn't no way he was going to get the other two's heads whacked off before one of them made it all the way to where I was and I didn't even think. I just grabbed up the shovel and swung it and I got to admit, a lot of what happened was just plain luck because I was acting out of pure desperation, but I caught one of them fuckers right in the throat with the tip of the shovel and off went his head. Mr. Bones yelled, "I got these. Fly up as high as you can!"

I didn't hesitate one single second. I kissed the Aztec bone for luck and shot straight up like a rocket and that demon was right on my tail. Just about the time I was hitting the treetops it got hold of my leg with one of his claws. It hurt like a motherfucker. He had a hold of me like a vise has a hold of a piece of iron and he wasn't about to let go. The higher I flew, the colder it got and I was getting enough of a chill that I wished I had wore a jacket. But something real strange was happening to the demon. As cold as I was, I could feel the demon's claw where it was holding on to my leg getting even colder, so cold that next to it ice would seem like it was hot. That was because demons live most of the time in the blazing heat of hell and when they come out, they are naturally going to feel cold even when it would be hot for us. All of a sudden, the demon turned completely to ice and exploded and turned into what looked like colored snow and fell back down to the ground. Not all of the demon exploded. His claw was still grabbed around my ankle. I stopped going up and hovered in the air just underneath the moon and took a good look. That claw was clenched around my leg so hard it had the circulation cut off in my foot. And there was a long cut from just below my knee to the middle of my calf from where the demon had scratched me with his razor-sharp fingernail. I smacked what was left of the claw with my fist and it broke up into smithereens. And then I remembered that Mr. Bones was down on the ground and for all I knew the last two demons was on him. So I jetted down there like I was the Green Lantern on a desperate mission. It was worse than I thought.

He'd managed to whack off both their heads. But without me to help him, he didn't get them in the sacks and they'd got their heads and bodies connected up again but they got them messed up, they got the wrong heads on the wrong body and all hell was breaking loose. Something about them getting joined up that way did something to their powers so that before where none of them could do Mr. Bones hardly any damage because he is nothing but spirit, now they could. He was flying every which way, in circles around the schoolhouse and in big loop-de-loops in the air and zigzagging in and out of the trees in the woods behind the school. He even dove down into the ground without even making a hole in it and then come up out of there someplace else. But he couldn't lose them demons. I looked around, but I couldn't see where the shovel was so I flew over to the woods with the idea of breaking a dead limb off of a tree and I did that and got a piece of a live oak and was heading over to help Mr. Bones out, which was just plain dumb luck. I wish I could say that I knew at the time that a live oak limb was the perfect one to get to go after a demon with because of it being crooked and you need something bent up and twisted to go after a demon because they have themselves gone all the way insane. Mr. Bones explained that to me afterwards. He said that it wasn't just dumb luck either. That purification thing he did to me makes you think of things you need to do without knowing why you are doing them. It's part of what being a hero is all about. A hero got to have that kind of natural instinct.

So anyway I went after the demon that was closest and kept speeding up even when I was getting right up to him and when I got there I clobbered him with that live oak limb as hard as I could and knocked his head right off. The other one stopped and looked around to see what happened and that gave Mr. Bones the second he needed to whack off his head with the hatchet. I can tell you right now, we didn't waste no time whatsoever getting that demon in the sack.

So now there was just two demons left to deal with. We dinged the bell and hollered and did everything we could think of to get them to come out. Finally, Mr. Bones said, "They're going to make us go in after them." I did not like the sound of that at all. Outside at least we could run (fly I mean) if any of them got too close, but inside, that could be a pretty dangerous situation. It would be like that fight I heard happened between two boys over in Jonesville where they tied their left hands together with a piece of rag and then fought it out with knives. The rag was so one of them couldn't chicken out and run off. The story goes that both of them boys died in the fight, one right on the spot when the other one got in a lucky swipe and slit his throat and the other one a hour or so later from bleeding to death inside. Once we were in the schoolhouse with the demons, there wouldn't be any escaping and I told Mr. Bones so.

"LeRoy, we ain't got no choice. We got to go in for Miss Wells's sake and you know that to be a fact just as much as me." And he was right, I did know that to be a fact. I just was hoping I wouldn't have to face up to it, like Jesus did in the garden before the soldiers came to get him. I told Mr. Bones I was ready.

"Now just because we got to do it don't mean we got to rush in there without a plan. Them two that's left ain't just the biggest and meanest of the whole pack, they are the smart ones too. They are the general and his first lieutenant and that means they are <u>real</u> smart."

I asked him what the plan was.

"Well, first off, once we get in there we ain't going to be able to talk to each other and give each other ideas, because they will hear what we are saying and know what we are trying to do. So whatever we going to think of, we got to think of it now before we go in. The thing to remember is that whatever it is they try to get you to do, you got to not do it. There ain't no way to predict what kind of trick they going to try to pull before we go in. All you got to know is that anything they say is going to be a lie. The best thing to do is to make like you are going to do what they say but do something else to trick them back. So the plan is to be smarter than them and not fall for anything they say." Then we made our plans and what our signals was going to be and when we were done with that he said, "Okay. It's time, LeRoy. This one is for all the marbles." Then he kind of took the lead, just a half step or so in front of me, but not straight out in front, more off to the side, so that we was going in like equals but with him in a position where he could get between me and the demons if it came to that. You can't put a price on that kind of friendship.

The general was sitting in Miss Wells's chair with his feet up on her desk and going through her roll book. That sent a shiver right up my spine because it meant he was figuring on going after the little kids when he was done with Miss Wells. The lieutenant was stuck up in the rafters at the back of the room. Mr. Bones looked at both of them, first the general and then the lieutenant and then tilted his head just a little bit the way he did a couple times I already told you about, and that was the signal to watch out because it looked like their plan was to come at us from two different directions at the same time.

Then the general demon, he started to hiss, like a breeze just beginning to blow up through a field of high, dried-up grass. The hissing sound started out real quiet and then got louder until it

was a voice, but it still had that hissing to it, which I figured was
his way of trying to keep us a little bit scared and off guard, but
I wasn't having none of that. "Hey, boy," he said, "how much
you want for that little piece of bone around your neck? I got a
girlfriend that trinket would look real good on."

I didn't say one single thing, even though the way that
demon talked, just the sound of it, made you almost believe what
he was saying. He could have said that Chicago is in Brazil and a
lot of people would have believed him, he was that slick. It ain't
no wonder so many people in the world get tempted into doing
evil things.

"How about it boy? I give you fifty dollars for it." And if I
did not know what he was up to before he said that, I sure knew
it then, because fifty dollars was a <u>real</u> lot of money back in them
days, a lot more than it is now, and way more than anybody would
pay for a "trinket" for a girlfriend. ~~Shit~~ Hell, a demon can go off
and kill himself a swan and pick a couple bones out of it and give
them to her if he wanted to. So for sure I knew now we wasn't
playing.

I pretended to go along. "Make it a hundred," I said. And
the demon said, "You got it boy," and reached around behind
him a little bit the way Mr. Bones had done when he got out the
bone in the first place and came up with a brand new 100-dollar
bill. I made like I was taking off the bone and when I did that,
Mr. Bones took a little stutter step like he was afraid I was falling
for the demon's ~~bullshit~~ lie and he was getting ready to stop me,
but I gave him a little wink out the side of my face and he relaxed
because he could see that I knew what was what.

The demon started floating over toward us with both his
hands out, one to give me the money with and the other one to
take the talisman, and that's when I said, "Hey there, General,
I got a better idea. How about I hold on to this here little bit

of worthless bone and you go ~~fuck yourself~~ back to hell where you came from." Well, if you up and told your old Aunt Betsy that she had the sweetest looking ass in four counties and you wished you could get underneath her dress for a better look at it, you wouldn't have seen a more surprised look than was on that demon's face. He stopped up short and kind of looked down at me for a second and then he got more pissed off than you think it could be possible for <u>anything</u> to be, man or beast or demon. And he come straight at us like a bolt of lightning and Mr. Bones yelled, "Run!" and that's just what we done, except we did it by flying, and that demon was right on our tails. We got one circle around the room before the lieutenant demon come down from the rafters and started chasing us too. Pretty soon the four of us was swirling around that schoolhouse like we was a whirlwind and the whirlwind was filled up with all kinds of light, what with the shining coming off of me because I been purified and the fire coming off the demons and the black lights coming out of Mr. Bones. For a second I thought we was going to get going so fast and tight in a circle that them demons would melt down into some kind of syrup like those tigers did when Little Black Sambo tricked them, except they would have probably turned into something more like hot sauce because they was demons. But demons is smarter than tigers and they kept their shapes and just kept coming. After about a hundred turns around the room, Mr. Bones yelled out for me to get up into the rafters and that's what I did, even though it didn't make no sense to me at the time. If I got up there into the peak of the roof, I'd be trapped with no place to run to. But Mr. Bones always got some trick going and when the general demon peeled off out of the whirlwind and came up behind me to the roof, Mr. Bones yelled again, "Now head for the door!"

I swooped over backwards like I was doing a gainer off a tree limb into the creek and that demon had to flip over too and when he did he got his feet against the roof to push off and come after me. That's when I saw Mr. Bones holding some kind of gun like I never saw before and he had it up to his shoulder and pulled off a round and the sound of it was louder than any gun I ever heard. Well, it was some kind of magic shotgun, because instead of shot coming out of it, pieces of light came out instead. They was like splinters of ice, lit up with the same kind of light as the Easter moon, a little bit like the glow I had on, but a whole lot brighter, and when they hit that demon, he just plain exploded and whatever he had inside of him that passed for blood plastered itself right up against the very peak of the roof and that was one demon that wasn't going to give us no more trouble. The lieutenant demon pulled up out of the whirlwind and pulled his head back so hard I was surprised he didn't whack his own head off doing it. He stood stock still for about as much time as it takes to sneeze and then he was out the door and off for parts unknown. I guess he had just about as much of us that night as he was ready to take. And then the whole night turned back into just a regular night, except for the Easter moon.

Me and Mr. Bones looked at each other and then we both broke down laughing like we was crazy demons ourselves. Even though Mr. Bones don't have to breathe, he was wheezing and trying to catch his breath he was laughing so hard, and I was laughing and wheezing right along with him. Mr. Bones tried a couple of times before he got out what he was trying to say: "How about I hold on to this here little bit of worthless bone and you go back to hell where you came from?" And then he went on laughing some more and me right with him. When we got ourselves calmed down, Mr. Bones looked up to where the moon was, halfway down to the horizon. We had been at it for a lot longer than it felt like when we was exercising them demons. Mr. Bones said, "We still got a lot to get done and we better get moving on it if we are going to get you back before your mama wakes up."

So we grabbed up the sacks and headed off for the hills. From up high where we were, I could see that there is a lot of things going on at night that don't go on in the daylight. People go out into the woods at night and them people is doing just the kind of things folks do at night that they don't want nobody to see. One place, I saw a whole band of white folks dancing naked around a big bon fire and they was every few seconds letting out a big yell, "Praise Baal!" At another place I saw a girl who couldn't have been 15 doing a long string of strangers. Some man who looked a lot like her but a lot older too was sitting off to the side with a shotgun and the men had to pay him first before they even got to look at the girl. She must have had one hell of a reputation to get that big of a line, all of them ready to pay up without even so much as a peek at her first.

And there was ghosts everywhere. Up in the air over the hills with us and just over the ground and some weaving in and out around the trees like they was looking for something that they had lost. When we got to the big hills, there was more ghosts there too. Some of them had a table and chairs set up right on top of the biggest hill and they was playing cards. One of the ghosts pulled out a six-shooter and blowed off the head of the ghost sitting across from him. The ghost that shot the gun said, "You goddamn motherfucking cheater. Give me back my fucking money!" And the ghost that got his head blowed off said, "Jesus Christ, man, give me a goddamn minute to get my head back on!" Then he did just that, put his head back on. "Here's your fucking money," he said and then reached back and came up with a whole basketful of rattlers and threw them at the ghost who shot him. And then every single one of them ghosts started laughing even harder than me and Mr. Bones did after we got done with the demons.

While we was looking around for a good place to land and bury the demon heads, I said to Mr. Bones, "How come it is folks always got to be so brutal with each other, even after they're dead?"

"Because they are scared, boy. And because they are crazy. You see them ghosts playing cards? Every one of them got a single place they supposed to be and every night they all sit in their place, every one of them, and every single one of them is stone-cold crazy because they don't know what is coming next. That's the thing drives people insane. You never know what the next thing is going to be, either when you are alive or when you are dead. And that is surely a fearsome thing for just about everybody, not knowing what the next thing is that's going to happen."

And then I said to Mr. Bones, "But I like not knowing what's going to happen. If I knew what the next thing was going to be, I would be bored completely out of my mind and have to think about killing myself, except there wouldn't be no thinking about it because I would already know whether I did it or not. Man, that can't be no fun at all."

"That's because you are one in a million, boy. Ain't too many folks think the way you do. They are too busy being scared about being scared. They are like a slave who says being a slave is a good thing because you don't have to pay no income tax."

"Mr. Bones, there is not one single place in the world where that makes sense."

"Don't I know it, boy. But it is the way things are."

By that time we had ourselves a good place to bury the sack of heads. It was along a little ridge that didn't have no roads running near it and too muddy a place for hunters to wander into by accident. We found a spot on top of a little hummock of scraggle grass and set the sacks down on it. Mr. Bones handed me the shovel and told me to start digging. You would think that muddy ground is easier to dig in than dry ground, but it ain't. Mud is a lot heavier than just plain dirt. And besides that I was tired from the fight with the demons and my leg was hurting where the demon had got ahold of it. Mr. Bones saw me having trouble and at first I thought he was going to laugh and ~~break my balls~~ give me a hard time, but he didn't. He just put his hand on my shoulder and said read gentle, "I got it from here." He took over and him digging was just a blur. He had a perfect grave dug out in about a minute. Six feet long and three feet wide and six feet deep. He dug it the way a grave is supposed to be even though it was filling up with water at the same time he was digging deeper and deeper down.

He stuck the shovel in the pile of muddy dirt and took up the sack and tossed it in the grave. The splash it made sloshed the brown water all the way over the sides of the hole. The sack started sinking down in the water and when it did, you could hear gurgle sounds coming out of it. I think the water was making up for the lack of air the demons had from not being connected anymore with their bodies, and the sound they was making was a scared sound and a sound like you would think a person would make when they was losing the one thing in the world that was most precious to them, and for just a second I felt sorry for them. But then I remembered that they had come here in the first place to rip Miss Wells into shreds of raw meat and I knew they got what they deserved and me and Mr. Bones had a obligation to keep them from trying that with anybody else. But what I learned from that second of feeling sorry for the demons is that knowing what is the right thing to do and going ahead and doing it is two altogether different things. Doing it is a whole lot harder than thinking about it.

Then just as fast as he dug out the grave, Mr. Bones filled it back in and said, "Let's get out a here." He grabbed the sack with the bodies and we went on a beeline because sunup was getting closer and closer. Mr. Bones took the lead instead of staying close beside me because he knew where we was going and I got to say that as easy as flying is when you know how to do it, keeping up with Mr. Bones ain't. I don't know how it happened but keeping up with him actually got me out of breath, which is a strange thing because you don't move nothing when you fly, flying being a magical thing. But it was a true fact that I was worn out by the time we got to Mr. Bones's elder trees. They was in a little circle in the blackest part of the woods. Their leaves had a shine to them in the moonlight like they was made out of gold and even though there wasn't no wind, they made a sighing sound like a breeze was blowing through them. There was about a hundred graves already dug and filled in in the spaces between the elders. This wasn't Mr. Bones's first rodeo. Mr. Bones dug out another perfect grave and buried them demons' bodies. When he was done, I stomped on the dirt to help and let out a little yelp because my leg was hurting so bad. "Let me see that," Mr. Bones said. He kneeled down and took my foot up in one hand and with the other one pulled back on the tear in my pants where the demon had clawed through it. "This ain't good," he said. "Demons has got poison in them and it comes out through their claws when one of them grabs a hold of you. If we don't get you fixed up right now, you will end up in real bad shape."

I got bad lightheaded and almost fell down, except Mr. Bones reached around me and picked me up in his arms and took us off on another beeline, this time straight north. I passed out about then so I can't tell you anything about the trip. When I came to, I was laying on a cot in some old cabin and there was a real old man with long gray hair holding a lantern in my face. I reared back to give him a smack and I heard Mr. Bones say, "Whoa there, LeRoy, he's going to help you." Then he said to the old man, "What do you think?" Which was real weird because it meant somebody besides me could see and hear Mr. Bones, but I didn't realize it at the time on account of my leg hurting so bad had me not thinking straight.

The old man pulled up my pants leg and said to Mr. Bones, "It ain't good, but I think you got him here in time." He set the lantern down on a table and said, "I'm going to make him a poultice, be right back." The old man headed for a work table on the other side of the cabin. It looked a lot like the witch's work table, but with not as much vials and jars on it. He did about six things all at once, most of which I couldn't see what they were, but I did see him take a wood spoon and reach into a jar with it. The jar had a flat kind of spider web in it, all up and down the sides, the kind a tunnel spider makes. I heard him say, "Sorry, fellow, but I need this for a patient. You can build yourself another web, but he can't build himself another leg." The old man beat around in there with the spoon like he was mixing up some biscuits batter and then pulled out the spoon and the spider web was wrapped all around it. Then he put that in a jar with some herbs and bugs and mixed that all together and came back.

He got a rag and some water and started washing my leg and I can tell you for sure that as soon as that damp rag touched my leg, I felt like I was on fire, and I let out a yell. I tried not to, but I couldn't help it. The old man said, "I'm trying to be easy as I can, but that demon left part of himself on you and demons can't stand water and that is what you're feeling. If you can stand it for just a minute more, I'll have all of him off of you and it won't hurt like that anymore." (Now that I think of it, that must of been part of the reason them demon heads was making so much noise when we threw them in their watery grave.)

I said, "Just do what you got to do."

By the time he got done washing my leg, it was hurting a lot less than when he started. He spooned up the poultice and smoothed it out over the scratch like he was putting icing on a cake. Wherever he laid on the poultice, my leg stopped hurting altogether and when he had the whole scratch covered up, it didn't hurt at all. "How's that feel now?" he said.

"Pretty good, can't feel nothing."

"What we owe you?" Mr. Bones said to the old man.

"Nothing for now. Maybe a favor on down the road."

"That's fair. We got to be rude and get going now."

Mr. Bones and the old man shook hands and I could tell that they had a respect for each other that is the kind you got to earn over a long time, most likely it took years for them to get to the place they was.

We went outside and started off for home. While we was flying there, the purification I had on me was getting dimmer and dimmer. By the time we got to my house, I was just my old natural color. That's when I remembered about my ripped pants leg. "Shit, Mr. Bones!" I said. "Mama is going to kill me when she sees this tear in my pants."

"Don't worry about it, boy, I got it covered. You think I can know how to kill off a pack of demons but can't fix up a pair of pants?"

We landed out behind the shed and he did that thing he does where he turns himself part way around and looks like he's rooting through a basket and came back around with a needle and thread. "Sit down," he said. In about a second, he had the rip all sewed up. I looked at it and all the stitches in the cloth and before I could get it out that having stitches in my pants wasn't going to be much better to Mama that the rip was, them stitches just started disappearing, one at a time until they was all gone and my pants leg looked like it hadn't never even been ripped. "Getting over your amazement, boy?" Mr. Bones said and chuckled a little.

"Guess I am," I said.

"That's it for the night then. We best get inside. It will be light pretty soon."

Mr. Bones flew in through the top of the roof, heading for his place where he could watch me while I was asleep, and I headed for the porch. I had to walk because Mr. Bones had took back the gift of flying. I went to sleep and nobody was ever the wiser and everybody was safe except for the demons.

So that is the end of The Killing the Demons Adventure. Wait until you read the next one. It is even harder to believe, but it is every bit as true as this one.

Brigard County, July, 1993

LeRoy said it would be better if Harmon went in and he waited in the car. Harmon came back with the shop manual and said Gardner wasn't as pissed off as he had been but it was just as well LeRoy didn't go in. The only reason he said they could have the manual was so he could tell LeRoy again what he thought of him and did LeRoy want to hear it. LeRoy said he already heard it a dozen more times than would have been one too many. They drove to LeRoy's bridge and carried up to the car what things LeRoy would need for now. They drove down through the Crossings and crossed over the river on the ferry and followed the river road back to the house. They took LeRoy's belongings up to the apartment. Harmon showed him where everything was and how to work the shower. LeRoy asked did Harmon have an extra blanket for the couch and Harmon told him he could use the bed. LeRoy said he couldn't let Harmon sleep on the couch, he'd be fine with it, way better than the bridge that was for sure. Harmon looked at him with a smile half-contrite.

Jesus, Harm.

Harmon spread his hands and shrugged. What can I say?

LeRoy shook his head and rolled his eyes and asked Harmon was she calling him Billie yet. Harmon said she wasn't but she knew his whole name if that's what LeRoy wanted to know.

I'll tell you what I want to know, William Harmon.

What's that?

How long you think it'll take us to fuck up this time?

Maybe we won't.

And maybe if we start eating newspapers and green jello, we'll shit hundred-dollar bills.

Tabernacle Parish, October, 1962

The men got out of the car with purpose, the man from the still and two others, one of them carrying a shotgun. They strode in step toward the porch and Jigger came from behind the house snarling and they shot him. The dog writhed in the grass trying to breathe, a soft cloud rising from the heat of its intestines snaking out in the cold October morning. LeRoy came out of the house and they took him by the arm and dragged him off the porch and Agnes stumbled out screaming and they grabbed her too. Whiskey ran out from the barn and the one with the gun leveled it at him. Whiskey stopped and stood motionless.

Where's it at? the man from the still said.

Whiskey measured the distance to the men and how far it was to Agnes and LeRoy and he measured the intention in the men's eyes and saw that he had lost and said buried in the vegetable patch behind the barn.

You got a shovel?

Whiskey tilted his head toward the barn. In there he said.

The one holding LeRoy told him to sit on the porch steps and don't fucking move. LeRoy looked at Whiskey and Whiskey nodded for him to do it.

The third man went in the barn and came out with a shovel and went around back and in a short while returned with two jugs and said they're all there.

The man from the still said you got a lot of names, Daniel Watson. You think I'm so fucking dumb I couldn't figure out how to find the biggest nigger anybody ever saw around here?

He took the shotgun from the man on the porch and told his companions to get all the moonshine in the car except for one jug and bring it to him. He walked up to Whiskey and clubbed him with the shotgun and Whiskey went to his knees but not all the way down and the man clubbed him again and this time he fell. The man unscrewed the lid from the jug and said you need it bad enough to steal it, you should have some. He poured the moonshine over Whiskey and then he lit a match and asked did you ever see how good hundred and fifty proof burns? He dropped the match and set Whiskey on fire and turned around and said let's go.

The Amazing Adventures of LeRoy James

I Die Saving the Princess

I'm going to get right to it this time: This adventure starts out
with me splattered on some rocks and plain out bloody and dead
as you can be. Being dead is a strange thing. At first not only
couldn't I move, but I couldn't even look around to see what my
situation was. I wasn't scared though, which I would have been if
I was still alive at the time, because landing on those rocks would
have hurt like hell. But being dead, I wasn't feeling anything at all.
Being dead is at times a blessing in disguise.

The reason I was laid out on the rocks is I had to jump from
a big cliff because a whole army was chasing me and they was
all armed with spears and lances and terrible swift swords. I was
pretty sure I was going to escape all that fury though, on account
of I wasn't wearing any heavy armor like they were and could
make better time. I could hear them panting and wheezing behind
me and would have been home free in just a couple more minutes
except for the cliffs. I should have taken a second and got my
bearings instead of just taking off. I ran east when I should have
headed north, and now I was dead on account of it. You got to
take every little detail into account when you are on an adventure.
Don't never leave anything to chance, because when you do, it
will fuck you up every time and being splattered out dead on the
rocks at the bottom of a cliff is about as fucked up as you can
get. So I had a choice to make when I came up on the cliffs: Jump
and <u>maybe</u> die or stand there like a slave in a cotton field and for
<u>absolutely fucking sure</u> die. So I jumped.

Not being able to look around didn't mean I couldn't see. I could see, just not a lot. Only what was right in front of my eyes. I was laying on my stomach on a big rock and my head was hanging out over the edge of it. I could hear too. I remember hearing a lot of cheering going on up above my head. It was that damn Arab army that chased me off the cliff that was doing the cheering and gloating over what they thought they did to me. But they didn't do it do me. I did it to myself. My choice, motherfuckers!

I could hear the waves too, breaking loud just a little off to my right. Man, I just about made it. I had calculated pretty close but still didn't make it out all the way to the ocean. If I had took a running start or if those cliffs had been sticking out just a little bit further, I would of hit the water instead of the rocks and been this very second swimming to safety. Who'd be cheering then? And then it got quiet up above me and I knew they had got tired of looking at my corpse and went off. Sayonara amigos!

I reconnoitered the best I could, given that I was dead and couldn't look around, but when you are in a bad situation, you got to do what you can, even if that's not a lot. Doing something might not get you out of it but doing nothing is a surefire guarantee that you will be staying in that bad situation. Once I got a good focus going on, I saw a bunch of fire ants way down below drinking from a pool of blood and it took me a second to figure out that that was <u>my</u> blood they was drinking. I tried to move my eyes a little bit to see if I could check out what was going on with the rest of me, and pretty soon I could move them a little bit, and then I was sorry I did, because right there not ten feet away there was a hyena on another big rock staring at me. He was checking to make sure I was absolutely dead before leaping across the chasm between us and moving in. I sure could have used Mr. Bones right about then, but I had told him I didn't think

I needed him on this trip, it just being a minor rescue mission, nothing magical in it.

I should maybe back up and let you know what I was doing there in the first place ("there" being Arabia). There was an Arabian prince who had got himself into a mess. He fell in love with the daughter of the sultan of another kingdom. He saw her taking a bath in an oasis while he was out hunting. He went right away to the sultan and asked if he could have her hand in marriage and the sultan gave them his blessing. Then the prince asked the sultan could he take his daughter out on a date and the sultan said yes but only for a walk out in his imperial garden and on the condition that the prince didn't let anything happen to her, because she was the apple of the sultan's eye. The prince made a solemn vow that he would defend her with his life, and off they went. (Just between you and me, what happened next I think happened because the prince had pussy on his mind and let that distract him from keeping a lookout. Pussy is maybe the most dangerous thing there is in the world, even for sultans and princes. Once you get it on your mind, it's hard to think altogether straight about business.) Well, the prince started reciting some of that Arabian poetry that makes women helpless against any man's advances when they hear it. He got so into it that he clasped his hands together like he was praying and because the particular poem he was reciting at that moment had something about the full moon in it, he gazed up at the moon with the most romantic look he could muster up while he was reciting. And that's all it took. While he was looking the other way, a whole gang of soldiers from the sultan's archenemy jumped up from behind the bushes and some of them grabbed hold of the prince so he couldn't protect the sultan's daughter and the rest of them grabbed her and dragged her off. The ones that was left behind with the prince gave him a good one right in the stomach so he couldn't breathe or even talk and fell down completely helpless on the grass. They give him a good kick in the back while he was down for good measure and told him, "Good luck with the sultan," laughing their asses off while they were heading off to join up with the ones who took the princess.

The prince knew he was in for it no matter what he did. If he went back to the palace and told the sultan what happened, he stood a pretty good chance of getting his head chopped off right there on the spot and if he didn't, the sultan was going to find out anyway and make it his life's work to track the prince down and do him in. It was your classic fucked-if-you-do and fucked-if-you-don't situation. But the prince was actually pretty brave for a rich guy and decided to face the music and went back and told the sultan what happened.

The sultan was righteously pissed off, like you would expect. But he was smart too and he let the smart part of him take over, because the main thing he wanted was not to kill the prince but to get his daughter back safe and sound. He could take care of killing the prince after he got her back. So he said to the prince, "You got exactly three days to get Serena back." (Serena being his daughter's name.) "She ain't back by then or if she is and got one single scratch on her, I am going to start with your toes and work my way up until you will be screaming for me to finish the job. I am going to slice off some of you and boil some of you off with boiling oil and I am going to let starving rats loose on your balls. If there is any of this you don't understand, you better ask me about it right the fuck now, because I absolutely ain't playing."

The prince knew better than to ask any questions. He didn't even take time to prostrate himself down on the floor like you are supposed to do when you're getting ready to exit yourself out from the sultan's royal presence. He just gave the sultan a quick bow that was the absolute minimum you could get away with and still show the proper respect and beat it the hell out of there.

The prince knew he was still in a pretty big mess. Getting out of there with his head still tied to his neck wasn't even close to getting him out of the woods. He had to figure out a way to rescue the sultan's daughter and he was totally clueless to even think of a way to put together a plan to get the job done. That afternoon he hooked up with some of his other prince buddies back in his own kingdom and they tossed around some ideas. One of them said he thought he knew about somebody who could help the prince out and that somebody was me. He had got word about my other amazing adventures from all the way across the sea and said that from what he had heard of my reputation, if there was anybody that could help the prince out, it would be me. They made a couple calls and found somebody who had my phone number. At first I wanted to turn the man down because I was due for a vacation from all this adventuring, but he sounded so sorrowful on the phone that I couldn't say no, him sounding so forlorn and like a lost little girl. So I told him I would help him out and told him to send a magic carpet over to pick me up. Well, that carpet was at my door in less than five minutes. I didn't figure this was going to take all that long so I didn't even bother to pack a change of clothes. I just jumped up on that carpet and said Giddy Up. That's when Mr. Bones asked if I didn't think maybe he should come along and I told him this little bit of an adventure wasn't even going to get me to the point of breaking out a sweat and he could just lay up for a day or two and rest up, but he sure would have been useful to have when I was laying dead on the rocks.

That's just a little bit of background to get you up to speed on why I was where I was at. I don't need to go into everything that went on to get you to the point of the soldiers chasing me across the desert. The real part of the adventure was what came after.

So there I was laying dead on them rocks, and just being able to move only a little bit, when I hear something that sounds like a waterfall. Just as I turned my head in the direction the sound was coming from, it stopped, and there right in front of my eyes was two angels hovering in the air next to the rock. From my angle I couldn't see their faces, just their robes and some of their wings sticking out from behind them and waving back and forth real slow, just enough to keep them up in the air but not enough for them to be moving around. They glowed with a pure white light. I could hear them talking between themselves but they was talking in some foreign language, probably Hebrew if I remember my Bible School right, and I couldn't understand what they was saying. They went on like that for a good long time and just when I was about getting ready to say something to them, that waterfall sound started up again. It was their wings beating. They moved in on me and both of them grabbed an arm, one on each side, and picked me up and the next thing I knew, I was flying through the air, way, way up, so high the rocks I was on looked like little pebbles on the beach. They just kept on taking me higher and higher up and before too long I couldn't see the ground or the ocean at all. I still couldn't see their faces but I kept trying and then something got my attention off to the side and I looked that way and son-of-a-bitch, don't you know the angel on that side was barefoot and his feet were black! I looked over at the other one and he was barefoot too and <u>his</u> feet were black too, but lighter skinned than the first one. Now this was a by-god, for-absolute-fucking-real revelation. From all the pictures you see, nobody in a million years would have guessed there are black angels, but there they were. That is one of those things that until you see it wouldn't of made no sense, but when you do finally see it, makes all the sense in the world and you wonder why you never thought of it before. If there are black and white and red and yellow people, it is an absolute fact that there got to be black and white and red and yellow angels, and who better to send for a black man than a black angel. Just goes to show you never know what you don't know but should. BUT: as strange as the revelation about the angels was, the next revelation that I was about to get would make the truth about the angels sound like 2 plus 2 makes 4.

Pretty soon I see this big green hill off in the distance, and you could just see the top of it at first, like it was over the horizon and we were coming up on it from on high. A little at a time, the whole hill came into view and the closer we got to it, the more details I could make out. The first thing looked like a moat house from a fairy tale with a big golden gate in front. The whole yard in front of the moat house was all filled up with flowers, every kind of a color flowers could be and little pools of shimmering water. Streams was flowing out of the pools and magic animals was drinking from their pure waters and gamboling in the grass.

The angels flew me down next to the moat house and lit on the grass like they was thistle seeds parachuting to rest, they came down that soft and easy. A pure white bench made out of marble stuck out the side of the house and the dark-skinned angel told me to sit on it and don't go nowhere. They were going to go let the boss know I was here and somebody would be out in a minute to take care of me. The light-skinned one pulled out a ring of gold keys and jangled through them until he got the right one. He unlocked the gate and the two of them pulled it open. It didn't creak or nothing, but that gate was <u>heavy</u> because it took both of them pulling with all their might to get it open. I don't know whether they just didn't care or if they just didn't feel like doing all the work of closing the gate back up because it was so heavy, but they left it open regardless. Now that was a powerful moment of temptation for me. Anybody who has got any curiosity at all and sees an open gate that looks an awful lot like a celestial gate is going to want to go in to Glory. I confess I was getting pretty close to doing something that I might of regretted later on when I heard somebody coming out.

It was another black guy! This one didn't look like he was an angel, more like the picture of Friar Tuck in Robin Hood, with a long brown robe that went all the way down to his feet. He had one of those hoods up over his head like all those friars have, and when he got up to the bench he pulled it off to be polite and that's when I saw he had his hair in a little afro. I remember thinking, "Nice touch." He asked if I minded if he sat down on the bench with me and I told him to help himself, wasn't my bench. He smoothed out the underside of his robe like he was a polite little girl making sure not to show her backside when she sat down.

He put his hand over his mouth and got that look people in charge get when they're about to tell you something ain't right about you and they are deciding whether it actually is a good idea for them to let you in on it. Finally he said, "Sir, I don't have a ticket for anybody for today. Which doesn't mean you aren't supposed to be here. It could just mean that the paperwork's got tied up someplace. It don't happen too often, but it happens."

"Where's here?" I said.

"This is a way station, there's lots of them. And that might be it. You might just have got the wrong pickup team. You maybe are supposed to be at another station. I'm going to go check that out. You wait right here. I'll be back as quick as I can." And off he goes back inside like the angels and pretty soon back he comes, but this time he's got <u>another</u> black guy with him and this one must really have been some kind of big shot because he was about twelve feet tall and had on a white robe, shining like it was made out of light. I was getting passed up the ladder which definitely meant something serious was going on. Anytime in my life I ever got passed up the ladder, there was always trouble waiting for me at the top rung. This one didn't bother sitting down. He just said he was sorry this was taking so long and thanked me for my patience and asked me a couple of other questions starting with did I realize I was dead. I wanted to say, "No fucking shit!" but knew that with this guy that was not the way to go, so all I said was, "Yes, sir. I do know that."

"You scared about that?"

"I'm LeRoy James. It's going to take more than being dead to scare me."

The Friar Tuck guy sucked in his breath like he just got kicked in the balls and got a look on his face like he was about to see something nobody could look at and not turn into stone or at least go completely insane. The big guy waited a second and his voice got real deep and he said, "We got that covered if it comes down to it." I realized that I had gone too far and didn't say anything else. Pissing off a powerful celestial being ain't a good move no matter how you slice it.

Then the big guy got this real distracted look and held his hand up to his ear and nodded. And then him and the Friar Tuck guy went off a little ways so I couldn't hear what they were saying and they whispered at each other for a good long time and then the big guy glanced at me once more and inside he went. Friar Tuck came over and sat back down and put his hand on my arm real gentle and says, "LeRoy, what I am going to tell you is maybe the most important thing you are ever going to go through, so you best pay close attention and do just what I say. You okay with that?"

"I'm listening."

"You going straight to the top to get this whole thing figured out. What was going on there with Michael, was God talking to him about you." (Michael is one of the archangels and that is the second most important job in heaven. Friar Tuck had my full attention after he said that.) "God told Michael he is going to handle this one himself. That hardly ever happens, so I can't give you all the etiquette you supposed to know because we don't got all that much experience with it. But what I can tell you is that no matter what, do not lie to God. If he asks you if you jacked off this morning and you did, you tell him yes, even if it embarrasses you. He already knows anyway. I will repeat that about the worst thing you can do to piss him off is to lie about something. You just go and ask Eve if you think that ain't so. Second thing is don't say anything until he is ready to hear it."

"How will I know when he's ready."

"You'll just know. You got any questions before I take you in there?"

"Am I supposed to bow or anything or take him a burnt offering or some frankincense or something?"

"No. That was in the old days when folks didn't know better. God is way past that these days. Just be a real person."

If being dead won't make you nervous, getting told you are about to meet God face to face sure ~~the fuck~~ will and I don't mind saying my palms was getting pretty sweaty. Friar Tuck asked me was I ready and I just looked at him and nodded. But what kind of question is that? You ready? To go see God?

TO BE CONTINUED

Brigard County, October 1975

Pewter-gray clouds twined in the sky and the rain came like pale wraiths, and wind in gusts came with it, so that the rain's shrouds billowed out before it and draped back, and billowed and sagged again. Overnight the rain had gathered in rills and rivulets, which by late morning washed gravel from the roads into yards and fields and flooded pastures and gardens and ran furious in roadside ditches and the river swelled. Eli looked out from his window to the barn where Jesse's trailer was withdrawn and where Emma stood at the barn door in a worn cloth coat, trying to tend her Coleman, to keep the fire outside but herself dry within the barn's dim harbor. Eli foraged about in his front closet and found an umbrella and put on a jacket and went out to her and told her let's go inside and warm up. I got coffee on. He let her argue with him for a while and then he turned off the gasoline and said I'll take you one at a time and she stopped arguing and called to Sarah Anne in the trailer to get her coat. Eli took the girl first. Her teeth chattered and she held herself close against him and clutched her coat tight around her neck, but the rain came full upon her even though he tried to hold the umbrella over just her. By the time he returned for Emma, his jacket was serving no purpose and his shirt clung to his skin. He said she might want to think about getting a change of clothes for her and the girl, the ones they had on were going to need dried out. She went in the trailer and came back with a trash bag swollen at the bottom and twisted at the neck and he took her across to the house, the umbrella of no more use on this second trip that it had been on the first.

Inside, he took them upstairs and showed them where there were towels and the extra room they could change clothes in. He went up to his room to dry himself and to change and remembered the coffee was perking and pulled on fresh jeans and went back down barefoot and bare chested, toweling himself. The coffee had just started bubbling over, the stove's blue flames fluttering yellow and sparking against the brown foam. He turned off the burner and was setting cups out when Emma came down. He asked her how they took their coffee and would they like something to eat. Again she tried to argue and again he talked past that and said he was just getting ready to make his dinner, he always ate his big meal about this time and all he was going to do was fry some pork chops and potatoes and it wouldn't take any longer to make a few more, being as the fry pan he used was pretty big. Emma said at least let her fix it, just tell her where everything was. He told her the pork chops was in the refrigerator and the potatoes under the sink and where to find the bacon grease. Emma set to work and he picked up his coffee and said he was going to go take a shower and finish getting dressed.

He met Sarah Anne on the stairs. She wore a faded house dress limp across her slender hips, the dress wrinkled from its passage stuffed down in the trash bag, her hair in tangled tendrils. She looked at his bare shoulders and flushed and looked another way and turned sideways to let him pass. She smelled like the rain. He asked her did she feel better and she said softly she did. He went on up, feeling her looking at his back all the way to the landing. He walked along the hall until he heard her stepping down and went back and called to her would she like a comb. She looked up and nodded. He told her to wait right there and got a comb from the bathroom. She flushed again and said thank you when he handed it to her. He told her there was a mirror in the front room and she took the comb and flitted down the stairs like a sparrow flying off with a stolen scrap of bread.

When he came down, Emma was forking the pork chops onto a platter. The table was set and a bowl of fried potatoes in the center and sliced bread. He said it was nice of her to do all that, he most of the time just got a plate and took it in and put on the television while he ate. He said sometimes he didn't even use a plate, just ate out of the pan. If it wasn't something too greasy, sometimes he didn't even use a fork. Emma told Sarah Anne to pour more coffee and the three of them sat and passed around the food. Eli said when you work nights you have to have your big meal in the middle of the day, but he never could get used to it. Makes every day seem like a Sunday and after you eat, you should be taking a long nap, but you got things to do. Emma recalled how Jesse worked nights for a while and it took him a couple of hours after he got home before he could go to sleep and was it the same for Eli. Eli said it was. He just watched television until it went off the air or sat outside when the weather was good until he got settled down enough. And then you end up sleeping until close to noon. By the time you get a couple chores done, it's time to go to work again.

Sarah Anne kept her eyes down and took tiny bites, her small hands fluttering over her plate and then hiding in her lap. He asked her if it was warm enough, he could turn up the heat if she was still cold. She tilted her head without looking up and said she was okay.

Emma tried not to look around at the room. Eli said he knew it was a mess, but in his experience, it only got so bad and then settled into the way it planned to stay for just about forever and he'd got used to it. He said he sometimes cleaned up a little bit, but he was afraid of doing too much in case the only thing keeping this old house together was that the dirt was caked up like concrete and the termites was holding hands. Sarah Anne giggled and blushed.

They heard the Fleetwood come into the driveway, and through the window, Eli watched Jesse drive over to the barn and he and his son go in and after a while come back and run across the yard to the house in their yellow slickers, their boots splashing in the pools they ran through. They knocked on the door and Eli yelled for them to come in.

Jesus, Jesse said and wiped his face with his sleeve. Eli got up and took a dishtowel hanging from the stove's door and handed it to him. Jesus, he said again. He wiped his face and said he never remembered when it rained this hard and gave Ashley the towel. Eli asked them were they hungry. Jesse said they already ate, but that coffee smelled good. Emma got them cups and poured everyone fresh coffee and they sat. Ashley lit a cigarette and Eli pushed an ashtray toward him to set it in, but the boy kept it dangling in the corner of his mouth and squinted through the smoke rising into his eyes.

Jesse said it was a good thing they got the roof fixed before this happened, it could have flooded the whole inside and they would have had to start all over. He said they were coming to turn on the electric in the morning and then they could move in and it was a sweet deal for everybody what with Sweeny putting up the money to fix the house and outfit the still and they could live in it for nothing long as they kept the liquor coming. And even better, Sweeney was taking care of the selling end and Jesse was going to get half of what he took in. Sweeney said them niggers across the river wouldn't be able to get enough. All Jesse had to do was keep the juice flowing. He said him and his wife was grateful for everything Eli did, putting them up and all, while they got situated. Eli let what Jesse said about niggers pass and said don't worry about it, he was glad for the company.

They finished their coffee and talked for a while. Jesse stood up and looked out the window and said the rain had slacked off and they better get to packing up before it started up again. He went out, his family following. Eli watch them fold the Coleman and put it up. Jesse backed the Fleetwood into the barn and he and Ashley undid the trailer's wheel chocks and wrestled the trailer onto the hitch and set the safety chains. They took up the lawn chairs set out on the barn's packed-earth floor and folded them and found room in the back of the wagon in which to stow them. And they went on like that, packing and rearranging and going into the trailer and coming back out carrying some domestic object and sometimes putting it in the back of the wagon and sometimes returning it to the trailer. And then Jesse stopped and threw up his arms and spun around from what he was doing and faced Emma, who stabbed her finger in his face, and they argued in pantomime in the gray afternoon, the barn's open doors framing them like actors in a silent film. Jesse came stomping back across the yard to the house.

Jesus Christ he said. Fucking women. He said he knew Eli done more than enough and if it was just up to him he wouldn't ask, but Emma didn't think the girl should be staying in the house before it was better finished what with the cold weather coming on and like he said, if it was up to him he wouldn't ask. But was there a way Eli could see his way clear to letting the girl stay here for another week or so, just until they got some furniture in the place and had the heater going. Won't be but a week or so. You got my word on that.

Eli said hell it didn't make any difference to him, he wasn't hardly here that much anyway and quiet as she was, she sure wouldn't be any kind of a nuisance. Jesse said Emma made him say Sarah Anne could earn her keep doing something around the house and was there a little something she could do. Eli told Jesse to look around. What do you think?

Brigard County, July, 1993

The sunset reflected off the river's sheen and glowed smoldering and muted upon the house and upon Harmon on the ground and LeRoy up on the ladder working at the old paint, his scraper raucously squeaking. Harmon called up didn't he know that was about as annoying a sound as he ever heard and LeRoy said he knew. It pretty much sounded like a duck shitting sandpaper eggs. Harmon said they should call it a day.

LeRoy came down and reminded him that when the parts came in, Harmon was going to be on his own, and he had had about enough of this shit work, him being a master mechanic and all, and this menial labor being way beneath his station. Harmon told him he didn't hear him calling it a shit job when she paid him. LeRoy wiped sweat from his forehead with a red bandana and said he was right about that. It's only shit work when you're doing it. Harmon said he was going to get cleaned up and go sit by the river. LeRoy said it sounded good to him and he'd be down in a little bit and went up to his apartment.

When he returned, Edna and Harmon were sitting in the Adirondacks, looking across the water to where the sky glazed the far bank liquid red. LeRoy walked down to join them. Edna handed him a beer from the cooler and told him Harmon said it would be a few more days before they could start painting. LeRoy said he knew it took them longer to finish scraping than they thought it would. She said she didn't care. She knew they weren't slackers. They sat and drank their beers and watched the light fade and the sunset drift from reds and yellows, down through dark blues and purples and then to black, the sun a darkening drum sliding down behind the colors. A bright star appeared, downriver and low. LeRoy said did Edna ever wish on a star and she said not since she was a little girl. LeRoy said he made a wish every night. Edna asked him what he wished for and LeRoy said he wished them fucking boat parts would get here. Edna switched on the electric lantern. LeRoy said why did they think they made them to look like old-time kerosene lamps. Harmon said did that mean LeRoy was working up a story to explain why that was. LeRoy said who? Me?

Edna wanted to know what they were talking about. Harmon told her she didn't know it but LeRoy here thought he was some kind of master storyteller, and he acted like you had to coax him into it, but all he was doing was waiting for somebody to ask him. LeRoy said he didn't know no story about why lanterns looked like that. He just asked because it came into his head that there wasn't any reason for a fake lantern to look like a real one and they had to admit it was kind of dumb.

Tell a different one then Edna said.

I need a beer or two more to get started on. A master like me has got to be in the exact right mood.

Harmon, who was slightly drunk already, handed him two beers. They watched a barge slip down on the darkened river, its running lights reflected brown in the water, its engines churning in a visceral grumble. A crewman called something to a shipmate. LeRoy said things were louder at night, especially scary things and Harmon said here we go. LeRoy began his story.

Back home there was these two half sisters. Their mother Jemima got married twice. First time was to a preacher. Hell of a preacher too. He would come on while the choir was still singing and he went right on with them, swaying and got his arms up in

244 • No Place to Pray

the air and his big old black leather Bible in one hand and a white handkerchief in the other for wiping the sweat off his face. That's how hard he'd be singing. And he put out a lot of sweat preaching too. I tell you that man could hypnotize you whether you was a believer or not. He saved a lot of people. I seen him one time call forth sinners at a camp meeting and the worst gambler there ever was came up to the altar just a bawling his eyes out and he let spill out of his gambler clothes about every kind of sin there is and he laid it all right up there on the altar. A straight razor and a pistol and a deck of marked cards and a half pint of Jim Beam and another deck of cards with dirty pictures. The preacher covered up them cards with the dirty pictures soon as he seen them because there was little kids around, but he left all the rest of it for a lesson for the congregation on what sin could do to you. That gambler just kept on wailing and weeping and said God could have it all and he wasn't gonna do none of that no more, just save him from the flames of hell. He kept yelling, I promise, I promise. O God, don't let me burn.

One Sunday that preacher was preaching so hard he had a heart attack and died and left his Jemima with a baby girl and no money at all and the church had to get a new preacher and she had to move out of the manse and didn't have no idea what to do or where to go. So she decides she will pray on it, her thinking praying is about the only hope she got and it was kind of like a reflex, her being a preacher's widow and all. But you got to be careful about that kind of thing because even though it don't work most of the time, when it does work, it's got a power you can't never expect what it can do.

LeRoy stopped and asked Edna would she hand him another beer. He opened it and sat looking out over the river. He said it was pleasant sitting out like this in the evening and it was just perfect warm enough. He said did they ever wonder if fish sleep.

Edna said go on.

Go on what?

With the story. What'd she pray for?

Oh yeah, kind of got lost there for a minute. Well, old Jemima takes her baby girl and goes way out in the woods and it's a real quiet night and she can hear every little animal that's stirring the leaves and some bigger creatures poking around in the dark too. She can hear the leaves falling down, it's so quiet. And not just when they hit the ground, hears them brushing the air on the way down too. It being so quiet tonight is what made me remember about her. So she finds herself a clearing and waits for the moon to come up so she can be bathed in its pure light and be glorified by its power, only she didn't think that all the way through because if she would have remembered her Bible, she would have remembered that the moon is the lesser light of the night and nothing good comes out of the night and that goes for lesser lights too. Anything that is the lesser is going to be real fucked up, kind of like it's got a inferiority complex. Anyway, after a while up comes that moon, but it's got a strange cast to it, like it's red and silver at the same time, and she'd look at and it would be red as blood and then she'd squint a little bit and it would be like a pure silver goblet some Chinese slave girl just polished. She gives up trying to figure out what omens that might be portending, and you know before you even get started that that was going to turn out to be a big mistake. One rule you got to have is don't never turn your back on no omens. You're just asking for trouble.

LeRoy said he had to go to the bathroom and stood up and said he'd be back in a minute. Edna said couldn't he finish the story first. He told her it was a pretty long story and he couldn't hold it for the whole time and started up for the house. She told him why didn't he just go over there in the weeds and LeRoy said that would be pretty ignorant wouldn't it? She said she'd seen men piss

before. He walked beyond the reach of the light and unzipped and
went, the hiss gliding on the warm evening air back to Edna and
Harmon. LeRoy returned and sat. That's better he said. Edna told
him to go on with the story, her voice beginning to thicken.

LeRoy said okay, but give him a second to remember just
where he was, he wanted to make sure he got it right. Edna told
him he stopped when he got to the omens. LeRoy said he could see
she was in a hell of a hurry but you can't rush a good story. Then
he went on.

So Jemima gets down on her knees in the moonlight and she
prays and says to God he had took pretty good care of her and
the baby up until now and she knew he was only testing her and
she didn't want to take that too lightly, but you can't eat a test and
please send somebody to marry her and whoever he sends she will
take that as a sign that she's supposed to marry them. She goes on
praying like that and she had it in her mind when she went out in
the woods that she would pray until dawn and that would show
God how sincere she was, and how strong her faith was, but it was
starting to get pretty cold and the baby kept waking up and fussing
and she would have to quiet her down before she could go back
to praying and it was getting to be a pretty hard night. And then
she had a real dumb thought. She didn't say it out loud. She just
thought to herself, I wish to fuck he'd either give me an answer or
send a goddamn sign. And right that second there appeared before
her a man who was naked all except for a feather loincloth and a fur
hat made out of about a half dozen different kinds of animal skins,
including skunk. He's got all color stripes painted on his face and
brass earrings and rope sandals and he's holding a scepter made out
of driftwood with a boar's skull nailed to the top and the skull's got
these big tusks on both sides wound up in curlicues and red eyes
blinking at her even though it'd been dead a long, long time. And
she says, shit.

Jemima sees that she is really fucked, because you can't make God a promise and then break it and she is going to have to marry this voodoo witch doctor and she thinks about what that is going to be like and she says oh shit again because the next thing she gets into her head is what he's got underneath that loincloth and if it's forked at the end and how bad is it going to hurt. What she don't know is he has got all kinds of powers she can't even imagine and one of them is reading minds and he says to her I aint going to hurt you. You are my beloved. And she falls for it right away and he takes her off to his secret cavern way back in the woods and he's cooing sweet things in her ear the whole way and what she doesn't know is that he is putting a spell on her and by the time they get there she is thinking he is of a lovely countenance and she is in love. And that night she conceives and next summer she's got another baby girl. You got to think about this for a minute. There's two sisters and one of them is the seed of a preacher and the other one is the seed of a witch doctor. You just know there's going to be trouble down the line with a combination like that.

LeRoy stopped and asked if there was any of that Crown Royal left. He didn't know about them, but he was about ready to take the next step. Edna said there was and she would go get it, but she didn't want to miss any of the story and don't start up again until she got back. LeRoy said he'd wait. She struggled to rise from the Adirondack and giggled and said she didn't think she needed the Crown Royal. Harmon said he did. She went up and came back with the bottle and three glasses. She kept dropping the glasses on the grass and picking them up and dropping them again and finally yelled down she needed a hand and LeRoy went up and helped her. Harmon said he'd take some of that. He took the whiskey and poured a shot in LeRoy's glass and more than a shot in his own. Edna said go back to the story and LeRoy did, but unwound the tale teasingly, a little bit at a time. He told about how them two little girls was inseparable and would touch their foreheads together and laugh and then when somebody came into the room, they would make like they were laughing over something in a picture book instead of the thoughts they just passed between them. He jumped around to when they were a little older and drove the old man down the road crazy because he tried to get them to sit on his lap and the one girl summoned down an angel to tell him God was real displeased with what he was doing and then right after the angel left, the other sister summoned up a demon who breathed fire on the old cocksucker and scorched his face and half burnt off his clothes and the old man up and threw himself into the swamp to put out the fire and drowned instead. It was a terrible death, the old man sucking mud down into his lungs and him thinking at the last second he could have cried out to God for forgiveness but couldn't with his breath all clogged up like that and his last dying thought was shit, I am going straight to hell and he went totally insane at the moment of his death.

LeRoy kept on going. Things the girls did when they was in school and then when they was becoming young women and how they seduced the town mayor and then blackmailed him to keep them from spreading around what he did and how they performed animal sacrifices. Every once in a while LeRoy would meditate on how you would think good and evil would be pure enemies but these girls was living proof that good and evil are just two sides of the same coin. Like there are animal sacrifices in the Bible and that's supposed to be good, but let a witch hold an animal-sacrifice party and she gets strung the fuck up, even though they are the exact same thing. Something got killed and burned up either way. And if that wasn't enough to declare the truth of good and evil being just different parts of the same thing, just think about what are the two things in the whole universe you absolutely do not want to piss off. One of them is God and the other one is the devil and that pretty much says it all. He told about the sisters going off to the big city and was on their way to getting famous and then the real story was about to start and the sisters was going to meet their match and you would never in a million years guess who that was. And everywhere in the telling LeRoy laid in sinister eyes shining in the darkness and foul mists and signs in the sky and evil characters slinking in the shadows.

Then he said he was out of gas and couldn't finish it tonight.

Edna said he had to and he said he was just too tired. She leaned her elbow on the chair's arm and again said he had to finish the story. Her elbow slipped and she hit herself above the eye with the butt of her palm. She laughed and said she thought she was drunk. LeRoy said that made two of them. He told her he would tell her the rest of the story tomorrow and she pouted like a child and asked did he promise and he said he promised. He worked himself up from the chair and took another beer from the cooler and said if she didn't mind, he'd come down in the morning and clean up. He said goodnight and Harmon slurred goodnight back and LeRoy went up toward the garage, his white shirt dimly luminous in the moonlight, marking his path as he ambled and meandered across the yard as if he had been ordained for no other purpose than to wander.

Edna got up and stood unsteady and Harmon almost got up, but fell in the limestone and said fuck. Edna giggled again and helped him and together they made it up to the house, their arms across each other's backs, Harmon stumbling and falling once more, Edna nearly falling with him, but not quite.

In the house, Harmon dropped heavily on the bed, one leg dangling over the side. Edna undressed and kneeled down naked and untied Harmon's shoes and pulled them off and began working at his pants, her fingers oddly thick, so that his belt became a difficult thing of great complexity and she could not undo it. She said for him to help her and he gently brushed away her fumbling fingers and tried to sit up but could not. She stood and leaned over and kissed him, but what came into her mouth was not him, but the Crown Royal. She put her breast to his mouth and passed it teasingly over his face. He snored and she stood, a bit of drool cold and sticky on her breast. She told him to wake up and laid her hand on his cheek, which he waved at in his sleep as if brushing away a fly. She kissed him again, resting her hand lightly in his groin, but from where he had gone, there would in this evening be no return. She groped around in the pale light and found her robe and put it on and went out again into the night. She stood unsteadily on the porch and felt her breath quivering in her chest and her hands trembling. There was a pack of cigarettes and a lighter on the table. She lit one and sat and smoked it part way down. Flicking the butt out into the yard, she saw LeRoy's light still on. She arose and crossed the stretch of damp grass to the garage and went up the outside stairs and knocked.

At midmorning she came down and back to the porch where Harmon sat with a cup of coffee, his bloodshot eyes looking past her. He told her the coffee was still hot and she started in without saying anything back. He took her hand as she went by and she held it for a moment before going in.

The apartment door opened again and LeRoy came and Harmon told him too about the coffee. LeRoy went inside and came back with a cup and sat. After a while LeRoy said he thought he needed something more than coffee. Harmon said maybe there was a little Crown Royal left and they went down to the river and there was some, but not much. They poured what there was of it into their cups. The beer bottles strewn about the chairs winked elfin-like and mean in the harsh morning sunlight as they came in and out of the shadows the two friends cast.

LeRoy said I don't feel much like scraping paint.

Me neither.

You mad?

No. All for one and one for all, right?

Billie?

What?

She made me promise to finish the story.

So finish it.

Which one was it and how far did I get?

Tabernacle Parish, August, 1963

Whiskey awakened once more from the same nightmare: the heat charring his face, the blue flames pulsing in the systole and diastole of fire, scorching him to the black of soot and scarring him with a many-pointed star clinging to his neck and face. He touched the star's webby threads to assure himself that the burning had been only a dream, that the star was indeed a scar and not a fresh wound. But then he thought only-a-dream don't matter, because the hurt in a dream is as bad as any hurt you can get in the world.

Sometimes in his dreams the star on his neck was a primal leech-like thing risen up from the muck of a swamp to suck the blood out of him and all of his strength with it. Every time the dream went that way, he awoke feeling like the star was humping him and he felt beaten and diminished and afraid to go back to sleep.

He reached out in the dark and rested his fingers on Agnes's bare milk-white shoulder, lightly so as not to disturb her sleep, the touch a kiss sent through his fingers and just that hint of a kiss was enough to whip up his heart so that it raced in his chest and he had to clench his fists tight and roll the other way to keep from cloaking himself around her and to keep the sound of his heart from awakening her.

He slipped from the covers and sat on the side of the bed and listened to the dark, not the sounds of the things that lived or came alive in the dark, the insects and night birds, the house's clapboards creaking, the soughing of the air as it eddied and rose in pockets of warmth and chill, setting the trees gently shaking and coughing like a sick old woman. But listened to the dark itself, the groaning so low that Whiskey had to still his own breath to hear it, how it opened up cracks in itself, inviting him in, murmuring come unto me and lay your burden down. When he let go his breath again, it warbled from his throat like an injured bird, bruised and swollen.

He stood up and gathered his clothes and picked up his shoes but then laid the shoes back down on the floor and slipped barefooted into the kitchen and set the clothes on the table and stood there naked, not moving, feeling the darkness seep into his skin and down through his flesh, marking him deep inside like ink drawing itself on his bones. Standing in the dark he thought of all of the dead things he ever saw in his life, dead animals and dead people, those newly dead and those dead for a long time, and it came into his head that every time he had seen a dead thing, it seemed to be looking up at him from a deep well of misery and what the dead thing wanted above all else was to still be alive. Whiskey wondered how it could be that such creatures could be so wrong, how they could have forgotten the pain of being alive and how could it be that they might wish to be in such agony ever again.

He dressed in the dark and went to the screen door and let the cool night air waft about him and the smells of the night with it, the damp smell of grass and the thick sweetness of honeysuckle and the terrorized smell of small prey animals being put to bay. The screen door creaked as he opened it and he hesitated, listening to hear if his opening of this door into the world outside had awakened either of them, but the house remained quiet. He stepped onto the porch, the grain of its worn wooden floor speaking to him through the soles of his feet like a letter someone had written to him in delicate, swooping handwriting. Whiskey thought about how in his entire life, he had never written a letter to anyone. What was that like? To sit at a table with a pencil and put down the day and say in the letter Dear Agnes. And then wonder what to say next and then to say it. What if it was wrong what you said? What did people do after they sent a letter and then thought that what they said was not what they really meant, knowing there was no way to take it back once it was in the mail? It wasn't just the words in letters you can't take back. You can't take back mistakes either, undo an unkind word or heal the bones you just broke in another man's face or what you stole from somebody you didn't even know. Or what they stole from you.

He picked up the shotgun lying across the arms of the rocker and leaned it up against the house's yellow clapboards and sat down and began the endless rocking that was all that filled his days now, rocking through the long dark winter and through spring and into this dead summer of air too thick to breathe. He flexed his bare toes so that they lifted him and rolled him back. He shooed a mosquito away from his face and thought of all of the things in the world his rocking mimicked, the baby in its cradle, the waves in the ocean, a dragonfly swaying at the top of a long thin weed. He remembered the different ways he had himself rocked in this life. As a child lying in the bottom of a boat, lulled into daydreams filled with sun and water. Staggering home from a night in town, the stars spinning when he looked up and the road under his feet seesawing when he looked down. Him and Agnes locked together, the slickness of being inside her and the slickness of their sweat mingling as they slid back and forth across one another. Her and LeRoy rocking him in the dirt to snuff out the pale blue fire, its ravenous tongue lapping up all of the parts of him that he had been proud of and leaving him forever stained with this ragged scar.

A blackbird tentatively chirped from the plum tree, the center of its eye black within the orange circle of its gaze, its eyes like polished stones liquid with black light, hard as his used-up soul, the bird shaking its voice like a ghost trebling a warning in a corridor that ran the long course of distance between everything that was alive and everything that was dead, as if the bird were saying I am

the archangel's shadow come to lead you home. The bird shaking
out its voice meant the day was almost here and the inevitability of
its coming was nothing he could stop, not a thing that could yield
to his will even if he had any will left.

Whiskey got up from his chair and took up the shotgun and
reached into the rafters of the porch roof where he kept his just-
in-case shells and took two down and loaded both of the gun's
chambers as the blackbird released itself into full song, the pale
light of the sun beginning its pitiless odyssey across the sky.
Whiskey stepped from the porch onto the damp grass, the dew
baptizing his feet, and walked straight and tall to the springhouse,
through the door with its still un-repaired hinge, now a thing that
would never be made right. Whiskey thought of all of the things
in his life he had left undone, each of them a broken promise.
He went into the springhouse and sat on the bench, the smell of
vegetables and fruit rotting on the shelves around him beckoning
him on to this thing he was about do to. A cricket chirped. A frog
splashed into the well. The swamp maple gently brushed a branch
against the wall outside as if it were trying to reach in and caress
Whiskey's cheek and croon gently like a mother that it was all right,
just go ahead. She would hold him in her arms while he did it.
Whiskey stood up and stuck the gun's cold muzzle beneath his chin
and pulled both triggers.

The thunder of the gun rolled in and Agnes awoke and thought of
LeRoy and would he be afraid of the lightening and remembered
there was little of the child left in him and he would scoff at the
storm. But there was no sound of wind and no hiss of rain and
thus no thunder other than the absence on the other side of the
bed and she came up from the bed and ran to the boy's room but
he was already pulling on his pants. He wriggled from her grasp
and darted through the kitchen and out into the world, Agnes
racing after him, screaming for him to stop, their bare feet dimpling

the wet grass, their arms flailing parodies of each other, Agnes's reaching to embrace and shield the boy from this unbearable thing and LeRoy's pumping for speed. He made it to the springhouse first and by the time she caught up, he was standing stock still in the doorway, his head canted like a crow deciding if the lump of carrion on the floor was worth pecking at.

O Jesus Agnes said and said it again and it was all she could say. She wrapped LeRoy's gangly body up in hers and he fought her for a moment and then molded into her as if she still carried him in her womb. They stumbled together back through the wet grass and sat on the porch steps. Agnes held her boy and considered what she could do and thought Whiskey would take care of them and then remembered and was ashamed of herself and again said O Jesus, hopelessness snaking cold and poisonous through her veins.

She told LeRoy to get dressed and run and get Pastor Johnson and he told her it would take too long and she should come with him, but she told him no, she would be all right and somebody had to stay. In her mind she thought in case dogs set upon the body in the springhouse but she told LeRoy it was in case the deputies came there would be somebody here to tell them what happened. Go put your shoes on and get a shirt she told him and he went in and came out dressed as she had said. Run she told him and he went off and Agnes watched him until he went around the bend and she went inside the house.

LeRoy knocked on the pastor's door and his wife answered and he told her his mother sent him to get the pastor and she told him he had gone last night to the church to work on his sermon and if it got too late, he would sometimes just sleep there and was it something she could help him with. LeRoy told her no and went back out to the street running and on toward the church until his breath gave way and he had to slow to a walk. A white man came toward him and LeRoy looked him in the eye and didn't even see he was there and the white man went to backhand that snotty little nigger and then thought better of it and just muttered to himself that little motherfucker. Someday he was going to wish he was white. LeRoy went on and came to the church.

The wide red door was locked. LeRoy went around back and up the stairs leading to the door into the pastor's study and knocked and waited and knocked again, but no one came. He tried the knob but the door was locked. He stepped back toward the graveyard and yelled up to the pastor's window and considered throwing a stone at the window, but did not. Asleep or awake the pastor would have heard him. He was not here.

LeRoy went through the painted wooden gate to the graveyard and looked behind the sagging old oak where the pastor sometimes went to pray, sitting on the ground with his Bible in his hands and his eyes closed, but he wasn't there either and LeRoy thought maybe the pastor and he had missed each other, that the pastor had got up early and taken some other route home to give him time to practice his sermon. He thought about going back to the pastor's house, but if he had gone some other place and LeRoy missed him again, his mother would be that much longer alone. He thought of Miss Wells.

Miss Wells's front door was open behind the screen door and LeRoy ran up panicky with hope and went to knock on the screen door's frame when he saw them all the way through the living room to the kitchen table upon which Miss Wells lay, a shiny white nightie pulled up over her hips and the pastor standing naked before her, her taut legs clutching his back. Even from the porch he could hear her sucking air in so hard it sounded like she was dying and fighting for just one more breath and the pastor with his hands spread on the table at her sides, his arms straight and rigid, his veins bulging like bark on weathered tree limbs, a rattling gurgle deep in his throat as if he were trying to cough up some feral thing that had taken residence there, his jaundiced haunches thrusting and sweat dripping down from his face onto the firm belly of LeRoy's teacher.

Tabernacle Parish, 1967

Among other injuries in the years after Whiskey died, Agnes had her jaw and both eye sockets broken and her shoulder dislocated. She was raped more than half a dozen times before finally a customer choked her to death in the cab of his pickup because he didn't like the way she was blowing him. He shoved her out with his booted foot, zipped up his jeans, and slammed shut the door. As the tires spun gravel into Agnes's surprised dead eyes, he muttered to himself that he could have got that good at home for free. When he remembered the money, he stopped the truck and went back and looked around under the stars for her purse and took from it that which she had stolen from him. And a little bit more for his trouble.

The Amazing Adventures of LeRoy James

I Get Out of a Real Bad Scrape

So when I left you off, Friar Tuck had just asked me was I ready to go in and see God and all I did was nod "Yes." We went in the gate side by side. The angels I told you about closed the gate behind us. Then the light-skinned angel took out his keys and locked the gate up and him and the dark-skinned angel gave me a little wave and flew off. I watched them until they was just little dots way up in the mists and then they was gone.

Friar Tuck took me down a path that was paved with gold. At first there was just the path and then there was some little temples and some houses, everything made out of gold or silver and all crusted up with precious jewels. There was diamonds and emeralds and rubies all over the place, even hanging down off of some little trees like they was just apples or peaches anybody could pick if they wanted to. And there was plenty of folks around to pick them if that was in their minds. All kinds of folks. People in ordinary clothes like you would see on the street, just sort of window shopping. And people in robes and other kinds of old-fashioned clothes. I saw a Japanese geisha girl sitting beside a little pond with about a million silver fish in it and I wouldn't of been surprised if them fish was made out of real silver and wasn't just the color of silver. One place had about a hundred India women with them little red dots on their foreheads all singing some foreign song. They was in a big circle and all hunched down on their knees. Every once in a while they would stop singing and all shout together something that sounded like Selah, but I couldn't be sure because they didn't say it almost mean the way I remember the preacher saying it in church. Off

to the side in a field of white flowers there was a bunch of hairy
Christians in white robes dancing like banshees and singing that
chantey song they got and banging on tambourines. One place we
came to had a river running across it and a bunch of Baptists all
lined up on the shores getting ready for their turn with a preacher
who was standing in the water with a white suit on. One by one
he immersed them and when they come up out of the water, they
had golden haloes spinning around their heads. This was turning
out to be one fascinating adventure full of things I never seen
before. I was starting to be glad about being dead, otherwise it
wouldn't of happened that I got to see all those things.

Friar Tuck led me in between all those buildings and temples
and into a golden meadow that had a gazebo made out of white
lattice wood all covered up with wild roses right in the middle
of it. Friar Tuck said, "I can't go no further than this with you,
LeRoy. The rest of it you have do it on your own. This is your
very own lonesome valley. The door is around on the other side."
He turned around the way we came and started back down the
golden path but he didn't get too far before he faded out, a little
bit at a time until he disappeared, and I was all by myself, just me
and a little breeze and some birds chirping away.

The golden path curved around the gazebo and I took it
until I came to the door. It was a lot further to that door than I
thought it would be. That path kept getting longer and longer the
more I walked on it, so that even though the gazebo only looked
on the outside like it was the same size as any gazebo in the park,
it must have been a mile across. I stood there kind of rocking
back and forth trying to decide if I should go in or not because
of what Friar Tuck said about waiting for God to make the
first move. Then a deep voice come out from the depths of the
gazebo. "Come unto me," it said. That voice went right inside me,
the way loud music does when the bass is turned all the way up

and makes you vibrate. No ~~fucking~~ doubt about it. That was the
very voice of God talking to me. I took myself a big deep breath
and stepped inside. It was dark in there, not real dark, but enough
darker so I had to blink my eyes for a second to get them dialed in
to the different light. I expected the inside to be all filled up with
heavenly vessels and candlesticks like it was the granddaddy of
all temples. But all there was inside was a tongue-in-groove wood
floor painted pure white and a white bench where God was sitting
looking away from the door. He said, "Fear not. Just come on
over." I started going to the bench and when I was about halfway
there God turned around and looked me right straight in the eye
and I fucking near had a heart attack because God was <u>black</u>, just
like Friar Tuck and the angels. And not just regular black, but
pure dark-skinned black, like pure-blooded <u>African</u> black. Black
as onyx. Once again, it was a good thing I was dead, because after
you are dead, you don't shit no more at all because you don't need
to eat anything to keep alive or I would have for sure shit myself
right on the spot.

God laughed and said, "You'll get used to it quick enough."

Friar Tuck was right. I could tell from the way God laughed
that it was all right for me to take a turn and I said, "How come in
all the pictures of you, you are white?"

He laughed again. "I don't have control on the pictures
people want to make. They see what they want to see. But up here
there is no want-to-see. There is only what there is. You ought
to see some of the looks I get from rednecks when it dawns on
them what's going on. Sometimes I go down to the front gate
and meet some of them myself. My favorite was when Jefferson
Davis's time come and he waltzed in like the Queen of Sheba and
handed me his hat and coat and told me to fetch him a bourbon
and branch and said how this place sure did seem like home and
how considerate it was for the Heavenly Creator to provide him

his very own house nigger. He could see how he was sure going to enjoy his eternity. I handed him back his hat and coat and said, "These are yours, not mine, except I'm pretty sure you aren't going to need anything to keep you warm where you're going. And then I presented myself in my full glory and he got <u>real</u> white and fell down before me and laid himself flat out on the ground and wept like a little girl. Sometimes I send for him and ask him if he thinks he can find a way to redeem himself and he goes into this long speech about how everybody including preachers had told him from when he was a little boy that Negroes was just fulfilling the divine order of things and what he did was what he thought was his duty to protect the order of things and he really never did want to do it and if he could have another chance, he'd do better and whatever else it took to make things right but please don't send him back there where it was <u>really</u> bad because the next bad news he got right after I sent him to his just reward is that the devil is black too. You talk about torment! But I have no intentions of ever letting him off the hook. I just bring him up here to play with him a little is all." Then he patted his hand on the bench and said, "Here, you have a seat. There's something I have to tell you."

This wasn't looking too good and I got a picture in my head of me sharing a room with Jefferson Davis. But God laughed again and said, "Nah, nothing like that, at least not right now. Just sit down. There's something I have to explain to you and it's going to take a while is all." Man, you can't keep nothing from God. Soon's you think it, he got it. The only thing you can do is try not to think about it. You think that's easy? Just try it sometime. Try being someplace where you are about half scared to death and don't go thinking about what's scaring you. You pretty much <u>can't</u>.

Anyway, I sat down. God had a book in his hand. Don't ask me where he got the book from, because it wasn't on the bench and there wasn't any flash of light and puff of smoke where it materialized out of and I didn't see him reach into a pocket and pull it out. It was just there.

"This is your book of days."

"That one little book for everybody?"

"Nope. Just for you. Everybody's got their own book." God held it up and bent the back of the book and let his thumb slide over the pages and let them riffle so I could see. Every page had something wrote on it except there was a lot of empty pages at the end.

"That's a lot of writing," I said. "Where do you get the time to do any controlling of the winds and the tides and perform miracles?"

"I don't do the writing. I just do the judging. I have a whole army of angels to do the writing for me."

"Does it say where I'm going to end up?"

"That isn't what we're worried about right now. But if it was, you are right about fifty-fifty. There's some rough stuff in here you ought to give some thought to changing. Put you more over in the plus column. But we got a different problem right now and that is your book doesn't say nothing about you supposing to be here on this day."

I didn't say anything to that. And it didn't surprise me too much neither. I don't mean I wasn't surprised like I expected him to say I wasn't supposed to be there or predicted it. I mean I was starting to get over being surprised at anything that was happening. Where God lives is one ~~fucking~~ weird ~~ass~~ place and I must have been getting used to it.

"I'll show you," God said. He opened up the book to the last page that had writing on it and let me read a little bit. I couldn't read the whole page, because when I tried to, there was little shadows floating in and out over the words. He didn't tell me, but I could see that that was God blocking out the parts he didn't want me to see. But the part that he did let me see had the date for that day and it said beside the date: "LeRoy got in a little over his head and didn't see the band of Arab warriors and they was on him. He took off across the desert and the band of warriors was right behind him."

"That's exactly what happened," I said. "How does that prove you got the wrong man?"

"It doesn't. What does is there's no final line across the bottom of the page. If this was your last day, then whichever angel who writes your story down is supposed to draw a line under it with ink and write THE END underneath that. Then he is supposed to hand the book over to Gabriel." (In case you don't know it, Gabriel is another archangel and his job is to kill people and send them up for judgment.) "But look what comes after that day."

He handed me the book and sure enough underneath the day I got chased by the Arabs there was the next day's date and a empty space. No line. No THE END. God said, "They were getting ready for tomorrow, which means you wasn't supposed to end up dead on them rocks."

"So what happened?"

"That's what we're trying to figure out. I got the Archangel Michael working on it. How about we take a little walk while we wait for him to get back to me?"

What was I going to say to that? "No thanks, God, you go on ahead. I think I'll just sit here in this gazebo for a spell. It's so nice and cool in here and the wild roses smell so good"? No way you are going to say something like that. You are going to say, "Yes, suh, that sound like a real fine thing to do, suh, take a walk around." Which I did, except for the "suh," because I didn't want God picking up no sarcasm from me, even if it was a habit I most of the time can't help.

That "little" walk turned out to be something else. He had me walking up long mountain passes and deep valleys and prairies and on beaches with orange sand and ancient, mysterious jungles and anything else you can think of, including more streets paved with gold. Alongside one of them gold streets there was a palace made out of ivory and jade. There was bunches of Arab women sitting around in them baggy pants they got that show off their asses and halter tops that don't leave a lot to the imagination and I thought, like any red-blooded American would have done, "Them's some damn fine pieces a ass," and God gave me about the dirtiest look I have ever got and I could see how one look from God could turn you to stone and that I better get my mind on something else if I didn't want that to happen to me so I started thinking again about those pictures where God is white and I remembered about Jesus. Before I could think I just came out with it, "But Jesus is white."

"What are you talking about?" (Like he had to ask!)

"You being white in the pictures is one thing, but it is a stone-cold fact Jesus is white because Jesus is a Jew in the Bible which mean it's true, and you can't get no whiter than being a Jew."

"Oh, yeah," God said. "That."

"That what?"

Just that quick we was back in the gazebo and sitting on the bench.

"LeRoy, you're smarter than just about anybody we get up here and I know you're going to keep after me until I tell you, so we might as well get it over with." That sounded a little bit like God was about to get pissed off at me and a little bit like he was showing me some respect. Not being able to tell, I decided just to keep my mouth shut and listen.

"It had come nigh unto the time for the Savior to be born and I started down to take care of that bit of business. I don't go down myself too much. Just once in a while to speak out of a burning bush or something like that to keep folks honest. Most of the time I send archangels to do the heavy lifting. So whenever I do go down, I always stop off in France for some of that French wine, cause I never know when I'll get the next chance. So that's what I did and hooked up with some French moonshiners and they brought out their best stuff. Well, we were at it all the better part of a day and then on into the night until the sun was coming up. I told them, 'That's got to be it for me, I got business.' And then I started off to pick me out the right virgin to conceive with my seed. Now the plan was to make it to Ethiopia, but I was woozy from near twenty-four hours of drinking wine and nothing on my stomach and got off course and ended up landing in Galilee. I saw right away as soon as I landed that I was in the wrong place and started calculating another course to get me where I wanted to go and then I saw Mary walking down the road. She had on this blue skirt that came close to showing everything she had and her feet sticking out of her sandals was so comely I couldn't stand it and that was that. Now Jesus was going to be white and there wasn't going to be any going back on it. I sat down by the River Jordan and thought things over. At first I thought I ought to just get myself over to Ethiopia and finish up like I planned to start, but that wasn't going to work either. Then there would be two Jesuses, one white and one black, and can you imagine what kind of trouble that would stir up? There's been enough trouble over the ages with folks fighting over just the white one."

I asked him how come he just didn't go back and get rid of the first Jesus, maybe unwind time so it never happened.

"It isn't that easy. Unwinding time isn't the problem. I do that a lot. The hard part is I'm not allowed to change nothing I personally did because I'm not allowed to fail. ~~Got to be fucking~~

~~perfect all the goddamn time, every fucking second, and I can't~~
~~never take nothing back. I'm just stuck with what I got.~~"

Just then God perked up his head and said, "Come on in," and the Archangel Michael entered into the gazebo. Him and God got together over in the corner and whispered back and forth and then God must of told Michael to go off and take care of something, because Michael took a step back and gave a little bow and left us alone again. God said, "Okay, we got it figured out. There was a little mix up on the weather. You had the right idea jumping off the cliff to make it to the sea. There was supposed to be a big wave waiting for you to land in, but it got missed."

"How come?"

"Things don't always go exactly according to plan. There's a whole lot going on in the universe and a plan is just a plan, not a guarantee. The way it works is that I got different angels in charge of different things. About a hundred are in charge of the winds and the seas, and they have a lot going on. The one that was supposed to be looking over you when you got to the cliff had a sudden emergency dealing with a tsunami over in Japan."

"So he just decided not to show up?"

"It happens sometimes. Not a lot. Just once in a while. When it does, we try to fix it up best we can. Worst case I ever had to deal with was Daniel in the lion's den. What was supposed to happen was that when the guards opened up the lion's den and went to throw Daniel in it, Daniel would get this surprised look on his face and say, 'What lions?' And then he would laugh right out loud and say something like, beasts of God, come forth, or something like that. We was going to leave the details up to him to make it look more natural. And then everybody would hear what they thought was the lions coming out and start bolting for the doors. But instead of lions, it would be lambs and Daniel would lay down beside them. There was going to be a miracle, just not the one in the Bible. After a while Daniel was going to get up and conquer the guards that tried to do him in."

"So what happened?"

"Daniel got ripped all to shreds is what happened. You get a lion mad, he's going to do what a lion's going to do. And then he ended up here when he wasn't supposed to be, like you are. Once he got thrown in the lion's den, we couldn't make it the other way, because the guards and everybody would see the trick. So what I did was have Michael take him back, but this time close up the lion's mouths behind closed doors where nobody could see that trick. That way Daniel got to fulfill his prophecy."

"So it all worked out."

"Not all the way. Because of that mess-up, I ended up with thirteen generations of American slaves all singing 'Didn't My Lord Deliver Daniel' every Sunday morning and being patient like Daniel waiting all night to get let out and depending on me to free them from bondage when they should have been rising up to smite the Philistines who was oppressing them like Daniel was supposed to do with the guards. A total mess. Sent a regular angel to take care of things where I should of sent a archangel."

So I said, "What you going to do about me?"

"This won't be as hard as with Daniel. Michael will take you back in time to right after you jumped and he's going to rise up a mighty wave and it will do two things. First off it's going to wash your body that's on the rocks out to sea. Then he's going to put you in a new body that's going to be just like the old one, clothes and everything, and toss you in the wave. That way when the Arabs come up on the cliff and look out, all they're going to see is your body being swept out to sea and they will still think you died. After that it's up to you what you do about saving the sultan's daughter. Now before we do this, you got to give your solemn pledge to keep this whole thing to yourself. I don't need no more false preachers and prophets trying to work out another prophecy on account of you not being able to keep a secret. You have to keep this just between you and me." I gave God my solemn pledge and was trying to say goodbye and thanks for the tour, but it was already too late. I was already in the sea and swimming for my life. One thing I can tell you about God from my personal experience is that when he makes up his mind to get something done, ~~he don't fuck around. He fucking just plain out do it.~~ he does it.

You probably want to know what happened after that with the prince and the sultan's daughter and how I saved them from the prince's own stupidity ~~and stiff dick~~. But after telling you about what happened from my adventure with God after dying, the rescue mission seems pretty boring. So for them who wants to know, I'll tell it real quick so you are not hanging. Everybody else can just go to the next chapter.

My problem the first time was I did a frontal assault and right in the middle of the day, just marched right in the palace front gate and said, "Give her up you son-of-bitch." Which turned out to be not so smart because there was way too many of them for me to handle. This time I did it smart, I waited till midnight and then threw a silk rope I found next to a tent outside of the palace walls over them walls and shinnied up. I dropped down like a cat and watched real careful to see where there was the most comings and goings and that would be where the princess was. Once I figured that out, the rest was easy. I just snuck up on that side of the palace and knocked out any guard I came up on. Some of them put up a fight and I had to kill them. I kept on until there wasn't no guards left and I was at the sultan's daughter's bedroom. I jimmied the door and went in and put my hand on her mouth so she wouldn't yell and when she woke up, told her not to be scared, I was a friend. I told her to grab anything important and then held her up in my arms and beat it the hell back out across the palace grounds being careful not to trip over any of them guards I killed. Getting over the wall carrying her was easier than I thought it was going to be because she was light as a feather. She just wrapped them perfumed white arms of hers around my neck and I grabbed another silk rope that was laying there on the ground and threw it up, and up the silk rope we went. Her breathing on the back of my neck on the way up almost got me started but I held back OK and once we was on the ground I was safe from temptation. I grabbed up the reins of a camel and hopped up on his back and reached down and pulled the sultan's daughter up behind me and we hightailed it out of there for the sultan's palace. He was so glad to see his daughter he offered to give me a bag of gold for my trouble but I must of had a spell of insanity because I said, "No just give it to somebody who is hungry." Then he said to his top guard, "Go get that motherfucking prince!" I said, "Hey look, since you was about to give me a treasure and I didn't take it, how about you give me something else instead?" He said, "What you got on your mind?" And I said, "Don't be too hard on the prince. That boy is in love and that has a way of destroying your good sense. Maybe think about cutting him some slack. You must of thought some good stuff about him before this all happened, giving him your daughter's hand the way you did."

The sultan calmed down a little bit and said, "I'll think about it."

"Well, I got to be getting back," I said. "You got a magic carpet handy?"

The sultan waved his hand and his main wizard came in with a carpet and unrolled it on the floor and up it came and stayed there in the air kind of waving up and down. I kissed the sultan's daughter on the cheek and climbed up on the carpet and gave the sultan a salute and off we went, flying swift as a shooting star in the moonlight over the Atlantic Ocean.

Mr. Bones was sitting on the porch waiting for me when the magic carpet left me off, just laughing his ass off and trying to catch his breath. I could see he didn't have no plan about letting me live this one down, and he never did.

Brigard County, November, 1975

A shotgun? A fucking shotgun?

Jesus Eli, what were you thinking?

I was thinking I didn't want to get shot.

You do know staying away from her was a better way of not getting shot, don't you?

It wasn't like I started out trying to get in her pants.

Not even a little bit?

Maybe a little bit. Jesus Harm, nobody could've stood it.

Jesus Christ, Eli.

So what's next?

Jesse told me I gotta marry her or else.

And you are gonna do that?

I am.

LeRoy said now he was just being thick headed.

Why not? She keeps good house and you got no idea what she had backed up inside her. And she's real easy to look at, you got to admit that. What more could you want?

I can think of a couple things.

Harmon leaned on his shovel and said to LeRoy it looked like they was going to lose him and who would've ever thought Eli'd be the first to go.

The engineer came out and waved to them it was time and they went out from the cupola and Eli ambled down the tracks and signaled up to Bean in the crane they were ready. LeRoy said to Harmon they should take Eli out and celebrate. Harmon said more like they should go buy him a one-way ticket to anywhere else. LeRoy said it didn't much matter, they was going to lose him whichever way. Eli returned.

We decided to throw you a bachelor party.

When?

Right after work.

Bean trawled his crane from the end of the yard, its steel wheels sparking on their rails, the hook trailing. He brought it up and stopped and braked and slid through the pendulous momentum of the hook and held it there so that it hung down dead still as if sculpted from the air. Eli went inside and pronounced it clear and dragged out the dropping cable. They threaded the cable's eye through the great hook and dragged the line through pulleys and attached it to the post upon which the cupola's pair of half-moon doors were braced. Bean lifted and the post sprang free and the doors fell and spread open and swung once on their great iron hinges with a dull clang, and the cupola shat the last of the heat, slag and ash and half-molten rails, a mountain of flaming refuse down which tumbled dwarfish avalanches of burning coke falling from star-like brilliance to a gnarled and angry orange as they rolled. LeRoy signaled to Bean vaguely visible behind his pitted windows that they were clear. Bean lowered the hoist and LeRoy lifted the cable off and dropped it on the ground. They put the hose to the fire and the steam racing up through the cupola spread an acrid sulfuric stench and the smell of burnt metal and the sour smell of wet ash. LeRoy asked Harmon whose turn it was to go up inside. Harmon said it was Eli's but he was going to take his turn for him. Eli was going to need every bit of his strength. That little piece of ass was going to drain him white and LeRoy said did he think that would work for him.

Where to first?

How about Harrisville?

I got a fiancée.

Shit, most of who goes there's married. Being engaged aint any kind of obstacle.

Nuh, I had enough of that. And I don't think they altogether forgot us yet.

Lone Pine?

Good as anyplace.

They drove there and went in and Harmon told everybody it was Eli's bachelor party and Eli drank for free, people he didn't even know sending over drinks. Girls danced with him and some of them pressed themselves up against him and asked wasn't there anything they could do to keep him from doing something stupid and he asked them what they had in mind. They winked and said you know what and he winked back and said he was spoken for and they said come back if it don't work out. They drank until last call and ordered three shots each and had a contest in which whoever drank down all three shots without touching them with their hands and not spilling any was the winner. They all lost. They staggered out laughing and got in the car and said what should they do next. LeRoy said he had a couple cases at his place and Harmon asked him were they cold. LeRoy said one of them was and if they got that far, they wouldn't care if the other one was or not. They drove over the bridge and through town and down to LeRoy's in a light, soft rain. Harmon rolled down his window and held his face to the night and let the rain come upon his face. Eli, lying in the back seat, told him to close the window, it was fucking cold back here. Harmon said he was just trying to make sure he didn't nod out, being there was a lot of night left.

They sat drinking in LeRoy's front room. LeRoy turned on the radio and said he had some leftovers if they were hungry and they said sure. He set out what he had on the coffee table and Eli said some of it looked kind of moldy, didn't it. LeRoy said hardly any of it's more than a couple weeks old and that's just spots in front of your eyes and Eli said he never seen no green spots before and LeRoy said there's a first time for everything. They remembered things they had done and when they had been in trouble together and how they got out of it and what bones they had broken in the effort. LeRoy said he was going to miss all that and Eli said he wasn't going anywhere. They drank some more and Harmon said was Eli sure about Harrisville, they never closed over there and it might be his last chance for some strange stuff. Eli said if he wanted any strange stuff, he could just come around and listen to them bragging, them being pretty fucking strange themselves, and besides, he was too drunk to go anywhere. Harmon admitted they were all a little on the strange side and said he was too drunk too. Eli said he had to piss and got up and went to the bathroom. Harmon and LeRoy lamented the impending loss of their friend and it didn't matter what Eli said, once you get that chain around your neck you are righteously fucked. LeRoy said if he ever decided he was going to get married for Harmon to knock him out and tie him up out in the woods someplace until he came to his senses. Harmon promised he would. They talked for a long time and Harmon asked aint he been gone pretty long? LeRoy said yeah and got up and left the room and came back laughing. He's passed out on the floor. Harmon said he guessed that meant the party was over. LeRoy said guess so and left for his bedroom. Harmon lay on the couch, his forearm across his eyes and after a while got up and turned off the radio and the light and lay back down and slept.

In the morning, LeRoy was up first and his rattling around in the kitchen woke Harmon. Harmon went in the bathroom to piss and gave Eli a little shove with his foot and said rise and shine cowboy. Eli rolled over and squinted up with one eye and said Jesus Christ turn the fucking light off. Harmon said if he did that he wouldn't be able to see to piss and would get it all over Eli instead of in the commode. Eli struggled up from the floor and told Harmon to hurry, he was going to piss himself if he didn't. Harmon said he better go first then and went out and on through the back door and pissed in the weeds behind the cabin. He waved his dick around trying to draw a little heart on the ground to show Eli and said to himself he was still drunk and went back inside.

Eli sat at the kitchen table holding his head. LeRoy stood leaning against the sink, a coverless paperback open in one hand, his thumb pressed along the bottom of the pages like he was a preacher searching a testament for a text from which to preach a funeral sermon. Harmon said Skeeter you read too much. Sooner or later it's going to fuck up your brain. LeRoy said it was too late, it was already pretty fucked up.

He laid the book face down on the counter and swished around a coffee pot and said there's enough for everybody and did they want him to heat it up or was cold good enough. Eli said boil that shit. God knows what's living in there. LeRoy put the pot on the stove and turned on the gas and went to the sink and fished around in the dirty grey water and came up with three mugs and rinsed them under the spigot and set them on the table. While they waited for the coffee to heat, Harmon said they still had close to four hours before they had to be at work and he didn't know about them but he didn't think they had shown Eli the proper respect he deserved and they should celebrate some more. LeRoy poured the coffee and said it sounded like they needed a plan. Eli said if the plan had anything to do with going out again, coffee wasn't going to do it. His kind of headache needed a beer and was there any left. LeRoy said did it matter if it was cold or warm and Eli said fuck no. LeRoy said that was good because he forgot to put the other case in the refrigerator, it was in the basement. Harmon said bring up the whole case. The three friends drank a couple warm beers each and their coffee and Eli said that was better and he was getting hungry. Harmon said they would take him out for dinner and it would be on him and LeRoy. LeRoy said speak for yourself. Then he asked Eli what he felt like and Eli said a steak, a real fucking bloody steak. LeRoy said Ruthy could do that and she wouldn't mind them staying there until the three o'clock ferry and LeRoy drove them there.

They went in and sat at a table. A row of hobbled and bent old men sat perched on the stools along the counter like a flock of blackbirds hunched down against the wind on a telephone wire. Ruthy came out from the kitchen and told LeRoy she hadn't seen him for a while and was he getting too good for old Ruthy and he told her never, she was the woman of his dreams and he been busy was all. They told her Eli was getting married and they were celebrating and she said she could tell. They told her they wanted big steaks and make them bloody and forget the potatoes. LeRoy told her while she was at it, bring them some of that special coffee she kept in the back and she said they didn't look like they needed it. LeRoy said nobody *needs* it. Eli said he did. Ruthy asked were they sure and LeRoy said he was so sure that soon as they got Eli married off, he was going to come back with a big bouquet of roses and a diamond ring and beg her to marry him just because of that coffee. She gave him a tender slap on the back of his head and called him a nappy-headed little smartass and went back to the kitchen.

Catfish came in and saw LeRoy and strolled over, lanky and loose limbed, and asked him where he been. LeRoy said around and asked Catfish how the museum was working out. Catfish said he decided the museum idea wasn't so smart and he was turning it into a store instead. If there was anything they needed, he probably had it. LeRoy told him Eli was getting married and they was going to have to buy him something nice for a wedding present and did he have anything like that but not real expensive in case the marriage didn't work out. Catfish blinked his good eye and thought and said he had a seven-day windup mantel clock. It kept pretty close to perfect time and sounded out the quarter hours just like a church bell. Harmon said that sounded like a good idea for a present because all the time Eli was going to be spending in bed, he wasn't going to have no time at all for winding clocks. Except his own once in a while to get rested up. LeRoy said he heard that after you been married a year, winding yourself up was pretty much all that was left. That wildcat you thought you married turned out to be about as horny as a sack of turnips and about that lumpy too.

Ruthy came with the steaks and coffee cups with bootleg whiskey. LeRoy took a sip and gasped and said Ruthy, you better bring us some cokes to cut this with and she laughed and said she thought she was dealing with grownup men or she would have brought the cokes out in the first place. Eli took a sip and said holy fuck, that's Jesse's! That shit is a hundred and fifty proof. Don't smoke when you drink it, you'll set yourself on fire. LeRoy lit a cigarette and took another sip and rasped out, see? No fire. Then he said that was the last he was going to take of it straight, he'd wait for the cokes. Son-of-a-bitch. They marveled at the unlikeliness of coming by accident upon Jesse's whiskey in the middle of celebrating Eli getting engaged to Jesse's daughter. Eli said it just goes to show that what goes around comes around.

One by one the blackbirds along the counter ruffled their feathers and brought forth money and laid it down and descended from their stools and ambled out to calls of take it easy and don't forget and other such farewells, and soon the bachelor and his squires were the only ones left in the diner. LeRoy wanted to know how it happened. Eli said I don't know, it happened. LeRoy said nothing just happens.

It maybe didn't just happen, but it didn't happen all at once neither. One night I come home and there's a sandwich on the table and a little note that said she thought I might be hungry and all the i's is dotted with little hearts. And then pretty soon it was every night and then she started waiting up for me and one night after I was finished eating, she went to wipe the table and leaned over and the top of her housedress is all loose and she aint got a bra on. And fuck. I mean. Jesus.

How'd Jesse find out?

I don't know. Must've guessed. All I know's I'm sleeping and I hear him yell you cocksucker, get the fuck up, and I roll over and there he is with a double barrel pointed right at me, and Sarah Anne starts in screaming and the old lady comes in and she's crying and that fuckhead brother of hers comes in and the only thing on his mind is getting a look at his sister naked. Hadn't been for the shotgun, I'd've smacked the smart right off that boy's face.

If it been my daughter, I woulda shot you.

You aint got no daughter.

None that I know of.

They told Ruthy bring them more of that coffee and pretty soon they didn't care about the cokes and then a trickle of men came in dressed in work clothes and picked up bag lunches. Harmon said oh shit, time to go to work. Eli said why didn't they just say fuck it and go someplace else. Harmon said we already missed too much. He hollered over to Ruthy how much and she brought over the bill and Harmon and LeRoy split it and wouldn't let Eli pay any of it. They gave her an extra ten dollars and said they appreciated her letting them take up the table for the whole afternoon. On the way to the door, LeRoy said don't forget, next time you see me, I'll be carrying a dozen roses and she said be careful driving. LeRoy said aint I always?

They had done this enough times that they didn't have to conspire among themselves to stifle back any involuntary smirk or on how to convey themselves as sober and sullen as they passed through the guard shack, to look like any other brace of tired men trundling grudgingly to work. The guard didn't even look up at them. Shuffling with the resignation of laborers, they made their way to the locker room and opened their lockers, their thick fingers struggling with the combinations. Eli said fuck I can't see the fucking numbers and LeRoy opened his for him. They took off their everyday clothes and jammed them into brown grocery bags and took down the filthy work clothes they'd hung up the night before. Eli smelled the armpits of his denim shirt and said fuck, this has gotta be the last night for these. Harmon said you been saying that every night this week. Don't she wash clothes?

She washes clothes.

So take them home.

She aint home. They took her off until we get married.

I knew we should've gone to Harrisville.

You better be careful. It aint going to take much more to talk me into it.

LeRoy and Harmon said it looked like they had a plan for after work and this was turning into a hell of a party.

They went out of the locker room and past the toilet with its doors open and the grimy toilets grinning from the open stalls and across the gritty concrete floor and out into the din of the main floor. They waited for a crane hauling a hulking ladle of molten iron to pass and crossed over to where Palmer stood waiting to give out the night's jobs. He looked hard at them as they came up, but they gave no outward sign of drunkenness. Just stood and waited. Palmer gave out the jobs and told them shakeout was short a man. After the heat was done, Eli should go work shakeout on the side floor. When Palmer left to go to the office, Eli said shit he hated that shit work and LeRoy said didn't he mean he hated work period. That too Eli said.

While the heat ran, Eli worked below, tracking the loads and shoveling buckets of limestone in the hopper among the iron scrap and steel rails that Bean brought with the crane, the metal clinging to the swinging magnet like castaways grasping at a life raft. He measured out traces of manganese and nickel and marked off on the engineer's chart with a pencil what he had done. Harmon and LeRoy worked above, forking coke into massive counter-weighted steel wheelbarrows in five-hundred pound loads and dumping them into the hopper as it rose up clanking on its chains and belched out its load into the cupola's gaping maw wherein blue and yellow flames spiraled upward and the firebrick glowed orange, the color wavering as if in pain.

They took their break at the end of the heat, drinking bad coffee from the machine. Eli said again how much he hated that fucking shakeout and how come they didn't give it to LeRoy. It was about his turn. LeRoy said sometimes you eat the bear. Eli threw his cup on the slag pile and said complaining about it aint going to get it done and rose heavily and almost fell but caught himself just in time. LeRoy asked him could he see straight enough to hit the flasks and he better be careful he didn't sledge himself in the face. He didn't want to make himself uglier than he already was. Eli said look who's talking and went off to the side floor.

Harmon and LeRoy stood and LeRoy said I got an idea. Come on.

He led Harmon outside to the narrow handling yard set between the foundry and the fence and took him down the tracks sunk in the concrete to the scrap bin and said that's perfect. He put on his gloves and leaned two sheets of mild steel against the wall and went to the cabinet and took out the torch and turned on the gas. He put on goggles and threw a pair to Harmon. He slid the striker and a rush of orange flame billowed roaring from the torch. He turned up the air and the flame narrowed and hissed pale blue and transparent. He took the torch to the steel, the hose writhing in the black sand and began cutting. Harmon said what the fuck? LeRoy cut out a figure from the first steel sheet, doll-like with hair curling and then another taller figure from the other sheet. Harmon laughed and said let me. He cut half moons through the chest of the small figure, the irregular scallops cooling as he drew the torch in an arc, the melted steel congealing in small globules as it wound down from white to red and then to soot black. LeRoy said make nipples and Harmon burned holes roughly centered in the jagged breasts. They stepped back and admired their work. LeRoy said make a cunt and while Harmon added that detail, looked around and saw a length of round stock and said give me the torch and tacked it at an upward angle from the groin of the taller figure, a gargantuan erection. Harmon said we don't want to give him something to brag on, make it shorter. LeRoy cut off most of the length so that what remained was a boyish stubble of a prick. He stepped back and dropped the torch, its flame snuffing out when it hit the sand. Harmon said let's make it like they're holding hands and they wrestled with the figures and leaned them in and out and set them this way and that until they found a pose that mimicked the carriage of young love. They stepped back and again giggled and laughed hard, doubling over and slapping each other on the shoulders.

Oh fuck. I'm going to shit myself.

Let's get him.

They went up the tracks and in the narrow door to the side floor where Eli, his face coal black from smoke and burnt sand, was about the task of severing flasks from still-smoking castings with a sledge, the sounds of the blows lost in the tumultuous thunder of the shaker bar. They went over and yelled that Palmer changed his mind and he wanted him to cut scrap. Eli waved up to the small crane and the operator nodded and went on with his work. They went out to the yard. Eli said was he ever fucking glad, you couldn't hardly breathe in there. Harmon and LeRoy followed behind him laughing and he said you drunk fuckers are up to something. They struggled to get out that they weren't up to nothing.

When Eli saw the graven caricatures, he set his arms akimbo and said he knew they were up to something. His two friends made little kissing sounds at him and then set to laughing so hard they had to hold each other up. They said it was a wedding present and did he want them to help him smuggle it out. They said they would look real good welded onto posts and stuck in the ground in front of his house. Maybe use the poker he already had up his ass for the post. He said he was going to smuggle them out all right, he was going to cut them the fuck up and shove the pieces up *their* asses and sneak it out like that. He went to get the torch and saw it wasn't in the cabinet and saw the hose. He picked up a striker and traced the hose to the torch, stumbling slightly in the loose black sand, and pulled up the torch by the hose and held the striker beneath the tip and LeRoy remembered he never turned off the gas and before he could yell out a warning, Eli squeezed the striker.

A yellow globe flared from the spark, enveloping his hand, and hesitated and fed its own strength and swirled about him and down along the sand, seeking out the eddies of acetylene pooling invisibly among the piles of scrap, igniting these backwaters and drawing their separate fires into itself, and there erupted from these allied fires a raging conflagration and a tornadic, roaring wind and the force of it blew outward and took up Harmon and LeRoy as if they were debris to be scattered and tossed them against the fence, the chain link rattling as they slid down to fall upon the concrete. The whirlwind greedily drew up within itself all the fragments of scrap and steel among which Eli stood and flung them all ways. A sheet of spinning steel caught him in the back and sliced through his spine, stopping only when its sharp corner edge protruded from his chest. He fell backward, the steel behind him propping him up in the sand like a new-world satyr, half man and half iron, squatting to shit, a posture from which better to gaze heavenward. He looked down at himself and the steel jutting from him and the blood spurting from the wound and muttered oh fuck, and turned to look at Harmon and LeRoy, his face blistered, his eyebrows gone, his hair ablaze. The blood stopped coming as his body gave way altogether, and a roiling sphere of fire rose up hissing from the scrap pit and cupped itself into the yard's metal roof and split apart and raced outward in massive teardrops of smoke-trailing flame.

The Amazing Adventures of LeRoy James

Me and Mr. Bones Rescue the ~~Princess of Mars~~ Mermaid Princess

After I got back from seeing God and fixing things up between the sultan and the prince, I decided to take a break from adventures and just live like a regular person for a while. But deciding to do something and people letting you do it is not the same thing and word was getting out about my amazing feats. I didn't tell anybody about that being dead adventure because God swore me to secrecy, but there is a society of magical creatures and they have a way of gossiping among themselves, just like everybody else, and it was pretty hard for them to keep quiet about me dying and going to heaven and talking to God and going back in time and not dying after all. I should tell you that when I say magical creatures, I'm not just talking about fairies and genies and things like that. I have to include in there beings like angels and heroes and even demons who have seen the light. (There is nothing worse than a demon who has got religion. Once they have come over from the devil, they are worse than preachers. The way they will gospelize you so hard, you will end up wanting to choke the ~~shit~~ Holy Ghost out of them. They think it's their way or the highway. But at least they are no longer out there terrifying children and ripping the flesh off of people's bones and stinking up the place with their foul breath. But when it's all said and done, I guess religion is religion whoever has it and you should respect it, regardless of how they started out.)

Anyway, all these creatures were talking about me and God, so word couldn't help but get out and one of the heroes who heard about it was the sailing ship captain Alexander Buchanan. You have probably not heard of him, because he doesn't like to brag about himself. But he has done a lot of good saving people when their ships are sinking and helping lost explorers get through treacherous waters and fighting off pirates. Captain Buchanan got himself into something that was a little bit out of his league. What happened was that one of Neptune's merman's had gone rogue and kidnapped the Mermaid Queen's baby girl and was holding her for ransom at the bottom of the sea and the Queen asked Captain Buchanan if he could maybe help her out. She asked Neptune first, but he told her no. (They had a thing once, way back, and he was still holding a grudge over her dumping him.) Him being a sailing ship guy, Captain Buchanan didn't have no way of getting ahold of a submarine, which was the only way he would have had to get down there where the baby Princess was being held captive and there wasn't a lot he could do, so he told the Queen he would call me and see if I could take care of it. I told him I would give it a shot. What else could I do? Somebody in trouble, you ought to do what you can.

After I hung up the phone, I knew that this wasn't something I could handle on my own and went out in the yard and summoned Mr. Bones. (Also, I had learned my lesson when I went off to help out the sultan by myself and I wasn't in the mood for going through that being dead thing again.)

So Mr. Bones appears, but around back of the house just up from the riverbank where I couldn't see him, and he says

Brigard County, July, 1993

Edna and Harmon awoke at the same moment on a warm and sweet Thursday morning. She reached to him and they fell into each other beneath the sheet, the morning breathing itself into them through the window screen and the sounds of the morning mellifluous. They made love with indolent patience and great tenderness and when they had finished, stretched like cats and lay enveloped in each other with the innocence of infants until they heard LeRoy call that breakfast was going to get cold and was they going to sleep all day. They arose reluctantly and put on robes and came out.

LeRoy stood at the stove flipping pancakes, a platter of sausage patties already steaming on the counter. He told them he'd been making enough noise out here he could've woke up a dead man and when they didn't come out, he was afraid he was going to have to eat it all by himself and then go shopping for a funeral parlor and how about Harmon help out a little bit and pour the coffee while he was finishing up. Edna kissed him wetly on the cheek and asked if that felt alive enough to him and he said she was making his day just a little bit better than perfect and handed her the sausage platter. The three of them fluttered about the table like small birds coming together to alight and took their places. They passed the platters around and sipped their coffee. LeRoy said they better get to it if they wanted to get anything done today and Edna said why did they have to get anything done today. The morning was half gone already and they should take the car and go someplace, just get in and drive. LeRoy said she knew it would put them even further back on getting the house painted didn't she. She said who the fuck cares? and they all of them laughed, Harmon and LeRoy with some remnant of shock they still could feel and she because they did. Come on she said, you know you want to. They admitted that they did. Edna said she was going to take a shower and get dressed and LeRoy said him and Harmon would clean up the dishes while she did.

They worked at the kitchen chores until Edna came out in high heels and a clinging, bare-shouldered dress that reached to mid-calf, a long silk wrap draped loosely about her upper arms. Jesus LeRoy said. Looks like we're going to have to wear clean shirts. She said she'd wait for them on the front porch and they went their different ways and came back again, freshened and expectant and met on the porch where Edna sat with three frosted cocktail glasses on a tray before her, snippets of green leaves sprouting from crushed ice. LeRoy asked if those were what he thought they was and she said you know they are, what do you expect from a lady? They sat and the three of them sipped their juleps until only ice remained, taking their time and admiring the day. Edna took the tray and the glasses inside and came back out with the glasses refilled and again they took their time. Edna laid her hand on Harmon's arm and asked where he thought they should go. Harmon said there was some pretty country across the river above town. Edna said let's go then and asked LeRoy if he'd back the car out. She told him to put the top down too, but she wanted to drive.

She drove them upriver and across the bridge as far as Merchant, her hands on the wheel light and delicate from the bourbon, and asked them which way to go. LeRoy told her to drive all the way out until Merchant changed from street to road and he'd tell her where to turn. They went past the River View and Jones's store and on through Merchant's maze of litter, leaving behind the river's and the town's smells, the town's stained streets and its stained citizens and came out into rolling country, green and fragrant. The road carried them along pastures where cattle grazed and through small copses of maples and pines and through ripening corn fields and past country homes where women in faded house dresses tilled their gardens. LeRoy told her to turn at a fork in the road and they went on a little way and came to a gas station with tables in the back looking out over a hazy valley. Edna said they needed gas and pulled in. A young attendant came out and looked at her and at LeRoy. LeRoy told him it was okay, she only looked white, she was passing, and fill her up. LeRoy nodded to Harmon in the back and said he's the one you got to watch out for. He's purebred redneck through and through. Edna stifled a laugh and pointed to a sign in the station's window, Cold Beer, and said they should get some and sit for a while.

Harmon went inside and bought a six pack while the boy filled the tank. Edna parked the Lincoln and they went around to the tables. Harmon asked Edna was she man enough to twist the cap off and she showed him she was and asked if he was and he tried to show her, but his hand kept slipping and he gave his bottle to her and said guess not. She laughed and opened it and handed it back. LeRoy opened his and they touched bottles and said cheers and drank and looked down into the valley and across to the hills limning it in the translucent distance. Edna said Harmon made a good choice, the view reminded her of sitting on her grandfather's porch except you couldn't see as far there as you could here. LeRoy said the view reminded him of a Bible verse.

She asked which one.

Yea, though I walk through the valley of the shadow of death, I will fear no evil, and Edna finished it for him: for thou art with me.

They drank their beers and started on the second round. Edna said she was going to see if they had a restroom. She said she'd meet them in the car and walked off with her bottle. Harmon took the pill bottle from his pocket and tapped two into his hand and swallowed them down with beer. LeRoy asked him was he going to be okay for this. Harmon said he'd be fine as long as he could get up and move every once in a while.

The Lincoln felt cloudlike and elegant in Edna's hands as she guided it back out onto the road, the sunlight shapeless around them. The road bent in a long sweeping curve down toward the valley and for a while there were neither farms nor houses and she bent with the wooing road and let it take her where it would. They passed a pond from which the scent of spring water rose and a chorus of small frogs sang. A pair of barn swallows flew across in front of them, spinning and swirling, trailing liquid atticisms which Edna read, and in them found some ineffable answer to a question she had not before thought to ask. She told Harmon there were tapes in the glove compartment and to pick something they could listen to. He went through them and said it was all classical and she said those were her husband's and they didn't have to listen to it if they didn't want to, they could find something on the radio. Harmon said no, he used to listen to this kind of music sometimes and it was a good day for it. He slid a random tape into the player and the sounds of strings rose and fell and rose again, mimicking the rise and fall of the Lincoln over small hills. Edna pressed down on the gas and went a little wide on a turn. LeRoy said hey there, maybe you want to ease up a little bit, we aint in that big a hurry. She told him it was the music and slowed the car. Harmon said if classical did that to her, it was a good thing she didn't bring any of her rock and roll tapes.

Sometime during midafternoon they came to a rustic restaurant set back from the road, its lot sparsely graveled. Beside it a sooty smoker smoldered, embraced in the scent of imperfectly combusted oak and blue vapor rising. LeRoy asked if anybody else was hungry and Edna pulled in. Harmon said he couldn't remember the last time they was here and LeRoy said let's hope they don't either. They got out of the car and walked up to the porch where old men sat in bent hickory rockers smoking pipes. They nodded to the men as they passed.

Inside, a stout, sweating man in a greasy apron told them to sit anywhere they wanted. Harmon asked where Edna wanted to sit and she started for the tables where several couples sat at the front wall lined with open windows facing toward the valley and then turned and led them to a dark and quiet corner. A waitress came and asked what they wanted to drink. Harmon told her to bring them a pitcher and she asked what kind. He said if they still had Stroh's to bring that and she left. Music came on, a country ballad of lost love and regret. LeRoy said that songs like that just went to show that love aint everything it's cracked up to be. Edna asked if he was sure about that. He said he was ever since the fifth grade when a little blue-eyed girl broke his heart for the first time and he never got over it. Sometimes he still dreamed about her. The waitress returned with the pitcher and asked if they were ready to order. Edna said she never even looked at the menu. Harmon said there wasn't no reason to look. The only thing to get here was the ribs and asked how hungry she was. Edna said pretty hungry. Harmon told the waitress to bring them three full racks and a bowl of extra sauce and she asked if he was sure. He said if they didn't finish them, they'd take the leftovers home. More country music came on and LeRoy filled their glasses from the pitcher.

A couple rose from one of the window tables and paid their check and left, the girl's willowy hips brushing her young man's as they went through the door. Edna asked if they ever wanted to be that young again and they all three of them said they did and then

LeRoy said if it meant he had to learn all the same lessons over again the hard way, maybe not. Harmon raised his glass and said here's to maybe not and they all said it and drank. The waitress came back with the ribs and laid a stack of dish towels on the table. Edna lifted her knife and fork and LeRoy said not like that, just break one off and use your hands. He showed her, ripping one from his rack and dipping it in the sauce bowl. He took up a towel and wiped his hands and face. See? he said. Every bit as clean as a fork. They all went at the ribs like children until they were gone and the towels lay heaped on the table like bloody rags. Edna asked what was next, she didn't feel like going home. Harmon said there was lots more places on up the road and he was up for it if they were. He waved for the waitress and she brought the check. Edna asked how much it was. Harmon told her and she laid enough money down for the ribs and a generous tip and said let's go find what's up the road.

Out on the porch they paused and looked out toward the valley tilting obliquely toward the sun languishing just above the horizon. Edna said they were in there longer than she thought and took each of them by the arm and they went down the steps with an exaggerated grace. One of the old men hawked and bent over the arm of his rocker and spat on the blue-gray floor. Edna came up sharp, twisting herself from Harmon's and LeRoy's arms and started back. She stood on the first step, at eye level with the man and looked him in the eye and with no trace of laughter said was there something he wanted to say to her. The old man hawked and spat again and put his pipe back in his mouth. Harmon and LeRoy looked at each other and went to her. She brushed their hands off her and asked the man again. He looked back at her and through his teeth clenched on his pipe stem said if he had anything to say to her he would have already said it. Harmon put his hand firm around her waist and this time would not let her go and took her to the car. LeRoy asked her did she want him to drive and she said she was good. They all got in and drove off, Edna chafing until LeRoy got her laughing when he said if he was ever in a bar fight and she was there, he was going to make sure he was on her side and would she mind if he put her in one of his adventures, maybe make her a Viking princess or something.

They went back to the promise of the day, stopping at one place and then another as the afternoon slipped into evening and Edna lost track of where they started and where all they had been. A vague memory of another homespun restaurant where they'd had their supper. Wagging tongues of candle flames in amber café lamps. A cabernet stain bleeding into a white table cloth and a remembered curiosity as to how the stain came to be. LeRoy saying she should try to keep it down. A man politely suggesting they might be more comfortable in the bar. Perched on stools around a high table, her heels hooked on the cross rail. Tequila shots. Struggling with the complexities of salt, shot, and lemon. Hysteria of laughter. A monster of a man in a black suit telling them he was going to have to ask them to leave. Her offended shout that she would not leave. Harmon appearing beside her, telling her let's go, they had another place they wanted to show her. A dance hall with music she didn't care for but to which she danced anyway, eyes closed, shoulders lolling. Smoke and strangers' faces, endlessly. Hanging rag-like from Harmon's arm at the door of yet another roadhouse and someone saying not tonight folks. Back into the heat of the summer night. Listing to the car on loose ankles. Asking did they just throw her out. Her wrap slipping repeatedly from her shoulders. The effort of rearranging it and the effort of trying to remember how to open the car door. LeRoy laughing and saying he got it and give him the keys. LeRoy opening the back door and helping her in where Harmon again materialized. Escaping down a long narrow road, the stars wavering streaks above them. Her face and hand in Harmon's neck, the stubble on his cheek arousing her. Stroking his chest. Opening his jeans and stroking him there. Licking her fingers after. Holding her hand to his face and giggling, asking him if wanted some too. Wiping her hands clean with her wrap and throwing it up into the glassy night and looking back to watch it twirl in the car's wake and disappear. Laughing and scrambling over the seat as they sped down the road to do for LeRoy the same favor.

Brigard County, August, 1993

Edna interrupted Harmon's and LeRoy's work to tell them the lawyers called and she was going to have to go home for two or three days and could they help her with the driving. LeRoy asked her where home was and she told him and he said that was on the high side of close enough to drive in one day.

LeRoy looked at Harmon and back to her. The phone rang before they could say anything. Edna said it was the lawyers calling back and she'd come talk to them some more when she got off. She said it was probably going to be awhile and went back inside.

Harmon told LeRoy there wasn't no way he could make a five-day trip. LeRoy was going to have to do it by himself.

Damn, Billie, me and you both know it aint me she wants going with her.

Please Skeeter. You got to figure something out.

Talbot Arms Hotel, August, 1993

It was after nine when LeRoy pulled the Lincoln in front of the Talbot Arms Hotel. A top-hatted doorman walked up to the car staid and erect, a bellhop following. He bowed and opened Edna's door and extended his white-gloved hand and said good evening Mrs. Connor. Welcome. She took his hand and swung her legs to the curb, her knees and ankles tight together, and rose demurely from the car and said thank you Carson. She turn and looked at LeRoy, his mouth slightly agape, and told him to open the trunk. He stared, bewildered, and she said again, the trunk, LeRoy. The luggage? He turned and popped the trunk and got out and went around to the back, but the bellhop was there before him and said quietly that it was his job. Edna waited and looked at LeRoy again and beckoned him with just a lilt of her finger and he came to her. The doorman led them to the hotel's wide stained-glassed facade and held the door for them, tipping his hat as they went in.

A black-jacketed, bow-tied young man greeted them at the desk. He said we have your suite ready Mrs. Connor and turned a leather-bound registry toward her on the pink granite counter. He handed her a fountain pen and asked if she needed a room for her driver and she told him no. His eyes clicked to LeRoy and back again and he handed a room key to the bellhop, who had come up behind them pulling a brass-plated luggage cart gleaming in the light of the lobby's crystal chandeliers. As she signed the registry, the young man said that if there was anything she needed, to just call. She asked him would he have someone take care of the car and again he looked at LeRoy, but said of course.

The bellhop led them to an elevator and pushed the button and took them up. The doors opened to a mirrored-lined reception room and he bowed and gestured for her to step out and went to follow but stopped when she said LeRoy's name and the bellhop waited for him to go first. Again the bellhop went before them, taking them down a broad hallway deeply carpeted to a set of enameled white double doors and unlocked and opened them and bowed as had the doorman, gesturing Edna and LeRoy in. He left the cart in the hall and carried in the bags and asked Edna where she would like them. She pointed to a small bag and told him to put it in the extra bedroom and everything else in the master bedroom. He asked was there anything else. Edna said no and as he was leaving, slipped him a twenty-dollar bill. He touched the brim of his cap with his finger and nodded, backing himself into the hall and closing the doors.

Edna sat wearily on a sofa and asked LeRoy if he was hungry and he said he could eat. She pointed to a mahogany table by the window and said there should be a room service menu and pick something, maybe something light. He scanned the menu and said they have chicken salads. She told him to call room service and order two and a bottle of wine. LeRoy looked at her puzzled. She said the number should be on the menu. He asked her what kind of wine and she told him to tell them to recommend something. He made the call and then sat on the sofa across from her and asked her what all that Mrs. Connor stuff was about. She said she and her husband used to own this hotel. She got up and went to the window and stood looking out, her fingers trembling on her lips. LeRoy followed her and put his arms around her from behind and laid his cheek on her neck. She turned and took his face in her hands and he kissed her, warm and full, and let her pretend he was Harmon.

Nathans County, August, 1993

LeRoy drove into the dilapidated motel's nearly vacant lot. He said that given where they was it was probably better if he stayed in the car and she got the room. Edna went inside and came back out into the hot and muggy night a few minutes later. LeRoy drove them around to the back and carried their luggage inside to the smell of must and mold, the aged wall air conditioner clanking, and came out again. They walked across the highway to a tavern, steadying each other and weaving. They went in to maudlin country music and dusty animal heads on the wall and plaques with fading photographs of hunters many years dead commemorating successful kills. They ordered sandwiches and beer.

Edna asked LeRoy what time it was. He looked to the bar and the clock behind it with the legend *Ask for Labatt's*. Almost midnight he said. She said she wished she hadn't said they should take side roads home and they hadn't made so many stops. It was nice at first she said, but if they'd stayed on the interstate, they'd be home by now and she'd be asleep in her own bed. Beside Harmon LeRoy thought. Aloud he said it wasn't much further, they'd be home by late morning.

They worried at their sandwiches and after a while two men in work clothes came to the booth and hovered over them. Edna asked was there something they wanted and the one a little bit older than the other asked Edna did she want to dance. She looked up and told them to go fuck off. The man's face flared red and he leaned his hands on the table and his voice turned cast iron hard. What did you say to me? Edna tried to slap him but missed.

You fucking bitch.

LeRoy said whoa, fellas, she's drunk.

The man seethed and said he didn't care what she was. His friend put his hand on the man's shoulder and said don't you think we been in enough fights for one night?

Depends on if this nigger's got any balls.

Not tonight I don't LeRoy purred. How about I buy a round and we everybody just take it easy?

I don't drink nothing from no fucking nigger.

The friend said she don't want to dance. Let's go. They turned and went to the bar, the angry man muttering fucking witch eats with a nigger but won't dance with a white man. I'd like to slap that fucking silver spoon right out of her mouth and shove it up her ass. His friend said that no doubt she was too tight back there and the best he'd be able to do was bend the spoon and that would be a waste of a good silver spoon and they laughed at how clever they were and sat at the bar, telling the bartender to set them up again.

Edna's head bobbed on her neck. She studied her hands as if some many-legged oddity of nature had crept up upon their table and she was trying to make sense of it.

You can't let them talk to us like that.

I didn't let them do anything. They did it on their own.

Why don't you do something?

First off there is two of them and only one of me and second off, I am way too drunk.

Edna tried to throw what was left of her beer in his face, but only spilled it on the table. She set the mug down and glared at him and said she was going to the bathroom. She wove away. When she was out of sight, an old and shrunken catamite slithered from his stool at the bar and came across the floor in a crouching gait and wormed himself into Edna's place.

The little man waved to the waitress and told her two drafts. He smiled, his tobacco-stained teeth a crack in his cadaverous face. With a delicate, papery lisp he said women aint the answer to everything. He laid a finger on his cheek and canted his head demurely with a vampish moue.

I aint that drunk.

How drunk would you have to be?

Pretty fucking drunk.

The drafts came and the little queer said you look pretty fucking drunk already, maybe one more would do it. LeRoy drank and the wretch drank. LeRoy was dimly aware of Edna standing by the table where the men who had bothered them had stood. He looked up. She said it seemed like he found himself some better company than her and far be it for her to get in between them. She was going back to the room. She turned and wove again, this time to the door. The man who had challenged LeRoy nudged his partner and nodded to her going out. He whispered something to his companion and they laid money on the bar and rose and went to the door themselves. LeRoy started to stand to go after them but the old man draped his foot across his and said one more? LeRoy nodded and slumped back down. He didn't move his foot. What were the chances they was going to try something? he thought. And if they did, they'd be sorry they had, she could handle them. He took the beer mug from the waitress's hand before she could set it on the table.

Brigard County, August, 1993

LeRoy rolled the Lincoln into the driveway, both he and Edna staring straight ahead, his eyes desperately repentant, hers burning. Late morning sun shone down on cars parked randomly aslant in the front yard, muddy parallel ruts trailing in the grass behind them. LeRoy turned off the engine and told Edna to just stay in the car for a minute so he could see what was going on. He found a length of galvanized pipe in the garage and stalked furtively across the yard, holding the pipe at the ready. He stepped lightly on the porch and stood a little aside and peeked into the living room through the open front door and into the kitchen beyond and saw Darryl at the table. He lowered the pipe and went in. O Jesus he said.

Beer cans and beer cans, some upright on tables and some on their sides on the sofa but most on the floor. A pile of ash and butts on the carpet where an ashtray had fallen. Cigarette burns on the coffee table and a shattered lamp. And everywhere a rising binge smell of spilled beer and food left out and piss and vomit. LeRoy went into the kitchen to accost Darryl. Ab sat at the table, with him one of Ruby's girls and a young girl maybe not even legal, well on her way to becoming one of Ruby's girls, dressed in nothing but one of Edna's blouses, the buttons open, parading her not yet sagging breasts mottled with love bites. LeRoy told her to go put her clothes on and she said she couldn't find them. He said maybe they were in the car and go look and she said who the fuck did he think he was and maybe he should go fuck himself. Ab told her if she knew what was good for her, she'd shut up. The man had a pipe. The others stared numbly at their beers. Darryl looked up inquisitive and bereft and said we're out of cigarettes. LeRoy searched his pockets and found a pack nearly empty and laid it on the table and the young girl grabbed for it and the others flapped her hands away in a flurry like rats after a scrap of garbage.

Where's Harmon?

Darryl pointed toward the bedrooms. LeRoy leaned the pipe up against the table and went down the hall, kicking aside the cans that lay there, making a path through them and saw where Harmon had punched at the walls, the plasterboard indented and in places broken through, the pure white of the rough edges incongruous to whatever dark farce had transpired here, a smudge of blood on the wall where his fist had found a stud. If Harmon had broken his hand, LeRoy would have to take him to the hospital. No Jesus he said. Please. I can't.

Harmon and another of Ruby's whores lay naked and asleep on the bed, the girl's gaping mouth slowly winking like a blind eye as she snuffled moist snores. Harmon's lips were bruised and lacerated from the beer can tabs his swollen fingers had only been able to partially open. Rust-brown ribbons of blood from his split hand and wounded mouth streaked the beer cans strewn on the floor around the bed. The girl rolled her head and looked up at LeRoy and asked was he next and he told her to get dressed and get out. He jostled Harmon's shoulder until he awoke and asked him was he all right. Harmon coughed wetly and nodded. LeRoy said let me see your hand. Clotted gashes ran across the bruised knuckles. LeRoy checked that the fingers were all aligned and asked him could he make a fist and Harmon did, grimacing but a little when one of the cuts opened and seeped a drop of blood. LeRoy said to himself at least there's that and told Harmon he had to get up and Harmon said fuck if he did.

LeRoy said she's out in the car. Harmon blinked and thought and raised up on an elbow, looking out over what he had made of the house. O Christ. He worked himself to the side of the bed and went to stand and clenched his teeth and said fuck and LeRoy asked him where his pills were and Harmon said in the bathroom. LeRoy went out and down the hall. He opened the bathroom door and gagged. Fuck he said. Vomit in the sink and on the floor and the smell of bad whiskey. But most of the stench came from an oozing mass of shit flowing slag-like down the side of the toilet and pooling on the floor. Someone had tried to wipe away that part of it which had been laid down on the seat and thrown the towel in the tub, the toilet seat filmed dull orange. LeRoy wondered if the girls knew they carried traced on the backs of their thighs the fecal refuse of somebody's wracked and poisoned body. He found the pills on the sink and took them and a glass of water back to Harmon, then went to the others in the kitchen and told them to get the fuck out and they started in to argue with him and he took up the pipe and slammed it down on the table and said right the fuck now! Darryl asked could they take the beer with them. They got up shuffling and said they would have to look around for their stuff. LeRoy told them to hurry it the fuck up and went outside to where Edna was coming across the lawn.

She started toward the house and LeRoy got in front of her and said there was people in there that shouldn't be and he threw them out. She should wait until they was gone. Edna pushed him out of the way and watched as two girls came out, one of them half naked, and two men, each with a case of beer, the four of them all looking some other way than at her. She went up to them and asked them what the fuck they were doing in her house. Darryl said they was invited and she could see they was going couldn't she. They got in the cars and backed out across the grass, gouging more ruts. Edna looked at LeRoy and said was this what she thought it was. LeRoy tried to answer and she just put her palms up and said don't. She went in, LeRoy trotting behind her, through the front room and past the kitchen and past the bathroom's hellish stench and on down the hall to the bedroom where Harmon sat struggling with his jeans and the naked whore had fallen back asleep.

Edna slapped him. Hard. Get out she shouted. And slapped him again. She turned to LeRoy who stood with his hands begging and his jaw hanging down. And take your fucking nigger with you, she said, the blade of her voice slicing through the threads that had briefly woven them into the trinity they had all of them deceived themselves into believing they might have been.

Brigard County, August, 1993

Harmon and LeRoy sat on rusting folding church chairs beneath LeRoy's bridge, a stained styrofoam cooler filled with beer cans immersed in creek water standing askew between them. I'm sorry Skeeter Harmon said.

LeRoy said he already told him he was sorry and he already told him back it didn't matter. She was about mad enough at me when we got home to pull the trigger anyway. You was just the last straw. Look on the bright side. We damn near set a record.

Harmon said we gave her a pretty good time for a while there, didn't we?

She gave us a pretty good time too. You got to admit them hand jobs in the car that night was a nice touch. But aint that always the way it goes? I wish that just one time it would have been their fault.

Harmon said there's something I want to do.

What?

Go see Davy's grave.

What for?

I been thinking about it for a while.

Why you want to drag all that up now?

When else would I drag it up?

Harmon turned around to face down toward the river and asked if LeRoy thought he could get a car from one of his Crossings neighbors and maybe drive him out there.

Catfish'll let me use his.

Since when did he get a car?

Since the railroad finally cut up his rail cars for scrap and he went to working nights for the ferry.

What's he going to do when they finish the bridge?

Something else.

LeRoy asked Harmon could he make the walk or did he want LeRoy to go get the car and come back and pick him up. Harmon said he could make it on his own if LeRoy didn't mind stopping to rest now and again. He got up and said let's go and they went up through the nettles and down the road toward the Crossings and came up to Catfish's shack where Catfish sat in an aluminum lawn chair, rubbing the neck of a gray-nosed mongrel hound. They passed civilities between them and remarked on the heat. Catfish told them he would offer them beer if he had any. LeRoy said he wondered if Catfish wouldn't mind them letting them use his car and Catfish told him just make sure to put back whatever gas they used and pointed to the battered old Packard sulking beside the house, its rusted out fenders patched with roof flashing fastened down with sheet metal screws. Keys is in it he said.

They thanked him and got in the car and for a moment after LeRoy turned on the key and pressed down on the starter button with his foot, the solenoid only clicked. He tried again and the starter caught and the car coughed to life and settled to a rough and ominous idle. Harmon asked if LeRoy thought it would get them all the way to the church. LeRoy said it was a righteous mission wasn't it. But just in case, he wasn't going to shut her off. He slipped the Packard into gear and gingerly let out the clutch. The car bucked forward. It'll go LeRoy said. Only question is will it stop?

He put in the clutch and pressed the brake pedal. The wheels groaned and lightly squealed. He said it'll stop a couple more times. Harmon said if Catfish was working he ought to be able to afford something better than this. LeRoy said you know Catfish. If it aint old and worn out, he don't trust it. He pulled out onto the dirt road and drove upriver toward town and on through and up the curving ramp to the bridge. As they rose, Harmon watched its rusting arches sweeping upward like arms lifted and its flung gossamer girders and willowy concrete pilings rising from the river, the bridge wishing to be borne heavenward but too deeply rooted in the river's mud to ever fly. He remembered from far in the past sitting in some taproom conversation with a wizened old man who'd morosely intoned over a glass of murky whiskey, everybody want to go to heaven but nobody want to die.

LeRoy said if he had a shop and his old tools back, he could turn this antique into a thing so sweet angels would pay to ride in it. Be worth a fortune. Harmon said like Black Beauty? LeRoy asked did Harmon remember how him and Eli would get in Black Beauty's back seat and LeRoy would drive and they'd be back there with cigars in their mouths like they were rich and LeRoy was their chauffer and they'd all three of them get laid.

Hell of a car.

Wish I never sold it.

What you got for it kept you in the cabin a few more months.

Wouldn't have mattered. Everything's gone anyway.

Everything.

They were right to fire us.

I know.

They could've called the sheriff.

I know that too.

Why you think they didn't?

Who knows why the fuck anybody does anything?

You think we should've kept our heads down all these years?

Sometimes I do. Sometimes I wonder how come we didn't go up even more. Maybe if we'd took bigger chances things would've turned out different.

Once over the bridge, LeRoy again turned to where the road swept away from the river and up through a cut in the ridge. The land opened out and lay flat as a lake and they went on until they came to a church. Harmon got out. LeRoy asked him did he want him to go with him and Harmon said he didn't think so.

Harmon walked across the dirt lot and across the grass and hesitated at the gate opening into a grove of gravestones off a bit from the church. He steeled himself and then walked in among them. Past ancient tilted slabs, milk white and stain-etched in dark lines running down like black tears and past stones barely a century old, still shining with a lacquered sheen, and others even younger and some just born. In places the stones had toppled and some had split apart. He came upon a grave where the only remaining memorial was a stump of limestone in the ground ragged like a broken tooth. He wondered did they use the plot over again when all evidence of whoever lay buried there was erased and did whoever it was who had arrived there first welcome the company or did it remind them how dead they were, the newcomer making it just that much worse. He stopped and looked across the field beyond the church. Thin lavender streaks ran through the sky though dusk was hours off and again he went on among polished granite stones on paths worn to brown grass and bare earth packed hard and dry and around which stood stone vases of wilted flowers like drowsy sentries. Harmon thought of the foolish virgins. He wondered if he had ever gone with a virgin and thought back upon those women he had been with and could also remember and decided he probably had not and wondered then if that was yet another thing to regret and walked on.

From the car LeRoy watched through its blue exhaust and his heart reached out to the man wandering monk-like among the graves and thought how God had made of misery the only everlasting truth there was. LeRoy got out of the car and leaned back against the hood and went on watching. He lit a cigarette and waited.

Harmon wove through the graveyard's maze of death and came upon Davy's gravestone flush on the ground and spent some time not looking at it and then looked down and read. *Then were there brought unto Him little children.* LeRoy went on watching as Harmon took a blue bandana from his back pocket and wiped his face and neck and LeRoy again considered whether to go to his friend and decided to see what happened and if Harmon went to his knees he would go, but otherwise he would not.

Harmon looked back toward the car and LeRoy raised his hand holding the smoldering cigarette and Harmon nodded and looked at the grave again. He whispered toward the ground and turned and walked back the way he had come and leaned against the car beside LeRoy.

Billie, you ever think what would've been different if I didn't piss off the chief and we ended up in the same cell?

No.

Me neither.

LeRoy asked Harmon was he ready and Harmon said he was, but he needed to make another stop. Just start back the way they came. They got in the car and LeRoy drove it out onto the macadam, the car's tires raising little ripping sounds as they separated themselves from the melting tar. As the road began its rise to the ridge, they came upon a dirt fork and Harmon said turn here and LeRoy slowed the car to keep it from bottoming its broken springs on the stone-hard ruts. LeRoy said how far? Harmon said a couple miles. The road went through a stand of silver maples and up to an old deserted house. Harmon told LeRoy to pull in. A flock of scrumming grackles foraging alongside the road flew off in collective panic. The house was slowly shedding its asphalt skin like a dog with mange, the black felt showing leprous through its brown faux brick. The porch roof sagged. No window was unbroken.

What're we here for?

I got to get something.

Harmon got out of the car and LeRoy started to get out and Harmon said he got it and he wouldn't be long. LeRoy said that didn't look like a safe place to go into by yourself.

What place is?

Harmon walked through tall brown grass in the side yard and around to the back and went up a set of concrete steps and through a doorless frame and into the old mudroom where the dog had lain dozing and where the old man kicked it, growling for it to get out of the fucking way and the place where the dog nipped the old man's calf, ripping his workpants and drawing blood. Harmon felt again the angry stare like flames in the furnace licking against the mica door and the old man's voice straight and cold as a steel rail. If I get home tomorrow and that fucking dog's still here, you are going to wish you never seen it.

Harmon went on into the kitchen where sufficient light came in the broken windows to make out the debris-littered space where the family had taken its sullen meals. He saw him again astraddle her, his knees on her shoulders, beating her, screaming where did she hide his fucking car keys. He closed his eyes and it went away and he opened them again to scattered beer cans and candles stuck fast to cracked saucers with their own wax. A rat looked at him from a dark corner, back on its haunches, licking a condom it held in its yellow-clawed paws. The rat dropped its supper and rattled off.

He went across to the cellar door and started down and stopped and came back and took up one of the candles and lit it and went down. He held the candle up above the dirt floor and breathed in the smell of cobwebs and mold and the cellar's cold damp fecundity. He looked about and located the old lantern still hanging from a nail stuck into a floor joist and took it down and held it up by the bail and shook it and heard kerosene slosh about inside. He set the candle on a shelf and turned up the globe and again took up the candle and set it to the ragged wick and it took hold, sputtering and smoking. He adjusted the wick and set back the globe and wiped the dust from the blue glass with his sleeve and there was enough light to see by and by that light entered into the fruit cellar.

Smashed jars lay on the floor, the bounty they'd once held oozing across the dirt, thick and fetid. He held the lantern before wide wooden shelves lined with newspaper, curled and with misshapen titianesque rings where rats had pissed. He saw the red crest of a black widow and held the lantern toward her and she scuttled away. Looking about, he found a length of lath and took it up, and swept away from the shelves the tattered curtain of webs strung between them. He reached through and felt about and came out with a short length of chain and held it loosely and let it retake its circle shape and studied it. With his thumbs he rubbed away the threads of dust lacing through the links. He read the dates on the thin aluminum license tags and was chastened by how long ago it was. He thought, you think you will forget but you don't. Not ever. He folded the collar over into a figure eight and braceleted his wrist with the double loop, the license tags dangling down like charms. He took up a sheet of the newspaper and read by the lantern's light. Read of a brawl and two men in custody and another dead. A burglary solved. A missing child. A fire. Down in the lower corner a photograph of a young woman, bright-eyed, and the caption *Teacher of the Year*. He turned the paper over and read *Beloved husband and father*. He let the paper flutter downward and went out.

He turned down the lantern's wick to snuff out the flame and hung it back on its nail and took up the candle. The lantern might have hung another decade had he not touched it, but moving and resetting it dislodged the nail from the dry-rotting joist and the lantern fell, the globe shattering and kerosene leaking across the floor. Harmon considered flinging the candle down with it, but went to the stairs and up and blew the candle out and tossed it on the floor among its brethren. Let the house come down in its own time from storm and wind, from frost. Let it fold in upon its foundation as it struggled against surrender. Let it creak in its bones and feel pain and long for death and not find it. Fuck the house and fuck the memories residing here.

He went out and turned and stared at the back of the house, where someone had sprayed JESUS SAVES and a cross beneath the words and where someone else had amended the short sermon in a different color JESUS ~~SAVES~~ SUCKS, the arms of the cross circled and reformed as drooping testicles and the shaft of the cross with a bulbous head hanging down from which tears of semen dripped. He went around and got in the car and LeRoy asked him was that a choke collar and Harmon said it was.

Must have been a big dog.

Harmon didn't answer. LeRoy put the car in gear and they drove back not talking. When they got up on the bridge, Harmon told LeRoy to stop. LeRoy said right here?

Right here.

Harmon got out of the car and slipped beneath the railing separating the roadway from the pedestrian crossing and stood leaning against the railing. He took the collar from his wrist and played with it idly as he looked down into the muddy water. And then with a sideways flick of his hand like he was dealing cards, he threw the collar out into the air, the chain spinning like a wheel of tarnished silver, twirling all the way down and catching the sun just before it slipped into the water. He got back in the car and LeRoy asked him was there anyplace else he needed to go and Harmon asked him if maybe they could stop by the doctor's on the way through town and get another prescription.

LeRoy asked how much money they had.

Whatever you got.

We're okay. I got enough left over from my last pay to cover the gas and the pills and a couple bottles of whiskey.

Might as well be millionaires.

They ran their errands and took the car back to Catfish and thanked him and said whatever they could do to return the favor, just ask. Then they walked back in the direction from which they had just driven, the chattering cries of cicadas splattering down upon them like rain.

Brigard County, September, 1993

Edna led the realtor through the house. For a while he took notes but stopped when they got to the hall to the bedrooms. She showed him the boathouse and the garage and its apartment and then they went into the kitchen and sat at the table. He told her a place like this with the extra apartment and the boathouse should go for three hundred fifty thousand, maybe a little more, but no way he could get that for it in this condition. The carpets was all going to have to be ripped out and a lot of the sheetrock, not to mention finishing up outside with the painting. And it was going to take some doing to get rid of the smell.

She said your commission's seven percent? He nodded. She left the room and came back with her checkbook and wrote him a check for twenty-five thousand dollars and asked him did he have a seller's power-of-attorney form. He ruffled in his briefcase and handed the form to her and she signed it and slid it across the table and told him to fill out the rest himself. She gave him a set of keys for the house and told him to get what he could for it. Buy it yourself if you want. He looked at her packed bags by the door and asked about the furniture and she said do whatever you want, burn it, sell it, give it away. She didn't care. The realtor told her he'd see what he could do and left with the smirk and gait of a pimp. Edna went up to the apartment and got the boat's title from her husband's desk and signed it with the notation *Estate administrator* and came back and made coffee and took it out on the porch to wait for the men from the marina.

While she waited, she watched the river slithering grayly by, dotted here and there with fishing boats, the last of the summer people. She remembered Harmon coming out of the boathouse, how she had at first thought he was a vagabond and then later learned he was a refugee. She wondered if that made a difference and decided it did not. We are all of us refugees.

A boxy, silvery boat with the marina's name painted on the side drifted down and turned and came in bow first against the bank. A man walked into the bow and spat in the water. The front of the boat let down deck-like and he walked across to the bank and started for the porch. Edna got up and pointed to the boathouse and the two of them angled there from their different places, Edna taking her coffee with her. They met at the door and she went in first, the man following. The boat still hung where Harmon and LeRoy had left it. She gestured to the rumpled cover on the deck and reminded him to take it. She asked if he knew how to get the boat down and he said he got it. She handed him the title and he gave her a check. She looked at it and wondered what LeRoy would have said about the amount and considered backing out of the agreement, of simply letting the boat drift out into the water to founder upon a sandbar. But she just asked him if he needed anything more from her and he said he was good. She went back to the porch and watched while they poled the boat out into the river and took it in tow behind their silver boat and began churning upstream.

She went in and rinsed her cup and took out the grounds and filter from the coffee maker and threw them in the garbage and rinsed the pot and lay it upside down in the rack next to the cup. She tied up the garbage bag and took it outside to the trash can and rolled it to the road and went back for her bags and took them out on the porch and locked the door. She carried the bags to the driveway and opened the garage door and got in the Lincoln and pulled it out and lowered the top. She put the bags in the back seat and got in again, reaching into the glove compartment for her sunglasses. She pulled onto the road and turned down toward the ferry and thought through the first hundred miles or so of the route she had plotted last night, the first miles she would drive on her way to her new home in the desert.

Brigard County, September, 1993

The morning came when Harmon could no longer rise from the warped plywood bed in LeRoy's shack. O Christ he said and LeRoy, dozing in an old kitchen chair, awakened and asked him what it was and Harmon said he'd fucking shit himself and turned his face to the wall. LeRoy laid his hand on his friend's arm and said it was okay, he got it. He turned down the oil lamp and pulled back the blankets and undressed Harmon who kept saying O Jesus. LeRoy told him don't worry, he seen it before and that tiny thing wasn't nothing to get all that excited about. Harmon weakly laughed and grimaced with the pain of it and closed his eyes against his ghostly nakedness. LeRoy took up a bucket and said he was only going to be a minute and went out and filled the bucket from the thin trickle of the creek and came back and dampened a rag and wrung it out. He said this was going to be pretty cold and bathed away what of the filth he could from Harmon's groin and legs and leaned him up and washed his ass. Harmon shivered. O Jesus.

LeRoy gathered up the blankets and the bucket and went out again and rinsed the blankets in the creek and hung them on a wire strung between two of the bridge's wooden posts and threw the water from the bucket back into the creek where it would mingle once more with the waters from which it had come and resume its pilgrimage down to the river. He went back and covered Harmon with a ratty topcoat. He told Harmon it was going to take a while for the blankets to dry and did Harmon want him to help him put on a clean pair of pants and Harmon said what the fuck for and was there any pills left. LeRoy said they had plenty and filled a cup from the water crock and laid two of the white pills on Harmon's tongue and held his head and helped him drink. Harmon said he never would have thought it was going to get this bad. LeRoy said he knew, he knew.

LeRoy said he was going to go in town and get a couple things and would Harmon be okay. Harmon nodded. I'll be quick as I can LeRoy said and snugged the coat around Harmon's neck and fluffed the sack of rags beneath his head and told him to try and sleep if he could and went out, closing the door behind him. An hour later he came back, leading a procession of derelict mendicants. They came single file down the road's broken asphalt and across the bridge and through the thicket of nettles still green on the bank, their hands held high to keep from being stung. They went in one-by-one and stood mute before Harmon, their rehearsed condolences forgotten, their eyes downcast, trembling and pigeon-toed like children about to be beaten, and they shuffled back out and away and regretted their silence. When again they could speak, they did so in clipped knowing phrases. It's a damn shame they said and it goes to show you never know and how come you think he kept it to himself? And they went on like that all the way back to town, platitudinous and as fatuous as farm boys gawking at a carnival strip show.

Harmon whispered LeRoy shouldn't have done that, but his damp eyes said thank you. LeRoy said you always done for me.

Harmon drifted. He hazily remembered the things the two of them had shared in their life along the river, the bar fights and the jail cells and the women. The inviolable trust of each in the other. He slept and awoke and slept again and there came unbidden memories that for years had festered within him into the pus of shame.

He again laid the gun's muzzle behind the dog's ear and pulled the trigger and the dog summoned the strength of its ancestors as it hissed out a defiant breath, refusing to die, its legs twitching, and the boy knew that in his naïve attempt at mercy he had inflicted a wound and pain beyond all imagining. He fumbled to reload and the shells fell scattered in the carpet of teaberry and moss and with his fingers shaking finally found one and ejected the spent round and managed to get the rifle reloaded and the bolt shut. He placed the muzzle straight on and square between the dog's eyes so that when he pulled the trigger, he was looking deep into that suffering heart and the dog folded upon the ground complete and altogether dead.

Through a door, the terrible thunder and the thud of a gun striking the floor and the blood seeping out from under the door into the hall. And lying down in the blood rank and warm and then ghoulishly cold, gluing his face to the wood floor like tar.

Lying cold beneath a storm, where he was but one of many bundles of rattling bones cohabiting this ossuary that is the earth. Spindled clumps of driftwood gray and brittle. Pale, veined stones. Fossilized dogwood blossoms.

At his feet the eviscerated body of a field mouse. Bleached grass, opaque and white like the frozen spittle of angels, in a drought-plagued field upon which his young brother had bled out his life from the gaping mouth of his shoulder, the boy's arm ground to mush in the corn picker's steel teeth. The boy screaming among the stalks of dead grass where lay the carapaces of dying beetles drying up in the heat, the scurrying bodies of wolf spiders flickering over them. The tail of a blacksnake disappearing into a burrow as if it were a demon's tongue slithering back into the foul mouth from which it came, torment's portent handwritten in thin black hieroglyphs.

And the memories went on so. Faces cartwheeling into crisis. Felonies prowling like machines through the ineffable presence of darkness. Snow-filled fields of burnt corn bending on knees thin as knives. Dragons too old and centered for ultimate answers. Sinners guessing their grades. Three jacks and a broken glass scattered across a felt-covered table at 7:30 on a Sunday morning. Savage girls on street corners, black streaks spidered about their eyes like pity bleeding from a mother. The quickening that was neither lust nor anticipation, hard edged as a crucifix and as amorphous as confession. A flapping mad-eyed preacher peddling redemption, his yellow grin written and rewritten in the crooning cadences of incrimination. An orphan child with a moldy crust of bread. Young soldiers pitching hand grenades into huts and the flames billowing up oily and dark and the soldiers shooting those who dared to flee, their heads exploding as they ran.

He arose from the bed's sweat-stained ticking and looked about and stepped forth into a day devoid of evening and morning and beneath the trellises of the bridge like a triplet of crosses, stood barefoot on the creek water and went on down the way toward the river. He looked up at two full moons circling each other. The sky mauve tinged. Downstream, the creek divided and forked and merged in the distance back to a single line. He walked on, the water cool beneath his feet. He passed a concrete jetty outstretched over the water and crumbling, a tributary of detritus dribbling down the bank, the jetty moaning in quiet pain through thrust out rusted rods like fractured ribs.

Out in the middle of the river he looked up unto the hills and to the trees clothed in sere, yellow leaves, their branches still as the moment between breaths. He walked between shores beaded with droplets of light, oil stains meandering on the water, their wavering spectra. A mannequin sculpted from tattered rags hanging by its neck in the noose of a frayed rope. Smoldering trash. Two naked men lying together back to chest in the brown grass, one crying, the other grunting. He nodded to a drunk old man fishing from a skiff, the reflections of his glazed eyes enameled on the rippling water.

He walked to where the city lifted up from the river, its terraced streets cut into the hills, and sought in that distance the houses wherein he had dwelled, wherein he had sought oblivion and not found it, and wherein he had lain with whores. An old woman came down a litter-strewn street and sidled up an ally and fluffed out her skirt and squatted and pissed. Two boys in leather jackets passed a bottle in a paper bag back and forth between them and lit cigarettes and threw the bag in a trash can and went into a diner. Dime store girls came out from the end of their shifts and young men took them on their arms, the girls' hips swaying in their pleated skirts. He walked on.

He came to the bridge and looked up. He heard a truck navigate from shore to shore above its swooping rusting buttresses, a bestial crossing over oblivious to the ethereal suchness through which it lumbered. He watched remnants of lives fluttering down from above, falling through the air to seek refuge in the water, the river calling come unto me. Through the confetti of falling faces he glimpsed stars and the stars moved not. He envied their placidity.

From the river the drowned arose and slept among its eddies and drifted upon the water like soiled bridal veils, and the river stopped and moved on and stopped again, the stuttering moments between what has been and what is yet to be, and the drowned awoke and some languorously whispered vows of eternal devotion to each other and sang softly and returned to their sleep, sinking again beneath the embracing waters. And from others there arose a howling like the howling of wild beasts, a drunken, marauding army spreading out over the earth, their pounding hooves like drumbeats, and finding no pure souls from which to extract their vengeance, turn themselves one upon the other.

His flesh and his bones gave themselves up to the nether light, and he opened as a net and the waters of the earth sieved through him, its rains and its rivers and its seething seas.

An osprey descended from beyond the bridge, its single-minded eyes fiery behind its executioner's mask, its talons unfolding like thorn-petaled tulips as it drew down upon him and reached into his chest and wrenched forth a slimy, writhing thing and turned, its wings heaving with the weight of its dark burden, and rose screeching over the river and away and was gone. He lifted up his face and raised his arms and, closing his eyes, said it is finished. Beneath the echoing vastness of the bridge, the river took him.

LeRoy raised his head at the death rattle and breathed a long and mournful sigh. He stood and cupped his hand beneath Harmon's slackened jaw and with the gentleness of a new mother pressed the gaping mouth closed and caressed Harmon's cheek and smoothed his hair and folded his friend's arms across his swollen belly and bent over and kissed his forehead. He snuffed out the lamp and went out from his ramshackle hut into the predawn quiet, his steps in the creek gravel enlarged within the chapel of the bridge's dry timbers. He lit a cigarette, the flare of the match a momentary beacon, and smoked, the streaks of the smoldering tip writing in the dark a missive in the indecipherable script of mystery. He looked down toward the river hidden in the unbounded night but flowing still with power beyond all understanding.

He wept.

The Story of My Life Continued

By

LeRoy James

Yesterday I packed up and left my bridge. I can't say it was a bad place to live. It kept out the rain, and the shack I built under it did a fair job of keeping out the wind. And there wasn't much traffic to bother my sleep as the bridge only connects a one-lane dirt road. Sometimes kids came down there on motorcycles and woke me up. But not often enough you would call it a nuisance. The name of the creek is Red Bird Creek. Which is an exaggeration. It is just one of maybe a thousand little streams running off the hills into the river. Red Bird Creek is so little, they wouldn't even have had to build a bridge over it. They could have just run a culvert under the road. But lucky for me they never did, because you can't live in a culvert. Water always will rise inside a culvert and flood you out. When the water is low, you never think it will rise up again. But it will. A bridge is better for staying dry.

I left for different reasons. One is that keeping out the rain and the wind wasn't going to be enough anymore. It is almost October now and living down close to the ground and beside water like that, even if the wind and the rain don't get in, the dampness does and is worse during the winter. It comes up from the river. Sometimes it comes up in fog and sometimes it just comes up. But it always comes. Every year the wet gets into my knees and my fingers deeper than the last year and makes everything harder and harder. Living out there close to the weather makes you older than you are and things get hard for you sooner that they do for people who live their whole life in a house and even though I am not that old compared to people who live in houses, I am starting to feel like I am and maybe I will have better luck downriver. Reason number two is my friend Harmon died. With him gone I don't have anything here I care about.

I packed up what things I would need and could carry and put them in a duffle. I made sure to bring my composition books. I am writing in one of them now. (But you know that because you are reading it.) I waited until after it was dark and went down Red Bird to the river and went upriver on the bank a little ways until I came to the summer houses and found one that the people were still in and borrowed their skiff. I rowed upriver into the current and found the channel and let it take me. I drifted down to the island and rowed in and tied up and built a fire even though it was a warm night for this late in the year and I didn't need it to keep off the chill. I didn't bring anything to cook either, so the fire was just for light. The wood was wet and the fire was throwing up sparks because of it. I sat Indian-legged for a while, but I got cramped up so I just sat with my knees pulled up and put my arms around them to keep myself sitting. I sat there and thought about the things that have happened since I came here. For some reason I remembered hearing a girl singing "On the Wings of a Snow White Dove," and I was rocking back and forth to the sound of it while I was remembering her singing it. I hummed along with her for a while and pretty soon I sang some of it and went back to humming the song for a little bit and then I laid down on the ground and watched the stars. And then I started thinking about Mr. Bones.

If you have read my other composition books, you know about me and Mr. Bones. I have not thought about him for a long time now, but I thought about him there on the island because of the darkness between the stars and how that part of the night is as black as he is. I got up off the ground and went down to the water and looked across to where I had come from and said real soft, "Mr. Bones, I know I have ignored you for a long time and have no right to ask, but if you could see your way to doing me one last favor, could you come down and talk to me? I expect you have moved on to be a new person's bodyguard, but if you got a second, I would appreciate it."

I listened for him to come. I listened behind me for a rustling in the bushes as of the spirit, and I listened for him out on the water like maybe he would walk up out of the river and the black water would be running off him like he was a monster in a movie. While I was waiting, I practiced thinking what I would say to him, what I would ask him for. I decided I would remind him of the time I died before I was supposed to and how God fixed it so that he sent those angels to take me back in time so I would land in the water and not on the rocks. I was going to ask him if he could go to heaven and see if he could talk God into doing that for Harmon. Send him back to before he died and while he was at it have him land way in the back mountains of China where there would be a wizard with a secret herb medicine that would draw the sickness out of him. But he never came. And I waited for him a good long time. I finally went back by the fire and laid down on the ground. The next thing I knew it was morning. I looked over toward the water and there right at the river's edge was a crow pecking around. Garbage washes up on the island's beach and the crows come for that. I thought for a second that maybe it was Mr. Bones come after all. He is like that. He will do what you want but make a joke out of it. I said, "Hey, Mr. Bones, is that you?" And all the crow did was caw and fly off. When I was little, I read a story that told why the Indians decided crows was black. The Great Spirit painted all the birds by hand. Red birds (like my creek) and blue birds and yellow wild canaries and every color of bird there is. They lined up and waited their turns for him to paint them. He asked the birds what color they wanted to be and they told him and that was what color he painted them. Then they flew off and any little birds that hatched out of their eggs would be the same color they was, so the Great Spirit didn't have to paint them over again. He just had to do it once and it was forever, for the birds he painted and all of their seed for all generations. The crow was the last in line and when it came his turn, the Great Spirit was all out of colors. He used them all up with the other birds and all he had left was black. He told the crow he was sorry but he was going to have to be black and that was that. I think about what it would have been like to be that crow and what I would have said. Which would have been different than what I think I might of said. And the crow would of been like that too. The crow would want to say something with a lot of balls in it like he didn't care and wasn't afraid, like, "Fuck, Great Spirit, black is just another color. Knock yourself out." But what really would have happened is he would have just bowed down his head and leaned over and took his medicine. I have been taking my medicine for as far back as I can remember, so I think I know what the crow must of felt like.

There have been only five people in this world that I cared anything about. My mama and her friend Whiskey and my Sunday school teacher and my friends Eli and Harmon. All but one of them is dead now and gone before their time and the other one might as well be. I never had a wife or a serious girlfriend. Mostly I went with whores. I like them better. There is something more honest about a whore that you don't see in a lot of women. And they can think too, even if most people figure you got to be real dumb to be a whore. I knew a whore one time who said being saved wasn't enough. That after that, you had to get sanctified. She was a Nazarene until she got kicked out for whoring. She couldn't stop whoring even when they told her they would throw her out if she didn't. She didn't have no choice. She didn't know how to do anything else. It is funny about all those different churches. Like how they have different ways of being baptized. They will even argue over it. Even my mama said there was a right way to get it done. But I'm not so sure about that. It seems to me everybody gets baptized their own way. You get baptized in the water of your own life. You walk out into the river of your life and sink down in it and when you come back up, whatever it is your life is made out of, comes dripping off you and you are soaked in it forever, just like the crow, and you might as well say hallelujah praise Jesus because that's the way it is going to be.

I am writing this on my new skiff. Every second I am further away from that town. I do not think I will miss it. I will miss some of the places I lived in though. Like that cabin I lived in for a good long while until I couldn't make the payments and a room over a store and off and on, in a whorehouse. I won't miss living under the bridge. I worked some good jobs there too but I couldn't never hold on to them. Sometimes it was somebody else's fault, but down deep I know most of the time it was my own fault. Like every time when I was a mechanic, I would lose the job because they don't like it if you don't show up first thing in the morning. If they tell somebody their car is going to be ready on a particular day, the customer will not like it if they have to hear an excuse why it wasn't ready. Especially if the excuse is that the best mechanic you got decided today was a good day to have a righteous hangover. My friend Eli had a thing he would say about being to work on time. He said once you start showing up on time, the next thing you know, they expect it.

I think you can tell that I am running out of things to talk about. I am winding down and going from thing to thing with no direction to it at all. But I don't want to stop. When I started these books, I was sure they would make me a million dollars.

But they have not made me one single cent and lots of times I have wondered why I kept on coming back to them if I was never going to get anything out of it. Sometimes it would be a couple of years between writing down my adventures, but eventually I would get back to it. It wasn't a thing I could stop thinking about and sooner or later, there I would be, scribbling in my books. That is how I feel right now, but it is getting dark. Me and my boat's shadow has got itself stretched out almost all the way to the east shore and is just about ready to disappear into the nighttime, so I have to stop, whether I want to or not. You got to be able to see if you want to write anything down. And not just shadows. You got to see what's making the shadows. I am going to sleep on the water in the skiff tonight. When I wake up, I should be a long ways downriver. Then I will start up again. Maybe I will finish telling you about the time me and Mr. Bones saved the Mermaid Princess.

James Carpenter lives in the New Jersey Pine Barrens
with his wife Rosetta.

Acknowledgements

To those who lift me up and lead me on — To my wife, Rosetta, without whom not only this but nothing is possible. To my children, J and Chris, whose strength, courage, and capacity to love inspire me always. To Marta and Mila Carpenter, proof positive that grace and joy do abide in the world. To my early readers, who rescued me from hubris, Erin O'Connor, Jean-Michele Rabaté, and Andrew MacDonald. To my extraordinarily gifted editor, Joan Leggitt. To Walt Davis, Keith MacDonald, and David Belmont for their frank conversations about race. To Wayne Knight, Dan McGrenehan, and Greg Reagle for the examples of their spiritual quests and for reminding me that spiritual progress is measured not in miles covered, but in lives touched. For my close friends in South Jersey and on Walnut Street—they know who they are and why. To the members of the Sangha of Seabrook Buddhist Temple. To Alice Mattison, Frankie Lambourne, and Sharon Black. And to my brothers, Wayne, Don, and Paul Carpenter—we made it out, not everyone did.